Also by K. Aten:

Embracing Forever:
Book Two in the
Blood Resonance series

K. Aten

Mystic Books
by Regal Crest

ISBN 978-1-61929-424-0

First Edition 2019

9 8 7 6 5 4 3 2 1

Cover design by AcornGraphics

Published by:

Regal Crest Enterprises

Find us on the World Wide Web at
http://www.regalcrest.biz

Published in the United States of America

Acknowledgments

I'm sending a huge thanks to Micheala, who puts up with my excessive comma usage, bad grammar, "fatty" prose, my love of the word "just," and last minute cleaning of house on my manuscripts. I want to thank Regal Crest Enterprises, Cathy, and Patty for putting up with my excessive questions, and for supporting me in this journey. Thanks to Kari for not reading this book (because vampires just don't do it for me) but still encouraging me every step of the way. Lastly I want to say thank you to Ted, because even though you didn't care for this series you still read the books and helped me bring the best novel forward with each one.

Dedication

This is the third novel I wrote after being bitten by the bug back in 2015. I wrote Embracing Forever after someone commented online that my stuff was good and I should write a sequel to show a potential publisher I had longevity with my writing. She went by the name Nicole and worked with me back and forth until the book was complete. When I faltered after comparing myself to another great writer, she reassured me that I didn't have to be the same as my idols to also be great. It was my first experience with a beta reader and I'm so glad it was positive. Though I wasn't convinced I could actually get published until I got a huge shove from my current beta reader, Ted.

This book is dedicated to those people who shove you, show you, and guide you when you most need it. For writers it can be a friend, a spouse, beta reader, or a random fan online. Listen to them. If they don't give up on you then you shouldn't give up on yourself.

"Every writer has their own gifts. It is when we go outside of ourselves and start comparing is when we do an injustice to us and the other writer. Kelly you are very talented and I believe you have a specific gift. Winter (Pennington) has hers, as I do. First take the time to learn your craft." ~ Snl aka Nicole

Chapter One

SARAH COLBY SAT on a stool, bellied up to the kitchen counter in her sister's house. Technically it was her house too but she didn't consider it as such. She had only stayed with Annie for about eight months when she had returned to Columbus the previous year. During that time, Annie's girlfriend had moved in and Sarah moved out to live with her own girlfriend. No, it wasn't her house but it was another home to her. Sarah and her sister, Annie, had always been close, despite their ten-year age gap. But after the death of their parents eight years before, their bond changed and grew even deeper. Perhaps it was the shared tragedy they had both experienced, or because they were forced into more of a parent/child relationship, but responsibility and grief had forced Sarah into a role she neither wanted nor was prepared for. Still, she managed because there was no other option where Annie was concerned.

When Sarah left to travel the country and play her own music, it was one of the hardest things she'd ever done. Besides the fear of venturing out into the unknown and living off her own skill and talents, there was also the fear of leaving Annie behind. But Annie survived and so had she. The singer smiled as her sister droned on about one of the regulars at the bar she managed. They sat opposite each other at the counter with two matching glasses of milk and a half-eaten package of cookies between them. The two women had looked similar for years but when Sarah finally cut her long hair down to shoulder length like Annie's, they looked more like fraternal twins than siblings with a large age gap between.

At first glance Sarah seemed the more striking of the two with her rare green eyes. But Annie, being all of twenty-three years old, had youth and a gorgeous smile to offset her average hazel peepers. The cookie chat was a tradition that began long before the death of their parents. Each time Sarah came home from college, they would retreat to Annie's room to gossip about school, girls, and music. Their bond survived everything life had thrown at them, starting with their parent's death. And right now they seemed normal, laughing and giggling at each other's stories. Their choice to ignore the patiently begging husky at their feet was completely human, if a bit heartless. But they were not normal. The past year of their lives had shown both that not only were the monsters real, sometimes you loved them.

Duke sighed and rested his head on Annie's thigh. Feeling sorry for the pathetic canine, she got up and got a treat from the cupboard. Sarah shook her head and smiled. "You're going to spoil him."

Annie scoffed. "Right. And Keller doesn't have half a dozen different kinds of treats in the cupboard next to her wine fridge?"

Sarah laughed knowing her sister was right and continued her story. "So anyways, we had to do a lot of explaining to the instructor when I accidentally threw Keller halfway across the room."

The younger woman looked confused. "I don't understand, you two are ridiculously strong. Why the sudden need to take kickboxing? When did you even decide this anyway?"

Sarah hummed under her breath and tried to come up with the words to explain something that had been a deeply personal decision. She knew she could talk to Annie about anything, but it was difficult to put her emotions and feelings into words unless it was through the medium of music. With music the expression of emotions and feelings came easily to her. Sarah wasn't just a musician because she had a knack for playing. She was a musician because deep inside her there was a melody always waiting to come out. "Well...Keller and I did a lot of talking about it actually. She pointed out that all it takes is a gunshot to the head and it's all over. After the freak that was running down people in the community last year, we just wanted to be as prepared for stuff as possible. As for when we decided all this, it was a couple months ago." She cocked her head to the side, eyes unfocused in thought. "Maybe sometime around the middle of January. I think it was shortly after I asked Keller to marry me."

Duke immediately went to work when the floor was covered in a fine spray of cookie crumbs. "Holy shit! What did you just say?" Annie stared at her commitment-phobic sister in shock.

Sarah's eyes widened, realizing she had forgotten to pass on some important news to her little sis. So she did the only thing she could think of. She played dumb. "Um, the middle of January?" Annie slugged her in the arm so she elaborated. "So yeah, I kind of asked Keller to marry me."

"Are you freaking kidding me? And you're just now telling me months later? God, you're such a clam sometimes, Sarah! Seriously, I'm your damn sister and you never told me this." Sarah shrugged contritely so Annie questioned her further. "Why? I mean first you were afraid to move in with her, and then you were hesitant to even call her your girlfriend." She reached over and felt Sarah's forehead. "Okay, who are you and what did you do with my sister?"

The older Colby gently slapped her hand away. "I guess it was finally time to admit everything I had been feeling. I want to spend all my days and nights with her. And our bond—" she searched for the words. "The bond between us keeps growing with every touch and look. It's not just that she's in my blood, she's in my head, heart, and soul. And I wanted to show her how much she means to me by offering her the rest of my life." When Annie stared at her like she'd grown another head, she added, "I know I'm not normally so sappy but, eh, it's all true." After admitting her feelings to Annie, she waited for panic to creep in. Sarah was used to keeping her emotions held tight inside. She had to put her own feelings and dreams on hold to raise a young woman who was grieving and rebellious, and after that it just became a habit. The singer found that life was a lot easier to deal with when she didn't let her emotions dictate her behavior. Despite all the strangeness and drama of the past year, she thought her deepening emotional bond with Nobel Keller was by far the most frightening.

Annie sat back on her stool, cookies forgotten. It was rare that Sarah would speak so freely about what she was feeling. It was almost more shocking than hearing about the engagement. "No, I mean, wow. That's, uh—that's a really long time." She picked up a cookie and tried to downplay her skepticism. "Are you sure? I mean, have you set a date or anything?"

Green eyes closed across the table and Sarah blew out a breath. She searched one last time for that familiar bit of emotional reticence but didn't find it. When Sarah opened them again they were full of surety and she smiled at the younger woman. "Absolutely. And no, we haven't set a date. It's not like there's a rush now is there?"

"Hmm, good point. So do you have a ring or anything?"

Sarah scratched idly at her temple. "Well..." Seeing the expectant look on her sister's face, she reached into the left pocket of her jeans. The sound of the ring hitting the counter was similar to that of a nickel. Then she reached into her other pocket and withdrew its twin. Annie scooped up the one on the counter and peered at it. The ring was beautiful with a band that looked like intertwined vines and a setting that appeared as if little thorns were holding the stone in place. The only difference in the platinum rings was the ring size and the color of the gemstones. The smaller one was set with a gorgeous emerald, and the larger was set with the bluest of sapphires.

The younger woman's eyebrows shot up in surprise. "You carry these in your pocket?" When her sister nodded, she yelled. "Are you insane? These must have cost a fortune!"

Sarah cracked up at Annie's indignant expression. "Well, it's not like I'm worried about getting robbed. And I just picked them up today. They are from some company out of New York, and I had to go sign for the package at the post office."

Annie nodded. "Oh, that makes sense. So when are you going to give Keller's to her? Does she know you bought rings?"

The older sister laughed again and put the rings back into her pockets. Then she reached over and tugged her curious sibling's earlobe. It was a habit from youth that she'd never given up. "I haven't told her yet, you nosey thing! And I don't want anyone to spill the beans to her, okay?"

Annie laughed. "Okay, I got the message loud and clear. But you better do something horribly romantic! I could help you come up with a plan if you're out of ideas."

"Oh, I'm sure you could. However, I feel like this is something I have to do myself."

Annie smiled fondly at her. "Well the rings are amazing, sis, so I think you'll do fine."

Sarah swallowed the emotions that her sister's approval brought up. Not for the first or millionth time, she wished her parents were still alive. So many pivotal moments in the Colby sisters' lives had been missed. But the Colby women were well on their way to making new families of their own.

Annie picked up another cookie. "So, are there any other big announcements you need to tell me, or is that all?"

The older woman grabbed another cookie too. "Well, I spoke with the band I used to jam with way back when. I asked if they would play with me to record my newest album. They all agreed, and I already have time booked at Studio Seven. We are getting together next week to go over the songs and discuss arrangements."

Annie raised an eyebrow. "The Standalones?" When Sarah nodded, she whistled. As the assistant manager in charge of Voo-doo Pony, the live music side of The Merge, it was Annie's job to find talented artists to fill their bi-monthly music gigs. The Sip and Chug music spotlight was still going strong after nearly a year and had gotten nothing but rave reviews. Sarah had been the first artist signed to play the series when she returned from the road the year before. Now that she's releasing another album, Annie thought it may be time to bring her back for another gig. Instead of telling her sister that, all she said was, "Hmm..."

Sarah laughed and shoved her shoulder. "I know that look! You're thinking now that I'm releasing another album, it may be time for me to play at The Merge again."

The younger woman made a face. "I hate it when you know what I'm thinking. What are you doing, using your creepy mind powers?" She waggled her fingers in the air toward her sister, doing a poor imitation of a cartoon mind reader.

The singer had to take a quick swallow of her milk to avoid choking on her cookie. "Oh please, you're an open book to me. I've known you since you were born, it's not like it's hard to figure out what your always scheming mind is thinking of."

"Whatever! I'm just here to support you, like always. That way when you finally get picked up by a record label and hit the big time you can spread around your mountains of wealth!" She winked to show Sarah that she was just kidding. Annie was quiet for a few seconds and then remembered what she was going to ask Sarah. "Hey, can you do me a quick favor?"

"Sure, what do you need?"

The younger woman stood and walked to the counter next to the refrigerator. "I dropped some papers back behind the fridge and they wedged in the coils. I'm worried they could be a fire hazard. Can you move it out so I can get them?"

Sarah gave her a confused look. "Why don't you just ask Jesse to do it when she gets home from work?"

Annie crossed her arms and a dark look came over her face. "Because she's going to Louve's farmhouse for training right after work. So she won't be home until later, and I don't think it's safe to leave papers back there."

The singer raised an eyebrow. "Okay, back up for a second. What has your panties in a bunch right now? Is it Jesse, Louve, or Jesse's training?" While Sarah was speaking, she nonchalantly walked to the fridge and lifted it. Then she carefully backed away from the wall until Annie could retrieve the papers. Once the papers were in hand, Annie quickly moved out of the way so Sarah could put the fridge back.

"You're such a show off!"

"And you're avoiding the question!"

Annie crossed her arms over her chest and leaned against the counter. She sighed. "I'm not a fan at the way everything went down last year, and I'm still really pissed that Louve let Marcel stay on. He was responsible for Jesse getting hurt! On top of that, Jesse says one of Louve's troupe has been coming on to her a lot. Her name is Marie, and Louve has them paired up for self-defense training because they're about the same size. Apparently the chick is having a hard time understanding the word *no*."

Sarah nodded in understanding. "Sounds like you're the Colby with green eyes now!" At her sister's scowl, she reassured her. "Seriously though, I get it. I'm really not happy about the Marcel situation either. Nor am I happy that another one of Louve's people is stirring the shit between you and Jesse. Do you want me to have a talk with her?"

"Who, Louve, Marie, or Jesse?"

The older sister laughed. "Well I'd speak with Louve first, and then probably have a few words with the bitch that's been sniffing around your *extremely loyal and devoted girlfriend*." Sarah gave her sister a significant look as she stressed the last five words.

Annie ran a hand through dark locks. "Yeah, yeah, I know she's as loyal as can be. But I still don't like it. Maybe I should have a few words with Marie. I already introduced myself once, so it's not like she hasn't seen firsthand that Jesse is taken. But she made some comment about me being weak. She seemed almost prejudiced against the fact that I'm normal."

Sarah walked over and grabbed her arm, forgetting her own strength for a second. "Promise me you won't confront her."

Annie pulled her arm away. "Easy killer! And it's really no big deal, Sarah. I just want to have a talk with her, that's all."

Sarah grabbed her carefully but firmly by the shoulders and looked into her eyes. "No, promise me! Confrontation is what led to half this mess in the first place. Please, Annie, pinky swear you'll stay away from her and that you won't go over there without me or Keller. In return, we'll stop in to see how Jesse is doing at her next training session this weekend. If we can't put some fear into this Marie, I don't know who can."

Annie thought about it for a few seconds, then held her right pinky in the air. "Okay. But just a warning, she's already been trying to get Jesse to go hunting with her in the woods behind the farmhouse. Apparently she brags at how the rush of bringing down game is almost sexual. She's told Jesse in detail how it feels to have their warm blood sliding down your throat as their heart slows to a stop." She shuddered at the thought of it.

The older woman started laughing. "Oh my God, does she

know anything about Jesse? She won't even eat her steak less than well done. I'm surprised your girlfriend didn't upchuck on Marie's shoes."

Annie muttered, "I wish she would have." Her face broke into a smile as she pictured exactly that. "I guess you have a good point, she's certainly not going to win her over with that. Since I can't go over there without you, can I ride over the next time you go? I would like to see how Jesse is doing in her training. She's been working with a guy named Alain for the mental exercises and control. I know it's only been a few months, but her changes have been a lot smoother. And she can change back and forth quite easily now. There's still pain but, eh." She shrugged to play off the last comment but it was a difficult subject for the younger sister.

Sarah vividly remembered the agony and suffering that Annie's girlfriend went through the first few times she saw her change. It wasn't just the screaming that set the singer's teeth on edge, it was the sounds that the younger woman's body made as it shifted and became something else. She mentally shook herself out of the sadness caused by Jesse's pain and suddenly remembered what happens when Jesse changes back. Sarah chuckled at the thought while she cleaned up the cookies and her glass. "Another reason I'm glad we don't live together anymore, if she's changing easier and more frequently than before..." The younger woman blushed bright red at how sexually charged Jesse became when she changed back to normal. She whimpered a little, and blushed even more when Sarah laughed again. She busied herself by taking care of her own glass and wiping down the counter. Sarah finally took pity on her. "Why don't you just ride over with Jesse, we won't be far behind you. I'm sure it will be fine."

Annie nodded. "Okay, that sounds good. I promise to stay out of trouble." She held up two fingers and Sarah pushed her hand down.

"Put those fingers away, you were never a scout and you're not fooling anyone! Especially when I know where those fingers have been!"

Annie made a disgusted face. "Really, you went there? You're my sister!" Sarah just laughed again.

Without even thinking about it, both women went into the living room and took seats on the couch, immediately putting their feet up on the old coffee table. Sarah kicked at her sister's socked food with her own. "So what else is new with you? Keller mentioned that The Merge is a big sponsor for Columbus Pride

this year. How is that going? Did they put you in charge of sched-
uling the music acts yet?"

The younger woman looked at the ceiling, mentally crossing
her fingers. "They did actually, probably because The Merge is
the only gay club that has live music. And about that..." She
turned innocent hazel eyes to her older sibling and gave her a
look that had worked many times over the years. "Would you
please, please, *please* be one of the performers for Saturday, June
eighteenth? I've managed to get a lot of the best Sip and Chug
bands to sign on, but I still have a few more slots to fill."

Sarah sighed. "Annie."

"I know, I know, it would be early afternoon and the hottest
part of the day. The sun'll be bright, and it'll be a real bitch for
you. But I know you can do it, please think about it?" She gave
another dose of pleading eyes. "I'll even bring a bottle of SPF 100
for you."

Sarah snorted. "That stuff is like white grease paint, it never
rubs in! Besides, sunscreen only protect against UVB rays, not
UVA. So it wouldn't do me much good." She thought for a minute
and finally gave a long sigh. She hadn't played live since she was
infected the year before. She really wasn't sure what to expect
from playing in front of so many people. She'd have to talk with
Keller about how different it may be from what she was used to.
"Fine, I'll do it. A short set in a tank and shorts shouldn't kill me.
Keller and I will just have to do some feeding at the club later."
She was jostled as Annie turned and gave her a big hug.

"Yes! Thanks, sis, you're the best!"

"And don't you forget it! Now you owe me one. Where is the
festival this year, did it change venues?"

"No, it's still at Battelle Riverfront Park. I have three months
to have the stage, equipment, and artists all set. Oh, and I'm in
charge of the stage show advertising as well. I still have two more
slots I need to fill, and I'm really not sure what to do there."

Sarah immediately had an answer. "Why don't you ask
Louve if she wants to showcase her circus troupe? I know she
doesn't have John Kaydell anymore, but her new DJ is just as
popular. I bet she could put together a couple of acts with a good
dance mix going. That should keep the crowd fired up."

Annie's face lit up. "Oh my God, that's perfect! You're a
freakin genius! And yeah, I'm bummed that John Kaydell has
moved on from our fair city. I heard he moved to Chicago, probably making twice as much. That dude is in serious demand!" Now
that her last immediate problem was solved, she changed the sub-

ject back to her sister's condition. "So how are you doing? Has feeding at the club gotten any easier?"

The singer thought about all her sessions at the club with Keller, and their aftereffects. "It's weird." She waved her hand in the air. "I mean, it's kind of cool and, um, hot. But it's all so strange still. I have to let my shield down, and it feels like all those people are inside my head."

"That does sound weird. But how does it work?"

Sarah wasn't really sure how to put the entire feeling and process into words. "It's—it's like being in the pouring rain. All the sexual energy is there around me the minute I open myself up. And I sort of open as wide as I can and swallow it down. Then all that energy just becomes part of me and, um, I'm sure you can guess. Just think about how Jesse is when she changes back."

Annie covered her eyes. "Yeah, I don't need any more detail, thanks. But that explains why the office door is always locked when you're at the club together. Lynn was complaining about it last week."

Sarah blushed. "Yeah." They sat in silence for a minute then Sarah looked at her sister. "Do you want to take Duke to the dog park before I head home?"

The younger woman raised an eyebrow then glanced out the window. "Well, I don't work tonight, but it's pretty sunny. Are you sure?"

Sarah followed her gaze. "Yeah, the sun will offset the chill. Besides, I'm wearing a hoodie." Both women laughed as they stood and made their way to the door. Duke was already seated near his leash, duster tail sweeping across the hardwood. He was well aware of what "dog park" meant. Annie opened the door, letting the sunlight stream into the entryway, and then glanced back at her sister with a worried look on her face. Sarah laughed at her expression and gave her a light shove out the door. "Let's go, it's not like I'm going to burst into flames or anything."

Annie finally lightened up and laughed as well. "No, you and Keller save that for the club."

"Brat"

"Freak!"

"Childish little dribbler!"

"Bloodsucking fiend."

"Hey!"

"Well, if the fang fits."

They continued to tease each other as they walked the two blocks to the dog park. It was a good thing there were no neighbors outside to hear them; it was hard to say what they'd make of the Colby sister's conversation. One thing was obvious though, the two women who looked and acted so much alike loved each other very much.

NOBEL KELLER WAS sitting in her office at The Merge. After wrapping up her call, she took an odd minute to play by spinning her chair around as fast as she could. Sadly, the chair couldn't keep up with her and she heard a cracking sound a split second before she was dumped on the floor. "What the—?" She stood up and looked at the broken chair. "Well shit." It was after she got down on her hands and knees to see if she could fix it that a stocky butch woman knocked on the office door as she walked in.

"Keller, could you take a look at..." She trailed off when she didn't immediately see her boss. Then she noticed her on the floor with the broken chair and snorted. "Seriously, another one? That's the third chair you've broken this year and it's only March! What the hell do you do in here?" Keller, ever the laid back boss, just grinned at her and wiggled her eyebrows up and down. Lynne groaned and covered her eyes. "I don't even want to know."

The bar manager stood and grabbed a tissue from a box on a nearby shelf. While she cleaned the chair grease from her fingers, she gave her assistant manager over Spin a more serious look. "What's up?"

"Julie and I were going over the inventory for Spin, and we're missing two cases of beer, and a few bottles of vodka. Do you know anything about that?"

Keller made a face. "Oh damn, that's my fault. They were running drink specials at the last Sip and Chug, and ran out. I had Sal grab the stuff from Spin's inventory, and I meant to write it down later. Sorry, Lynne, separate inventories for the two clubs gets a little tricky sometimes."

Lynne smiled. "It's all good, boss; I just wanted to know where it went. I didn't want to find out we had another skimmer again."

The assistant manager turned to leave the room but before she could get out the door, Keller called her back. "Hey, could you do me a favor and check to see if we have another chair in the store room?"

Lynne grinned at her. "I can already tell you that we don't.

Looks like you'll be sitting in a bar chair until you can make it to the office supply store." She laughed. "Have fun with that!"

Keller threw a stress ball at her but she scuttled out the door too fast. Instead it bounced off the door frame and knocked over a potted plant. "Well shit!" She looked at the spilled dirt, then back at her own broken chair, and contemplated just going home. She knew Sarah was supposed to be hanging out with Annie today, and after that she had two clients. Feeling slightly irritated and tired, she threw herself onto the well-worn leather couch. There was a part of her that was happy at the fact that Sarah's music instruction business was picking up and her lover was getting ready to record a new album. However, when her own schedule was added to the mix, it seemed like they had to constantly scramble to make time together.

After spending a lifetime looking for the one person she was capable of bonding with, the bar manager was starting to resent every little thing that kept them apart. Keller had lived a long time and knew how quickly life could come and go. Perhaps it was time to move on from this job and do something that better complimented Sarah's career. If there was one thing that a few centuries of life could give, it was the time to learn how to be successful at a variety of careers. And of course a few centuries of smart living provided the money to not need a career at all. Keller smiled, glad she had worked out some things in her head. Now all she had to do was talk to Sarah about her ideas for their future.

Thinking about her lover never failed to fill her head with the image of the singer's gorgeous green eyes. Unfortunately her day-dreaming was short-lived when she caught a glimpse of the broken chair next to her desk. With a sigh, she shoved up from the couch and pulled on the hoodie that was hanging from the coat rack. Then she grabbed her keys and wallet from the desk drawer. After making sure the laptop was logged off, she headed out of the office. On her way through the bar she called out to Lynne, who was in deep discussion with her lead bartender, Julie. "I'm making a run to the office supply store. Do we need anything while I'm there?"

Her affable employee paused in what she was doing. "Yeah, we need printer paper and some more shipping labels. And look into a chair that's a little sturdier this time, huh?"

Julie grinned at Keller. "You broke another one?" She laughed aloud at her petite blonde boss. "Maybe you should go on a diet, Keller!"

Keller squinted back at her. "Yeah? Well maybe you should be busted back down to bar-back."

Julie held up her hands in surrender. "Just kidding, boss, you look great! Have fun chair shopping!"

Her chair-killing boss nodded once. "That's what I thought." She walked out the door to the sound of laughter.

SARAH ARRIVED HOME that evening nearly an hour after Keller. When she opened the door to the condo, Duke ran in and immediately went to his food dish. The musician was surprised to see the lights dimmed, music playing, and the dining room table set. She could also smell the tantalizing aroma of Thai Guys express coming from the bags on the breakfast bar. This prompted her to hang up her hoodie and go search for her girl-friend. When she found the short blonde, all the moisture from her mouth migrated elsewhere. Keller walked out of the bath-room wearing a thin silk robe. Gazing at the smaller woman's erect nipples, Sarah said the first thing that came to mind. "Aren't your feet cold?"

Keller laughed. "You're not looking at my feet, love."

Sarah smirked. "No, I'm most definitely not. Do you blame me? And I think it's cruel that you're teasing me with both Thai Guys and a silk robe."

Keller walked up and wrapped her in a warm embrace. "I'm definitely not cold, and I think you're overdressed."

Before Keller could back away again, Sarah tightened her grip. "Not so fast!" The deep kiss pulled a moan from both women as tongues worked magic on their sensitive teeth. Reluc-tantly Sarah pulled back. "Oh God, we're never going to get to dinner at this rate. And I'm starving!"

Keller looked at her lover with nothing but hunger. "I am too, and I know exactly what I'm having." Before Sarah could say a word, Keller picked her up and deposited her on their bed.

Sarah laughed at her girlfriend's enthusiasm, as Keller fin-ished unbuttoning the oxford she was wearing and reached for the clasp of her bra. "Our food is getting cold."

Keller never strayed from her task. "We have a microwave."

Sarah started to say something else but it came out as a hiss as Keller enclosed her nipple with warm lips. She shuddered against her silk-clad lover as Keller increased suction and put her tongue to work. The singer nearly went over the edge when a smooth leg came out of the robe and pressed firmly against the crotch seam of her khakis. Despite wearing the restrictive pants, Sarah did her best to writhe against the hard thigh when Keller switched to the other nipple. However, before she could get too close to relieving that ache, Keller pulled back. Looking dismayed and thoroughly aroused, Sarah tried to pull her down. "Where are you going?"

The bar manager smiled as if she were holding a secret. Straightening the robe, she slowly backed up until she could unbutton Sarah's pants and slide them off. Sarah quickly removed her open shirt and bra at the same time. When Keller stopped her from taking off her panties, she was confused. The confusion didn't last long as Keller lowered her shields and a wave of lust rolled over Sarah. At the same time, Keller lowered herself to the woman lying on the bed. Sarah reveled in the feel of silk against her naked skin, and nearly came when she realized what Keller was hiding under the robe. Knowing Sarah's love of large toys, she picked one of the bigger strap-on attachments, and she was also wearing a vibrator underneath for her own pleasure. Sarah's breathing increased as Keller teased her with the toy through the thin fabric of the panties. When she leaned down to give Sarah another deep probing kiss, she rolled her hips, making the woman below her whimper. Not very big on patience, Sarah gave a little growl and grabbed the smaller woman's ass. Desperate for more contact she gave her lover an intense look of need.

"You're killing me here!"

The heat in the room went up another notch when Keller ripped the panties from Sarah's body and stroked the toy through her wet folds. Once she was sure the strap-on was well lubricated, she took her time working the toy inside, despite Sarah's desperate pulling.

Sarah pleaded. "Love please—I need more." Keller reached down and realized just how wet her lover was. Sarah tried one more time. "Please..."

Giving in, Keller turned the vibrator on and sucked in a breath at the sensation that rolled through her. At the same time she buried the toy deep within Sarah. The emotional and psychic feedback took them beyond the simple act of sex. She began with a slow pace until Sarah started moaning almost continuously. The vibrator was spiraling her own pleasure higher, tightening things down low. Keller knew they were both close so she leaned down to whisper in Sarah's ear. "I can see your pulse and I want to taste you." When she ran sharp teeth along the singer's neck, she felt her hair gripped tight in Sarah's fist.

"Do it!"

Keller immediately pierced the flesh below her mouth and was rewarded with a rush of hot blood. Between the backlash from feeding and the pounding of their bodies together, their orgasm was instantaneous. It rolled over and through them, back and forth until they were spent and twitching. The vibrator that had felt so good moments before became too much. Keller detached all the toys and dropped them to the floor in record speed. Panting and sweaty, Sarah turned to her girlfriend. "I'm still starving, and you owe me another pair."

Keller started laughing. "I'll buy you twenty!" The running joke was that Keller loved ripping Sarah's underwear off, and both women thought it was a big turn on. It was why Sarah seldom had any matched bra and panty sets. Panties were just too expendable.

After lying in each other's arms a bit longer, physical hunger eventually got the best of them. Sarah picked up their clothes while Keller took care of the toys. Sarah dressed in a soft baby tee and pajama pants and went to reheat the takeout. Her lover rejoined her a few minutes later wearing something similar. Even though they'd lived together less than six months, it was hard to tell from their familiarity and the comfortable routine they had established. Sarah was surprised at how quickly she had grown accustomed to her life with Keller. The singer had never lived with a lover before, her fear of being tied down and of commitment in general had kept it from being an option. Keller, on the other hand, had lived with a variety of people since she was first turned centuries before. She had lived many lives and the most important lesson she had learned from them was how to adapt. However, nothing could compare to waking each morning with one's soul mate, the person you were bonded to for life.

The move served to do more than simply bring them closer together physically. It had done a lot to get Sarah past her fear of relationships. They had their comfortable routines, but they also reveled in their passionate nights and all those moments of humor in between that were the telltale signs of a solid connection. Staring at the revolving plate of the microwave prompted Sarah's moment of introspection. She smiled at the how afraid she had been before she fully committed to the mystery that was Nobel Keller. Her thoughts were thoroughly derailed by the familiar Pavlovian ding. It took very little time before they found themselves shoveling in food like starving wolves. Sarah moaned as the first taste of Mongolian beef hit her tongue.

Keller watched her with a lust-filled gaze and felt things tighten once again. "Stop that."

"What? It tastes delicious! And you can't tell me you're wound up again already."

Keller laughed. "Did that really just come out of your mouth? Do you know me at all? Everything you do winds me up." She paused for a second, then made a face and amended her statement. "Okay, so not everything."

Sarah growled in return. "It was one time! It's not my fault you didn't own a plunger!" Keller laughed at her girlfriend's bright red blush. The remainder of dinner was had in companionable silence until they both decided to speak at once.

"I wanted to talk to you about something—"

"So, Annie talked me into another gig—"

They both stopped and laughed until Keller waved the singer on. "You go ahead. What did Annie talk you into?"

Sarah looked carefully at her lover and she knew instantly that she had killed the lighthearted connection that had been set in the bedroom. She suddenly had doubts about picking up extra things to do with her already full schedule. They had been struggling to find time together lately, with their contrasting work schedules. It wasn't so bad until Sarah started seriously writing the music for her new album, and her client load doubled. She knew how much Keller missed her when she put in long days, and Keller worked the occasional long night. But now she'd committed to Annie, and there was no way out of that without leaving her sister in a bind. "She asked me to play in one of the open time slots at Pride this year. I know it's probably going to be sunny as usual, but I should be okay, right?"

Keller felt a flash of irritation that she quickly tamped down before Sarah could feel it through their bond. She wasn't happy at adding another task that would take time from them, but in all reality Sarah was doing it for her. Annie was her employee, and filling gigs for the upcoming Pride festival was part of her job as assistant manager of Voodoo Pony. Officially, she was supposed to submit all the performers to the Pride committee for approval, but they had pretty much given the younger woman *carte blanche*. It was hardly surprising after Annie worked so hard to make the Sip and Chug spotlight such a huge success. So Keller only had herself to blame. She should have foreseen Annie asking Sarah to play. *Well shit.*

Instead of saying everything that tumbled through her head though, she merely smiled. "I think that's great, and you should be fine for a little bit. Based on every Pride festival I've seen, the bar will be packed after and we'll both feed well that night." The vampire thought for a second before adding another suggestion. "You should also see if you can play a live gig before then, so you can get a feel of what it will be like with all that additional feedback." It was another thing added to Sarah's already too full schedule but it was also something that Keller thought she would need before performing at something as large as the Columbus Pride celebration was supposed to be.

Unfortunately for Keller, Sarah had felt that initial flash of irritation and regretted saying yes to her sister. She set her fork down, focusing on her lover's displeasure and completely forgetting about the bar manager's suggestion at the end. "You're mad, aren't you?"

Keller was startled. She was always surprised at how far along her lover was in the development of her mental powers. When it came to strong emotions, there really wasn't much she could hide from her anymore. Seeing the sad look on Sarah's face, she tried to explain. "I'm not mad, merely a little unhappy. And it's not about the Pride festival, it's about our lack of time together overall. Actually, this is what I wanted to talk to you about. I wanted to run something by you, to see what you think."

Sarah looked at her with slight apprehension. "What is it?"

"Well, I know we've been struggling to find the time to be together. And while that is completely normal for most couples because they don't have any other choice, I realized that I *do* have a choice. I've grown bored with my work managing The Merge, and I'm ready to take on something new. What would you think if I quit my job there and helped you with your career?" Seeing the incredulous look on her girlfriend's face, she added, "Or, I could be a professional dog walker and I'd use Duke as a reference for my skills."

"You really want to quit working at The Merge? Seriously?" Keller nodded. "So what can you do? I mean, what are you trained for?"

The bar manager laughed at Sarah's reaction. "Well, I can do a lot actually. I've had a long time to pick up skills. I can fly planes, I've fought in wars disguised as a man, I can play a few different music instruments as you know, I've managed a variety of businesses, and I got a doctorate in psychology back in the eighties."

Sarah's jaw dropped. "You're kidding me, right?" When Keller shook her head no, Sarah mumbled under her breath.

"*Jesus.*" A myriad of things went through the singer's head. Some days it seemed hard to believe that her lover was something as fantastical as a vampire. Hell, it was hard to believe that she herself was also! But then there were days when Keller would bring up something that happened a century ago as if it were merely another memory, or she'd pull out some previously unknown talent. It was days like those that really hit home how different she was from everyone else; how different they both were. She took a minute to compose her thoughts then asked the most important question. "What do you want to do?"

Keller reached over and took Sarah's hand. "I want to be with you; that is all that's important to me. I'll admit that I've been a little restless lately. I really enjoy traveling and living in new places, but I understand if you're not ready to leave Columbus yet. You've got Annie and your career here. But eventually we will have to move on when it becomes obvious that we're not aging. And I just want you to know that I've got a lot of options for us when that time comes. I have a handful of properties in Europe, just as many in the United States, and a couple more scattered around. I've learned to make the fact that I have to move on into a joy of rediscovery, rather than a sorrow of loss. We can reinvent ourselves over and over, and explore every little thing you've ever wanted to learn." As the words left her mouth, Keller was acutely aware that Sarah knew intimately about the sorrows of loss. In some ways, the death of Sarah's parents would make it a little easier to move on when the time finally came. Soul mates or not though, if they were going to stroll happily into the long future, they would have to do it together.

Not letting go of her lover's hand, Sarah sat back in her chair. "Wow. I guess I've been so busy with immediate life and all the changes we've been going through lately that I never took the time to look at the big picture. So you're saying that instead of stressing about the choice between being a private music instructor and opening my own recording studio, I can have both? I could do one until I tire of it, then move on to the next in a different city."

Keller grinned. "Yes, that's exactly it! It's whatever you want to do, love. And I'll help you in any way I can."

Sarah smiled tenderly, and lifted the smaller woman's hands to her lips for a gentle kiss. "Thank you. Now, what are *you* going to do?"

The bar manager released her hand and started eating again. Between bites of food, she laid out her plan. "Well, I think I'm going to give Joanne Markham my notice and tell her I'll stay until Pride. That should give her plenty of time to find a replacement. As for Annie, I'm certain she'll be fine no matter what. She's very talented, and any manager coming in is going to realize that he or she has a gold mine running the Voodoo Pony. She's made quite a name for herself in a short amount of time."

"So have you. I just wish..." Sarah trailed off, unsure how to put her disjointed thoughts into words.

After a minute of deep thought, Keller prompted her. "You wish what?"

Sarah shook her head. "After all we've been through, I just wish we could start someplace new, all four of us. It's too bad there isn't something that would utilize all of our skills."

Keller snorted and started laughing. "What, you mean something that would keep a manager and jack of all trades busy, and occupy a musician, a band promoter, and a computer geek guru? I think you already know what would work, should the time ever come when all four of us want to move on."

Sarah nodded. "Did I ever tell you that having a recording studio was one of the options I considered when I returned from touring? I didn't choose it because it seemed like a lot of work to take on by myself. But you do have a really good point. Maybe it's something we should bring up the next time we see the girls." She suddenly remembered her other promise to Annie. "Which reminds me, I told Annie we'd go check on Jesse's training this weekend, out at Louve's farmhouse. One of Louve's people has been causing trouble between them, and I still don't trust that Marcel. So we can bring it up to them then. Okay?"

"Yeah, that sounds fine. I'm not working this weekend, which is probably a good thing. It'll give my office furniture budget a little break."

Sarah cracked up laughing, and began clearing the table. "You broke another chair again, didn't you?" Keller gave her an embarrassed smile before picking up her own plate and carrying it toward the kitchen. Sarah's laughter followed her through the condo.

Chapter Two

DESPITE KELLER'S BOREDOM with her professional life, and Sarah's busy schedule, the weekend rolled around fast. Saturday found the two women driving north on I-71, heading for Louve's farmhouse. It was situated on about twenty acres, east of Alum Creek Lake. The edge of her wooded property ended where the woods around the lake began. It provided plenty of land for her people to hunt and run off excess energy. As Keller's midnight blue Audi started up the long driveway, the women got their first good look at the place Keller's old friend called home. Louve was an old acquaintance from decades before; she had been married to the woman who had infected Keller with the vampire virus. Eventually Catherine, Louve's late wife, went crazy and started killing children. Keller was forced to end her suffering when Louve asked for help.

Now Louve was manager and part owner of a circus-themed nightclub that was located in an old gothic church in downtown Columbus. It had become one of the most popular nightclubs in Ohio. They had a standing invitation to come out and train with Louve's people, but the past few months had been a little strained. They had spent a few no-strings nights of passion with the small Frenchwoman, but Keller and Sarah were still unhappy with Louve's decision to continue employing the man who had attacked Annie's girlfriend. Jesse recovered of course, but will suffer a lifetime of side effects. The nerdy younger woman seemed to take it in stride though, declaring that being a werewolf was kind of cool. However, Keller and both the Colby sisters had seen the pain Jesse had gone through at the beginning.

As Keller followed the dirt drive back, Sarah noted the large three-story white farmhouse that was beautifully shaded by trees and sported a wraparound porch. The shutters were deep red, as was the front door. Next to the house was a three car garage in the same color scheme and behind that a shed. At the back of the cleared area, near the tree line, there was a huge pole barn. That was where the drive ended. Keller parked next to Jesse's car, and they made their way inside. The door entered into a good size lounge area with a large flat screen TV on the wall, couches, and a kitchenette complete with trestle table and chairs. The rec area also featured a ping-pong table, a foosball table, and a pool table.

One door was open and led to what looked like an office. Upon inspection, the other door led into a large locker room. That was the door they took. They paused just inside the locker room when they heard someone yell.

"Stop! Get your hands off me!"

Sarah looked at Keller in panic. "That's Annie!" Faster than a blur, the women ran toward the younger woman's angry voice. When they rounded the corner into the shower area, they saw Annie pinned against the wall near the showers by the large and menacing figure of Marcel. Sarah yelled at him. "Let her go!"

Surprised by the interruption, he let go of Annie's wrists just in time to be grabbed and slammed into the concrete floor by a very pissed off Keller. Anger seemed to boil out of the man so Keller slammed his head into the ground twice more to knock him out. They certainly didn't want a werewolf with a temper and known self-control issues to turn furry with Annie in the room. She looked at Annie, who was busy rubbing her wrists. "Are you okay, A?"

The younger woman grimaced. "Yeah, just a little bruised. Thanks, Keller." She glanced at her sister, who was strangely quiet. Sarah was staring at Marcel wearing a look of rage. Her fists were clenched and breathing was ragged. Concerned, Annie went to her. "Sarah?" She could feel her sister's arm trembling beneath her hand.

Keller's head jerked up at the strange note to Annie's voice, and she noticed the interaction as well as the state of her lover. "Shit!" She immediately understood the problem. Sarah was caught in an emotional loop that was linked to Marcel. She immediately pulled the taller woman away from the unconscious Marcel and sent wave after wave of positive emotion through their bond. Between that and the feel of Keller's arms around her, Sarah slowly snapped out of her rigid anger. Keller looked at Annie. "Go find Louve, please. Something needs to be done about him. We will keep an eye on Marcel until she gets here." Once Annie was gone, Keller turned Sarah's face away from the prone man so she could look in her eyes. Being very reflective of her moods, Sarah's green eyes were dull and stormy with anger. Keller tried to soothe her with voice and gentle touches. "Hey, it's okay. He's not going to hurt anyone, it's okay."

When their eyes met, Sarah took a shuddering breath and a look of dismay came over her face. "Oh my God, I wanted to kill him!" She started to tremble again for a completely different reason. "I could have killed him, couldn't I? What's wrong with me?

I've never felt like that before!" Her sudden lack of emotional control terrified her. She'd never been so completely taken over by anything. That, coupled with the fear for her sister, had her nerves jangling.

Keller led them both over to a nearby bench where they could still keep an eye on the man who had caused them so many problems over the past few months. "Sarah, listen to me. In much the same way your change has increased your physical and mental strength, it has also made you a lot more receptive to the strong emotions of others. Because werewolves emote so much more than humans, you were caught in an emotional loop with Marcel. It was your anger that made the connection, but it was his rage that continued to fuel yours. I really didn't think we would encounter something like this or I would have warned you. I'm so sorry."

Still shaken from the experience, the singer did her best to move on. "How do I prevent that in the future?"

Keller regarded her silently, aware that the taller woman was trying to push the incident behind her. "All we can really do is be diligent with our shields when being confronted by an emotional situation. I suspect you dropped all of your protective walls the moment you saw Annie in danger and your own anger just invited his in. So to speak."

Sarah ran her hand through her dark hair and blew out a breath. It was a habit that she had unconsciously picked up from her lover. She tried to downplay her initial terror and still shaking hands with humor. "Jesus, maybe I should be taking those meditation and yoga classes with Jesse!" She couldn't help looking worriedly toward the man who was still prone on the concrete a few yards away. "I wanted to kill him, and it took everything I had to merely stand still and not move. Could I have actually killed him?"

The bar manager followed her gaze and noticed the subtle signs that the French-Canadian was starting to come around. She turned blue eyes toward her lover. "While they are very fast, and extremely strong, werewolves are no match for us unless we've been severely drained. You saw what I did in just a few seconds. I fear that if your rage had taken complete hold of you, he would be dead right now." Though the words were not what Sarah wanted to hear, she nodded in acceptance of the statement. Peering at her for a few more seconds, Keller abruptly stood. "Now, keep your thoughts well-guarded. I want to make sure he doesn't get away or do something stupid before Louve gets here."

Louve came rushing in just as Marcel was getting to his feet. He snarled and made like he was going to lunge at Keller, but she stopped him with a mere look. Even an angry werewolf knew when he was looking into the face of his potential death. The petite brunette walked straight up to the bloodied man demanding answers with her heavy French accent. "What is going on here? What have you done now, Marcel?"

Marcel's handsome face turned red in anger at being singled out like a naughty boy. He scowled at his boss. "Your pet vampire attacked me when I was having a discussion with the little human." He stepped toward the small woman in challenge.

The mottled red of his skin stood in stark contrast to his pale blonde hair. Sarah thought he looked like a boy scout, but he acted like an ass. A dangerous ass. "That human is my sister, and you hurt her when you had her pinned against the wall!" She looked around, noticing for the first time that Annie was missing.

Louve saw the searching look and reassured her. "I sent Annie into the training room with Jesse and Alain. She was still very much upset." The Frenchwoman then turned her attention back to the man who had become such a thorn in her side. She let him come to America to work for her as a favor to his uncle. And despite the unfortunate incident below the nightclub when Jesse had been infected, she really had hoped she could help him get his anger under control. She could see now that was never going to be the case. With a brief glance at Keller, she addressed the angry young werewolf. Looking straight into Marcel's eyes, the petite androgynous Frenchwoman seemed to grow in size as she let her alpha personality have full reign. "What is this? You dare to challenge me, to challenge your Alpha?" Her power wrapped around him, trapping his own inside his skin. It wasn't so much a chastisement as it was a swat-down. While Marcel was powerful, he was no Alpha and certainly no match for Louve's age and experience. She shook her head at his look of simmering fury. "I can no longer overlook your behavior, Marcel. You have brought dishonor to my troupe and to my name, and I'm sending you home. You will not speak with my friends again, nor will you go near them. Go pack your bags and I'll have one month of severance pay waiting for you by the end of the day."

The man snarled at her then forcefully shoved his way between Sarah and Keller. Keller looked at Louve. "I'm going to follow a little bit behind him to make sure he heads back toward the house and not anywhere near Jesse and Annie." She followed the path that Marcel took, leaving Sarah and Louve alone in the locker room.

The singer didn't say anything, her mind still reeling from the events of the past twenty minutes, and her own reactions to them. She felt more than a little raw at the discovery that she could carry so much anger inside her. Louve broke the awkward silence. "I am truly sorry, *ma belle chanteuse*. My continued failures have caused pain to you and your family. How can I make it up to you?"

Sarah knew the small brunette was sincere, but she was also aware that her words carried more than the meaning of simple reparation. Werewolves and vampires are naturally drawn together. Werewolves emoted an overwhelming amount of energy, and vampires lived to swallow that energy down. Keller had been feeding off sexual energy for centuries and had recently shown Sarah how to do it. However, it was not without risk to one's self control. Louve had been seeking that 'socket and plug' connection for decades, since the death of her vampire lover Catherine. Sarah knew that the Frenchwoman wanted more of the commitment-free nights of passion between the three of them. However, with all that had been going on lately, and with their anger at Marcel, it had not happened in a while.

She gave Louve a small smile. "Firing Marcel is definitely a step in the right direction. The worst of the damage is permanent though there is nothing we can do about that." When Louve started to speak, Sarah interrupted her gently. "However, allowing Jesse to come here and train each week helps a lot, so thank you." Louve stepped closer and reached out a hand. Sarah could feel the energy rise in the room and strengthened her mental shields to prevent another incident like when she first met the she-wolf. Louve had overwhelmed her with power and stolen a kiss the first night they met, and it was only Keller's intervention that broke the energy that had ensnared Sarah. Needless to say, the singer wasn't happy when she came out of her stupor and made her displeasure well known with Louve. They'd worked things out since, but the beginning of their acquaintance was rocky.

Keller returned before Louve could make contact. "Well, he's gone. But a skinny blonde woman met him as he was heading for the house and I could hear them shouting from the pole barn. She kissed him and then he stalked away. I'm afraid he also tore up your lawn with that muscle car of his when he left. That is definitely not a happy guy."

Sarah looked at her curiously. "Who kissed him, did you get

a name?"

"He called her Marie but I don't know who she is."

They turned toward the singer when they heard her growl. "That's the same bitch that's been sniffing around Jesse and causing problems for my sister!" Sarah could feel the anger that was simmering just below the surface. The knowledge that the two troublemakers seemed to know each other wasn't helping to keep her emotions under control.

Louve looked up in concern. "Oh, what is this? Another one of my people is causing you trouble?" Sarah took a deep breath in an attempt to calm down, and passed on what Annie had told her a few days prior. She mentioned how Marie wouldn't leave Jesse alone and wasn't doing a good job of accepting the word no. She also explained that Marie called Annie 'weak' to her face and seemed to be prejudiced against the fact that she was human. Louve scowled at the new information. "I know that Marie has a very dominant personality. I will speak with her and let her know that your young wolf is off limits. As is your sister." Her eyes were sorrowful. "Again, I am so very sorry that my people are causing you problems. I will ask Alain to help keep an eye on them. He is very good at soothing the angry and dissatisfied ones." She had her reasons for keeping Marcel, despite how much she regretted the decision now. And she thought maybe it was time to explain those reasons to Sarah and Keller. "I can tell you the story of how Marcel came to join my troupe, if you'd like to come up to the house for a drink. Are you interested?"

Keller glanced at Sarah and the singer shrugged. "I just want to run and check on Annie, and then we can talk. I don't have any clients until this evening." Keller nodded and Sarah left the locker room in search of her sister.

Louve watched the departing woman with curiosity. "How is she doing?"

"Surprisingly well. She's finally accepted everything and has been learning all she can to control her new power. While she is no match for me in strength and speed, she has fogged my mind twice."

The Frenchwoman looked at her in shock. "*Mon Dieu!* Seriously?" Keller nodded. "That is unheard of in one so young. Even Catherine, who was a little older than you, could never do that."

"I know. Sarah is very strong mentally and she has a creative mind that lets her see her powers in a way I never considered. She also has an enormous amount of control. If it weren't for that I'm afraid your angry wolf would be dead right now. When she saw

Annie get hurt she dropped her shields and got caught in a loop fueled by his rage and her anger."

Louve looked at her in shock. "You didn't warn her that could happen?"

Keller gave her an angry look in return. "No, I haven't had the chance. I certainly didn't think that would be a priority but clearly your wolves are out of control!" Keller was actually surprised that Louve didn't have a better handle on her people. The Frenchwoman had always been a very good Alpha. Certainly not one that would allow her people to show guests such rude behavior. And she would never have tolerated such disrespect from her troupe members before. Keller wondered what had her friend so distracted that her pack would fall to such delinquency.

Louve didn't want Keller to focus on the disarray of her pack members. She knew that she was putting too much of the day-to-day running of things on Alain. She had also been suffering from depression since coming to the United States. Louve had been lonely for a long time and hoped that a fresh start would be good for her. Unfortunately, moving to a new country seemed to only make her more aware of how alone and different she was than those around her. She could not turn to someone in the troupe because she was their leader, their Alpha. She wanted another lover like her Catherine but with the connection that Sarah and Keller shared. And the further she moved forward in life, the more aware she was of that emptiness in her heart. Louve held up her hands in surrender. "*Oui*, you are right *mon ami*. I am very sorry for that. She is good now though, yes?"

Keller sighed and ran a hand through her hair. "Yeah, Sarah's fine. I had to talk her through it. I also warned her to stay well-guarded around wolves."

The French woman put a hand to her chest, mock wounded. "*Aie*, you cut me to the quick, *mon ange de sang*! Surely you do not want to guard against all of us?" Once again, Louve's special brand of sensual energy filled the room. But Keller had centuries of experience and rather than let it overwhelm her, she opened herself up and swallowed it all at once. Sadly for the she-wolf, the vampire did not let any of the usual feedback escape to her friend. Keller gave her a little smirk, knowing what the woman was trying to do. Louve's lips turned to a pout. "You do not play fair; it is rude to take without giving. Your lover would not have been so cruel"

Keller laughed and then turned serious again. "Consider it a payment for all the trouble your people have caused us. As for

Sarah, she would have been overwhelmed and you know it. I won't let your tricks make things more difficult for her. If she wants us to spend the evening with you again, the choice must be hers alone and not influenced by your lust."

Louve gave a single contrite nod. "I understand. But please remember how difficult it is for me, especially with two of you so close. You pull me and I fear I become nothing more than a bitch in heat when you're near."

Sarah walked in to hear the end of Louve's sentence and laughed. "Oh Louve, we already knew that. Something tells me you have no problems finding someone to share your bed."

The small brunette shook her head sadly. "It is not the same."

Keller agreed. "No, it's not."

After a few seconds of awkward pause, Louve spoke again. "Come. Now that you've checked on *ta soeur*, we can speak of other things." They followed Louve to the main house as she rambled about all the updates and changes she had made to the property. They entered through the back door into a large open kitchen. There was another roughhewn trestle table in the open dining area, open to an industrial quality gourmet kitchen. As they moved through the house, Sarah thought it had a very open European feel to it. It was spacious and bright, with simple décor and comfortable seating. Louve led them through a large pocket door into a den. "I'm going to leave you here for *une* minute, while I go check on Marcel's room and make arrangements for his severance pay. I will return shortly."

When she was gone, Keller sat next to Sarah on the loveseat. "Are you all right?"

Sarah glanced at her, slightly confused. "Sure, why wouldn't I be?"

"Saraaaah." Keller drew her name out. "You know what I'm talking about. Your reaction to Marcel...do you need to talk about that? I know from experience how frightening it is to be caught in a rage loop." She paused. "I also know you don't deal with emotions well."

She didn't get mad at Keller's assessment because she was well aware of her own shortcomings. Instead, the singer analyzed the feelings swirling in her head. It *was* frightening, which was exactly why she didn't want to talk about it. Sarah had a tendency to keep all her fears internalized, shoved down so deep that only her unconscious mind would access them. She had nightmares for years after the death of her parents. Sarah especially didn't want to talk about it now that she knew Keller had spent time as a trained psychiatrist. No, there was no point in bringing up things that were best forgotten. "I'm fine, I promise. It's over and done and you've told me how to prevent it in the future so we're all good, okay?"

Keller didn't believe her soul mate but she knew that pushing the issue wouldn't get anywhere with the stubborn singer. Instead she waited a beat and then pointedly changed the subject. "So what do you think about the rest?" She waved her hand around, indicating the room and their situation in general.

Sarah cocked her head thoughtfully, curious eyes roaming around the room. "I think the house is gorgeous."

Keller bumped against her shoulder. "Not about that, about Louve and *this* situation. All of it."

Sarah sighed and leaned back against the cushions. "I'm glad she finally got rid of Marcel, but I don't trust him. I also don't trust the fact that he and that Marie are apparently good friends or more. As for Louve, well I know what she wants from us and why. But while I think of our nights together as a fun bit of enter-tainment, I have to wonder if it's really good for her. Shouldn't she be looking for someone she connects with?"

Keller rested her elbows on her knees. "I know she was deeply in love with Catherine, but I don't believe they had bonded. They were not soul mates the way you and I are. How-ever, I think her experience with Catherine has left her both lonely and afraid to really look for something more meaningful. It's a defense mechanism to keep people from getting too close emotionally. And the facts are, there just aren't many vampires around. That is the bond she is looking for."

"Is that your professional opinion, Doctor Keller?"

Keller smiled at her girlfriend. "It was Doctor Phillips then, and perhaps."

Sarah laughed and shook her head. "I can't believe you never told me that you have a doctorate in psychology!"

"Yeah, well it's completely irrelevant now. It was decades ago. My name is long out of circulation not to mention the fact that my age doesn't fit. I'd have to completely re-educate myself." She shrugged and made a face, indicating her interest in that par-ticular option. "As for the rest, well I'm open to the occasional night with her. You have to admit, a werewolf does make for a nice snack." She smiled thinking about the significant amount of energy vampires got when they drank from people with *other* blood. It was a huge rush and power boost.

They were interrupted by Louve's laughter as she reentered

the room. The Frenchwoman smiled at Sarah's look of dismay. "Have no fear, I have heard her say those exact words many times over the years. There is no shame in enjoying a beautiful woman, or two, for whatever the reason." She sat on a matching chair, adjacent to the loveseat. "I pledged to you a brief history of Marcel and his family." Remembering her promise of a drink, she stood abruptly and walked to a fully stocked bar on the far side of the room. "What would you like to drink? I can mix something, or I have wine, Blue Moon, and soda."

Sarah spoke up. "Blue Moon? What is that?"

Louve smiled. "Beer. Jules, my sword swallower, is from Michigan and brings back the most wonderful beers. In the summer the brewery has something called Oberon. It is *magnifique!*"

Keller raised an eyebrow at the petite brunette. "Since when do you like beer?"

She got a sly smile in return. "Oh, I've definitely expanded my horizons over the years. I will be sure to save you a few bottles the next time he brings some back. Maybe you two can share more drinks with me this summer, hmm?"

Sarah answered for both of them. "I think if this Oberon is as good as you say, you can count on it. Until then I'll try the Blue Moon."

When Louve looked at Keller, she nodded thinking she'd at least try this new brew. While the vampire had grown to like beer over the past few decades, she was a bit of a beer snob. "I'll have the same, thank you."

Once they all had drinks in hand, two beers and a red wine, Louve began talking in her heavy French accent. "Marcel's uncle is a very old friend of mine. Before we moved to North America, we both ran in the same circle in Paris. Raph was one of my very best friends for decades." She paused and looked at Keller. "I was a mess after Catherine died, you remember?"

Keller nodded. "Yes, and I am truly sorry for that."

Louve waved her apology away. "No need for sorry, I do understand. But it was still hard for me. Raphael, he was a good friend and he kept me out of trouble many times. He even saved my life when I was convinced I could go on no more. So you see, I owe him. Unfortunately, the one thing he wanted more than anything else was something I could not give."

Seeing the sadness and regret on her face, Sarah spoke up. "He loved you, didn't he?"

"Oiu, he was very much in love with me but I never saw him as more than a friend. Eventually, our friendship was strained because of it, and he decided to leave France for good and go to Quebec. There he eventually met a woman who loved him as much as he loved her. They married and had a brood of sons, and together they all run his farm. His brother, Jean, and Jean's wife, Adrienne, moved to the farm a few decades ago, so now the farm is truly a family business."

Sarah looked confused and peppered Louve with questions. "But how? I mean, weren't they werewolves? Did they have kids before or after? And are the children werewolves too?"

Louve laughed, and the energy she emitted crawled up her guest's spine, eliciting goose bumps and a shivers. "Oh, there are two ways you can become a werewolf. One is through contact with our claws, whether they accidentally pierce your skin or on purpose." At Sarah's startled look, she explained. "Some cultures purposely infect others, as part of a ritual. But I will not explain that to you today. The other way is for two infected werewolves to create a child. That child is guaranteed to carry the werewolf gene and will change with the onset of puberty. If only one parent is a werewolf, there is a chance le bébé will be human. Raph and his wife are both werewolves, so all his children were born with the blood. However, his sister-in law is not. She is privy to the secret of us but has no wish to change. Because she is human, her children were not all werewolves. Marcel is their oldest, and he was born human."

She paused to sip her wine before continuing with the story. "Raph explained that the boy seemed to take issue with his cousins and some of his siblings who had the gift, while he was always left behind. Raph also had believed that Marcel was never satisfied with the farm life. According to Raph, Marcel begged to be infected his entire life, and it wasn't until the boy was a man that Jean and Adrienne consented. Raph had concerns that were well-founded. Marcel has issues with his anger, and many times it took both Raph and Jean to keep him from trouble. Eventually, Marcel wanted to leave the farm for a bigger city. Knowing someone would need to keep an eye on him, Raph contacted me with his request."

She sighed. "After so many times helping me out, I felt like it was the least I could do for my old friend." Louve turned to Sarah with a look of regret. "I really had no idea how poor his control was, and I am very sorry that Jesse had to pay the price of my miscalculation." When Sarah looked down at her hands, Louve cast her gaze toward Keller. "And I am also regretting the fact that I did not send him home after that incident. It seems I am becoming *insensé* in my old age. Forgive me, mon ami."

Keller held her gaze. "I understand about old debts, and I too have had my fair share of mistakes. All we can do is move forward from here."

Sarah finally raised her eyes and nodded at the Frenchwoman. She was not so easy to forgive, but mistakes she had made aplenty. Who was she to judge? Her main concern was Annie, and the safety of all four of them. "Yes, let's definitely move forward."

Noticing empty bottles, she stood and cleared them away. "Would you care for another?" When dark and light heads nodded assent, she made her way to the bar and returned with two more beers. "I have brought a few new ones for you to try, since you seem to enjoy the American microbrews." She handed a bottle of Sundog to Keller and a bottle of Amber Tease Ale to Sarah.

After both tentatively took a swig of the new beers, Keller grinned. "Hey, this is really good!" She turned to Sarah. "Would you like to try it?" The singer smiled and nodded before handing her own bottle over. Almost as one, they exclaimed "I like this one better!"

All three women burst into laughter, but Sarah and Keller kept their new bottles. Louve clapped her hands in delight. "Excellent!"

After taking another swig of the Sundog, Sarah let her natural curiosity out to play. "Where did you say these beers are from?"

The small brunette across from her grinned. "They are from breweries in Michigan. Who knew American beer could be so varied and subtle with its flavors. It is not wine, but eh, it is quite good, no?"

Keller held up her bottle and read the label. "Grand Rapids. Isn't that the second largest city behind Detroit? I've never been there."

Sarah nodded. "I played there once while I was on tour. They have an amazing live music scene. With all the bars and pubs, they have an incredible array of talent hitting their open mic nights. I actually played at a brewery downtown. I opened for another popular band and the crowd was very receptive and laid back." Sarah remembered that particular gig with fondness. It paid well and the crowd was amazing. The sporty blonde butch she spent the night with was also a pleasant memory. Jamie was only in town for a night, just like Sarah, but what a night it was. Yes, Grand Rapids was a nice city with a Riverwalk that was quiet and dark after midnight. One of the things she loved about touring the country for her music was the sense of exploration and adventure that met her with each new city.

Every word Sarah spoke aloud burrowed deeper into Keller's brain. She had been contemplating alternatives for when they would inevitably have to leave Columbus. If she truly wanted to open a recording studio with Sarah, then maybe this Grand Rapids would be a good place to look. Active nightlife, live music scene, fairly large city, it had all the things they would look for when it came to relocation. "Maybe we should visit this place and check out some of the breweries and music ourselves, hmm?"

Her lover gave her a delighted smile. "I think that would be amazing."

After a few seconds pause, they both shook themselves free from the loaded look. Louve sighed and gave them a sad smile. "What I would not give to find a mate that would like to travel with me. But alas, I am alone and now tied to the circus."

Sarah looked at her seriously. "You don't have to be alone, Louve. Maybe you should take a vacation and see what or who might be out there for you."

Even though she knew the singer was serious, Louve could not help releasing a tinkle of laughter as well as another rolling wave of lust. "Ah, but you know what they say in America, all the best ones are taken." She looked curiously at Keller, then Sarah. "But perhaps you are right in that I am in need of a holiday." Wanting a topic change, Louve addressed Sarah. "So Keller tells me that you do well with your training. She says that you are quite strong mentally."

Sarah blushed lightly, sparing a quick glance at her girl-friend. "Yes, things seem to be going well. Despite knowing all about Keller and the things she needed to do to satisfy her hunger, it is quite different when I'm the one that has to do those things." She took another swig of her beer. "And physically it is very different. I broke three guitar strings the first time I tried to play after my change."

Keller spoke up. "It is better now, but still difficult. We started taking kickboxing classes but I think our instructor is getting suspicious. Sarah nearly threw me across the room in our last session." She turned to Sarah. "I don't think we should go back there again, it's too risky."

Sarah agreed with a sigh. "I think you're right. But I still need to work on control and we just don't have the space at the condo."

"*Mes amis*, I have offered the solution to you many times. Why do you not take your training with us? We are not all circus acts and wolf training. You can ask Jesse yourselves, but we also teach self-defense."

The two vampires appeared to mull it over for a few seconds, then looked at each other. Keller shrugged. "It makes sense, they would be better to train with than humans. We would still have to temper our strength with them, but we'd be getting the training we want. I have had enough instruction in the past to save me from those more extreme circumstances. However, I will be the first to admit that I've always relied more on my mental powers and brute strength than any real fighting skill."

Sarah snickered at the thought of the small blonde using "brute strength" on anyone then nodded in agreement with her about the training. "You're right of course, and we'll be able to keep an eye on Jesse. I made a promise to Annie to look out for her." She looked at Louve and answered for both of them. "That sounds great, thank you."

The Frenchwoman stood and collected empty bottles again, then made her way out of the room at a fast pace. "Come, come, I will introduce you to Alain. He handles the day to day business of the circus and sets the schedule for training." Keller chuckled at the energetic she-wolf but her and Sarah had no choice but to follow her just as fast.

Their meeting with Alain went well. He was a short, stocky man with a friendly easy-going personality. When Keller asked Jesse if she'd be willing to switch her training to Sundays, she readily agreed. Sarah saw the look of relief in Annie's eyes when she found out that Jesse would be training with them. It all seemed to work out perfectly.

However, one person did not seem happy about the arrangement. Marie overheard the plans and had words with Louve in the corner. The words were loud and unhappy. Eventually she stalked out, roughly brushing her shoulder against Sarah's, nearly knocking the unsuspecting woman down. Keller immediately went to work to soothe her lover's temper and it wasn't long after that the four women found themselves heading home.

Louve could sense her control over her troupe slipping and knew it wouldn't bode well down the road. She thought perhaps she would speak with Alain and see if he thought she was failing as their leader and boss. He had always been honest with her in the past.

Chapter Three

SARAH AND KELLER had been training with Jesse and Alain more than a month when Sarah first began having problems. She began to feel drained by the end of each day but she didn't want to say anything to her girlfriend. Sarah was used to dealing with stuff herself and didn't like to admit weakness of any kind. Keller had given Joanne Markham notice that she would be quitting before the Columbus Pride festival. While the bar manager had been busy looking for her replacement, she had cut back her own hours slightly.

Unfortunately Sarah kept getting busier. On top of the training with the werewolves, she was also still giving private lessons for her business, putting together a set list for the festival, and filling in all her free time at the studio recording her new album. The musician was exhausted and felt like she hardly saw her lover any more. Feeling the drag of her schedule more acutely than normal, Sarah decided to take a couple nights off from the studio. It was a Friday night and she knew Keller was off the entire weekend so they would have a couple days to spend together. Keller wasn't there when she arrived so she poured herself a glass of wine and sat on the couch for a few minutes to relax.

"Sarah...Sarah..." The brunette woke with a start. She looked toward her lover, then the darkened windows of the condo. Sarah glanced over at her untouched glass of wine, confused. Keller sat next to her and gazed into her eyes. The blue never failed to entrance Sarah. The hunger she felt for her lover was more than just biology. It was emotional, visceral, and on some level, spiritual. Her attention was broken when Keller spoke. "Are you okay?" Keller took note of the dark circles under her soul mate's eyes and the uncharacteristic deep sleep. She had called her for a few minutes before Sarah finally woke. Worry nagged the back of her brain.

Sarah gave her a weary smile and tried to brush off Keller's concern. "I'm fine, I just didn't realize how tired I was. I had plans to come home and make us dinner, and then have my way with you. I'm sorry I fell asleep, I just feel so run down." She cocked her head in thought for a few seconds. "Are you sure I can't get sick? Because I feel like I'm coming down with something." She laughed slightly, trying to play her words off as a joke. But her attempted humor was hollow, much like she felt.

Alarm bells clamored inside Keller's head with Sarah's admission. She suddenly had an idea what was wrong with her girlfriend. "No, we definitely can't get sick. However I fear you've been working so hard lately that you're burning more energy that you can take in. It's been weeks since we've had a chance to feed at the club. I think what you're suffering is similar to when I got injured last year and nearly died." When Sarah gave her a startled look, she rushed to reassure her. "It's not that bad; however, you do need to feed as soon as possible."

Green eyes stared back at her in confusion. "I don't understand, I fed off you a few days ago. We feed off each other regularly, and you've gone longer without draining energy at the club. Why isn't that enough?"

Shaggy blonde hair shook with Keller's head. "It's not the same for a few different reasons. I'm a lot older and I have a much greater capacity than you do. I can take in a lot more when I feed, which means my energy will last a lot longer. And also I think it's because we are only feeding off each other. I suspect that maybe we are both suffering from weak blood, so when we feed off each other it's not rejuvenating us. We need fresh blood."

"So what do we do? I don't think I could feed off just anyone, and I definitely don't want to do it without you. It's too sexual and it would feel weird now. And you said that that was the only energy that would feed us."

Keller thought for a minute, going over their possibilities in her head. "While we can technically feed on ordinary neutral emotion, it typically has no real power to it. Sensual energy is ten times stronger than average emotion. For instance, even I would be hard pressed to make a meal at a conference of dentists. That being said, we still have a few options. We can try to pick someone up together at the club, we can find someone outside the club for a quick snack in an alley and wipe their memory, or we can call Louve. You know she would be willing."

Sarah seemed to ponder the ideas. "What do you think is the best for us?"

The shorter woman sighed and ran a hand through her already messy hair. "Well, I've done all three plenty of times, but I'll admit it is a big difference when approaching the problem as a couple. Perhaps the safest would be Louve. But I also don't want it to look as if we are seeking her out either. I don't want anyone to know that we are weakened right now." What she didn't admit to Sarah was her impression that Louve seemed a bit off lately. Her long-time friend was losing control of her troupe and her emotions, and Keller didn't want to distract the Frenchwoman any further. She only hoped that between Louve and Alain, they could get things back on track again with the wolf troupe.

The singer tapped her bottom lip in thought. "What if we leave it to chance? Why don't we go to the Temple du Loup tonight to feed on the energy? If she is there, you know she will offer a night together. If she's not there, perhaps we then try to pick up someone from the club. There's usually at least one person willing to participate in a threesome. What do you think?"

Keller looked at her strangely. "Have you done this before, set out to pick someone up for a threesome?"

Sarah blushed and scratched at her temple. "Ahh, it was years ago, when Jill and I dated. Neither one of us wanted to seriously settle down. As a result we had many wild nights with a third."

It was a grinning blonde that leaned in close and whispered in her ear. "Wild nights, hmm?" She ran her sharp rapidly elongating teeth along the helix of Sarah's ear. "Were they as wild as ours?"

Sarah shuddered with sudden arousal. "Definitely not."

Keller looked at her lover curiously, often wondering but never asking about Sarah's relationship with her ex-girlfriend turned best friend. "What ever happened between you and Jill to cause you to break up? Did you love her? I mean, were you in love with her?" She was legitimately curious, and she was always interested in gaining little insights into Sarah's personality and past. While they had shared a great many things about their lives, Sarah was definitely the more closed between the two of them. Sarah Colby had many layers, much like an onion. She liked to hide her emotions beneath layers of superficial thoughts and smiles.

Sarah stiffened, not expecting the question in the middle of a conversation that was headed to places a lot less serious. She thought for a few seconds trying to come up with a sufficient answer. "We did love each other. We were actually best friends through high school, but we didn't start dating until college. We didn't date very long though because I think neither one of us really wanted to settle down." She frowned. "We broke up right after my parents died. I guess I just wasn't the same person after that, and I had too many responsibilities. I couldn't deal with a relationship on top of everything else."

Keller's eyes widened with a sudden flash of insight into her lover's personality. "Did you break up with her?"

Sarah shrugged. "I mean, it was mostly mutual but yeah, I broke it off. It was..." She sighed, struggling to find the words. "I guess I still loved her at the time. I just couldn't, you know? And after so many years, she's just Jill. We're best friends, who sometimes hook up. But there's no romance between us." Tired of dredging up old memories, she grasped Keller's face in both hands and pulled her close for a kiss. She swirled her tongue around Keller's sharp teeth, caressing the sensitive canines until Keller was panting with desire. When Keller did the same to her in return, she pulled away to see that her lover's blue eyes had gone dark with need. "I can assure you that no one in my life has come close to matching what you do to me. Now, I believe we were going out tonight, which means I need to get ready. Off with you!" She pushed Keller back from the couch and stood. With a wink at her gobsmacked lover, Sarah headed for their bedroom to get ready.

Two hours later they were standing in line to get into the club. It wasn't nearly as long as the line on Saturdays because Saturday was the only day the circus troupe actually performed. Keller cast another glance at Sarah's outfit. "Not that you aren't hot in anything I've seen you wear, but I don't understand why you chose that shirt to go with your jeans when we're supposed to be looking for a third." She pouted. "The shirt totally covers your ass."

Sarah glanced back at her and smirked. It was near eleven and the people in line were not paying them any attention. "I chose the shirt on purpose, and I have other attributes to offer besides my ass you know." They got to the front before she could add any more, so she dug a twenty out of her pocket and handed it to the doorman. Just inside they showed their ID's and got their hands stamped. Rather than proceed through the familiar revolving door, Sarah pulled Keller off to the side.

Keller looked at her in confusion. "Don't you want to go in?"

Sarah gave her a mysterious smile. "Of course I do, but I want to explain my outfit to you."

Blue eyes looked up at her in surprise. "Lass, you don't have to do that. I think you look gorgeous in anything and as long as you're comfortable I'm happy."

"Oh, I'm happy too. Come here and find out just how happy I am." She pulled Keller into her arms and spun them around so the blonde's back was against the stone wall next to the rear entrance of the church. As Sarah pulled her into a kiss she bent her knees slightly and rubbed the front of her jeans into Keller's crotch.

As soon as the distinctive lump rubbed against the front of Keller's own jeans, she moaned into her lover's mouth. Pulling back, she turned darkened eyes toward the singer. "I can't believe you wore that out!" Even after knowing Sarah for a year, the singer continued to surprise her. Keller would have never expected Sarah to do something so daring. Sometimes it seemed as if every single day opened new facets of their individual lives to each other.

Sarah gave her another enigmatic smile. "Do you like it?" When Keller whispered "yes," Sarah's voice lowered. "Do you want me to use it on you right now?" She gave another roll of her hips and felt Keller shudder against her once again.

While Sarah was typically more emotionally reserved than Keller, she was also a little wilder in her ways. Keller's reserve had much to do with the fact that she had to learn to live below the radar for most of her life. As a vampire who lived for centuries, one learned very quickly to not be noticed. But despite the quiet reserve brought on by centuries of self-control, Keller enjoyed being tempted into Sarah's fresh antics. "You're killing me here! Of course I do, I—" She was interrupted when a large group came through the door laughing, clearly having started drinking at another bar. She pulled Sarah's head down so she could whisper in the singer's ear. "I want to find a dark corner somewhere and show you just how much I want it!"

Sarah took a deep breath and imagined she could smell Keller's arousal, or maybe just her own. While the strap-on under her jeans seemed like a good idea at first, she didn't realize how much it would affect her. It rubbed against her clit deliciously with every step, not to mention the way it fit inside. It wasn't uncomfortable, but it wasn't completely comfortable either. She sighed and pulled back from Keller. Seeing her flushed face, Keller laughed delightedly. "What's the matter, love? Has the toy got you all hot and bothered?"

Sarah took another step back and ran a tremulous hand through her dark hair. "You could say that. Definitely no dancing tonight, or we're going to give everyone a show!"

Keller held out a hand. "Let's go get a few drinks and calm you down, then we'll see about a show."

Sarah moaned. What had she gotten herself into? Despite having no circus performance on Fridays, the club was surprisingly busy. They had to fight their way to the stairs that led to the next level. While the bar on the second floor didn't have much of a wait, there was still a crowd watching the people on the dance floor below. So after each downing a shot and grabbing a couple of beers, Sarah suggested they check out the third floor. The top level wasn't anything more than a small area across the back of the church, with mere walkways along the sides. They knew from experience that there was an elevator door that would be at the end of the walkway on the left. They decided to take a seat on one of the low couches while they sipped their beer. Between the alcohol and the fact that Sarah was no longer moving around, the singer's arousal had cooled a bit. At least until Keller set her beer down and quickly moved to straddle her lap. Heat shot straight to her core. "Oh God, what are you doing?

Keller smiled and rolled her hips, enjoying the way Sarah's eyes fluttered closed. She leaned down and captured her lover's lips in a hot kiss. When she pulled back, she winked at the woman below her. Rubbing herself on the toy that was hidden below denim was serving to turn herself on as well. Keller enjoyed the slightly parted lips and whimpers that Sarah couldn't seem to control. "Relax. I want to dance with you so I'm trying to take the edge off now. This way you won't be so sensitive later. I don't want another night with speed racer."

Sarah made a face. "You were just as bad that night yet you won't let me forget it!" The woman straddling her lap merely laughed and increased her grinding pace. Sarah's breath hitched. "Keller, we can't do this here! We are completely out in the open."

Keller leaned down and traced Sarah's bottom lip with her tongue. Then she moved near Sarah's ear and breathed the softest of whispers. "Can't we?" Keller knew exactly what toy Sarah was using. Not only did it put pressure on her clit, but it also had an extra portion that rested inside. She knew in that exact moment Sarah's muscles would be clenching around the hard length. She was both jealous of the toy, and jealous of Sarah. Later. She would get her own later. Knowing that they could indeed be found out any second, she opened herself wide to Sarah. Barriers down, the lust flowed freely between them. At the last second before they both fell over the edge, she leaned in again and took Sarah's mouth hard. Sharp teeth accidentally cut a lip, and the blood boiled in their veins. It was always like that, so hot and wet between them. And it was something that Keller would never take for granted after centuries without it.

As the orgasm swept through them, Sarah held the smaller woman's hips so she could thrust even harder against her. When it was over, they lay on the couch panting. Keller had fallen forward into her, resting her head on Sarah's shoulder. While sweat cooled, Sarah marveled at their connection. Sometimes it was overwhelming, but it was never less than amazing. One of the things Sarah noticed after her change was that instead of getting languid and sleepy after a really powerful orgasm, she now felt energized. The sex and connection they had was like fuel to their fire. Keller told her it was completely normal, and it was a good thing vampires had such amazing stamina.

Tonight, as with most nights, Sarah was in complete agreement. Not wanting to wait any longer, she stood with Keller in her arms. Both women shuddered again as Keller slid down her body and stood on her own two feet. Sarah watched her lover run a hand through messy blonde hair. Knowing her reprieve from the intense arousal of earlier was going to be short-lived, she wanted to get in that promised dance. "Come on, let's grab a few more drinks and do some dancing."

Keller growled at the singer's teasing look. "Oh yes, lets." After a few more shots on the second floor, they took their fresh beers downstairs to the main level. The dance floor was still packed when they forced their way on. They were lucky enough to find a place to set their sweating bottles before grinding together with the beat of the music. As Keller held her from behind, Sarah took the opportunity to tie the ends of her shirt under her ribs, leaving her belly bare and the fact that she was packing very obvious if one chose to look. Her low-slung jeans just barely covered the length of the toy beneath. As they danced, Sarah could feel eyes on them. Turning her head, she was surprised to see her friend Jill dancing nearby. What didn't surprise her was the heat Jill's gaze held. She smiled and crooked her finger to call the tall redhead over to them.

Jill looked at her ex curiously when she saw Keller step into view. The blonde seemed familiar, but she couldn't place the face. Sarah and Jill both considered the other their best friend, no matter how much time or distance was between them. But now that Sarah was back in town for good, Jill was starting to miss not seeing her friend. The veterinarian hadn't seen Sarah in months and wondered if this woman was the reason. However, the look of lust that Sarah was sending her way left her unsure. She shrugged and made her way through the crowd anyway. Maybe they were in an open relationship.

When Jill finally made it to their corner of the dance floor, Sarah gave her a fond smile. She leaned in close so Jill could hear her. "I'd like you to meet my girlfriend, Keller." Holding Keller's hand, she pulled the shorter woman near. "Keller, this is my closest friend, Jill."

Keller grinned. "The ex?"

Jill blushed slightly, wondering how serious Sarah was, and curious about how much the small blonde knew about their past. "It was many years ago, but yes. You seem familiar, do I know you from somewhere?"

The bar manager gave her a seductive look as she caressed the taller woman's hand in greeting. "Perhaps." Seeing the startled look on Jill's face, as well as the uncomfortable look that the redhead cast toward Sarah made Keller burst out in laughter and leaned close to her so she could be heard over the music. "Relax Jill, I'm just playing with you. I'm the manager of The Merge, so perhaps you've seen me there."

Jill blew out a relieve breath but was taken by surprise again when Sarah grabbed her by the hand. "Let's dance, we can catch up later!" Even more surprising was that the singer maneuvered Keller between them into a sandwich and winked at her. Curious. It almost felt like old times.

While Jill was busy grinding against Keller's ass, Sarah leaned down and spoke into her lover's ear just loud enough for Keller to hear and no one else. "What do you think?" Keller grinned and pulled her into a kiss. Understanding the bar manager's approval, she spoke again. "I think I could get us an invitation to her place." After she spoke, she worked her way around until Jill was in the middle of the sandwich.

Jill was only taller than Sarah by an inch, and she was well aware of what the singer was grinding into her. As soon as the realization hit, she forgot about the blonde in front of her and whipped her head around to look at Sarah. "You are not!"

Sarah smirked and pressed her full length into Jill. "Is there a problem?"

A dark red eyebrow raised toward her hairline as Jill abruptly stopped dancing. "Are you two serious?"

Keller came around to stand next to Sarah when she realized the two taller women had stopped dancing. Sarah took her hand and grabbed Jill's as well. She pulled them to the edge of the dance floor, near where they left their beer bottles. Sarah grabbed hers and took a swig, then offered the rest to Jill. They could hear slightly better since they were off to the side in the transept. That was the area that formed the cross-shape of the first floor of the church. Sarah gave her friend a smile. "We are very serious, but we also like a little adventure once in a while." She cocked her head. "What about you, do still enjoy a little adventure?"

Jill threw her head back and laughed loud enough to turn a few heads their way. "You never change, do you?"

Sarah gave her a look that was full of simmering heat. "Oh, I've changed plenty but that's a story for another day."

Jill looked from Sarah, to Keller, and back to Sarah. "Why not today? You two can come over to my place and *fill* me in." She licked her lips, suggesting more than just an interest in gossip. She waited, already anticipating a night of fun of which she hadn't seen in many years. Sarah's new girlfriend was hot, and Jill was definitely open to their type of adventure. "Well?"

Sarah looked at Keller with an unspoken question. Keller smiled and Sarah gave Jill their answer. "I think that sounds great. We'll follow, I'm assuming Sarah knows the way."

Sarah's old friend nodded and led the way toward the exit. The crowd was still heavy so they had to stay close to one another to thread through. When they popped out of the crowd near the back of the church, Jill abruptly stopped and turned toward Keller and Sarah. "One of you is good to drive right? You can ride with me if not."

The singer laughed, knowing that with her vampirism the alcohol wouldn't be an issue. Her body metabolized much too fast, so any buzz she had earlier was already burned off and she was left without any impairment. "No worries, we're good. We'll be right behind you." They went in separate directions when they got outside the club.

As they were walking to Sarah's SUV, Keller noticed her lover was having trouble. Sarah's lips were parted and she was breathing a little heavier than normal. Knowing that the toy was most likely the cause of her discomfort, Keller smirked. "Would you like me to drive?"

"God yes!"

When they were buckled into the Blazer, Keller looked at her lover. "Are you okay with this? Is this a good idea to do this with someone you know, that you are close to?"

Sarah cocked her head. "The more I think about it, the better I think it will be. I know she's open to it, I know she isn't expecting more than a good time. And I think between the two of us, we can both feed and cloud her memory of it without having to make her forget we were there." She frowned with her next thought.

"Besides, with the way I've been feeling lately, we have to do something." She looked at Keller. Her lover's face was dimly lit by the streetlights. "This isn't too weird for you is it, because Jill is an ex-girlfriend?"

Keller raised her right hand to cup Sarah's face. She opened her shield and connection to Sarah, and smiled. "Does it feel like I'm worried about anyone else? Our connection is everything. It is all there ever was, or ever will be; we are bound together for life." She moved her hand away and laughed. "I feel pretty secure in that."

Sarah smiled and rested a hand on Keller's leg while the shorter woman pulled away from the curb. "Okay then. Now, Jill lives out by Franklin Park so keep heading east on Broad Street. She lives on Auburn, which is right across from the high school."

The bar manager chuckled from the driver's seat. "A redhead lives on Auburn Street? Seriously? You know what they say about gingers..."

Sarah shook her head. "I wouldn't call her a ginger to her face or you'll be a bottom for the rest of the night." Keller raised a pale brow in disbelief and Sarah smirked. "Or call her a ginger, because having you bottom for both of us sounds kind of fun too." It wasn't long before they found themselves in a quiet residential neighborhood. It was well after midnight, so most lights were out in the surrounding houses when they pulled up to Jill's two story home. Sarah could see that Jill had beat them by more than a few minutes since multiple lights were on in her house. Sarah teased Keller. "Come on my bonny lass, the tall girls are going to make a proper lady out of you."

Feeling the slight heat of challenge, Keller let a little of her control slip as they walked up to Jill's front door. The wash of prickling power covered Sarah's skin with goose bumps. But the piercing bolt of lust from Keller nearly buckled Sarah's knees. "If I'm a bottom, it's simply because I want to be. We'll see who will be dominant by the time the night is through." In that moment when Keller's blue eyes met Sarah's green, the world around them seemed to disappear.

Sarah ran a tongue over suddenly dry lips. "I can't wait." The spell was broken when Jill opened the door.

Noticing the heated gaze between to the two women on her doorstep she chuckled. "Are you coming in, or are you going to give the neighbors a show?"

The tall brunette laughed in response and brushed past Jill on her way in. She made sure to rub against Jill's not-insubstantial breasts. "Shut up, Red, your neighbors are asleep."

Noticing the way Jill's nipples hardened with Sarah's touch, Keller paused when going by her. Taking the taller woman's hand, she brought it to her lips for a chaste kiss. Looking into the blue eyes of Sarah's friend, Keller let a little of her lust rush through the woman. It wasn't a clouding of the mind, just a light wash. With her voice purposely lower to prolong the sexual haze, she spoke, "Thank you for inviting us over, I hope our visit can bring you the pleasure you seek."

Jill gave a little gasp before shutting the front door again. Keller released her hand and stepped toward the waiting Sarah. Jill finally shook herself from the aroused haze and attempted to offer a little hospitality. "Would either of you like a drink? I have beer, wine, or water."

Keller and Sarah answered at the same time. "Water's fine."

After retrieving three bottles of water from her fridge, Jill handed over two of them to her guests. "Let's go into the living room where we can talk." She led the way through the open floor plan first floor to a spacious and well-decorated living room. After turning on the gas fireplace, she took a seat on an over-stuffed chair near the sofa. Sarah and Keller sat on the couch. Despite the arousal that was still coursing through her from Keller's words and Sarah's touch, Jill tried to make small talk. She genuinely wanted to know about Sarah and Keller's relationship. "So how did you two meet? Was it at The Merge?"

Sarah smiled. "Actually, Keller is Annie's boss, and we just kept running into each other everywhere." She shrugged. "We hooked up a few times and then we kept hooking up."

Keller laughed. "What can I say, I'm irresistible."

Sarah shoved her. "Oh please, you were the one who was conspiring with my sister to get me to move in with you!"

Keller protested. "We did no such thing!"

Jill's jaw dropped in shock. "Wait a minute!" She pointed at Sarah, then at Keller while she spoke. "You moved in with her?" When Sarah nodded Jill just stared. "Oh my God, you mean someone has finally tamed the untamable Sarah Colby? All your fans will be so disappointed!"

Keller cleared her throat and held up a single finger. "Actually, I can attest that she has not been tamed at all." She gave Jill a simmering look. "Would you like to find out?"

Just like that, the small talk was forgotten. All three of them stood then Sarah and Keller approached Jill. Walking right up to the taller woman, Sarah pulled her into a deep kiss. Sarah's arousal was already running hot from the toy, so she had to make a real effort to keep her teeth retracted. Meanwhile, Keller was plastered against Jill's side, with one hand running up the front of her shirt, and the other running down the back of her pants to squeeze the firm ass inside. Keller caressed Jill's soft belly skin and work her way up to lightly skim over the tops of her breasts, and then move back down again. When her fingers finally ran across achingly hard nipples, Jill gasped and pulled away from Sarah's mouth.

She turned her head and pulled Keller into a kiss. Sarah moved behind her ex and started grinding into her ass. It took less than a minute before she had to stop and back away because the toy nearly sent her over the edge. Sensing how close her lover was to orgasm, Keller pulled back as well. When Jill gave her a questioning look, Keller nodded toward Sarah. They both took in the parted lips and glassy eyes and knew she was right there, so close.

Jill smiled fondly, remembering the many times she had seen that look in Sarah's eyes. Grabbing Keller's hand, she addressed Sarah. "Let's move this to the bedroom, I want to see you fuck your girlfriend with that thing before you blow your top. Will alcohol help take the edge off?"

Sarah gave a shaky laugh and was joined by Keller. "If it's strong enough, and only for a little while, why?"

Jill grinned and led them into the kitchen. She let go of Keller's hand and grabbed three shot glasses from the cupboard before lining them up on the long breakfast bar. Then she opened her freezer and removed a bottle of Rumple Minze. After pouring generous shots, Jill grabbed the small thick glass and raised it into the air, waiting for her guests to follow. "A toast, to the freshest breath you can get after drinking alcohol!" With that, they each tossed back the one hundred proof peppermint liqueur. Jill shuddered. "Brr, that's good stuff!"

She froze suddenly when she noticed two pairs of eyes gone very dark with arousal. Sarah began to unbutton Jill's shirt while Keller poured another shot and moved the other two glasses out of the way. Once the shirt was open, Sarah released the bra's front clasp and Jill licked her lips in anticipation. She didn't have to wait long. Sarah grabbed hold of Jill's ass and lifted her onto the counter with ease. "Jesus, Sarah!"

Before she could say another word, she was gently pushed back to lie on the counter, gasping slightly at the chill of it touching her shoulders and back. Sarah unbuttoned Jill's jeans while

Keller waved the shot glass above her chest, trying to decide what she wanted to taste first. Distracted by the thought of the ice-cold liquid touching any of her bare flesh, Jill was barely aware of Sarah pulling off her jeans and underwear. She wet her lips in anticipation when she saw a heated look pass between Sarah and Keller. She smiled down the length of her body at her old friend. "Well, who's going to go first?"

Sarah merely smiled and Keller laughed. "Who says anyone is going to go first?" Before Jill could contemplate the meaning of her words, Keller poured the shot over both breasts and watched the recumbent woman arch her back off the counter. Nipples hardened in response and the small pink areolas puckered at the cold. At the same time, Keller took one of the hard buds into her mouth, Sarah slowly ran her tongue the length of Jill's sex.

Jill's reaction was immediate. She gripped Keller's head to her breast and hissed. "Oh God!" Keller took her time cleaning the liquor off Jill's chest. By the time she was moving to the other nipple, Sarah had inserted two fingers and was proving just how good musicians were with their hands. When Sarah felt her friend's thighs begin to tremble, she immediately pulled out. Jill was so turned on she couldn't stop herself from begging. "Please don't stop!"

Sarah smirked and tugged Jill's knees away from the counter, indicating she wanted the other woman to get down. "Come on, I'll give you what you want."

Jill groaned. "I don't think I can stand. And I don't remember you being this much of a tease, Colby."

Keller helped the taller woman off the counter while Sarah backed away from them. "I told you, a lot of stuff has changed. You'll just have to wait and see." When she caught Keller's eye, she nodded toward the back of the couch. "I see you have new furniture, have you tried it all out?"

Keller draped Jill forward, over the back of the couch while Sarah removed her own jeans and underwear and stepped up behind her. Keller knelt on the couch in front of Jill, leaving her head perfectly lined up with the tall woman's breasts. She took one into her mouth as soon as Sarah started rubbing the toy up and down Jill's wet slit. Jill warned, "Shit Colby, you know I won't last long like this!"

Sarah smiled at Keller, unseen behind her friend. "Oh, I'm counting on it." The toy wasn't too big, simply because it had to fit within the confines of Sarah's jeans, so it didn't take long to work it all the way in. She rolled her hips with each thrust and raked blunt fingernails down Jill's back. Between the movement of the strap-on against Sarah's clit, and the way it fit nicely up inside her, the singer's own pleasure was quickly ratcheting. Each thrust brought them closer and closer to the edge.

Sarah took a firm hold of Jill's long wavy hair and used it to pull her nearly upright. Just a little pressure, not a lot; exactly the way Jill liked it. Keller could see just how close her lover really was once Jill's upper body wasn't blocking her view. She pulled her mouth away from Jill's stiff peaks and watched the flush progress across both women's chests as they neared orgasm. Knowing her ex was one of those women who could come from penetration alone, Sarah picked up the pace.

With the sound of bodies slapping together and feminine panting, Keller let some of her lust roll through the other two women. She leaned up and kissed Jill's neck when she sensed the end was near. Like the crashing of waves, the force of orgasm pummeled the taller women. Timing it just right, Keller bit down and clouded Jill's mind completely with the energy they created. She drank just enough and used her saliva to heal the wounds by gently licking the neck below her lips. As soon as she pulled away from Jill, the redhead collapsed unconscious over the back of the couch and Sarah nearly followed her. With only a minimal shudder, Sarah pulled out of her ex and then removed the toy from herself. Sensing her lover's legs wouldn't hold her, Keller was around the couch in a flash, catching her. "Easy, love."

Jill came to less than a minute later, just as Sarah's legs firmed up and she was able to stand on her own. With hands resting on the back of the couch to support herself, Jill threw a thoroughly fucked look over her shoulder at the other two woman. "That was hot! Who's ready for round two?"

Keller shot Sarah an incredulous look and the singer responded with a laugh. "What can I say? I chose her for her stamina, not her brains."

The woman with the doctorate in veterinary medicine stood up and swiped at her ex. "Right after we first met I began tutoring her in algebra, and I chose her because she has a hot ass!"

"Whatever, Red, you remember it however you like. I'll always know the truth!" Keller smiled at their antics.

Jill snorted. "You do that!" After stretching her arms far above her head to help work the kinks out of her lower back, she turned off the fireplace and headed toward stairs leading to the upper level. "If either of you want to check out my new shower, follow me."

Keller called out. "We'll be right behind you." In a lower voice she addressed Sarah. "You're totally right, that was hot. I'm glad we did this." She squirmed a little, immediately noticed by Sarah.

"You're right on the edge, aren't you?" She lowered a hand to press against the crotch seam of Keller's jeans.

Keller shuddered and then moved Sarah's hand away. "I can wait. I want to see what's so special about this shower of hers."

Sarah gave her a smirk and turned toward the stairs. "Oh, you're gonna like it." And she was right. The shower was extraordinary. It was ten feet from left to right, and eight feet deep. The front and part of the right side were made of glass. On the left side was a tile bench that was three feet wide and ran from the glass front to the back wall. But the best feature by far was that the ceiling had a large rectangular showerhead that rained down in the center, and multiple detachable heads around the tile walls. When Keller and Sarah made it upstairs, they found Jill already in the shower beckoning them with a single index finger. They hastily removed their clothes and joined her. She immediately pulled Keller into an embrace and started feasting on the smaller woman's mouth. Sarah walked up and molded her wet body behind her lover. She reached around between the two women and cupped Keller's pert breasts in her hands, rolling the nipples between her fingers. She made eye contact with Jill. "I do believe we left someone out of our fun earlier. What are we going to do about that?"

Jill pulled away from Keller's mouth, leaving Keller panting with desire. "I have a few ideas. Why don't you go sit on the bench, all the way back?" Sarah followed her instruction, and Jill sat Keller in front of her, between the musician's legs. Then she knelt on the tile floor, with water spraying all around her. After draping a leg over each shoulder, she smirked up at the couple in front of her. "I'll trust you to hold her there and not let go." Sarah grabbed Keller's arms just as Jill dipped her tongue into the hot folds of Keller's sex. Keller squirmed and cried out, so near to release. Sensing that Sarah's girlfriend was close, Jill immediately filled her with two fingers and curled the tips as she thrust in and out. Jill worked her to a fever pitch and then stilled all motion, only to repeat her actions again. She did this three times until Keller was straining against Sarah's grasp.

When Jill started working her up a fourth time, she couldn't help the words out of her mouth. "Oh God, please just let me come!" Sarah nuzzled her lover's neck as she released Keller's arms. She put her hands to work immediately by rolling a nipple with the fingers of her left hand and running the right one down to rhythmically massage Keller's abdomen. Sarah teased her neck with sharp teeth as Keller started to shake with the pending orgasm.

Sensing Keller wouldn't be able to last another go around, Jill added a third finger and furiously sucked the hard clit between her lips. The explosion was almost instantaneous. Keller's back bowed away from Sarah as her entire body stiffened at the onslaught of pleasure radiating from her core.

Sarah refrained from feeding on the bar manager, knowing she could be seen by her ex. Instead, she shuddered from the spillover of arousal that leaked around Keller's shields. Then, like a puppet whose strings were cut, Keller's body suddenly went limp. Without opening her eyes, Keller spoke in a quiet voice, barely heard over the spray from the showerheads. "I love this shower."

Jill started laughing and was joined by Sarah. "Well if you think this is nice, you should see the bed! I don't know about you two, but I'm ready to be dry and horizontal! Not to mention I think we may have used most of the hot water in my jumbo heater."

Keller laughed as well and then glanced up at Sarah as Jill stood and turned the shower off. Blue eyes met green, and both women wondered how Jill had managed to take over this little tryst. She was like a cruise director, not that they were complaining. Keller lowered her voice even though Jill had already left the shower. "I want to taste her while you feed from behind."

Sarah's lips parted as a bolt of arousal caused her to throb. Just the thought of feeding while she watched Keller go down on her ex caused her breath to hitch. "Yes. I'll take care of it."

Jill returned to the bedroom with a few bottles of water just as Keller and Sarah emerged from the bathroom freshly dried. "I thought you guys might be thirsty." She held the bottles out to her guests. Keller and Sarah each quenched their thirst before setting the bottles on a nearby dresser.

Sarah was the first to move onto the bed. Completely nude, she crawled up to the head of the king size bed, leaning against the headboard. With a heated smile, she looked at Jill and patted the bed between her legs. "Come lean back against me, Keller is thirsty for more than water." Jill glanced at Keller as if seeking confirmation then crawled onto the bed to do as Sarah asked. Wet hair tickled Sarah's cheek as Jill nestled her ass against the singer's crotch. Sarah immediately wrapped her arms around Jill and took advantage of her unhindered access to the taller woman's breasts. She could feel a change in her friend's breathing when Keller started crawling up the bed with the smooth grace of a panther. Keller's eyes had gone dark as the combined lust of the two vampires flooded the room.

Jill was caught in the black depths of Keller's eyes, and the primal part of her brain tried to kick in through the wave of arousal. "Wait—" She started to sit up and Sarah locked her arms around Jill's upper body.

At the same time Keller secured her legs and whispered. "No waiting." Using only her tongue, since hands were needed to hold Jill down, she teased the writhing woman beneath her. In a matter of minutes, Jill was no longer trying to get free, merely squirming to test her bonds. Sarah knew it was a scenario that her ex was both familiar with and fond of. Keller let go of Jill's legs to bring her fingers into play, eliciting a cry of pleasure from the prone woman.

Sarah leaned close to her ear. "You like it when we hold you down, don't you? You like it when you can't get away."

Jill hissed. "Yes! Oh God—" She moaned under the deliberate onslaught of Keller's talented tongue and fingers, and Sarah moved her head down to kiss and nip at her ex's neck. Sarah cradled the woman's cheek and jaw in her right hand, as Jill's head canted to the side. Sarah was drawn to the pulse that pounded just below the surface of her skin. Jill rode the waves of pleasure higher and higher, and Sarah made eye contact with Keller. Both pairs of eyes were now dark and the skin around Sarah's fangs felt tight. She craved that friction, that hot wash of liquid down her throat. And Keller knew. Without a word between them, they both dropped their shields and crashed together. Jill gave a primal scream as she roared over the edge at the same time Sarah struck. Augmenting the pleasure felt by all three women, Sarah made sure that was the only thing Jill was aware of. Once she drank her fill, Sarah sealed the wound the same way Keller had in the living room. The strength of the triple orgasm had rendered Jill unconscious again, and Keller had collapsed between her legs as well.

After more than a minute, Keller raised her head slowly and her eyes were drawn to the drop of blood at the corner of the singer's mouth. Raising herself, she straddled Jill and crawled up the bed toward her lover. The kiss she bestowed on the musician cleaned the remaining evidence of her feeding.

As she pulled away from Sarah's lips, Jill opened her eyes. She gave a tired chuckle when faced with Keller's breasts. "Damn you two, all this glorious flesh at my fingertips and I'm too tired move!"

Keller laughed and sat down in Jill's lap. "What happened to all that stamina that Sarah bragged about?"

Jill looked at her wryly. "Well, between the two of you, you fucked it out of me." She took a calming breath, still basking in the afterglow. She gave a casual wave of her hand. "There's plenty of room for you to stay. Sarah, you know this already. However, I'm afraid I'm going to have to tap out from any more sexual activity. I was up last night on call with two emergency cases that came into the clinic and now I'm running on fumes."

Sarah turned her head and gave her a light kiss on the lips. "No worries, Red, we had fun. But I think I'm ready to head home now too." She looked expectantly at her lover.

Keller also gave Jill a light kiss and gently rolled off the taller woman's lap. "Yes, it was a great time. Thank you so much for inviting us over." She knew that she and Sarah were a big part of why Jill felt so drained and expected that she'd be done.

Exhaustion suddenly washed over the woman still lying on the bed. "Ugh, I don't even think I can move to see you out. Sarah, be a doll and lock up for me?"

Sarah winked at her. "You know it." Sarah shut the lights off on their way out of the bedroom. Downstairs, they quickly dressed and the musician found a paper sack from a popular high-end grocery store. She held it up so Keller could see before dropping the strap-on into it. "She's such a food snob!"

Keller laughed. "Well not everyone can live on pizza and Thai takeout like the Colby sisters."

Sarah cocked her head to the side and smirked. "True." She stood there for a minute, just staring at the woman in front of her.

Keller smiled. "What are you thinking about?"

Sarah's eyes and nose crinkled in mirth. "I'm thinking about how *not* tired I am, and wondering how fast we can get back to the condo."

"I'll drive." Laughter followed them out of the house on Auburn Street while the woman upstairs dreamed of being hunted by wild dogs outside her veterinary clinic.

Chapter Four

SARAH SLEPT LATER than usual the next morning. Keller was up making breakfast and didn't have the heart to wake her lover on her first weekend off in months. Twice in the middle of the night she was startled from sleep by her lover's thrashing. The singer had clearly been in the throes of a nightmare. Sarah had been having them a few times a week since the incident with Marcel. She never spoke to Keller about them and Keller was hesitant to inquire. Sarah tended to close down emotionally with difficult subjects. She was hoping that whatever was prompting the bad dreams would taper off with the passage of time, and with Marcel no longer in their lives. Her only company in the kitchen was an intently watching husky. Every time Keller walked past Duke, his great broom of a tale swept the floor hopefully.

By the time Sarah wandered out, breakfast was finished cooking. They ate in comfortable silence, enjoying the feast on the breakfast bar. Keller always stressed how important it was to get plenty to eat because of their condition. Besides a heaping plate of waffles with pecans and maple syrup, they had eggs, bacon, and sausage. Once breakfast was complete, they efficiently cleaned up the leftovers then Keller watched the sickening ritual of her lover preparing coffee. Keller shuddered as the third spoonful of sugar went into the mug. "Lass, I don't know how you can drink it like that. It's too sweet!"

Sarah nearly snorted her first sip of the hot coffee. "Are you kidding me?" She pointed at Keller's waffle plate. The only thing remaining of the three large waffles was the quarter inch deep puddle of syrup. "You put enough syrup on your food to choke a horse. Talk about the pot calling the kettle black, jeez! Come to think of it, this entire breakfast, while delicious, probably just clogged the rest of my arteries."

"Our arteries can't clog, love."

"Well, then it gave them a good scare!"

Keller burst out laughing, happy to finally see Sarah smiling and lighthearted. The dreams coupled with Sarah's physical exhaustion had given Keller a good scare, not food. "How do you feel today?"

Her question was met with a happy smile. "I feel refreshed,

rejuvenated even. It's crazy how just a little bit of blood can do so much!"

Keller started clearing the dirty dishes from the table. "Good, I feel a lot better too. I'm going to take Duke out and get the paper. Do we have any plans for today?"

Sarah smiled. "Well, we don't have any plans but I'm sure we can make some. The only thing we have scheduled is training with Alain tomorrow. Other than that we have nada. Maybe there will be something in the paper."

"Want to throw on some sweats and come with me? We can take Duke for a longer walk in the park by the river and grab the mail on the way back."

Sarah nodded. "Sure, I'll be right back."

Keller called after her girlfriend as the singer left the room. "Not that I'm complaining about the skimpy panties and baby doll t-shirt!" Five minutes later, the dishes were loaded in the dishwasher and both women headed out the door with Duke bounding in front of them on his leash. He pulled them toward the stairwell door and Sarah sighed, resigned to the fact that her dog refused to get on the elevator. When they returned forty-five minutes later, Keller grabbed a bottle of water and took the paper to the couch. Her eyes were immediately drawn to an article at the bottom of the front page. "Hey, Sarah?"

Sarah wandered in and sat next to her on the couch. "What's up? Anything good in there?"

"Have you ever heard of a wild animal attack near Columbus?"

Sarah tilted her head in puzzlement. "No, why? Did something happen?"

"Apparently two hikers were found up in Alum Creek State Park, both dead from a suspected animal attack. The article says investigators are speculating that it could be a bear or a pair of large coyotes but they weren't sure until they brought an expert in. Apparently the park isn't known for having large predators but park officials have said that it's not uncommon for them to wander in from farther off."

Sarah peered down at the paper in Keller's lap. "Isn't Alum Creek State Park near Louve's farm?"

Keller ran a hand through her messy blonde hair. "I believe she said it was on the other side of the lake." She turned serious eyes toward her girlfriend. Centuries of life had gifted Nobel Keller with superb instincts and she had learned to listen to those instincts. If this attack had anything to do with Marcel, or wolves in general, it would surely only lead to more nightmares for Sarah. "There is something off here, and I don't like it. Just a second." She went to find her cell phone, dialing as she came back to the couch. When it was answered, Keller spoke in rapid French, then seemed to listen for a minute and nod her head. "*Au Revoir*." The bar manager sighed again and tossed the smart phone onto the coffee table. She threw herself down on the couch in frustration and leaned forward to rest her elbows on her knees.

Sarah could feel the emotions swirling around in her lover. Foremost was worry, then irritation and disbelief. "Well? What did she say?"

"She said Marcel came back to pack his things and pick up his final check. He told her that he would be returning to Quebec and his family."

Sarah looked into her lover's serious blue eyes. "But you don't believe her, do you?"

Keller scrubbed her face with her hands and blew out a breath. The last thing she wanted to do was worry Sarah further but she couldn't lie either. "Oh, I believe *her*. I just don't believe him. Call it a gut instinct, but they found two sets of tracks by the bodies. And it worries me. We certainly don't need any deaths to draw attention to a community of people who are *different*."

The musician took her hand before it could rake through the messy blonde spikes again. She reveled in how warm and alive Keller felt. "What can we do?"

Keller gave her a look that carried the weight of helplessness. "Nothing. There is nothing we can do but wait and see."

HALF ASLEEP, ANNIE Colby squinted in annoyance. She had worked late the previous night, and since it was now Saturday, she knew she'd have to close again. The loud thump of music from the living room indicated that Jesse was up. She grabbed her cell phone off the nightstand and growled when she saw it was just after seven a.m. "What the hell?" Knowing her girlfriend would hear just fine, she yelled. "Jesse!" Then she covered her head again and waited.

Rapid thumping came down the hall and her girlfriend burst into the room. "What? What's wrong? Are you okay?" Jesse had become paranoid about Annie's safety since the incident at the farmhouse with Marcel. She knew the man was gone, but still she worried.

Annie peered out from under the pillow. Normally her obvious worry would prompt a fond smile but on just a few hours of sleep, it only set off more irritation. "It's seven a.m., why are you blaring music so early? I didn't get in until three."

Jesse wore a contrite look. "I'm sorry, babe. I guess I didn't realize what time you got home. I thought you'd just go back to sleep after I left for work."

Surprised hazel eyes met Jesse's brown ones. "Wait, you're working? Since when?"

The IT professional swallowed, realizing that she hadn't texted Annie to let her know her change in schedule. "Uh, since last night? My boss asked for a few volunteers to work this weekend, and I wanted some extra cash to upgrade my laptop. I was going to text you at work but I forgot." She smiled hopefully. "But hey, why don't you catch some more sleep after I leave and maybe we can do dinner and a movie later."

Annie looked at her in frustration. "Apparently you also forgot that I work tonight as well. I have to go in early and close, which means I'll be gone before you get home and you'll be in bed when I return. I don't get a night off until Sunday!"

"Well shit." She knew Annie had been on edge since she had been training with werewolves out at the farm. Between Marcel's threats and Marie's blatant disregard of their relationship status, things had been rocky at home. She wracked her brain trying to think of a way out of their situation. "Um, do you want me to call in sick to work?" Jesse never called in sick, and just the thought of it only served to ratchet up her anxiety. "I mean, I'm sorry but I guess I figured since you worked last weekend that you'd have this one off."

Annie ran a hand through her tangled dark hair. "Well, normally I would except Lynne and I are both picking up extra hours since Keller announced she was quitting. She's only there half the time, and we still haven't found another manager to replace her. So it's crazy right now." She leveled an exasperated look at her clueless nerd of a girlfriend. "But dammit, Jesse, no matter if I was working tonight or not, I don't appreciate an early morning wake up when I work the night before. Seriously, what were you thinking?"

Angry at her own stupidity and being called out on it like a child, she responded with heat. "I *wasn't*, okay? Jesus, Annie, I'm only human and I make mistakes." In a fit of temper, she turned and stalked toward the door. "You want some quiet, fine! I'll be out of your hair in five minutes, and then you can have as much quiet as you want!" Growling, she slammed the door as she left the room. The wood trim splintered as her wolf strength kicked in, and the door twisted on its hinges.

Annie stared wide-eyed in the direction of the hall. She whispered with equal parts fear and disbelief. "Holy fuck." She stayed that way until she heard the front door slam, albeit with less force. It took another five minutes before Jesse's car started and drove away. After that, exhaustion and anxiety caused Annie to curl into a fetal ball and fall into a nightmare plagued sleep.

IT TOOK FIVE minutes for Jesse to calm down enough to drive away. She sat in her car doing the meditation and breathing exercises Alain had taught her. She knew that losing her cool wasn't an option, so she had to get her anger under control. It was so hard because she loved Annie more than life and she was desperately afraid of losing her. Jesse thought back over the events of the past six months. First the city had been plagued by a string of violent gay bashings and after that things just got weird. Her girlfriend had been through a lot. Annie discovered that vampires and werewolves were real and had both her sister and girlfriend turn into them, respectively. It was lot to take in. And Jesse knew that despite reassurance to the contrary, Annie was still jealous and afraid of Marie. They'd only been together a year and they'd already fallen into a pattern where they never saw each other.

Dread pooled in Jesse's belly and slowly rose up to lodge in her throat. One year. Their one-year anniversary from the date they had become a serious couple was three days ago. "Sonofafuckingbitch!" The revelation that she had missed their anniversary caused Jesse to pull over to the side of the road in order to get her breathing under control again. The last thing her girlfriend needed was for her to think that she didn't care. When she finally arrived to work, she was five minutes late. It wasn't a big deal, and it wasn't like she'd get penalized for it, but Jesse was always early. Always.

Her coworker, Jason, peered around the wall separating their cubicles. "What's up, J? I almost thought you weren't coming in today, you're never late!"

Jesse sat in her chair and fired up her laptop. "I know, I know!" She ran a hand through her hair in frustration.

Jason looked at her in concern. "Are you all right?"

The brunette slumped in her chair. "We had a big fight this morning. I forgot to tell her I was working today. She worked late last night, I woke her up, and then it all went downhill from there. She's working a lot of hours lately and — I dunno. Oh, and to top it all off, our anniversary was a couple days ago and I totally forgot!" Her hair, shaved short on the sides and back but long on top, hung over her eyes in the front. She peered at him through the messy bangs.

"Oh damn. One year, right?" Jesse nodded. Jason whistled. "You know you're going to have to do some major ass-kissing, right?"

Jesse sighed. "You know the sad thing is that I don't think she realized it either. We've just been under a lot of pressure lately. And now I feel like we never see each other." Jesse had been pretty good friends with Jason since she had started working at the tech startup right after graduation. They had a great rapport. She knew all about his wife and new baby, and he knew all about her being disowned by her family, as well as about Annie, Sarah and, Keller. Well...he knew as much as he could be allowed to know. So Jason understood how important the Colby sisters were in Jesse's life.

He thought for a minute, trying to come up with some way to help his friend out. Finally he grinned. "You know, Resurrection is coming to town and they're playing at the Newport Music Hall on Sunday and Monday night. You should take a vacation day on Monday and see if there are tickets still available. Didn't you say Annie was a huge fan of their music?"

"Yes!" Jesse spun in her chair and logged into her laptop. After a spate of rapid-fire typing, she found what she was looking for. Not only were there still seats available, there were some in the front row. She quickly added them to her cart and went to the pay method. She lost a few seconds when her eyes bugged out at the price, but quickly typed in her PayPal information and completed the transaction. Two thoughts ran like a freight train through her head: *It's a good thing I'm working today* and *I don't need to update my laptop anyway.* "Done!" She gleefully accepted the earned high five from Jason.

He grinned at her, happy to help out. "You know what this means though?"

She looked at him curiously. "What, that I owe you one?"

He laughed. "Well, that too. But it also means you'd better find someplace nice for dinner." Jesse gave him a brief look of panic before spinning back around in her chair and attacking her keyboard again. He was still chuckling when he walked away calling over his shoulder. "If boss man comes by, let him know I went to drop the kids off at the pool."

Jesse grimaced unseen at his childish euphemism. "You're sick, man. I'm not telling him anything!" Meanwhile, she never stopped searching for the perfect restaurant. She had a plan, now she just had to get it all in place.

SATURDAY NIGHT AT The Merge was always busy. Annie had been running since she stepped through the door. She slept terribly, plagued by nightmares and thoughts of Jessie. She hated when they fought and hated the fact that her girlfriend scared her when she was angry. But she knew it would devastate Jesse if she ever told her that. It had taken them months to come to terms with everything when Jesse had been infected with the werewolf virus by Marcel. But even with all her training and meditation, Annie knew that her girlfriend wasn't perfect. The younger Colby sister was currently checking stock in the back room in a rare moment of calm. Since no one was around, she was chastising herself for her own cranky attitude that morning. "This is why I should never speak on little sleep and no caffeine, I turn into a raging bitch." Granted, Jesse was pretty clueless and sometimes didn't understand some things that seemed like common sense to others. Things like "you can't cook food twice as fast in the oven if you turn it up twice as high" and "if running the bathroom sink makes the water go cold while your girlfriend is in the shower, so too does flushing the toilet." And the newest one was "don't blast loud music a few hours after your girlfriend gets home from a double shift." Clearly that one was still a work in progress.

Once Annie confirmed the liquor quantities on the shelf, she sat on a nearby stool. She thought back to when she and Jesse had first started dating. It was so exciting to find someone she really liked. Much to her own sister's surprise, Annie had been saving herself for the time she fell in love. Once she finally gave in and had sex though, she and Jesse became ravenous. Of course, this only helped with their plot to get Sarah to move in with Keller. Now it felt as if they hardly ever saw each other, and the only time the younger couple had sex was after Jesse changed back to her human form.

Annie sighed. As much as she loved her job as assistant manager over the Voodoo Pony, more and more she wished she could just have a day job so she could spend more time with her girlfriend. Working nights got old after a while. Annie pulled herself off the stool and grabbed the clipboard she had set on the shelf. "I'm starting to think that Keller had the right idea to quit. Too bad we can't all be independently wealthy vampires."

Jesse had called Sarah and Keller, asking if they wanted to surprise Annie at the club. Even though her plans were mostly finalized for Sunday, she still felt bad for losing her temper on her girlfriend. They met Jesse at the house to pick her up, and even spent a little time helping the younger woman fix the broken bedroom door frame. Keller took one look at it and simply raised an eyebrow. Sarah was a little more vocal. "Is there something we should know, Jesse? Is everything okay between you two?" She leveled a green eyed gaze at Annie's girlfriend, a young woman that Sarah had come to see as another sister. "I don't have to worry about my sister, do I?"

Jesse realized in that moment how serious Sarah had taken the broken door. Her eyes got wide and she swallowed nervously. "Um, no! I swear Sarah, it was just a little fight and the bottom line is that I'm just a stupid jerk. I slammed the door and totally forgot my own strength." She went on to explained how it happened and how she planned on getting back into Annie's good graces. Keller left then to grab the tools from the basement and a few pieces of scrap lumber from when the contractors had remodeled the downstairs the previous fall.

Sarah nodded. "She loves that band. I think you made a great choice." Sarah told her a brief story about how she and Annie had gotten tickets to see Resurrection a couple years ago, on one of her many short trips home. It was during the time that Sarah had spent as a "starving" musician on the road. Truthfully though, she had never been a starving musician. She spent years planning and had plenty of money saved up, on top of the insurance money from her parent's death. Going on the road to play gigs around the country was never about making money. It was about the experience and getting her name out there. She had been chaffing at responsibility until Annie was old enough to be on her own. Once she got it out of her system, she was finally able to admit how much she missed home and family. That's what finally prompted her to return the year before. She cocked her head and Jesse noticed that it was exactly the same mannerism as Annie.

"Where are you going for dinner?" Keller returned, catching only the tail end of the conversation.

Jesse answered with a pained look. "I have no idea! We haven't gone out in forever, and I feel like I need to take her to a really nice place for dinner."

Sarah shook her head. "No, you should go someplace where they have good food and it's comfortable." When Jesse gave her a surprised look, she continued. "You'd have to dress up for a really nice place, and you're not going to want to wear those clothes out to a rock concert."

Keller had a sudden thought and cleared her throat to interrupt. When she had their attention, she dropped her own little bombshell. "I uh, hmm, I just happen to know the lead singer of Resurrection, and can get us all back stage passes for the show."

Sarah looked at her curiously. "How is it that you know a famous musician so well, and I don't? I was the one traveling the country singing for my supper, so to speak. I met a lot of people."

Keller winked at her. "Maybe I'll tell you the story some time."

The younger woman smiled at Sarah and Keller, and then her face fell. "Well, I would love it if you guys could come too, because I know how much Annie loves hanging out with you. And the back stage passes would be a dream come true. However, I know for a fact they are all sold out now. Jason tried to get tickets before we left work this afternoon and they were gone already."

Keller gave them both a wide grin. "Oh, don't worry about that. As a matter of fact, why don't you give your friend Jason your tickets, and I'll take care of the four of us. How does that sound?"

Jesse's mouth dropped open, and only one word came out. "Epic."

Sarah and Keller started laughing, but truthfully Sarah was just as excited. She loved the band as much as her sister. Keller looked from one brunette to the other. "Why don't you two figure out where to go for dinner, and I'll call my friend about the tickets."

The singer gave her a serious look. "You're sure your friend will come through? I don't want any of us to get our hopes up."

"I'm sure. Now if you'll both excuse me, I'll be right back."

Sarah and Jesse stared at her in awe as Keller walked back down the hall to the living room to make her call. Jesse whistled. "I can't believe she knows Grace Cadence! That's some fucking shit right there! Wait 'til I tell Jason!"

The elder Colby sister shook her head and smiled. "She continues to surprise and amaze me."

Jesse smirked and elbowed her girlfriend's sister. "I bet outside the bed too, huh?"

Sarah lightly cuffed the back of the younger woman's head. "Get back to work, pup! The sooner we fix this door, the sooner we can go see Annie." Jesse mock saluted and started measuring the door frame for a new slat of wood. She was just giving the saw a curious look when Keller returned with a big smile on her face.

"Better go call your friend Jason, because the four of us now have front row seats." Sarah leaned over and gave Keller a kiss in thanks. Jesse was a little more exuberant. With the hand not holding the length of wood, she punched the air. However, all three women's attention was drawn to the sound of splintering wood and her other hand.

She looked down, chagrined at her loss of control. The younger woman groaned when she realized she had just made more work for them. She looked at the other larger board on the floor, and then glanced over at the circular saw that Keller had brought up. "Damn."

Sarah looked at her humorously. "Do you even know how to use that?"

Jesse idly scratched her temple. "Um, no?"

Keller grabbed the tape measure and pencil off the floor. "Go call your friend; I'll take care of this."

Jesse beamed and ran down the hall. "Thanks, Keller!"

It took very little time to measure and cut a new slat to replace the broken one. It wouldn't be painted but at least it was functional. Once everyone was cleaned up, they all piled into Sarah's SUV for the trip down to The Merge. While standing in line to get in, Keller said they could just skip to the front. Sarah scolded her. "You're not the manager tonight, so we're going to stand here just like everyone else."

Knowing Sarah was serious about not working tonight, Keller made a crossing motion over her chest. "I swear, no work tonight."

When they got to the door, Teddy let the three of them in without paying cover. "Hey ladies, fancy seeing you here tonight. Just a heads up, we are busy as all get out tonight. Poor Annie has been running ragged trying to keep up." He smiled showing his friendly gap-toothed grin.

Sarah returned the smile. "Thanks T. We're actually here to surprise her, so don't say anything if she comes by before we can catch up to her."

"No problem, miss thang! Now go and try to stay out of trouble, I have a job to do and my boss is a real mean one." He winked at Keller.

Once inside the three women went to get drinks first. Keller led them through to the Voodoo Pony, since it wasn't as busy as the dance bar on Saturday nights. While Fridays they ran the Sip and Chug music spotlight, Saturdays alternated between special events. They had live bands, karaoke, talent contests, fundraisers, and even drag shows. Sure enough, they found Annie behind the bar, helping one of the new bartenders who seemed to be in over her head. A big smile came over her face when she saw her family walk up.

"Hey, this is a surprise!"

Keller walked behind the bar, despite the scowl Sarah threw at her. "I'll get Angela caught up, go say high to your sister and girlfriend."

Annie gave her a grateful look. "Thanks, boss!" She quickly made her way around the bar and threw herself into Jesse's arms. "Oh my God, what are you guys doing here?" She turned to Sarah and gave her a big hug as well. "And I thought you banned Keller from the bar this weekend, to give you guys some bonding time?"

Sarah tugged the younger woman's earlobe affectionately. "It's all good, A. And we're here because Jesse has a surprise for you."

Annie held up a finger and waved them toward Keller's office where they could talk and actually be heard. Once inside she shut the door and turned to her girlfriend. "What surprise?"

Jesse nervously ran a hand through the dark hair hanging slightly in her eyes. "Well, first I want to tell you that I'm an ass. I'm a totally inconsiderate jerk. And second, I remembered that Thursday was our one year anniversary."

A look of surprise crossed Annie's face. "Oh damn it was, wasn't it? Are you guys here to celebrate then?"

"Actually, the band Resurrection is playing at the Newport Music Hall tomorrow night and I got us tickets."

Annie squealed and threw herself into Jesse's arms. "Oh my God, I love that band! You're the best, J!"

Happily accepting the kiss she received, Jesse caught a glimpse of Sarah's uncomfortable face and reluctantly pulled away. Annie pouted and the young werewolf tapped her on the bottom lip. "There's more. When Keller found out how much both you and Sarah liked the band, she made a call to her friend and scored all four of us front row seats and backstage passes."

Annie looked at Jesse in disbelief, then over at her sister. "Holy shit! I bet you're on the moon right now, huh?"

Sarah laughed. "Oh yeah, definitely!"

The younger Colby sister looked back and forth between the two women. "So who's this mystery friend of Keller's that has such good connections?"

They were interrupted when Keller opened the door and came into the office. "My mystery friend is none other than Grace Cadence."

"No shit?"

Keller smiled. "No shit."

Sarah slapped her girlfriend's arm. "Did you really hear us through the door, with all the noise going on out there?"

The bar manager winked at her. "Yup. And someday when you become a big bad grownup vampire, you will too!"

The friendly slap turned into a not as friendly pinch. "Ass!"

Everyone laughed and Annie looked at the clock on the wall. It read eleven-seventeen. "So are you guys staying 'til close?"

Sarah nodded. "Yup. I want to drink and sing some karaoke!"

Jesse looked confused. "But you're a real musician; you can play all sorts of instruments. Isn't karaoke, like, beneath you or something?"

The singer placed a limp hand over her heart and let her high school drama training come to the forefront. "What? Why I'll have you know that karaoke is its own art form!"

They all laughed and Keller covered her face with her hand. "Crivvens!"

Sarah slapped her arm as they filed out of the office. "Just for that, you're going to sing a duet with me." The look on Keller's face cracked them all up again.

Everyone had a blast on the Pony side of the club. Sarah even talked Annie into coming up and singing with her. They covered the song "My Immortal" by Evanescence. They didn't just cover the song, they owned it. When they returned to their table, Jesse looked at her girlfriend in awe. "Babe, I had no idea you could sing like that!"

Sarah piped up. "She can play the guitar too."

Jesse looked at Annie curiously. "But you don't even have a guitar."

The younger Colby sister threw the older one a look of annoyance. "I don't have a guitar because I haven't played in years. Our parents had us both take lessons when we were kids."

The werewolf could practically feel the sadness rolling off her girlfriend. "What happened, A?"

Annie swallowed and felt Sarah's hand squeeze her shoulder reassuringly. "I stopped playing after our parents died."

Sarah smiled at her. "Maybe it's time you started playing again. I know someone who gives lessons for cheap." Her words had their intended effect and the four of them all laughed. Inside though, Sarah was remembering back to a time when it seemed like nothing would ever come between the sisters. Before all of Annie's rebellious drama, before the death of their parents. Annie used to love playing guitar with her sister, and Sarah adored her younger sibling so she always made time for her. When their parents had died, it was one of many things that seemed to get lost between them. Years and family therapy had returned them to their previous closeness, but a few things remained missing. Annie's interest in playing music was one of them.

The younger woman looked up at her sister. "Maybe." After that, they covered a popular song by Resurrection called, "Bite Like You Mean It", driving the crowd in the bar wild. And the last song they sang was a lesser known one called, "Anymore Pain" and it perfectly suited the sister's alto and soprano voices. Their flushed faces were practically glowing each time they returned to their seats.

Sarah turned to her sister. "I forgot how much I love singing with you, you're really quite good!" Annie merely blushed and shrugged.

As promised, the trio of women stayed until the bar closed and even helped with cleanup to get Annie out of work faster. They were the last ones to leave, with Annie closing and locking the front door, and setting the alarm. Hugs were exchanged and the two couples went their separate ways. Sarah had gotten a lucky parking spot right across the street. When Annie and Jesse walked around the back of the building where employee parking was located, they stopped at the sight of Annie's damaged car. All four tires had been slashed, the driver's window was broken in, and claw marks gouged the metal of the doors and hood. There was also dark red writing on the driver's door of the car. All it said was "MEAT."

Jesse's immediate reaction was disbelief. "Dude, what the hell?"

Annie immediately pulled out her cell and dialed Sarah's number. The voice that answered was reassuring on a lot of levels. "What's up, A? Did you lock yourself out of your car?"

Annie grimaced. "Oh, getting into my car is no problems. Unfortunately it's not drivable right now, someone vandalized it." She heard cursing over the phone, and then her sister's voice came on again.

"I'm turning around; we'll give you guys a ride home. And call the cops immediately! You need to report it."

Jesse lifted her nose to the air and gave a sniff, then abruptly jogged over to the driver's door. She reached down and ran a finger through the still wet paint, and then brought it to her nose for another smell. With a look of disgust, she bent down and wiped her finger on some crab grass growing from cracks in the pavement. She looked at Annie with worry. "It's not paint, it's blood!"

Annie could see her girlfriend's face go pale even in the darkened parking lot. "Jesse Michelle Cooper, you will not vomit on the evidence! Come here please."

Sarah's worried voice came over the forgotten phone again. "What's going on, A? We're almost there; you should hang up and call the cops."

"Jesse says the writing is in blood, Sarah. Please hurry, this is creeping me out! I'm going to hang up now and call the police."

The headlights from Sarah's SUV became visible around the building just as Annie connected to 911. She was explaining her situation when Sarah and Keller ran up to the younger couple, preternaturally fast. Keller walked around the car, making sure she didn't accidentally step in anything. Once Annie hung up, Jesse and Sarah each flanked a side to console the upset woman. Annie dropped the cell phone into her jacket pocket and cleared her throat. "They said they'd be here in about ten minutes." She glanced over at Sarah. "Can we go sit in your car until the police get here? I don't want to look at this right now."

The singer nodded. "Sure A." She handed Jesse her keys. "Why don't you two go chill for a few minutes while I talk to Keller." After she watched the two younger women get in her car, Sarah turned to Keller. "This wasn't random."

Keller looked at the sign in front of the car that said MGR Parking, then at the door of the car. "No, it wasn't."

Sarah gave her lover a serious look. "Will Louve believe us if we warn her about Marie?"

"I don't know." Keller sighed. "Why don't you get some pics with your phone and I'll give Louve a call and see if she can come over to see the damage."

Keller was speaking French into the phone when the police arrived. They took a statement and asked a few questions, then eventually called a tow company. They said it looked like some vandals that were out to have some fun. When Keller pointed out that she thought the writing on the door of the car was blood, they took a closer look. Eventually, they got some equipment out of the trunk and took a few samples and said their goodbyes. Annie was given a copy of the report and by the time the tow truck hauled her car away, it was just the four of them again. Sarah walked over to her sister and wrapped her in a hug. "Are you going to be okay?"

The younger woman closed her eyes and held on tight. "Yeah, I'll be fine. It just seems so personal, you know?"

Sarah made eye contact with Keller, over her sister's shoulder. "Yeah, I know. I'm sorry about that, A. I'm sure the police will do everything they can to find out who did this. Until then, stay strong. Okay?"

When they all loaded into Sarah's SUV, she turned so she could see into the back seat. "Do you guys want to stay in our spare room tonight? You're more than welcome."

Jesse turned to Annie, who was snuggled into her side. The brunette gave her a small shake of the head. "No, we're good, Sarah. But thanks for the offer. And we'll see you tomorrow anyway since we're riding together to the show."

With a promise that they would call Sarah and Keller if anything else strange happened, the younger couple was dropped off at Annie's house. Once the car was empty, Sarah questioned her girlfriend about the conversation with Louve. "So? What did she say?"

"Well, you probably figured out that she was unable to leave the bar to look at Annie's car, and she's pretty skeptical about there being any connection to her people. She said she spoke with Marie and that she seemed a lot calmer. Marie even apologized for the way she's been acting toward Jesse."

Sarah made a face as she parked her car in the garage by their condo. "I still don't trust her. But I suppose all we can continue to do is wait." She could see Keller looking at her, despite the gloom of the garage. Pale face and pale eyes were the only things she could make out.

"Yeah, that's about it, lass." When they walked into their building a few minutes later, they missed the sound of squealing tires outside. The rumble of a three hundred horsepower engine was distinctive as it faded away into the night.

ANNIE AND JESSE were lying in bed and Jesse could tell her girlfriend wasn't sleeping. Despite the fact that Annie had to be exhausted from working another twelve-hour shift, the younger Colby was breathing too fast for sleep, and every few seconds Jesse could hear her eyes blink. "You okay, babe?"

Annie swallowed the lump that was sitting in her throat. "No."

"Alain says that it helps to talk things out, even if it's not to another person. He says that talking things out helps purge whatever is upsetting you." Jesse paused. "I know what's upsetting you, but do you want to talk about it?"

Annie started to cry. "Why is this happening? I know it was her, but I don't understand what I ever did to deserve this. I'm just..." She trailed off when the emotion of it all became overwhelming. Jesse could only hold her tight and murmur little reassurances. When the tears slowed again, they lay in silence for a few minutes. Annie's voice was a broken whisper when she spoke. "I don't want to live in fear, J."

Jesse touched the other woman's cheek and turned Annie's face so she could look her in the eyes. "You don't have to live in fear. I'm here for you, and I'd do anything to make sure you're safe. And if that isn't enough, we've got two very powerful vampires in the family that could turn Marie into shredded wolf meat. So no more tears, okay? Things are going to be all right."

"Promise?"

The werewolf nodded unseen by her human girlfriend. "Nothing is going to take you from me. I promise."

The person standing outside the bedroom window smiled at the easily overheard words. A block away, she laughed quietly. "We'll just see about that."

Chapter Five

AFTER DINNER AT Barley's Brewing Company, the four women made their way to the Newport Music Hall. The hall itself was limited to a seventeen hundred person capacity, relatively small for a big name rock show, but it still seemed like feeding time at the zoo when it came to getting to their seats. The theater was set up much like any other, with the main floor seats directly in front of the stage. And the second floor balcony seats went along the sides and back of the space. The ceiling was covered in beautiful concentric circles and patterns, and the theme of the room was rounded openings and arches. Sarah could barely control her excitement, wondering what the band would sound like in such a location. The acoustics alone would make any musician swoon.

Resurrection was one of the bands that she covered on a regular basis when she was playing gigs. Their songs had always spoken to her on a deeper level, from the very first song she had ever heard by them. When she and Annie had been dealing with their loss, Sarah frequently turned to music as an outlet for all the emotions she kept bottled up. She continued covering Resurrection's songs years later because they fit really well with her own vibe and style. The band had a great sound and the crowd absolutely ate up the energy of their songs.

Annie was practically vibrating in her chair, seated between Sarah and Jesse. When Sarah looked at her sister, she got a big grin in return. "Excited?"

"Are you mental? Of course I'm excited!"

The singer threw her arm around the younger woman and gave her a quick hug. "I was just remembering how much I liked covering their songs when I'd play my shows. They have a crazy amount of talent. I'm surprised they haven't gotten bigger than they are."

Annie cocked her head. "You know, you're right! They have their own independent label and they don't tour much. It's like promotions for them are purposely kept at a minimum. And just for the record, I used to love hearing you play their stuff."

Sarah turned her lose and gave her arm a little shove. "Probably more than my own!"

Annie grinned and shrugged. "Eh, it's about equal. Have you

written anything new lately? I know you've been trying to get your album done but you always try your new stuff on me, and you haven't played anything for me in a while."

The singer frowned and Keller paid close attention to her answer. Sarah's nightmares were increasing and when Keller finally asked her about them, Sarah simply shut down. Keller knew Sarah wasn't writing anything new because of all people, Keller would hear it first. "No, I've been too busy with everything else that's going on." Her response was short and set off alarm bells for Annie.

"But sis, you *always* have some tune or lyrics rolling around in your head. Nothing at all?" She nudged her shoulder. "Come on, I promise not to judge too hard if it sucks."

Sarah gave her an irritated look, not liking the probing questions. "I said I haven't been working on anything new, and I promise to let you hear the first thing I come up with. Hush now, the band is going to come on!" She smiled, trying to lighten the sudden mood shift and distract her sister from the subject. When Sarah leaned forward to get a drink from her water bottle, Annie and Keller shared a worried look behind her head.

It wasn't very long after they were seated that the lights went down. The crowd quieted as if they knew something great was coming. Sarah waited, feeling the anticipation build in the people around her. Keller had shown her how to read the emotions without fully dropping her shields. It was like being adrift on an ocean of murmured feeling. There was a building excitement, and some other indefinable emotion that always preceded really good music, like everyone in attendance expected magic to happen for them alone. Sarah was curious how Keller knew the lead singer of such a famous band, but she knew she'd get her answer sooner or later. The only lights in the theater were a few lone beams that shown above each band member's spot. They were four white LEDs in a seething shadow of expectancy. Suddenly, a multitude of colored lights crashed over the crowd, and the band stood where previously they had not. No introduction for the three women and one man that now occupied the stage, only the beginning chords of "Digging in the Dirt."

Keller watched the stage with her lover and friends and enjoyed the music. But her mind automatically took her back to a previous lifetime. She remembered the seventies and a little garage band that used to play back alley clubs in the seedier parts of New York. Grace was just as charismatic then as she was now, and Colton hadn't lost that trademark grin. Neither woman on the stage in front of her looked like the hippie girls of her memory. Grace had long wild hair and was rocking in a black baby-doll tee with some low-rise threadbare jeans. Her black boots only added to her rocker persona. Colton, always the rebel, wore her hair in a perfect Mohawk and sported the drummer's go-to outfit of black tank and jeans.

She smiled at how the three of them used to make quite a team. When the second song started, she turned her gaze toward the man on keyboards. Mozzie was what Grace called him. Apparently he and his wife, Corentine, had joined them about seven years ago. Mozzie was a piano/keyboard virtuoso and had been known to bust out the piano accordion and even the dulcimer for a song or two. His wife Corentine played a variety of stringed instruments. She was master level in the double bass, cello, viola, and violin, but she usually stuck with the violin and cello with the band. From what Grace had told her, all four band members wrote and contributed songs. It was a very talented and well-rounded group, evident by the rapt audience and the rising energy in the theater.

About half a dozen songs into the set the band paused for a breather and for a chance to connect with the crowd. With a water bottle in hand, Grace's English accent carried throughout the theater. "So I'm going to tell you all something, this is one of my favorite American theaters. We played Newport a few years ago and the people are just the best!"

Colton's voice cut in. "You do know we're in Columbus, right love?" Her cockney accent lent to the comedic comment. The crowd laughed.

"Of course I know we're in Columbus, Ra-ta-tat! Look at this gorgeous theater, how can you not love it? And the fans are top notch!" She used the nickname that she'd always had for her lover and friend. It first came out as public knowledge in an interview five years ago and the fans ate it up. So now she used it whenever they were on stage. It annoyed Colton but made everyone else laugh. "As a matter of fact, one of my very good friends lives here and is in the crowd tonight." Sarah immediately turned to Keller and saw her lover smirk. The bar manager merely winked at her girlfriend then turned back to the stage as Grace continued speaking. "And my good friend has brought two guests with her, sisters, who are not only huge fans of our music but are musicians themselves."

Annie paled and Sarah whipped her head around to look at Keller once again. "What did y—" Her words were cut off by the lead singer on the stage.

The brunette with the electric blue guitar snapped her fingers and pointed toward the front row. She was trying to get the attention of the control booth and security. "Do you think you can bring them up here for me? Their names are Sarah and Annie Colby." She pointed again at the foursome sitting in the front row, and a muscular man in black walked up to the end of their section. More than a few people whistled and cheered from the crowd, recognizing Sarah's name from the local music scene.

Annie murmured. "I'm gonna be sick."

Seeing the flummoxed look on the women's faces, Grace encouraged. "Come on luvs, I won't bite."

Colton once again piped up. "But I might!"

With a side look at the rest of the audience, Grace added, "It's true, she does. And I only bite if asked." The crowd roared and the sisters had no choice but to follow the security guy to the steps that led to the stage.

As soon as Sarah hit the stage, she *felt* the band and unexpected clarity hit. Sarah looked closer at the four person group as they made their way across the stage and stood under the hot lights. Opening her shields, she could sense two swirling vortices of energy. One that went back and forth between Mozzie and Corentine, and the other flowed between Grace and Colton. They were both vampire/werewolf pairs. *Holy shit!* Her mind screamed in the shock of discovery. She spared a quick glance at Keller but could see nothing under the glare of the spotlights. However she did notice that Annie looked ready to pass out. She casually threw her arm around Annie and whispered out of the corner of her mouth. "Relax, A, and don't forget to breath." She gave a reassuring mental push and felt the younger woman take a shuddering breath as her emotions calmed.

Grace, now wearing a wireless mic, approached them with an acoustic guitar and continued speaking to the crowd. "Now these two ladies are going to do us a favor and help out with a song that a few of you might know. It's from our very first album and it's called 'Anymore Pain.' Sarah will join us on second part vocals and guitar, and Annie will help me sing the first part vocals." The acoustic guitar she handed to Sarah was lacquered black and equipped with a pickup. Grace pointed to the foot pedal on the floor and the guitar cable. Assuming it would be off; Sarah bent down to grab the cord and plugged it in, then hit the pedal to turn on her guitar.

Grace looked at her. "Good?" Sarah smiled and rattled off the first three chords to "Anymore Pain." The bandleader returned her grin. "All right, I'm going to leave you to it then. You can use that mic and I'm going to steal your lovely sister to share mine." Once everyone was in place, the lights went down and a single blue spotlight illuminated Grace and Annie. Then a yellow light came up on Corentine and she started to play. The haunting melody pulled from the strings of her cello put goose bumps up and down Sarah's arms. Sarah watched her sister and sent her another reassuring wash of emotion. She saw the younger woman immediately straighten and take a breath. The song was hauntingly beautiful with only one voice and the cello to carry the melody in the opening part. But with two voices in synch it became something else entirely. It was a sad song and the music soared with the pain of it. It started soft with just Annie and Grace singing. The first stanza was but an intro to a song about betrayal and loss.

I lost my way out in the night
I could not stay without a fight

Then the piano joined in, softly.

Out in the rain I shed my tears

Next were the two guitars, Sarah's and Grace's, giving a gentle crescendo of the music.

My soul was stained with all your fears

And finally, the entire band crashed together for the chorus. The hard driving guitars were balanced by the haunting keyboards and cello. And the drums drove the entire thing forward in the critically acclaimed rock ballad from their first album.

Let the pain out
Let the pain in
The memory of you
Is under my skin
Living on edge
Edge of insane
Don't let me feel
Any more pain...

All the instruments stayed after the chorus, but were hushed as the song continued. This was the part where Sarah joined in to sing harmony.

I would give all to hear you speak
But I won't call I am so weak
Stupid mistake burned for a kiss
Driven away it's you I miss

Once again the chorus crashed over the crowd. Pain of the song was amplified and lifted. It was truly heartbreaking and everyone in the house felt it.

Let the pain out
Let the pain in
The memory of you
Is under my skin
Living on edge
Edge of insane
Don't let me feel...
Any more pain

Grace made eye contact and Sarah understood that the bandleader was letting her take the hook.

I just can't eat
Still losing sleep
I'm half alive
Through...the...week
Living within
This empty skin
Searching for...the...words...
To begin

Back to the quiet story, Sarah noticed that Annie's eyes were closed. The younger woman was a study of concentration as her and Grace began singing the first part melody again.

Let me return I'll swear my soul
With you I'll learn as I grow old
Your beauty brings calm to my fears
There is nothing that compares

And finally they all brought the song home. They played it out to its glorious heights, leaving Sarah's pulse pounding in her veins and goose bumps marching across every inch of her body.

Let the pain out
Let the pain in
The memory of you
Is under my skin
Living on edge
Edge of insane
Don't let me feel
Any more pain
Let the pain out
Let the pain in
The memory of you
Is under my skin
Living on edge
Edge of insane
Don't let me feel...
Any more pain
Any more pain...
Any more pain
Any more pain...
Any more pain
Pain...

With the last chord ringing through the hall, there was silence. Then as if the crowd woke from a dream, there was immediate thunderous applause and screams. Sarah was caught in the moment, the music having taken her back in time to a place she had forgotten. One of the reasons she loved music was because it was the one place she had no fear of releasing all the emotions she kept bottled inside. The song they had just played was on Resurrection's very first album, the same album that Sarah listened to religiously after her parent's death and her breakup with Jill. Giving herself a mental shake, she looked at her sister standing next to Grace Cadence. Sarah smiled when Annie turned to look at her. Then she watched the younger woman get a hug from her rock idol. The elder Colby sister chuckled and used the foot pedal to turn off her cable, and then disconnected it from the guitar. A stagehand rushed out to grab the instrument then disappeared again into the wings. With her left arm draped over Annie's shoulders, Grace walked over and draped the other arm around Sarah. She spoke into her cordless mic once again. "Let's give it up for Annie and Sarah Colby everyone. Thank you both for helping us out!"

They were once again shown off stage by the security guard and escorted to their seats. Jesse hugged her girlfriend as tight as she safely could. "Holy shit, A, that was incredible! You were amazing, babe!"

Annie blushed. "Thanks." Slightly embarrassed, she turned her gaze back to the stage when the band started their next song.

Sarah laughed to herself, thinking the younger woman might be a little star struck. She turned to her own girlfriend and gave her a look. "You are a little sneak!"

Keller laughed and reached over to hold her hand. With a little smirk, she innocently asked her question. "So how do you feel?"

The singer's broad grin seemed to say it all. "I feel amazing; I'm so energized right now! I've never played in front of a crowd this size before."

"The energy that you feel is from the crowd. You haven't played live since you were infected but when you have that much energy focused on you it's quite a power boost. It's a good thing you only played the one song." Sarah looked at her curiously but Keller didn't get a chance to explain before another high energy song started, drowning out their conversation.

After the show, they were taken backstage to the dressing room where Keller was enveloped in a three-way hug between Grace and Colton. Grace was now sporting a pair of red- framed glasses, looking a lot like the stereotype of a hot school teacher. She was the first one to speak. "Look at you luv, we haven't seen you in a donkey's year! Why has it been so long?"

Colton glanced at Sarah, Annie, and Jesse, and smirked. "Well, clearly she's keepin' better company these days, that's for sure!"

Grace pushed her away. "Back off you tart, there's nobody here for you to ogle! Now, let's have some introductions, shall we?" Grace pointed to herself and Colton. "For the new ladies, I'm Grace Cadence, and this tosser is Colton Shep. We've known Noby for a long, long time."

Sarah raised an eyebrow at her girlfriend. "Noby?"

Colton laughed. "Cor, Noby, you didn't tell them your nickname?" She addressed the entire group. "It was when we used to play those seedy bars in the big city. You could barely take a jimmy without three people sittin' in yer lap. Bunch of gormless prats in them places! Anyway, we were always takin' the piss out of 'er for 'er name. Grace didn't want to call 'er Keller so that's when Noby was born."

Everyone laughed and Grace continued introductions. "Over here is our esteemed maestro, Mozzie Amaduk. And next to him is his beautiful wife, I don't know what she sees in him, Corentine Atieno. She is the most beautiful woman with a bow, next to Artemis herself."

Keller reached over and shook hands with Mozzie and Corentine and began her own instructions. "It is a pleasure to meet you Mozzie and Corentine. My name is Nobel Keller —"

She was briefly interrupted by Colton's loud whisper. "Noby."

Keller merely smiled and shook her head before continuing. She gestured toward each person as she spoke. "This is Sarah Colby, talented singer, teacher, and my fiancé. Next to her, is her sister, Annie, who happens to work as the assistant manager in charge of a local music club in town. And the brooding wolf that's last in line is Jesse Cooper. IT and electronics guru, she is the love of Annie's life." Both younger women blushed as welcomes and handshakes were exchanged.

A short while later Sarah found herself in conversation with Keller, Grace, and Colton, while Annie and Jesse were a few feet away talking to the married half of Resurrection. She smiled, knowing that this was one of the biggest days of her sister's life. Her observation was interrupted by Grace. "I haven't had a chance to say it yet, but you were brilliant up there tonight. Keller says you're a traveled musician too?"

The elder Colby blushed much the same way her sister had and laughed. "Yes, but not on your level. I taught for a number of years in a traditional setting, and then I toured for a few years playing in dive bars and pubs. Eventually I got tired of wandering and returned home. Now I play locally and give private music instruction. I'm average at best; I just have a knack for figuring out what the crowd wants sometimes."

"That's a load of tosh! Like Grace says, yer real ace on the guitar. I bet you've got a few or your own albums under yer belt too, huh?" Colton gave Sarah's shoulder a little poke to emphasize her point. Sarah nodded to the question about her own albums.

Grace laughed and grabbed the drummer's finger away from their invited guest. "Easy luv, it's rude to prod at our backstage VIPs." She turned her honey brown gaze back to Sarah. "But she is right, you play beautifully. I'd love to hear you play your own stuff sometime. And if you have some of your CD's handy, I'd like to take a listen. We don't have a lot of artists under our label, but we're always keeping an eye out for that special someone."

The entire night felt surreal. Sarah thought it was strange that Keller wasn't joining in, but she figured Keller was just letting her experience the band in all their glory. She cleared her throat before she could speak. "I don't have any CD's on me right now, but I can be sure to get you copies before you leave town." She wouldn't even contemplate that such an amazing band might want to sign her to their label.

That was when Keller decided to chime in. "She's actually working on another one right now. Her and a few musicians she used to jam with have been pretty busy at the studio lately."

Grace's eyes widened and she shot a glance at Colton. "It looks like you really lucked out mate. Your bird can certainly sing!"

The drummer at her side winked at Sarah. "And she's no boiler either!" Not completely certain of what they were saying, Sarah got the gist of it and flushed at their comments.

Keller threw her head back and laughed, her blue eyes twinkling. "Oh, I know exactly how lucky I am."

The bandleader shook her long hair back from her face and turned a calculating eye on Sarah and Keller. "And if I didn't know any better, I'd say you've finally bonded." At Keller's nod, she added, "Good for you!" Looking at Annie and Jesse, her next question was full of curiosity. "How is it that you are a vampire, but your sister is human? And does she know that you are all *other*?"

The short blonde smiled and answered for Sarah, knowing the events from the previous year were still hard for the singer to talk about. "Annie knows. I'm afraid we've all been through a lot over the past six months. I was forced to infect Sarah when she was nearly killed last year. She didn't deal well with it. Then there was a scuffle with some local werewolves that were helping us keep Sarah contained and Jesse was accidentally infected as well. Annie has done an amazing job handling everything."

The other two couples walked over as Keller finished speaking and Annie overheard the very end. "What have I been handling?"

Sarah laughed and tugged her earlobe. "The fact that your girlfriend is a scruffy bitch sometimes!"

"Hey, I *resemble* that comment!" Jesse protested good-naturedly and the rest of the group joined in the laughter.

Remembering her conversation with the married couple, Annie excitedly turned to her sister and Keller. "Do you know who Mozzie really is?" They both shook their heads. "He is the bastard son of a very famous eighteenth century composer."

They both turned their heads to take in the tall thin werewolf. Keller said the first thing that came to her mind. "Mozart was short." Sarah shot her a startled look. The certainty with which Keller spoke of things centuries old amazed her sometimes. It was easy to forget that her lover started her days in a more primitive time. The amount of history Keller must have seen was mind boggling to the extreme.

"*Ja, meine dame.* But my mother Magdalena was tall and thin. I can play like *mein vater* but sadly I did not inherit his level of genius for composition. But I do well enough with *meine Frau und Freunden.*" Mozzie had a pleasant tenor when he spoke. And while he spoke with the accent of his home country, his English was very easy to understand. He had short brown hair that curled slightly around his face, and he was sporting the beginnings of a scruffy chin-strap. His wife had her arm curled loosely around his waist. She wasn't as tall, but nearly so. Her long black hair and straight bangs provided a dramatic contrast to her ethereal skin.

She had a slight accent when she spoke but none of them could tell what her original language was. "My husband is so modest. He writes beautiful songs. They're just not as well known." She focused on Sarah. "I too would love to hear your music, Sarah."

Sarah was immensely flattered that such a talented group of musicians would be interested in her work. She was trying to think of a way to get her CD's to them when Keller spoke up. "I know you have another show tomorrow night, why don't I give you an official invitation to my condo for brunch mid-morning. Good food, great view, and both new and old friends. I couldn't think of a better way I'd like to spend my time. Let's say eleven?"

Colton immediately clapped her on the arm. "Blimey, Bob's yer uncle! We'll be there!"

Annie looked at Sarah. Sarah looked at Keller, and Jesse vocalized what the Colby sisters were thinking. "What?"

Grace laughed and translated for the Americans. "She thinks it's a great idea, and I do too."

Keller clapped her hands together. "Good, it's settled then." She glanced at Mozzie and Corentine then focused back on her old friends. "Now, it hasn't been so long that I don't remember what it's like right after a show. So we're just going to say our goodnights and look forward to seeing you all tomorrow." Sarah looked at her curiously but didn't speak. Instead the eight people all exchanged hugs and handshakes and went their separate ways.

Once in the car, Annie began chattering to Jesse in the back seat. Sarah started her SUV and drove toward Annie's house. Unable to contain her curiosity any longer, Sarah said what was on her mind. "I have so many questions."

Keller laughed. "I'm sure you do."

"First, what did you mean by remembering what it was like after a show?"

Keller looked at her from the passenger's seat. "You actually got a taste of it when you were on stage tonight. You know how there is a lot of energy when we go to a dance club? You haven't played in public since your transformation, but imagine standing on stage and having the energy of tonight's crowd directed at you for a few hours, instead of just the one song. It's not all sexual, which is what makes it bearable. But some of the songs..."

Sarah's eye's widened. "Oh. Yeah. That would be—hell. I'm surprised they didn't kick us out sooner."

The younger couple had stopped to listen from the back seat. Annie was the first to speak up between them. "So how is it for werewolves? You say vampires can take in energy, and that wolves emote it, but how does that much energy affect Colton and Mozzie?"

Keller tried to think of a good analogy to explain to everyone, including the one person who couldn't feel or sense the energy all around them. "So for a vampire, it's like being really thirsty and you're swimming in a pool of the most delicious liquid. The temptation is immense. It's a bit different for the wolves. They emote a high amount of energy all the time. That is why they have to stay so physically active, why they run the woods, have sex, etcetera. When they're in a place that is so full of energy, it's like two rivers meeting. The greater river, the crowd, will cause the lesser one to "back up." So it's a lot like when wolves change back to their human form. The skin feels too tight, all the emotions and senses are crammed into a little human space."

Annie looked at her girlfriend. "Is that how you felt tonight?"

"Not quite. While I could feel the pressure all around me, it was more like being in a ball pit at the kid's pizza place. Maybe it's because I was part of the big river?"

Keller nodded, though the two in the back couldn't see it. "Yes, that's a good way to put it. All the energy was being directed toward the stage. Energy that people give off is more like a hair dryer than perfume. Yes, if it is not dissipated it will eventually fill the room, much like a scent. However, it is often directed, whereas a scent simply fills the room slowly." She shook her head at the poor analogy, but supernatural metaphysics were difficult to explain on a good day.

Everyone rode quietly after that, taking the time to absorb the amazing night. Sarah's problems were temporarily forgotten in the wake of such soul-soothing music. Her stomach fluttered at the thought of the members of Resurrection actually wanting to hear her stuff and of Grace's mention of them looking for new bands to sign to their label. Enjoying the pipe dream of making it big, she smiled to herself in the dark.

THE NEXT DAY, Keller made a quick run to the grocery store for enough food and drinks for everyone. By the time people started arriving, they had all the ingredients for Bloody Marys and mimosas. They also had pans of waffles, bacon, sausage, hash browns, and all the fixings for breakfast burritos. Annie and Jesse arrived first, full of energy and excitement. Annie had the code to the front entrance, so there was no need to meet them downstairs. Keller had texted Grace the address and parking instructions the night before and the band arrived a little after eleven. Sarah noticed right away that Corentine was carrying her violin case, and she felt a flutter of anticipation that they might have time for an impromptu jam session after brunch.

There was a sideboard on each wall of the dining room where they arranged the food and drinks. There was plenty of room for the eight of them once Keller put a few leaves in the dining room table. The conversation flowed easily while the group enjoyed their brunch. Sarah watched the amount of food the wolves in the room ate with some amusement. They were the biggest and fastest eaters, even the mellow-seeming Mozzie.

Colton was the first to sit back in her chair and rub her stomach. "Aye, mates, that was absolutely scrummy!" She raised her Bloody Mary glass in front of her. "Cheers to the good food and great new friends!" Everyone raised their glasses with her, with a chorus of "cheers" going around the table. Jessie and Annie volunteered to help Keller clean up while Sarah showed the rest of the group around.

The condo was a very open concept floor plan. On the adjacent corner of the living room, with wraparound floor-to-ceiling windows, the grand piano sat. Sarah went to the touch screen built into the wall and lightened the window tint, as well as turned on the track lights above the beautiful instrument. There was a spot where the windows turned to brick wall, before the living room area. Sarah kept a variety of instruments there that she didn't need at the studio where she gave lessons. The collection consisted of a few different types of hand drums, an acoustic guitar, a banjo, a trumpet, and a wood flute that she had picked up a music festival a few years back. She continued the tour and they eventually ended up back near the piano.

Mozzie looked up from the keys he was caressing. "May I?"

Sarah nodded then remembered her CDs. Since Mozzie was now busy tinkering with a fancy tune she addressed Grace, Colton, and Corentine. "I'll be right back. I've got a couple copies of my first two albums in the closet." When she was digging around in the closet of the spare room, she thought she heard a familiar tune being played on the piano. "Oh shit, my notes!" She quickly found what she was looking for and returned to the living room in time to catch Grace's question.

"What are you playing Mozzie? I love it!"

Sarah answered. "It's called Blood of My Blood, and it's one of the songs that's going to be on my new album."

Mozzie flushed in embarrassment, realizing he had been peeking at another musician's notes. "Forgive me, I did not realize this was one of your original works. I merely saw the music sitting up here and began playing."

Sarah smiled at his uncharacteristic nervousness. The man always seemed cool and collected, even when the band played on stage. "It's fine, Mozzie." She took her old acoustic off the pegs set into the brick wall. "I can play the whole thing if you want?" Colton grinned and settled onto the floor with a Djembe drum between her knees. Sarah laughed. "Help yourself to the instruments. And if you want to play along, there are actually two copies of the song on the piano."

Mozzie gave her his own reserved smile, but she could see his eyes were twinkling at the thought of playing something new. Corentine sat on the bench with Mozzie without crowding him, and Grace took a seat on the chaise lounge. Without further ado, Sarah started playing. Colton waited a few measures to get a feel for the song then started a rhythm on the drums, her hands providing a good counterpoint to the melody. It had a bit of a funky upbeat blues sound that had even Corentine nodding along. By the time the piano part came in, Keller, Annie, and Jesse had finished cleaning up and settled in to listen. Grace had her eyes shut, listening intently.

When the song ended, all those not playing an instrument clapped their approval. Annie was not shy with her praise. It was something her older sister always appreciated. "That was great, Sarah; I hadn't heard that one yet. You said this is going on the new album, right?"

Sarah nodded. "Yeah, but it's not quite right. That's why I have the music here at home. I'm still trying to work out the center section, the hook."

Grabbing another acoustic from the stand next to the chaise, Grace spoke up. "What if you tried adjusting the fingering in that part, like this?" She perfectly played the refrain leading to the hook that Sarah was trying to clean up. But when she played the troubled spot it was slightly different.

The fingering was different but Sarah couldn't immediately figure out how. "That's it! What did you do there?"

"Watch." Grace repeated the fingering a little slower, then observed Sarah while she duplicated it. "Perfect, you've got it!"

Annie, who was cuddling with her girlfriend, also had some input. "You know, the hand drum in there sounds great with this song. But I think you need more. This would be a perfect foot stomper if you have a little drum solo before the third chorus. Like the drums are holding back the water, before letting it crash into the chorus one last time. I'm not saying for the album, but maybe in the live versions..." She trailed off, realizing she was giving musical opinion to a room full of musicians. "Heh, never mind."

Sarah already had her eyes shut, going over the song in her head. When she opened her eyes, she turned a slow smile onto her younger sister. "I think it's a great idea, A!" Turning to Colton, she added, "Do you think you can improvise something?"

The drummer grinned. "Sure thing, luv, let's give it another go, yeah?" The group gave a little laugh while Sarah counted it off to start again. Even Grace kept the guitar and joined in. The second time through went much better and they perfectly nailed the sound that Sarah was looking for. Colton gave a little drum flourish when they finished. "Yes, that was aces!"

"Wow, that *was* fun. And it was exactly what I was looking for. Thanks for helping me finish my song everyone. I owe you one!"

Jesse turned to her girlfriend. "That was hot! You should definitely start playing the guitar again! Now I really want to hear you."

Grace looked at the younger Colby sister. "You play too?"

Annie shrugged. "Not for many years. I'm afraid I'd flub more chords than not."

The bandleader winked at her. "Well why don't you come over here and show me. Perhaps Colton can give a quick drum lesson to Jesse."

The werewolf that was more nerd than musician immediately jumped up and bounded over to sit next to the drummer. "Sweet!"

After about five minutes of working with the younger women, Corentine took out her violin and suggested they play a song from their first album, one that Annie and Sarah would both know. Everyone turned to Annie and she thought for a second. "Stake My Claim?"

"Perfect.

The next song was even more fun since everyone was involved. There were a few missed notes but much more laughter. They joked around, mixed more mimosas, and continued to play for a few hours. Any time a song was played that someone didn't know, they'd either sit out or just join in the best they could. It was a true jam session and a real bonding experience for the eight people in Keller's condo. Even Keller picked up the flute and joined in with the merriment. And when the flute didn't fit with the song, she simply picked up a drum and added to the rhythm section. It was fun and lighthearted, and something the four Columbus residents desperately needed.

Eventually the band had to leave to get ready for their show that evening. They took copies of Sarah's two albums and made her promise to send them her newest one once it was finished. In return, they all signed copies of their newest album for Sarah, Jessie, and Annie. And Grace promised that they'd all catch up again when their North American tour was finished in June. The condo seemed strangely empty when the four members from Resurrection took their leave. Keller and Sarah were next to each other on the low-slung leather couch while Annie and Jessie shared the chaise lounge. One of the newly-signed Resurrection CDs was playing softly while they sat in the aftermath of their day of fun. Finally Jesse sighed and broke the silence. "That was awesome."

Annie, who was seated between her girlfriend's legs, laid her head back against the werewolf's shoulder and sighed too. "I need to start practicing again." Keller smiled and thought about their future and what the next life for all of them would hold. Sarah merely closed her eyes, head full of music as usual, though sadly it still wasn't anything new. What she didn't admit was that she was having a hard time finishing the song because she couldn't seem to write anything lately. It was as if the more worried she got about her sister, the more she just bricked everything off. But the emotions she was blocking were the same ones responsible for her writing. She had locked herself into an emotional prison and had no idea how to get out.

Chapter Six

"SOMETHING HAS TO be done, Keller!" Her food forgotten, Sarah's frustration was evident as she scanned a write-up on the second page of the paper. It had been nearly four weeks since their fun-filled day with the members of Resurrection. Sadly, real life had come back with a vengeance as Sarah immersed herself into the music once again and Keller upped her dedication to looking for a suitable replacement manager for The Merge. They were having a rare few hours together with a late breakfast before Sarah was to head off to give Saturday lessons at her studio.

Keller had just taken a bite of her toast when she looked up in concern. "What's up, love? Is the mayor closing another homeless shelter?"

Sarah turned the paper around so her girlfriend could see the article she was looking at. She started reading aloud because she was too fired up to wait for Keller to scan the entire thing. "After a rash of pet attacks and mutilations around the Alum Creek State Park area, officials are now convinced that the hikers found dead a few weeks ago were the result of a wild dog attack. They caution that a potential pack of wild dogs are loose in the area and are asking people to keep their pets indoors or well-monitored until park officials, animal control, and trained volunteers can track down the dangerous animals."

Keller snorted. "Are they idiots? Don't they know the difference between wolf and dog tracks?"

"I don't know the difference." Sarah turned the page of the paper and shoveled another forkful of eggs into her mouth.

"Well if the dogs are large enough, they do look similar, but wolf tracks are typically bigger than most of the largest breeds of domestic dogs. And this is definitely the work of more than one, but I don't know how many. We could do some snooping in the area where they found the bodies, maybe see what we could find out from the tracks..." Keller trailed off, not entirely confident in her own suggestion.

Sarah shook her head. "I don't know the first thing about woods, tracking, or wildlife. So I'd be no help there. Plus, I'm not a detective, Keller, I'm a musician. As much as I hate to say it, we should leave this to the police."

"I'm not a detective either, but the police are not going to connect wild animal attacks to a person, or people! Marie has seemed fine the last two Sundays we've been out to the farm for training. But I still don't trust her. And I think that both her and Marcel were involved with vandalizing Annie's car."

Sarah set her fork down and sighed, zeroing in on another small article in the crime section of the paper. "Oh look, there have been a bunch of burglaries in Lewis Center, Orange, and Westerville. So far the police have no leads." She looked up at Keller. "It sounds like someone is running out of money. And I know you don't trust Marie. I also think that her and Marcel are working together in *all* of this. But I just feel so helpless!" She tossed the paper toward the center of the table, out of the way of their plates. Her gut was telling her that the wolves were involved and she feared for her sister's safety. Sarah wasn't sure what she would do if something happened to Annie. Even contemplating the thought made things go dark in her mind.

Keller reached over and gently took her hand. She realized that most of Sarah's worry was for her sister, the one person in all of this that could not defend herself against potentially hostile werewolves. And after the death of their parents nearly a decade before, the singer was desperately afraid of losing her younger sister too. Sarah's nightmares had persisted over the past few weeks and Keller had been forced to help soothe her with empathy more often than not. She hated dipping into her lover's private thoughts and emotions without her knowledge, but something had to be done or the singer was going to run herself down again.

Luckily she only picked up vague images with the terror in the dreams. A couple she recognized as Sarah and Annie's parents, and Annie seemed to be most prevalent anytime she minddipped. She didn't want to take a chance of blurring Sarah's memories of her parents, so she had to be careful with what she did to calm the dreams. The bar manager wanted a distraction so Sarah wouldn't just obsess over the stuff that was out of their control. "How are you doing at the studio? I know you don't have any lessons tonight, but are you at a point where you can take a night off from recording? I think we should go out and get a recharge if we can. What do you say?"

The singer gave her an "oh shit" look. "I forgot to tell you that we finished the post production work on the album. I sent the discs out yesterday to be manufactured. It'll be around five weeks for production, so keep your fingers crossed that I'll have the CD's in time for pride weekend."

"Hey, that's great news! Congratulations, love! Maybe this should be a celebratory night out then."

Sarah smiled in appreciation of her lover's continuous support. "Should I text Annie to see if they want to join us?"

"Hmm, well I meant what I said about recharging our batteries. I'm not sure you want them around for that."

Sarah shuddered at the thought of being sexual around her sister. "Eh, not really. You want to hit Merge, or try something new?"

Keller looked at her, contemplating what her lover was in the mood for. "How about the circus tonight? All those emoting werewolves would make a tasty snack."

Sarah grinned and polished off the rest of her overly-sweet coffee. "Sounds good. Now, why don't you come shower with me before I head off to give my first lesson of the day." She turned and sauntered toward the bedroom. Keller took one look at the dog that was sitting next to her chair and quickly gathered the dishes and put them in the sink. The husky that had been patiently waiting for scraps gave a great sigh and dropped to the floor in defeat.

When their shower was finished nearly a half hour later, both women were clean and slightly more relaxed. As Keller dressed, she filled Sarah in on her schedule for the day. "Joanne and I have three interviews this afternoon. They are all second interviews so hopefully one of them is going to be the new Merge manager. Wish me luck!"

Sarah smiled and gave her a kiss on the lips. "I've got four lessons today but should be done around five-thirty. How about I call and make reservations at Vineyard?"

Keller raised a pale eyebrow. "Vineyard?" Vineyard was a popular queer-friendly restaurant that had a menu as diverse as its clientele. It was also the place where Sarah and Keller were first introduced. She smiled at the memory of that night. "I think that dinner at Vineyard sounds perfect, and long overdue."

"Me too! I'll make reservations for seven; that should give us plenty of time to get ourselves pretty and smelling nice." She winked at Keller before grabbing her messenger bag full of music notes and her guitar case. "Okay fang-babe, I've gotta go or I'll be late for Ethel's drum lesson!"

A pale eyebrow rose as Keller thought about the seventy-year-old woman who had started drum lessons the previous year. "She's not dead yet?"

"Nope. And now she wants to join a band that goes around

playing at nursing homes. Apparently it's a folk band that has two accordion players and a fiddle player already, and they're looking for someone on percussion. I'm not going to lie; I totally want to see them play." She grinned and shook her head. Snapping the lead to Duke, she opened the door to the condo. The good-natured dog had been going with her for months. He mostly stayed in the backroom while lessons were being given, unless it was a quieter instrument, then he'd come out and nap by the front window. "Okay, now I really have to run!"

Keller just shook her head at the wide variety of clients that Sarah taught. But she couldn't deny that she wanted to see them play too. If only for the novelty of it, and because she had probably been born long before most of the folk songs were written.

DINNER TURNED OUT to be a surprisingly romantic interlude for the *other* blood couple. They got ready in separate bathrooms and both made an effort to impress the other. It had been much too long since they had a real date. Sarah felt actual hunger when she saw her lover after they finished getting ready. She wanted to drink Keller down in so many ways. Teeth pricked her bottom lip and she smiled at how lucky she had gotten in life. With so many things and people that had been taken away from her, Sarah was glad that she still had love. Keller dressed in jeans, polished black dress shoes, and a dark gray vest. She was also sporting a starched white shirt with a bow tie the same brilliant blue-star shade as her eyes.

Sarah was wearing skinny jeans, black knee-high riding boots, and a light gray form-fitting turtleneck. Her shoulder length dark hair was hidden under a dark gray driving cap that was turned backwards. It was typical selection of outfits for two women whose dress-up tastes ran the gamut from beatnik to dapper. When they strolled into the restaurant five minutes early they cut quite an attractive pair to the surrounding patrons. Keller's black leather biker jacket with its heavy, off-center zipper seemed incongruous with the vest and tie but she didn't care. Sarah kept it classy with a slim wool peacoat. Dinner was delicious, both women having ordered dishes the other would like so they could share. Once the bill was paid, they still had time to kill before heading to Cirque du Loup so Sarah suggested a new destination. "Want to head to Forno for martinis?"

Keller had been enjoying her red wine, much the same way she had when they first met. All the sexual tension was still there between them but they were trying to save it up for later. "I think that's a great idea, lass." She finished her wine and set the glass down with a smile. As they were leaving, Sarah's phone vibrated in her back pocket. When she saw who it was, she held it up for Keller to see.

"Jill is free again tonight. She wants to know if we're working, or if we are interested in meeting her out for drinks and dancing." She cocked her head at Keller as the proud owner of the midnight blue Audi TT unlocked the doors. "What do you think?"

Keller leaned on the top of the car door of the convertible and looked at Sarah with a grin. "I think you should tell her where we're going and see if she wants to meet us." Jill was already seated at a table when they arrived at Forno. Keller laughed when she saw the red-haired woman waiting for them. "She must have texted you when she was already downtown."

Jill stood when they walked up to her table. She gave Sarah a long hug and then turned to hug Keller as well. "It's good to see you again, Keller." When she pulled away they all sat down. "I'm glad you answered, I was hoping I wouldn't have to spend an evening out on my own. Of course that means you're stuck with the awkward doctor who's more comfortable with dogs than people."

Keller looked at her in surprise then laughed loudly enough for the other patrons to turn heads in their direction. "Awkward is not exactly the word I'd use to describe you, Doctor, um, what exactly is your last name?"

Sarah smirked and chimed in. "It's Doctor Jillian Cole. We had lockers right next to each other in high school, that's how we ended up friends."

"That, and we both liked pu —" She was interrupted when the server walked up to their table. After Sarah and Keller ordered martinis, Jill finished her sentence. " — Um, we discovered we both liked girls. Of course that led to slumber parties, first kisses, and eventually becoming girlfriends when high school was over."

Sarah laughed. "Short-lived girlfriends!" She raised her martini when it arrived and toasted. "Let's hear it for not settling down until finding the right one!"

Jill laughed and added to the toast. "Let's hear it for finding the right one and still not settling down." She looked from Sarah to Keller, then back at Sarah, and winked. The suggestion was out there, and the night was still young. The tall redhead addressed her two friends, old and new. "So what brings you two out tonight, looking so fancy?"

Sarah answered. "Actually, we both had the night off and wanted to go on a long overdue date."

The veterinarian made a face. "And I foolishly invited myself along?"

She was saved by Keller. "Actually, no. We simply wanted to get dinner and eventually end up at Cirque du Loup. We haven't seen the circus act in a while and thought we'd check it out tonight. Have you been there on a Saturday?"

Jill shook her head. "No, I seem to always be working or too tired." She paused, wanting desperately to be honest with Sarah and her girlfriend. "And, well between eight years of serious schooling and my career, I don't have a lot of close friends other than Sarah, just casual acquaintances." She smiled and tried to downplay her loneliness. "I've always thought it looked cool in their advertisements, I just haven't had the time or company to go before this."

Sarah and Keller shared a look then Sarah said the first idea that popped into her head. "Why don't you ride over with us when we leave here? There's room in the backseat of Keller's car and it makes sense to only take one vehicle. It's really busy on Saturdays and parking will be crazy unless we pay for valet."

Keller raised an eyebrow and sipped her drink. "Oh, we're paying for valet. You don't think I'd let my baby sit on some derelict side street, do you?" Sarah and Jill laughed at the shorter woman's over protective behavior of her car. "Actually, let me send a quick text to Louve. Maybe she can get us in without the wait outside."

Jill looked at them curiously. "Louve?"

Sarah smirked. "She is the owner slash manager of Temple du Loup. You'll like her, she's *fun*."

Jill nodded and then read between the lines of what Sarah was saying. "Oh?" Sarah smirked. "Oh! Good, I like *fun* people." After two martinis, they all piled into Keller's car and made their way to Temple. Keller handed her keys to the valet then they walked right up to the bouncer, drawing protests from the people in the long line. All three women had left their coats in the car, so they were really glad Louve said she'd get them in as VIPs. The muscular man wearing jeans and a tight black t-shirt recognized Keller and spoke into the microphone clipped to his collar. Without waiting for an answer he gave Keller a short nod and waved them through the door into the foyer.

Inside was the ringmaster herself. She was wearing the same outfit as when Sarah first met her. It could only be described as ringmaster steampunk. Her short black hair was slicked back. A pair of goggles rested on the rim of her velvety top hat, and her bow tie was perfectly centered atop a glorious spill of cream-colored ruffles. The outfit was finished by black riding pants and riding boots, a vest and short jacket, as well as her always present cane. Louve was about the same height as Keller, which was significantly shorter than the five foot eleven inch Dr. Cole. And when Sarah looked at her good friend, she could see that the good Dr. Cole was blatantly checking out the Frenchwoman.

Keller leaned over and whispered in Sarah's ear. "Well, she said she's more comfortable with dogs—" Sarah elbowed her discretely and smiled when Louve walked over. The couple exchanged cheek kisses with the Frenchwoman before she turned to take in their companion.

Louve took a slow look up and down Jill's body, her roving eye leaving goose bumps along the much taller woman's arms. "And who is this belle *rousse*?" Jill stepped forward and offered her hand to the small androgynous woman in the steampunk outfit. When Louve offered her hand, Jill brought it to her lips. Charmed, Louve glanced at Keller. "*Elle est magnifique!*"

Jill winked at her and released Louve's hand. "*Pas presque aussi magnifique que vous.*"

Surprise and delight colored the short brunette's face. "Oh! *Tu parles français!*"

The veterinarian smiled. "*Oui.* Thanks to high school, college, and two trips to France. It is a beautiful country. Though it is probably less so without you there."

Sarah snorted as her ex laid it on thick, and it was Keller's turn to use her elbow. "Hush, they're twitterpated."

Sarah whispered. "twitterpated?"

Her girlfriend shrugged. "It's my favorite word from Bambi."

A dark eyebrow rose. "Bambi? You're what, more than two centuries old? I feel like I don't even know you!"

Keller laughed. "Hush! Let's break them up so we can get drinks and dance."

Louve heard Keller woman's words and turned to the whispering couple. She tapped her cane on the floor twice. "You have always been so impatient, Keller! But fine, if you wish to move into the temple proper, let us go." She held out her elbow for Jill, and the other woman was more than happy to twine their arms together. Luckily there was plenty of room for the pair to walk through the giant revolving wood door.

Hours passed like minutes as the threesome had fun dancing and watching the circus performers. For Sarah, it was a brief respite to all the worry and troubles that had been resting on her shoulders. And because she was noticeably more relaxed, it was a respite for Keller as well. Louve came and went often, not staying very long each time she'd find them. She was the ringmaster and had a job to do. Jill pouted each time the Frenchwoman had to go back to the stage. About an hour before closing time, Sarah and Jill went to the restroom and Louve used the opportunity to question Keller. "Does she know about us?"

Keller shook her head. "She has no idea. She's Sarah's ex-girlfriend from a decade ago, they're best friends now. Apparently they've been what she calls 'fuck buddies' for the past few years. Sarah and I spent the night with her a few weeks ago when we wanted some fresh blood. We both fed but we clouded our feedings from her memory. We were going to offer another night to her again but if you're interested we won't stand in your way."

Louve pulled her close and whispered in Keller's ear. "Who says we must choose, mon ami?" She wore a wicked smile when she backed away from her old friend.

The two taller women returned at that moment and Sarah looked at Keller curiously. "What are we choosing?" Her vampire enhanced hearing allowed her to pick up the end of what they were saying. Jill gave her a curious look, not having heard anything in the loud club.

Keller glanced at Louve, and then turned to give Jill and Sarah a smile. "Louve was just inviting us all to the apartment downstairs after the bar closes. I told her it was up to Jill to decide, since she rode with us."

Jill became the center of attention when three pairs of eyes turned in her direction. She focused on the green ones to the right, looking for any indication that accepting the invitation would be a mistake. When Sarah winked, she knew what answer she would give. "I would love to have a drink downstairs with you." Knowing what was implied, Jill was a little nervous when the bar closed an hour later. Her nerves faded quickly when she saw the layout of the apartment below the old church. And they disappeared entirely when she realized how comfortable Sarah was with the situation. They had known each other a long time and she trusted Sarah above anyone else.

Once they were all seated around the tastefully decorated apartment, Louve let her curiosity play out. She had removed her top hat, jacket, and boots when she came in the door and invited her guests to also make themselves at home as well. "So what kind of animals do you work with, Doctor Cole?"

Jill took a sip from her beer bottle and made a little face at Louve's use of her professional title. "Please, call me Jill or Jillian. There are no dogs in sight so I'm off the clock tonight!" Sarah snickered. She winced slightly when Keller pinched her side, but otherwise didn't say anything. "I typically work with small animals, pets and such. Once in a while we'll get something more exotic in like lizards, turtles, or wild animals. I spend one day a month volunteering at the animal sanctuary hospital north of the city, but for the most part it's pretty mundane. Give fluffy his shots, cut off some balls, or if he's too old then give him some blue juice."

Louve looked at her in confusion. "What is this blue juice?"

"Ah, well that's what we refer to the stuff we use to put animals to sleep. We call it 'blue juicing' them. Inside morbid humor, sorry. I'm not very good with humans I guess, I spend way too much of my time working."

The French woman rushed to reassure her. "No, not at all. I think you're very beautiful and eloquent."

Jill finished her beer at the same time as Keller. The vampire looked at her old friend. "Do you have something stronger down here in your little dungeon?" Louve stood and went over to the cupboard in the kitchenette. After rummaging for a few seconds she turned with a fat frost colored bottle in hand. "The label says Bruichladdich X4. Will this do?"

Keller's eyes widened. "Losh! That is what you come up with?"

Sarah looked at her. "I don't get it, what's brewackka—er, what is that?"

The bar manager shook her head in disbelief. "Tis only the highest-alcohol single-malt ever produced! It came about in the late 1600s. Its original name meant 'perilous whiskey' in Gaelic." She narrowed her eyes at Louve. "Where ever did you get that? Did you know that's one hundred and eighty-four proof?" Even Jill raised her eyes at that tidbit of information.

Louve raised a perfectly arched dark eyebrow. "Warm or chilled?"

Jill looked at her and smiled. "Whiskey? Warm of course!"

Sarah and Keller extricated themselves from the oversized chair and lined up for their shot. When it went down, it was both smooth and earthshattering. Sarah downed it and staggered.

Despite the fact that three of the women had *other* blood, even they felt the effects of the high proof alcohol. "Holy shit, that's some strong stuff!"

Jill looked at her ex-girlfriend, who had always been a bit of a lightweight. With no small amount of challenge in her eyes she spoke to the little group. "Let's have a second one for luck."

Sarah grimaced at her. "You're evil!" Louve looked at the other three women, then settled her gaze on Sarah who was the only one that made a face after the shot. The singer finally relented. "All right, set 'em up barkeep!" After their second shot, she leaned over and quietly whispered in Keller's ear. "Should I be feeling this so much? Despite all my special powers I feel half in the bag now!"

Her lover laughed. "It is quite potent but don't worry, your metabolism will take care of it soon enough."

Sarah nodded and decided to go with the flow. She looked up abruptly and turned to their hostess. "You haven't shown Jill the best part of the apartment!"

The veterinarian reached out and traced a finger over the back of Louve's hand. "But I've already seen the owner."

"Oh, you are very smooth. I've heard about you Americans charming the pants off unsuspecting women."

Jill smirked. "I would hope that you're suspecting by now."

Sarah interrupted before they could go any further down flirtation lane. "Louve." When she had the petite brunette's attention she prompted. "The bath. You haven't shown her the amazing bath!"

The Frenchwoman looked at the other three women in slight dismay. "Oh, where are my manners? I have not given you the tour!

Keller grabbed a few bottles of water from the fridge and waved her hand at Louve and Jill. "Go ahead and show Jill around, we'll be right behind you." When Louve and Jill left the room, she turned to Sarah and spoke honestly. "Does it bother you?"

The singer shook her head and smiled. "Actually, I think it's great! I mean, Jill has been single for a long time and can certainly keep up with Louve. I think if they can get over their baggage they could be good for each other."

Keller leveled a serious look at her. "Even if you are some of that baggage?"

Sarah cocked her head in that familiar Colby look of confusion. "What do you mean?"

Keller ran a hand through her perpetually messy spiked hair. "Surely you realize that Jill still has feelings for you."

"But we haven't dated for years, almost a decade!"

Keller shook her head. "Love, I don't think it matters. The heart doesn't forget. I get that you two have gone your separate ways emotionally and physically, but I can feel that she still loves you. Only part of that is your deep bond of friendship."

Sarah looked at her shocked. "I never knew! Maybe it wasn't a good idea to sleep with her a few weeks ago."

Keller pulled her into an embrace. "I also sense that she has a good handle on things. I don't think she wants you back, I simply get the feeling that she's lonely and that she wishes things could have been different between you."

Sarah thought about Keller's empathic impression of her best friend but only had a shrug in response. When she broke it off with Jill years before, it was after they had been fighting for a while. Sarah had been pushing the other woman away for months and Jill was desperate to get back the connection they had shared before Sarah had walled herself off. It was right after the death of her parents and Sarah had been shutting everyone out. Just as it was hard on the Colby sisters to lose their parents, it was also hard on Jill. The Colby family had become surrogates of a sort since her relationship with her own mother had never been very good. Jill resented being shut out when she too was hurting.

Eventually, Jill found the connection with someone else. Sarah broke up with her shortly after Jill admitted to cheating on her. More than once Jill had brought up that she thought Sarah pushed her away on purpose, hoping she would do something that would justify the end of their relationship. It took a while to get to the point where they could be friends again, but since then things had been good. Sarah's actions with Jill were just a few of the things the singer regretted during that time period. No, she hadn't handled her loss well at all.

Before her lover could wander too far down memory lane, Keller took Sarah's hand and pulled her toward the immense bathing room. "Come on, we don't want them to get too far ahead."

Sufficiently distracted from her spiraling memories, the singer laughed and allowed herself to be pulled along. "Keller, they just left. How much trouble could they..." Her words faded when they saw the trail of clothes leading from the door to the large in-set bathing pool. Jill was standing in the pool near the side while Louve was seated on the edge with her legs wrapped around the tall woman's hips. "Wow, they certainly move fast!"

The bar manager shot her an unrepentant grin. "Want to join them?" Sarah's response was a smile and the slow unbuttoning of her lover's jeans. By the time they fell sideways into the pool, Louve was well on the way to her first orgasm, or "little death" as she called it.

The next few hours went beyond the expectations of all four women. It was both comfortable and incredibly hot. By the time the three visitors were dressed again and ready to go, it was less than an hour until sunrise. Sarah and Keller were standing a few feet from Jill and Louve while they exchanged phone numbers. Louve gave the tall redhead one last embrace and a very friendly kiss before the two women walked back toward the door where Keller and Sarah were standing. Louve also bestowed an embrace on the singer and bar manager. "It is always a pleasure when you come visit me, mon ami."

Keller laughed and opened the door behind her. "I think the pleasure belonged to all of us." Louve had made arrangements for Keller's car to be left in the private lot behind the church. So when they left out the back door, her Audi was sitting un-molested a few feet away. "Jill, why don't you let us drop you off at your house. I don't think you're good to drive yourself."

Jill tried to protest. "I can just call for a cab—"

Sarah grabbed her arm. "No way! We'll take you home, and I can come get you later so you can pick up your car. Or you can take a cab then if you want."

"Okay, you win! Drop me at home and I'll call you later for my ride."

The singer thought for a second as they all got in the car. "We have a self-defense class today at three, we can swing by and pick you up around two. We'll drop you off at your car on the way. How does that sound?"

Jill nodded unseen in the backseat. "Sounds good. I'll call you sooner if I decide to take a cab earlier instead of waiting to ride with you."

It was only a matter of minutes when they pulled up in front of Jill's house. They made sure she was safely inside then found their own way home. Sarah's eyes slipped shut mere seconds after plugging her cell phone in to charge next to the bed.

SARAH DREAMED SHE was playing a show at the Cirque du Loup. She was standing on the stage in front of the knife thrower display. Keller was throwing knives at her while she strummed away at her old acoustic guitar. It was weird because no matter what notes she played, the same little tune came out. The tune was familiar, the tune was— Sarah bolted upright, realizing that her phone was ringing. She grabbed it, figuring that Keller must have put earplugs in due to the late hour they got to bed. She mouthed "It's Jill" to the sleep tousled blonde next to her and Keller nodded then turned back over. Seeing that they'd only been home a few hours, she answered with a groan. "You know you could have waited a bit longer to tell me you didn't need a ride to your car." At first there was no sound from the other end. Sarah was confused until she heard a faint whimper. Jill's voice was a broken whisper.

"S—Sarah?"

Instantly alert, Sarah got out of bed. "Jill? What's wrong, honey? Where are you?"

"Please...help. I'm—I'm hurt...home..." Her voice trailed off with a faint moan.

"Jill! What happened? Jill!" She tried to get a response but there was nothing on the other end. She turned toward her girlfriend as she began dressing as fast as possible. "Keller!" The half-asleep woman looked up and took out her earplugs. "We have to go now! Something is wrong with Jill, she wouldn't call unless it was an emergency." The couple made it to the veterinarian's house less than ten minutes after Sarah had first picked up the phone. They rushed to the door and immediately noticed it was ajar. Cautiously Sarah entered and began calling for her friend. "Jill? Where are you?" Keller stopped in the middle of the living room and Sarah stopped with her. On the largest wall were the words, "MORE MEAT."

"Oh God!"

Keller closed her eyes and took stock of the environment around her. "I smell bleach and blood, a lot of it. And—I can hear her, but it's faint. Upstairs!"

They found her in the large walk-in shower with an empty bleach bottle on the tiles next to the bench. Jill's broken body was on the bench across the far wall. Legs were twisted into compound fractures with broken bone sticking through the skin. But the worst damage was done to her fingers. Each digit had been smashed and twisted into an unrepairable mess. The injured woman's clothes were soaked with blood from all her injuries. Jill's phone was lying next to her head, still connected to Sarah's. She must have passed out right after talking to Sarah. The tall redhead's breathing was faint and shallow. Sarah knelt at her side and looked up at Keller in horror. "Why?" When she heard Jill's breathing begin to falter she shouted in anguish. "No!"

Keller quickly knelt and pushed Sarah back. "Move, let me try to save her." There was a faint pulse at her neck, so she quickly bit her and drank deep. Then Keller bit into her own wrist and let her blood flow between Jill's parted lips. After ten minutes, they both breathed a sigh of relief when Jill gave a great gasp and her upper body bowed off the bench. The virus had successfully infected Jill's weakened body, and it would only be a short amount of time before she was healed. Not wanting the victimized woman to wake with her bloody clothes on, Keller and Sarah began carefully stripping the broken woman. The couple quickly washed her while the bones knitted and the horrific wounds began to close. They dressed her in shorts and a t-shirt, then Sarah carried her friend into the bedroom where she would be more comfortable upon waking.

Keller sat on a chair in the corner of the room, and Sarah paced back and forth around the large bed. Every turn she would swear and worry. "What are we going to do? What they did to her — oh God!" She stopped abruptly as the reality of what was done to her best friend, her ex-girlfriend, began to crash down. Keller was up and had her arms wrapped around the sobbing brunette in an instant. The anguish was overwhelming in Sarah's voice. "They targeted her because of us!"

Keller held her lover, soothing with both words and washes of emotion. "I know, love, I know. But it's going to be all right, Sarah, we can get her through this. I promise she's going to be okay." Once Sarah calmed down, Keller led her over to sit on the bed near Jill. Then she pulled out her phone and dialed a number that had become too familiar lately. As soon as Louve answered, Keller began speaking. "Don't talk, just listen. Your stray puppy has gone too far, and it is past time he was stopped. You can call his uncle in Quebec, but I know that Marcel never arrived back home. Not only that but I'm pretty sure he's been working with Marie. Wolves have been attacking people and animals in the Alum Creek State Park, pets in the surrounding area have been killed, a rash of robberies have taken place in the area south of the farm. Now, mere hours after dropping Jill off at her house, she has been attacked!"

Louve's voice was loud coming through the phone. "Mon *dieu!* Is she all right?"

Keller sighed and ran her free hand through her hair. "No,

she is not all right. Half the bones in her body were violently broken. She was bleeding to death when we got here, and I was forced to infect her so she wouldn't die on us. We can't even report it to the police because Jill is nearly healed already. She is most certainly not all right! What are we going to do about these *dogs*?"

With each word that fell from Keller's lips, Louve's dismay grew. "Mon *ange* rousse! I am so sorry, Keller, but are you sure it was Marcel? Did she see him, or did you scent him at all?"

Keller shook her head, unseen by the Frenchwoman. "*Non,* whomever it was covered their scent with bleach. The only thing I could really smell was blood."

Louve sighed. "Okay, let me make some calls, and we will come up with a plan. I want to call Marcel's uncle just to be sure. It is not because I do not believe you, but I must let him know what we suspect and see what he has to say. I will also have Alain find and hold Marie until we can question her. If you give me a little time, I can be there *en une demi-heure.*"

Keller interrupted her. "Non. That would not be a good idea. I think she needs as few people here as possible right now. And none of them can be a wolf until she can process what has happened."

Louve was silent for a few seconds on the other end of the line, processing the meaning of Keller's words in the context of her connection to the beautiful veterinarian. It had been many years since the last time someone had so thoroughly intrigued her. Her answer was quiet and pained. "*D'accord.* I understand, mon ami. Please keep me informed of her well-being."

"Okay. We will be here until Jill wakes. She will probably need to stay with us until she comes to terms with all the changes she's just gone through. She has a lot to take in, not to mention dealing with any lasting emotional damage she may suffer from the attack. I will help her as best I can but I don't know everything they did to her. A lot can happen in a few hours."

Sarah urgently whispered her lover's name from Jill's bedside. "Keller."

Keller glanced over at the women on the bed. "She's waking; I have to go." With that, she hung up her phone and put it back into her pocket before making her way over to stand next to Sarah.

When Jill opened her eyes, she was disoriented. "That's weird, I would swear we all slept together at that apartment below the club. But clearly we're here at my house so..." She trailed off as bits of her memory over the last few hours started to come back. She moaned. "Oh God." The veterinarian shut her eyes again and images flashed behind her eyelids. She gave a little whimper and pulled her body into the fetal position. Keller leaned over and placed her hand on the tall woman's shoulder to reassure her. Jill merely cringed away from the gesture and yelled. "Don't touch me!" She remained on her side, hands over her head, murmuring the same words over and over again. "No, please stop. Please, no!"

Keller looked at Sarah with concern. "She knows you, you have to be the one to get through to her. We can't allow her to get trapped in a psychic loop or to spiral out of control now that she has the virus in her blood."

Sarah cast her a helpless look. "What do I do?"

"Reassure her that she's okay, that no one is going to hurt her." Before Sarah could turn back toward the bed, Keller grabbed her arm. "Speak slowly and softly, and no matter what don't let your fear or worry leak out, only send comforting emotions like love. She will be very sensitive right now on all levels."

Sarah nodded and turned toward the crying woman who acted more like a wounded animal than anything human. She slowly crawled up on the bed, careful not to touch her friend. "Jill, honey, it's Sarah. I'm right here; I won't let anything happen to you. Shh, it's going to be okay. Just look at me okay? It's Sarah." She repeated the same words for a few minutes before she started to get through.

Slowly Jill calmed. Her words faded and the rocking back and forth stopped. Keller could sense the traumatized woman's mind opening to Sarah. The veterinarian moved her hands from over her head and looked up at the singer. "Sarah?" Jill's voice was small and her mind was a whirlwind of remembered pain and fear. Her eyes filled with tears. "I called and you came."

"Keller and I both came, we're here to help." Jill sat up and grabbed Sarah in a tight embrace. She had no idea how strong she was and as a result Sarah winced slightly. "Easy, honey, let's sit up here for a moment, okay?" The veterinarian nodded, her tears already starting to dry into milky white lines on her cheeks.

Jill moved to lean against the headboard of the bed, and Sarah adjusted her own position so she was next to her. The red-haired woman spared a quick glance at Keller, and then looked back at Sarah in confusion. Seeming to take stock in her own body, her voice was full of trepidation. She looked down at her hands and ran them over her bare legs. "I don't understand. I was hurt. They hurt me! Was it—was it all a dream? I saw terrible things. Strange things."

Keller moved to the other side of Jill so that she and Sarah could both hold her. "No, I'm afraid it wasn't a dream, Jill."

Jill looked at her and lashed out in anger. She was afraid of her sanity after the things she saw. "You don't know what went on! The things they did, that they became...those things aren't real. I'm going crazy!"

Sarah placed a hand on her arm to calm her. "Jilly, she's not lying. I promise you, we will explain everything, but you have to start with this belief. I know it's scary to realize that monsters really exist."

"But how?" She looked back at her hands, the same hands she remembered as being agonizingly broken bits of bone and flesh. "And how am I healed?"

The singer took her hand into her own and gave it a gentle squeeze. "The same way I was healed when the guy that was running people down with his truck nearly killed me last year." Sarah's hands trembled at the memory of being run down. When Jill looked at her in surprised shock, she told an abbreviated story. "The gay basher was caught last year because Keller called in an anonymous tip after he hit me. I was out with Annie, and the three of us had just closed The Merge. I remember pushing Annie out of the way and after that nothing until I woke in the bar office. My femoral artery had been ripped open by a jagged bit of metal on the truck and I wouldn't have made it to the hospital in time. Annie knew that Keller was infected with a virus that could save me and she begged Keller for my life. Keller did it *despite* me telling her I would rather die than be infected. Clearly I got over my fears, and I've lived with this secret since."

Jill looked skeptical. She was a doctor after all, and such things did not exist. There were no monsters and there were no miracles. Except, she *had* seen monsters, and she was sitting here very much alive. "Why didn't you tell me?"

Sarah laughed quietly. "Excuse me, Doctor Cole, are you telling me you'd believe a story about me being turned into a vampire?" She shook her head. "Exactly. And it's not just my story to tell. Keller, Annie, and Jesse are part of this and for obvious reasons we don't want a lot of people to know."

"Okay, I think I understand."

Keller lightly cleared her throat. "Do you, Jill? You were dying in the bathroom when we found you; your body was broken beyond reasonable repair and you were succumbing to shock and blood loss. I was forced to save you the same way I saved Sarah."

Realization dawned over the veterinarian's features. "You mean—"

"You're like us now. You have the virus in your blood."

Jill drew her knees up to her chest and circled them with her arms. "I—this is a lot to take in. Sarah, you said something about vampires? Like *Dracula*, or *Twilight*? How is that real? Will I have to drink blood? Oh God, did you drink my blood?" Her knuckles were turning white as each new though tumbled over the next.

Sarah placed a hand over Jill's. "Hey, calm down okay? It's not all like the movies. We can feed on energy and emotions, as well as blood. We don't sparkle in the sun, but we don't burst into flames either. Our skin is very sensitive to ultraviolet rays so we have to take precautions or we can become drained or injured. Because we feed off emotions, we are empaths and psychics of a sort. What we have is very difficult to get. The virus is fought off by your body's natural immunity. You can only be infected when you are right on the edge of death. Our teeth will elongate when we are hungry, or sometimes horny. We need blood rarely, unless we are expending a lot of energy. We heal almost instantly, we are very strong and immune to disease. We are also barren, I—I'm sorry." She looked down at her ex and knew that the last part would affect her. Jill had always said that she wanted to have children someday, if she could find someone to settle down with. Now having her own children would no longer be an option.

When Sarah finished speaking, the room remained quiet. The silence seemed to expand around them the longer it went on. Finally Jill spoke up. "It's okay. I understand you needed to do what you could to save my life, and I'm truly thankful for that. What happens now?" She looked from Sarah to Keller and her face showed sadness. "Will I have to give up my career?"

Keller was the one who answered. "Not unless you want to. I've had many careers; you'll have plenty of time to try them all." When the veterinarian looked at her in confusion she elaborated. "You are going to live a very long life."

"Oh."

Keller pressed on before Jill could wander any further into the vampire tangent. "Now that you understand about us, we need to talk to you about your attackers."

The look of pain on Jill's face was expected. "I don't want to talk about it."

Sarah pulled her into a hug. "Jilly, we have to. We are all in danger unless we catch them."

Jill looked at her ex with suspicion. "Who is 'we?' You and Keller?"

The singer sighed. "No. Me, you, Keller, Annie, Jesse, and Louve."

"I don't understand. Who attacked me and why would all of you be in danger? You said monsters exist and—" She drew a shuddering breath and tears sprang to her eyes. "They were monsters."

Sarah kept her arm around the distraught woman. "I know, sweetie, and we need to catch them. Can you describe who did this?"

Jill closed her eyes and took deep breath. "There were two men and a woman—"

Keller interrupted. "Two men? Are you sure?" Jill opened her eyes in fear at the tone of Keller's voice. She nodded and Keller got off the bed. "Shit! I have to call Louve. Wait, first can you tell me what they looked like? Do you remember?"

The victimized woman thought for a few seconds and nodded. "One of the men was big and muscular, he had really blonde hair. The kind that looks almost white."

The singer murmured "Marcel" under her breath.

"The woman was blonde and skinny. They both spoke French. Clearly they didn't know that I'm fluent in the language. Her accent was different than his though."

Keller prompted her. "Did they say anything about why they were attacking you? Or anything about where they were staying?"

Jill shook her head. "They just joked that putting me in the shower would make it easier to clean up after. The other man was short and stocky and stayed mostly out of my line of sight. He was wearing a hat so I couldn't tell what color his hair was. He didn't speak at all and he—he usually held me from behind so I didn't see his face. They all—" She stopped speaking and shuddered. "They took turns abusing me, at first just pulling my hair, then by slapping and punching. Then they started really hurting me by breaking my fingers one by one. It hurt so much, and I was sure that I'd never practice medicine again." She started to softly cry.

Sarah looked at Keller in surprise. She hated making Jill relive the ordeal, but they had to know what the rogue wolves were planning and they had to understand why they were doing what they were doing. "All three of them hurt you?"

Jill whispered. "Yes."

Sarah instantly folded her into her arms and held her tight. "I'm so sorry, sweetie. I'm sorry all this happened to you and we'll do whatever we can to make it right."

Jill pulled back, remembering something important. "You don't understand, they — they changed. After they were done with me, they turned into monsters, like werewolves from all the horror movies we watched in college. How can we fight them?"

Keller laughed, surprising the veterinarian. "Have no fear, Jill, we are ten times stronger than any werewolf. They are no match for us, which is why they are playing all these games. All we have to do is catch them and I guarantee they will never be a threat again." She pulled out her phone. "Now, I should call Louve and let her know that it was Marie and Marcel, with one other unknown. If you'll excuse me." She turned and left the bedroom as the phone was connecting.

"I don't understand, how does Louve know who my attackers were?"

Sarah groaned and ran a hand through her hair. "Marcel and Marie used to work at the Temple du Loup. Marcel is the nephew of an old friend of hers. The boy had anger issues and Louve was trying to train him and rehabilitate him. She only gave him a warning last year when he attacked Jesse and infected her with the werewolf virus. But she fired him when he started harassing Annie. Marie wants both Marcel and Jesse, and hates that Jesse and Annie are together. She is prejudiced against normal humans. I'm afraid they are very angry with all of us and you got caught in the cross fire. They must have seen the three of us leave the club this morning, and they went after the only one they stood a chance against. I'm so sorry, this is all our fault."

"Did you know you were putting me in danger by being with me?"

"Of course not!"

Jill smiled. "Then it's not your fault. So stop beating yourself up about it, Colby! So Louve knows that two of her employees are werewolves, and she doesn't care?"

Sarah leveled a serious look at her friend. "Jill, it's called Cirque du Loup for a reason."

"Oh my God, they're all wolves aren't they? Even Louve?" The veterinarian shuddered at the thought of the woman she had been with a few hours prior becoming one of the monsters she had seen.

"Yes. We go there because just as vampires feed off emotional energy, and sexual energy in general, werewolves are like batteries. They emit a huge amount of energy, emotionally and physically. So when vampires and werewolves get together, it's like a plug and socket. All the energy we take in eventually gets released if we use sex as an outlet. So both the vampire and the werewolf benefit from a pairing. But you shouldn't worry about any other werewolves but the three that attacked you. I know Louve and a fair number of her circus troupe. They are good people."

Jill looked at her with disgust. "But they turned into beasts! That's when they really hurt me, when they started breaking larger bones and dislocating my limbs." She squeezed her eyes shut trying to block out the remembered pain.

The singer cocked her head in confusion. "Wait, did they scratch you at all? Would you remember if they did?"

"No, the woman kept saying for them to be careful in French. She also kept repeating the words, "*Ne rayez*." I didn't understand at the time, but now it makes sense."

Keller walked into the room and elaborated for her confused girlfriend. "That means do not scratch. So they had no intention of turning you, they were being careful not to do that. They merely wanted to make you suffer. But why leave your phone near you so you could call for help?"

Jill drew in a shaky breath. "That wasn't their intent at all. They taunted me with it, knowing that all my fingers were so broken they wouldn't function, and that I was in agony. They laughed at the fact that I couldn't call for help. That's why they left it by my head."

The singer looked at her ex curiously. "Then how did you call me?"

"Wake up you bitch."

Sarah looked at her in shock. "Excuse me?"

Jill chuckled. "It's a feature on my phone. When I have it running, I merely have to say that phrase to unlock it, then I can tell it to call a saved contact. That's how I dialed your number."

Keller shook her head. "Jings! The tech continues to amaze me."

Jill shrugged and got off the bed. Now that she had a better understanding of what was going on, she wanted real clothes on. She quickly stripped and pulled on a pair of well-worn jeans and a Henley. "So what do we do now?"

"First, I need to train you on how to shield yourself and instruct you on how to feed. I just need to do the basics today, but we will need to continue your training until I'm sure you have it all down." Keller gave the veterinarian a serious look. "This is non-negotiable. You think you're fine right now, but the minute we leave this house you will be bombarded by emotions and sensations like you've never felt before."

Sarah hopped off the bed too. "She's right. I almost went crazy. I even tried going after Louve. They had to lock me in the apartment below the club until Keller came to help me."

Jill nodded in acceptance. "So, what do I need to do?"

Keller smiled at Jill's willingness to meet her newest challenge head on. They just needed to take care of their friend, then the hunt would be on in earnest. What she hadn't said to Louve over the phone was that there was no longer an option for Marcel to return to Canada. With the death of two hikers, and the fact that they may as well have killed Jill, Keller knew that if the decision were solely up to her, she would not let any of them go. They were too much of a threat to let live. She wasn't going to tell Sarah that either. Keller knew what she would have to do and felt no remorse for it. Some skills you never forget and for her friends and lover she would become the "noble killer" again.

Refocusing on the women in the room, she gestured back toward the bed. "This won't take too long. I'm going to start by showing you how to build shields." In light of the traumatic events, they decided to skip going to the farmhouse for training. Instead they stayed with Jill and helped clean up the wall in the living room. As an experiment, Jill put all her weights on the bench press in her basement gym and lifted them with ease. She couldn't deny the obvious healing she received from Keller's "vampire virus," but her immensely increased strength really made it hit home how different she now was. That and she could feel her neighbors in her head if she concentrated hard enough. She also quickly learned that overextending herself led to a short-lived blinding headache. Keller tried to get her to come stay at the condo with them, but Jill refused.

Sarah was frustrated with her ex but Keller knew that Jill was better able to take care of herself now than most people. Even untrained, she doubted very much that the rogue wolves could overpower the veterinarian. Now they just needed to focus on finding the dogs and keeping Annie and Jesse safe.

When they left the house, Jill went into her garage and searched around until she found her old softball bag. She removed one of the aluminum bats and went back inside and took a seat in the recliner that was located in the only solid corner in her living room. Setting the bat across her lap, she drew her knees up until she could comfortably rest her chin on them. Jill Cole had been self-dependent most of her life. Her mother had barely engaged her as a child, and even less so when she came out. There was no way she would admit her level of fear to Sarah and Keller, but that shaking blackness of terror still clawed at her from the back of her mind. With her emotions on autopilot, she stared at the door and waited. Alone. No one was going to hurt her again.

Chapter Seven

IT WAS NEAR noon when they finally backed out of Jill's drive. The down-to-earth doctor had taken the knowledge of vampires and werewolves quite well, understanding that there are many things in the world that science had not yet been able to explain. But despite Jill's willingness to accept the stranger things in life, Keller knew that it would take a while before she could get over the actual attack. She could feel Jill's terror; it settled around the woman like an odor. It was what many referred to as the "stink of fear." As much as Keller would have liked to take it all away, she knew she could cause serious damage the other woman if she altered her emotions and memory too much. She helped her as much as possible by slightly clouding the emotions attached to the attack, but the long-term healing would be up to Jill. The bar manager was concerned about all their friends and family now. "I think we should swing by Annie and Jesse's house. Just to check on them and fill them in. We are all going to have to be more careful now that the rogue wolves have escalated things."

Sarah looked at Keller in the driver's seat with unfiltered anger. "If they touch Annie I'll kill them."

Keller glanced at her lover in concern, then turned eyes back to the road. "Let me handle them, lass. You just focus on protecting your sister. Promise me you won't attack them, just protect Annie. Okay?"

"No, I will not promise that. Of course I'll protect Annie with everything I have but I'm telling you that if they harm one hair on her head they'll regret it!" Keller let it drop. She knew she wasn't going to get through to her lover right now, not while the anger over Jill's attack was still so fresh. She could only hope that when the time came, Sarah would keep a level head. It didn't take long for them to arrive at the house and they were relieved to see both cars in the driveway. When they knocked on the door it was Jesse who answered. The nerdy younger woman was wearing her customary jeans and a comic book character t-shirt. She was full of boundless energy, as always.

"Hey you two! We didn't expect you to come over today." She craned her head out the door. "Where's Duke?" She had unexpectedly bonded with the husky after her transformation.

Sarah and Annie had actually taken Duke to the dog park a few times, together with a transformed Jesse. She said it was weird because he didn't communicate like people, but still fun. Annie was just happy to wear out her girlfriend for once.

Sarah answered her sister's girlfriend. "He's not with us; we didn't come from home. Where's Annie? We need to talk to you two." Jesse moved so they could come in. When Sarah walked around the corner into the living room, she saw her sister sitting on the couch, eating cereal and watching the cartoon network. She was immediately relived to see the younger woman. The fear she felt after seeing Jill's broken body had been clawing beneath the surface until she verified that her sister was safe. She couldn't even think about what she would have done if it had been Annie's body she'd found. She shoved the dark and troublesome thoughts down. "Some things never change do they, A?" The younger sister grinned and shoveled another spoonful of "magically delicious" into her mouth.

Jesse could sense the tension in the two visitors and knew immediately something was wrong. "What's going on?" Annie looked up at the tone of her girlfriend's voice and suddenly realized that her sister and Keller had just dropped by unannounced on a Sunday. She took one look at her sister's face and immediately jumped up and ran over to her.

"What happened? Are you okay?"

Keller grabbed Sarah's hand and pulled her into the living room. "Let's sit down and talk. Things have escalated with Marcel and Marie, and it's not good."

"What do you mean?"

Anger washed over Sarah's face and she answered Annie's question. "What she means is that Marcel, Marie, and an unknown third man attacked Jill this morning after we dropped her off. They assaulted her, breaking nearly every bone in her body while they were in half-wolf form, and left her for dead. Keller was forced to infect her just like she did with me or she would have died right after we got there."

Annie paled. "Jilly?" Sarah nodded. "Shit!"

Always the one for details, Jesse looked at them in confusion. "Three? Who is the other guy?"

"We don't know, only that he was stocky and was wearing a knit hat so she couldn't tell what color his hair was. She said he didn't speak and she never saw his face, just the back of his head. Jill's description of the other two perfectly matched Marcel and Marie, right down to the fact that they were speaking French."

Sarah looked at Keller suddenly. "They were speaking French!"

Keller looked at her curiously. "Yes, I just said that."

"No, Marie was speaking French to the two men. Jill said she was telling both of them to be careful in French. That must mean the third man must speak fluent French as well! You should let Louve know."

Annie looked at the older couple fearfully. "You think they're going to come after me next, don't you?"

Sarah looked at her for a second then nodded. Jesse was still trying to figure out who the third person would be. "Do you think they would have infected someone else in order to make more rogue wolves?"

Keller shook her head. "No. It would be months before the man could be trusted not to lose control. Plus, how many fluent French speakers live in Columbus that wouldn't mind murder and assault as a pastime?"

Sarah looked at her abruptly. "I'm serious, Keller, you need to call Louve right now and give her the full description that Jill gave us. The third man kept his head and face hidden and he didn't speak. What if he was the one in control, not Marcel like we thought? What if the third man is one of her people that we haven't met, or even one that we have? She needs to start looking on her end."

Annie snorted. "And I would have got away with it too if it hadn't been for those meddling kids!" When three serious looking sets of eyes turned her way, she immediately sobered. "I'm sorry, I know it's not something to laugh about. And I know I'm in danger, but I guess all the mystery just struck me as funny." She shrugged. "So what do we do in the mean time?"

Keller looked at the little group. "We're going to have to change our routine. Annie, are you willing to take a leave of absence from work?"

"Are you nuts? We have Columbus Pride in a month, and our manager is leaving." She gave Keller, her manager, a pointed look. "There is no way I can take time off right now!" When Sarah looked like she was going to protest Annie cut her off. "And I'm not going to either. This is my life and my career, and I'm not going to let them make me afraid to live it! We'll find another way."

The elder Colby sister punched the couch cushion next to her. "Why are you so stubborn? This is serious, Annie! They'll kill you!" Tears threatened but Sarah's anger at her own helplessness in the situation wouldn't let them fall. There was nothing she wouldn't do to keep Annie safe but the younger woman didn't seem to understand the level of danger she was in. Of all people, Sarah thought that Annie would understand her fear. Annie was the one who begged Keller to save Sarah's life the previous year. Yet Sarah's pleas fell on deaf ears when the situation was reversed.

Hazel eyes looked back at the closest thing Annie had to a parent. Annie knew her sister was overprotective, but she wasn't always right. But for Annie's own piece of mind, there were just some things in life that she had to do, regardless of what Sarah wanted. She trusted her strange family to have her back, and she didn't want to live her life in fear. "I said we'll find another way. Look, I won't ever go anywhere without one of you three. I won't even stay at the house by myself."

Jesse leaned toward her girlfriend and put an arm around her shoulder. "I'll watch out for her, Sarah, I promise."

The bar manger ran a hand through hair that had given up on any sort of style for the day. "Jesse, I know you're strong and that you mean well, and I know you'd give your life for Annie. But that is exactly what you'd be doing. You can't face three older werewolves alone. They will kill you and then they'll kill Annie."

"Why don't you stay with us at the condo?"

Annie wrinkled her nose in disgust at her sister's suggestion. "I love you guys, but with your vampirey-succubus thing going on, you two seriously scrump all the time! The condo is big, but it isn't that big. No can do, sis."

The singer raised an eyebrow. "Like you're one to talk! What about Jill then? She lives in that big house and she could definitely take care of you both. I also think she could use a little friendly company now since the attack. I'm worried about her being alone right now."

"Sarah, I love Jill, you know that. But she still calls me 'kid,' just like when you were dating."

Sarah gave a curious look. "What's wrong with that?"

"You dated, like, ten years ago! I'm not a freakin' kid anymore. Besides, I'm sure the last thing she wants right now is more strangers in the house!" Sarah sat back, slumping against the cushions of the old couch in defeat.

Keller thought about Jill's seeming fear and revulsion at the thought of werewolves. The attack had definitely affected her and potentially any relationship she might have with Louve. Maybe a little exposure of the "good kind" might help her come to terms with stuff. "Actually, I think Sarah has a good idea." When Annie shot her a dirty look, she tried to explain. "Listen, right now Jill is traumatized from the attack. She has dealt really well with being infected, and with learning that there are more things out there than we learn about in school. But she was tortured and left for dead, all by three people she watched turn into half-wolves. She was broken, Annie, as broken as a human can be and now she is alive and very much afraid. They turned into things she's only ever seen portrayed as monsters. She needs to see that not all the monsters are the bad kind, that some of them are people." She turned and looked at Jesse. "Do you think you can help with that?"

The young werewolf geek looked skeptically back at her. "I don't know, Keller; I've only met her twice when Annie and I have gone out. She seemed cool at the time but she has every reason to hate my kind now. And from what you've said, she could snap me like a twig. I don't want her to take all that anger out on me."

Keller shook her head. "I don't think she will. And I'd also like the opportunity to teach her how to feed on energy. Hypothetically, vampires can drain a werewolf enough that they turn human again, if they drink deeply of every bit of their energy. Now, I don't want to test out that particular theory on you, but I'd like to at least show her the basics of feeding on a wolf's energy." She looked back and forth between the two younger women. "Jill is emotionally vulnerable right now, and I sense that she could use all the friends she can get. Especially ones that she can talk to about all this. What do you say?"

Annie looked back at Keller, then glanced at Sarah. She stood and grabbed Jesse's hand. "We need to talk about this first." She turned to her sister and waved her fingers near her forehead. "And no listening in with your mind thing either!" After she dragged her girlfriend through the door to the kitchen, Keller turned to Sarah and started laughing.

"Doesn't she realize that we can just hear them from here and it has nothing to do with mind reading?"

Sarah shrugged. "I've explained it many times, she never believes me. You do realize that even if they agree, we still have to convince Jill."

Keller nodded. "I'm aware and I'm leaving that to you. She's your ex, you know her better than anyone else. I'm sure you'll find a way to persuade her."

Before Sarah could respond, Annie and Jesse came back into

the living room. Annie looked irritated but resolute. "Okay, we're fine with the plan. What do we do now?"

The elder Colby sister looked at Keller expectantly. "Yeah, Doctor Headshrinker, what do we do now?"

Keller thought for a minute. "Well, normally people would be more comfortable in their own home dealing with new things, because that is where they feel safe. However, I don't think that Jill feels very comfortable in her home right now. At least that's the impression I got from her before we left, despite all her reassurances of being fine. Why don't we all go over to our condo where it's kind of neutral ground?"

Everyone agreed with the plan, which left Sarah to make the call. Five minutes later she came back into the house, having stepped outside for a bit of privacy. "Well, she wasn't too happy about it, but I think she was less happy sitting at home by herself. I told her Annie and Jesse would be there and surprisingly she didn't comment. She seemed almost in shock." She looked at her girlfriend. "Maybe you were wrong with your assumption that she'd have a problem with wolves now."

Keller shook her head. "I don't think so. It's easy to be brave when you're not face to face with your fear." She stood and stretched. "All right, let's get this over with. Even vampires need more sleep than what we got last night."

JILL ARRIVED AT the condo around three in the afternoon. Though she'd never admit it, she was relieved to get out of the house and be around familiar faces. The hours she spent staring at the door felt like years. Sarah and Annie were playing guitars in the living room while Jesse tried to follow along with a tambourine. Keller went down to get Jill when she buzzed the intercom. Jill looked wary when she followed Keller into the elevator and Keller could make out the faintest traces of fear through the other woman's shield. Neither one for small talk, they rode in awkward silence to the fifth floor. Jill neither smiled nor emitted any other emotions until she walked into the condo and heard the Colby sisters playing. Then it was as if a calming blanket settled over the veterinarian and Keller watched the woman's face relax. She thought to herself, "Ah, familiar is good." The trio was so engrossed in what they were doing that they didn't even realized Keller had left, let alone returned with another person. Keller gave a little trilling whistle. "Hey, look who I found on the front step!"

Annie and Sarah both stopped, and the younger woman set her guitar aside and jumped up. "Jilly!" She ran over to her sister's ex. Despite all her complaining that Jill still called her "kid," Annie thought of her as an older sister. Jill and Sarah had been friends for a long time. With so little support and affection in her own house, Jill spent a lot of time at the Colby's. Annie practically grew up with her.

Jill accepted the hug with some trepidation but her smile was completely real. "Hey, kid, how's it going?"

Annie stepped back and scowled at her. "How many times do I have to tell you, it's Annie, you big ginger Amazon!" She emphasized her point with a poke to the chest. Jesse looked at her girlfriend in shock while Sarah burst out laughing.

The ginger amazon growled at her. "Big. Ginger. Amazon? Really? You know, kid, you're never too old for *the claw*." She held up a hand and spread her fingers wide, the same way she used to do right before tickling a young Annie Colby senseless.

The younger woman's eyes widened. "Eeep! I give, sorry Jilly. I won't call you ginger names anymore!"

Jill gave her a warm smile. "It's okay, A, I understand. So things are crazy, huh?"

Annie looked at Jill, then around at the rest of the people in the condo who were watching them. "Yeah, things are crazy. Life, you know?" She sighed then abruptly shook off her mood.

Duke was sitting idly by, waiting his turn to say hello. Jill followed Keller and Annie into the living room area to take a seat in the recliner. The big dog decided that was his cue to climb into her lap. Sarah immediately scolded him and stood to pull him down by the collar. "Duke, get down. You're not a lap dog!" He managed to wedge himself between the chair and Jill's hips, then sprawled the rest of his body across her lap.

"He's fine, leave him." She ruffled his fur and accepted his doggy kisses. "He's just a big lovey boy, aren't you, Duke? Who's my handsome boy, hmm? Who's my beautiful baby?" The two couples watched the veterinarian lavish attention on the husky. When she saw them looking she stopped what she was doing. "What? He's my favorite patient! He's not drama queen like literally every other husky I see." After accepting one more kiss, she patted her lap to get Duke to lie down. "All right, you got me over here, let's talk about the situation. I want you to fill me in completely, starting with last year and ending with now."

It took a while, but between the four women, they were able to paint a pretty good picture of what life had been like since

Sarah had been infected by the vampire virus the previous year. They explained all the things she'd had to deal with as she came to terms with having *other* blood. They also told Jill what it had been like for Jesse, after she had been infected by Marcel. Jesse talked about how difficult and painful the transformation was at first, even mentioning that her first form was the half-wolf thing that she saw her attackers change into. To lighten the mood a little, Sarah talked about Jesse trying to eat her first meal of pizza and Dr. Pepper after the initial transformation. Her story had all of them rolling in laughter, even the veterinarian. When they calmed down again, Keller laid out their plan to Jill, explaining that the trio would most likely go after Annie next.

Jill sat forward on the chair, tense. "I won't let them touch her! I'll be damned if she has to go through what I did! It was —" She took a shaky breath and shut her eyes. When Sarah broke up with her nearly a decade ago, she had been devastated. Even though half of the break had been her own fault. Jill had spent most of her life feeling alone until she met the tall gangly Sarah Colby. She had so few people in her life that she truly cared about that she couldn't bear to lose Sarah once they were no longer dating.

The biggest reason they became friends after the breakup was because Jill simply wouldn't let the singer walk out of her life. Sarah and Annie had been her family for so many years that it was something she would never willingly give up. Now, the friendship she shared with both women was one of the bright spots in her otherwise fallow life. Sarah looked at Annie and something unspoken passed between them. The younger Colby got up from her seat and went around the back of Jill's chair. Bending at the waist, she wrapped her arms around the stoic woman and just held her from behind.

"It's going to be okay, Jilly. Sarah and Keller will do everything they can to make them pay. You've got all of us so don't be afraid to cry, okay? We're right here, sis." Sarah got up from her seat and went over to Jill as well.

"You became an honorary Colby when we were freshmen in high school. That doesn't change just because we stopped being a couple. Let us help you, and you can help us."

Keller cleared her throat, catching everyone's attention. "Jill, anyone who could remotely be related to me is centuries dead. But what we have right here, right now, this is more family than I'll ever need. We are all family now, and we will get through this together."

Jill looked from one person to the next, until she came full circle around the four of them. "You're right, you're all right. We'll stick together and lean on each other when we need it." She turned to look at Jesse. "Is it true? Are you really like them? You can turn into that half-beast monster too?"

Jesse nodded, causing her dark hair to flop over her eyes. It was short on the sides and back, but the front continuously drove her crazy. She pushed it out of the way before she spoke. "Actually, I can turn into the half-wolf, or all the way into a wolf. Half-wolf is nice because I can still talk to Annie, watch TV, and eat people food." She blushed a little, remembering the pizza and soda story. "Well, with a little help. But full wolf is different, it's...freeing. To be able to run and sense things on an entirely different level is just awesome. It's really hard to explain."

The younger Colby sister laughed and walked around to sit on the arm of Jill's chair. "Actually, sometimes I take her and Duke to the dog park to play. It's pretty funny watching them together."

The veterinarian cocked her head curiously. "So do you speak dog? Does he understand you, and can you still understand us?"

"Oh, I understand people just fine when I'm the wolf, I just can't speak. But animals are different, they're cruder. It's like talking to a two-year-old, they only understand basic things." She thought for a second, then lobbed the idea out into the middle of the room. "Do you want to see?" When Jill paled, Jesse tried humor. "I mean, I haven't had my shots or anything and I've been looking for a good doctor in the area. You see I have this pain right here..." She trailed off, vaguely gesturing toward her side.

That worked. Jill cracked up laughing. "Oh God, that's exactly what my friends who are people doctors go through. Every time they meet someone who finds out they're a doctor they start talking about all their aches and pains!" The tension was finally eased in the room, which only left Jill curious. "Okay, so does it take long to change? Does it hurt? Is your anatomy the same inside when you change? How does that work?" The last question was directed at Keller, who seemed to be the most knowledgeable about things of *other* blood.

Keller looked back at her and smiled. "There's only one way to find out. Let's have Jesse change then you can give her a full physical. After that, I'll teach you how to feed on a werewolf's energy."

Jill nodded and Jesse shrugged. "Okay, everyone ready?"

Annie abruptly got up from the arm of the chair and headed to the far side of the condo. Sarah watched her walk away in concern, then looked back at Jesse. The young werewolf gave her a sad look. "She doesn't like to watch me change because she knows how much it hurts. She can't stand to hear me in pain. I mean, don't get me wrong, it's a lot better now. But it's still kind of agonizing."

Keller looked off in Annie's direction, then back at Jesse. "It will keep getting better until eventually you'll feel no pain, or at least you won't notice it. As far as werewolves go, you're practically a newborn. Stay strong, okay?"

The continually curious werewolf nodded in understanding. She began stripping down in the middle of the living room. Before they had come over to Keller's condo, she had dressed with the thought that she would have to change. She was wearing form fitting boxer briefs and a sports bra under her clothes. Jill watched intently as Jesse dropped down to all fours. The younger woman cried out and gritted her teeth and the three watchers could see all the bones in her spine seemingly pop outward. The popping and cracking sounds happened faster as the changes became more evident. She purposely stopped early so Jill could see her in the half-wolf form of her earlier attackers.

Jill swallowed and couldn't look away from the beast that was so much like the ones who hurt her. "Tha—that's what they looked like. Except their fur wasn't the same color."

When Jesse spoke, her voice sounded slightly lower and had a rougher quality to it. "This is my halfway, I wanted you to see it. I'll admit that Marcel and Marie are bad people, but not all of the monsters are monsters, Jill. I would give my life to protect any of you but like Keller says, I'm no match for them. I'm still new, still learning about all the things I can and can't do. That's why we need your help, because I can't protect Annie by myself." Her voice broke a little with that admission.

Jill gave her a hesitant look that still managed to be full of compassion. "I understand that; you make complete sense. It's just hard to reconcile you being different from them, when you look so similar."

The younger woman gave her a reassuring smile, or at least she hoped it was reassuring. It was hard to tell with partially protruded doggy-type jaws. "You can come closer; I promise I won't bite. Well, I only bite Annie, but she asks for it!"

The younger Colby sister came back to sit down as she was finishing her statement. "Well, I do ask for it, but I bite too so it's only fair."

Jill rose with uncertainty and approached the half-wolf creature. She reached out a shaking hand to touch Jesse's shoulder. Sarah noticed and her heart broke for her friend. She knew the fear would pass with time but on a deeper level the singer still felt responsible for Jill's attack. Sarah was convinced that if she hadn't invited Jill into their trysting, her friend would have remained untouched. Despite the shaking, Jill's hands pushed forward into Jesse's fur. At first contact her eyes widened in surprise. "Oh! You're so soft!"

Annie moved closer and snuggled into her girlfriend's side. "Yeah, she's totally cuddly. And she keeps me warm when I'm cold."

Suddenly it was the doctor looking at the werewolf, and not a frightened woman. "So like canids, your temp runs higher than humans. Interesting. How is your sense of smell and hearing, are all things enhanced the same way?"

Jesse nodded. "I heal fast, have faster speed, better hearing, and I can smell an amazing array of things I never even thought about before. It's like an entirely new language! Sadly, my eyesight is exactly the same. Annie says it's creepy that I have my human eyes when in wolf form. I think it's cool!"

"Can I see your other form?"

The younger woman nodded. "Sure, but I won't be able to talk and I won't be able to change back while I'm here."

The veterinarian gave her a curious look. "Why not? Do you have to stay a wolf for a while? Do you have to um, kill and eat something, just like the movies?" Jesse went quiet, and idly scratched at one furry ear. The Colby sisters and Keller all started laughing at her embarrassment. Jill looked to Sarah for an explanation. "I don't get it, what's the joke?"

Keller thought it would be a good teaching moment so she answered instead. "Jill, I want you to drop your shields just a little." She had noticed that the taller woman had completely blocked herself off to everything. While it was good for someone who was new to all the emotions and sensations that would be bombarding them, Sarah's ex needed to learn how to deal with those sensations at some point.

"But you said —"

Keller interrupted her. "It's okay, we are all safe here. I just need you to feel what werewolves will feel like in your mind. They put off an incredible amount of energy and you need to learn how to sense that. I will teach you to do that and to feed off that power." Slowly and tentatively Jill began lowering her shields. She was immediately aware of a low level kind of buzzing in her head. It wasn't unpleasant, just unexpected. When Keller sensed that she was open she spoke again. "Can you feel all that power that is coming from Jesse?" Jill nodded. "Well she emotes all that and more when she's in *other* form. So when she changes back to human, all those senses, power, and emotions are crammed into a small human package. So for most wolves, it can feel a lot like sexual over-stimulation. The bottom line is that it makes werewolves pretty horny." Jill made an 'O' shape with her mouth. "Now, open yourself to us and feel what is all around you. Feel the energy coming from each of us."

She was immediately aware of the three people with *other* blood. They felt different in her mind. If she had to assign animal breeds to each person, Jesse would be an Australian Shepherd. Quiet, intelligent, and high energy. Annie barely registered in her head compared to the other three but she was a Cavalier King Charles Spaniel. She didn't like to be alone for long, she was affectionate with family, and overall just a very friendly person. Ironically enough Sarah was exactly like her best friend Duke. Siberian Huskies were known for not liking to be alone, and were known for their affection, friendliness, intelligence, and energy. But the last person in the room, Keller, she was different. Not realizing that she was staring, Jill continued to look at the small blonde in front of her. Despite the woman's small physical size, mentally she was a giant. The image of an Anatolian Shepherd popped into her head and she had to admit it felt right. The golden giant was fiercely loyal and originally bred to guard sheep from wolves, bears, jackals, and even cheetahs. Her perusal was interrupted when Keller chuckled and the veterinarian wondered if the powerful vampire could actually read her thoughts. "What is so funny?"

Keller shook her head and smiled. "I find your analysis of us interesting, that's all."

Jill bristled a little. "Are you reading my thoughts right now?"

"No worries, Jill, empathy isn't that...detailed. But when you dropped your shields I caught flashes of your impressions of each of us. I simply found it amusing; quite astute, but funny none the less."

The singer cocked her head curiously toward her ex. "Analysis of us? Just what were you thinking?" Suddenly she burst out laughing, remembering a game Jill loved to play. "Oh God, which breed are they?" Jill smiled sheepishly and nodded.

Annie looked back and forth between the older women, clearly not remembering this game. "What the hell is that?"

Sarah snorted. "She was imagining us all as dogs."

The only werewolf in the group grinned, looking a little maniacal in the process. "Cool! What am I?"

"Besides a giant hairy nerd?" Jesse playfully snapped her teeth at her girlfriend for the unflattering description.

Jill sighed, realizing that she was going to have to tell everyone what was going through her head minutes before. She turned her gaze back at the enigmatic blonde. "Thanks a lot!" Keller merely smiled and raised an eyebrow as if to say, "well, go ahead." "Fine. Jesse, I see you as an Australian Shepherd...smart, work oriented, and energetic. Annie, you're a Cavalier King Charles Spaniel..."

Annie grinned. "Ooh, fancy!"

Jill continued over the younger woman. "...affectionate, friendly, and a little needy."

"Hey!" Jesse could be heard trying to cover a strange snuffling laugh.

Sarah looked at her ex, curious about what Jill had to say about her. "And what am I?"

The veterinarian laughed. "Besides a huge pain in my ass? You're Duke." The Husky looked up from the chair he had taken over after she stood up. His duster tail began to wag as he sensed eyes turned his way.

"Duke?"

Jill ticked off traits on the fingers of her right hand. "Sure. You're a lot like your sister in that you are both friendly, affectionate, and you don't like to be alone for long. But unlike Annie you have a high amount of energy and a need to roam."

"Interesting. And what about Keller? What is she?" Annie whispered the word, "pit bull," and Jesse laughed again.

The veterinarian turned her gaze to the younger two women. "Actually, the American Pit Bull Terrier is an amazing breed of dog. They are strong-willed, obedient, loyal, friendly, clownish, stubborn, courageous, intelligent, and affectionate. That would also be a good description for Keller, don't you think?"

Sarah laughed. "You sound like you have that whole speech memorized. Another one of your pet projects?"

Jill shrugged and smiled good-naturedly at her friend. "Actually it is. They get a bad rap across the country because of a few people training them to do bad things. But most every vet I know will tell you they are actually a good dog, that there are at least a dozen more aggressive breeds out there to watch out for. But anyways, we got off track. I think that Keller feels like an Anatolian Shepherd." Three blank stares met with her statement.

"Huh? What the hell is that?" Annie was never afraid to speak her mind.

"The Anatolian Shepherd is a big dog—" Again she was interrupted by laughter only this time it was Jesse. Jill scolded her. "I didn't say she looked like a big dog, you mangy mutt!" Jesse's mouth slammed shut with a meaty snap. And she wore a look of utter surprise on her doggy face. Annie doubled over in laughter, knowing that her sister's ex-girlfriend was kidding, but finding the look on Jesse's half-wolf face too hilarious not to react.

"Oh God, your face right now!" She quickly pulled out her cell phone and snapped a pic. Jesse growled and made a swipe for it but Annie quickly scampered out of the way and hid behind Sarah.

Jill cleared her throat. "Like I was saying, she *feels* big inside my head. I'm guessing that has something to do with your age?" When Keller nodded, she continued. "The Anatolian Shepherd is one of the biggest breeds. It is rugged and strong, and has superior sight and speed for running down predators. They are fiercely loyal and have been known to guard sheep from bears, wolves, jackals, and such." When Annie continued smirking, she addressed the younger woman directly. "I know I haven't known Keller as long as you have, but let me ask you a question. Who would you count on to protect you from anyone, no matter who it was?"

Annie cocked her head in that distinct Colby way then nodded. "You're right."

Even Sarah agreed. "Yeah, she's right, love. You feel very large inside my head." Jesse nodded as well.

Keller began to slowly clap. "Congratulations, you've all just learned a very important lesson. There is a difference between how energy feels in your head and how large someone feels in your head. Think of energy as something that is quick and strong, and it has nothing to do with age, power, or skill."

Jesse looked confused, her strong STEM background not fitting in with what Keller was saying. "I don't get it, how is a lot of power not related to a lot of energy?"

Keller thought for a second, trying to put it into terms they would all understand. "Do you remember when I said that the energy that werewolves emote was a lot like a river?"

Three out of the four heads nodded, Jill not having been part of the conversation about what it was like for werewolves to perform in front of a large crowd. "Where do all rivers eventually end up? Large bodies of water. There is a reason that vampires drink deeply from werewolves. We collect that energy and either release it, use it, or store it up. The more energy we take in, the less we have to drink blood."

"Okay, that makes sense. But what does that have to do with age?"

Keller smiled at how Jesse was always so curious to learn new things. The younger woman never stopped trying to learn about the world around her. "Well, the older we get, the more capacity we have. So while I would not have been able to store very much energy a few centuries ago, now I have a much greater capacity." Sarah flashed back to when her lover repeatedly slammed Marcel into the concrete floor of the bathroom out at the farm.

Suitably impressed, Jesse merely gave a quiet "Oh."

"Now back to the lesson. Jill, you can feel both how old the two vampires are, and how 'hot' the werewolf feels. Right?"

Jill looked at Keller and Sarah, and then turned her gaze toward the half-wolf. "You're right, the energy she emotes feels like heat but it flows toward me like water."

"Good. Now, we showed you how to feed on blood at your house this morning. I want you to remember how that felt. Think about the feeling of you opening your mouth wide and drinking down the flowing blood. I want you to open that hungry part inside your mind, and do the same with her energy."

Jesse grinned at Keller's words. "Hey, I'm like a Scooby snack!"

Annie pulled the brushy tale that was protruding out the back of the wolf's underwear. "You're an idiot, now hush!"

Jill concentrated for nearly two minutes and the silence was deafening. But she just couldn't get it. She growled in frustration. "I don't quite understand what you're trying to tell me or how it should feel."

Keller looked at the angry woman calmly, then turned to her girlfriend. "Sarah." Sarah nodded and walked up to her ex.

Sarah understood what her lover needed. The singer also had trouble the first time, but through her bond with Keller was able to "feel" how the other woman did it. While it wasn't a bond of soul mates, she and Jill also shared a bond of friendship and love. It would have to do. "Take my hand, and feel what I'm doing.

Open up your mind and just feel it."

Jill did as she was instructed and shut her eyes to block out other distractions. Even with her eyes shut, she could still sense the waves coming off Jesse. She could also sense that quiet power of the other two vampires in the room. She "felt" it when Sarah started opening herself. It was like she was opening her mouth in the middle of the pouring rain. With something other than her human senses she could see that hot river flowing into her ex-girlfriend. It was a slow stream and she sensed that the singer was holding back.

Quickly, before Sarah could stop her demonstration, Jill emulated her. She tried to open just a little, exactly like the woman holding her hand. However, without the practice and experience, she had no real control. Instead of opening just a crack, she fumbled wide open and quickly swallowed everything the young werewolf had to give. Jesse made a chuffing sound and immediately passed out.

Everyone moved at once, but quickest was Annie. She tried to catch her falling girlfriend as soon a she heard the strange sound but Jesse was too heavy. "Jesse!" She screamed the young werewolf's name, then turned a furious gaze to Jill. "What the hell did you do to her, Jilly?"

Jill looked mortified and frightened. "I—I don't know. I'm so sorry." She turned anxious eyes to Keller. "What happened, what did I do?"

Keller raised her voice to get Annie's attention. The distraught younger Colby was cradling her girlfriend's furry head in her lap. "Annie! She's okay, I promise." Turning her gaze back to the two taller vampires she explained what happened. "I told Sarah about the possibility that we could drink a werewolf's energy to the point that they would turn human again. You didn't drink that much, but you certainly took enough for her to momentarily lose consciousness. You were aided by two things. One, that she was focused right at you and Sarah. And two, that Sarah was also drinking from her. Don't worry though, she'll wake up in a few minutes good as new. The question is, how do you feel?"

Reassured that she hadn't harmed Annie's girlfriend, Jill took stock of herself. "I feel amazing! It's like everything is alive and more vivid. I feel strong, like I could run a hundred miles or lift a truck. Is that normal?"

Sarah looked from Jill to Keller. "Um, why isn't she, uh, *you* know?"

Annie snorted. "That was pretty eloquent for a musician and poet."

"Shut up, you mutt-lover! I mean why isn't she horny and wanting to hump the first thing in sight after feeding from someone else's energy? I think I've been doing it all wrong here."

Her younger sister snickered. "Or you've been doing it all right, heh." Sarah stuck a tongue out at the younger woman.

Keller smiled at her lover. "It has to do with the type of energy she fed from. Typically we feed from the sexual energy at the club, and it tends to blend with our own, making us feel it intimately. However, if it's just straightforward energy, like what you were both just doing to Jesse, it's completely clean of emotional contamination. We don't feed from that type typically, because it's not as strong enough to satisfy us unless we take it all. Which based on Jesse's reaction, it's a bad idea if you don't want to be found out. You can technically feed from any type of strong emotion, or *other* energy; you just have to be prepared for the aftereffect of the feeding. You can get "drunk" depending what, or whom, you feed from."

A strange look came over Sarah's face. "So can we feed from anger if we're faced with it?"

Keller's expression turned stony. "No. Never ever do that."

Sarah looked at her girlfriend curiously. "Why, what's wrong with it? What's the big deal?"

Keller walked toward her slowly. "You know what it's like after we feed at the club, how impossible it is not to be taken over by all the sexual energy?" Sarah nodded. "When you feed from strong anger or rage, you are also taken over by it. The taint of it will remain with you until you can expend enough energy to cleanse yourself again. It would be a lot like when you got caught in Marcel's rage-fueled emotional loop. Trust me, love, you can do a lot of damage and you wouldn't be able to control who you took it out on."

Sarah swallowed, remembering the feeling of being trapped in a circle of anger with the French Canadian werewolf. It wasn't pleasant and she remembered with sickening clarity how much she wanted to kill him in that moment. "I understand."

Keller reached up and cupped the taller woman's cheek. "Promise me you won't ever try it. Please?"

Sarah looked at the other three women in the room, then back at Keller. "I promise I won't do it unless I have no other options." Keller wanted a different answer, and wanted to press her point, but they were interrupted when Jesse started to wake up.

"Whoa, what happened?"

The bar manager smiled down at the younger woman and offered her a hand up. "You've been sucked dry, my friend."

The younger Colby snickered again. "And not the way you like, I should know."

Sarah looked at her in disgust. "Too much information!"

Jill just shook her head at all of them, a lot more relieved now that Jesse was back up and around. "Are we done here then? Because I don't know about any of you, but I'm starving." She looked at Keller. "Did I pass your test?"

"Well, you definitely need to work on your control but I'm confident you have the basics down."

"Good. Now let's order something to eat and discuss what to do next. What does everyone want?" Her question was met with a resounding "Thai Guys!" and she started laughing. Looking right at her ex-girlfriend she shook her head. "Some things really never change, do they, Sar?"

Ten minutes later Jill was off calling in everyone's orders and Annie was still doting over the perfectly recovered Jesse on the couch. Sarah took the opportunity to pull Keller into their bedroom where they could talk in private. Once the door was shut, Keller looked at her in concern. "What's wrong?"

"You tell me." When Keller gave her a confused look, Sarah elaborated. "It hasn't even been twelve hours since Jill was broken and left for dead. Of everyone in my life, she has always been the most practical and levelheaded, but this chill attitude is a lot for even her. She should be feeling something more right now, Keller, not the vague amount of fear that trickles in whenever someone mentions her attackers. Is this dangerous? Could she be internalizing it and is going to just explode later?"

Realizing that she'd been caught out, Keller sighed and ran a hand through her long blonde spikes. "She is internalizing her fear but not as much as you think. A good portion of that chill attitude is actually my fault."

Sarah looked at her in surprise. "Your fault?"

"By infecting her with the virus, she was left with no physical pain or damage from her attack. So to help speed her recovery along even further, I clouded her memory of it. I made it hazier and less sharp." Shocked silence met her words. "Don't worry, I've done it many times. It's very similar to the way we cloud people's memory of us. I didn't want to make her forget, I just want to remove her from it a bit. I've come across many attack victims in my time. I did more than just avenge them; I often tried to heal if I could. PTSD is very common with someone who has suffered extreme physical trauma or injury, more so if it's coupled with emotional trauma. I didn't want what happened to her to cripple her mentally."

She grimaced. "However, I have never met anyone as stubborn as your ex. I can sense that she is holding a lot of fear inside but she shows no signs that she wants anyone to help her. She has a wall up that goes beyond what I showed her this morning. Seeing you and Annie together when she walked in was the key to getting her to open up to us. I think she needed that familiarity."

Sarah was suddenly filled with wash of love for the woman in front of her. Every time she thought she understood her lover, the smaller woman would unveil another layer to her personality. The gratitude she felt on her friend's behalf was immense. "You're right, Jill has always been that stubborn. Her home life was never that great and she's always had a hard time connecting with people. When my parents died, I think she was nearly as devastated as Annie and I were. They were like second parents to her." Sarah paused for a second, thinking about what she wanted to say. "Thank you for understanding that Jill is more than just my ex. She is family to me and Annie, and we are the same to her. And thank you for helping her. I can never repay all you have given our family, and all you continue to give."

Keller nodded in understanding and gave Sarah a sweet smile. "Lass, you never have to thank me." She placed her hand over Sarah's heart. "Every day you carry me in here is all the thanks I'll ever need." She moved her hand then to the back of Sarah's neck and pulled the taller woman down for a kiss, a kiss that continued until they were interrupted by a knock on the door.

"Hey, thanks to my vampire super powers I know exactly what you're doing in there now. Come out and join us; food will be here in twenty."

While the food was being eaten, they came to the decision that Annie and Jesse would stay with Jill for a while. They'd close their house up and Sarah and Keller would take turns checking on it. They were hoping it wouldn't be any longer than a few weeks. It would take some juggling for everyone to adjust their schedules to accommodate around the clock protection for Annie, but no one wanted to take any chances. With Columbus Pride rapidly approaching, the coming weeks were going to be busy enough for the lone human. No one wanted to think about what would happen if the rogue wolves attacked again. All they could do is hope that the three slipped up and either Louve, or Keller and Sarah, were able to pinpoint where they were hiding. And Jill felt her first bit of relief, knowing she didn't have to return home alone. They were a family, and they would help each other.

Chapter Eight

TEN DAYS AFTER making arrangements for Annie's safety in Keller's condo, they were no closer to finding the rogue were-wolves. It was early Wednesday afternoon, and Sarah had a few errands to run before she needed to be at the studio for her first lesson of the day. Since the singer was busy, Keller made arrange-ments to meet Louve at a martini bar to discuss their situation. She was nursing her first drink when the Frenchwoman walked through the door. Keller didn't even wait for Louve's first drink to arrive. "Have you found out anything?"

Louve gave the barest shake of her head. "*Non*, we have noth-ing. I have spoken with Raph and he is coming to Columbus with his two eldest sons."

Keller raised an eyebrow. "What are they going to do for us? And who will be running his farm?"

"His wife, Rosaline, will be running it while they are away, and his brother and sister-in-law, Marcel's parents, will also stay in Quebec. He is afraid that Jean and Adrienne will not allow him to harm their son, even if Marcel proves to be a danger that needs to be eliminated."

The vampire was surprised that Louve's friend was willing to truly take care of the problem with Marcel. "Well, that is certainly good news. And when will they be arriving?"

Louve's drink was placed in front of her and they waited until the bartender walked away before the werewolf answered. "Raph said the three of them still have some arrangements to make so they cannot leave until this weekend. It's about a twelve-hour drive from the Village de Labelle, in Quebec. Their farm is a few kilometers outside the village. They will of course be staying with me at the farm house."

Pale eyebrows rose. "Driving?"

Louve nodded. "Yes, that is easiest for them in case he does not want to return home. They may have to subdue him for the trip. And if he is killed, it will be much easier to transport the body without involving the authorities."

Keller was skeptical. "I know the border between Canada and the US is pretty lax, but how would they pull that off?"

The werewolf gave her a little smile. "My people have their ways, as you should well know."

Keller nodded and sat for a few minutes thinking about all that Louve had said. They had known each other for a long time and the silence was not uncommon between them. Finally, she looked at her friend. "So what is the next step? Should we all meet again when Raph and his boys arrive?"

The circus manager nodded solemnly. "I think that is the best we can do for now."

"Has Marie said anything yet?"

Louve gave her a frustrated look. "Alain has spoken with her many times and she denies that she has been running with Marcel. She also denies that she has done anything wrong other than show interest in your wolf. I don't know what to do with her, mon ami. I have always been protective of my people, and I would hate for her to think I do not trust her word. She has consistently been loyal to the troupe. And if Alain says she speaks true, I trust him."

Disbelief washed across Keller's face. "Seriously? Jill's description was pretty spot on, Louve."

The Frenchwoman shook her head. "You said she described a skinny blonde wolf. I have three people in my troupe that match that description. I'm sorry, but without proof..." She shrugged, helpless.

Keller sighed. "Do you at least have a photo of her, maybe Jill can identify her. Though I'm not going to hold my breath on that."

Louve looked at her curiously. "Why would she not be able to recognize a photo?"

"I faded her memories to help her with the healing process. So I'm afraid the images that were so clear after the attack are not so clear now. I'm not sure how much she would recognize at this point. I thought it would help her..." She trailed off, regretting not thinking of having Jill identify Marie sooner. Instead of dwelling on it, she changed the subject. "What about the mysterious French speaking man? Any luck there?"

Again Louve shook her head. "I am sorry, but I have found nothing. Alain and I have spoken at length on this subject and neither of us can figure out who it may be. He said he is starting to regret this venture with me, but I know in his heart he loves the cirque. It makes me sad that this thing we have created is *étant déchiré en morceaux*." She made a ripping gesture with her hands. "Torn into pieces!"

Keller cocked her head. "Wait, Alain is the other owner of Temple du Loup? I knew you were only part owner, I just never realized the other owner was another member of the troupe. I assumed it was a silent partner back in France."

"Non, it is he. He is the — how do you say, the 'lesser' partner because he did not have as much *investissement de capitaux* to put into our venture here. But he says he is content with training the troupe and being the strong man. We each have our say in what the cirque does, and we each have a share of the profits. It is a good arrangement."

Keller finished her martini while she slowly digested the new information. Alain was an all-around unassuming man, and he had never said a word about being the part owner of Temple du Loup whenever Keller had spoken with him. She knew that Louve counted on the quiet Frenchman to keep their circus family together, and he seemed to have a very positive effect on the younger ones. "What would happen to the bar if something happened to either of you? Did you leave your percentage of ownership to someone, like Raph maybe?"

A delicate hand waved through the air as Louve answered. "Non, we are each the beneficiary in the case of the other's demise. We have known each other a long time. Alain is a good man. He had a rough life for many years before I found him. His wife and twin sons had been killed decades before. Whoever it was knew he had *other* blood and had chained him to a chair to watch the torture and death of his family. He said the person killed his sons last, one after another." She shook her head at the horror of it. "While he has been instrumental in getting the troupe and bar as far along as we have, I know he still suffers from their loss. I can only imagine what that kind of torment is like, or what it does to someone. It was difficult enough for me to lose my Catherine, but to lose one's wife and their own innocent little children? I could not bear such a thing."

Keller was shocked that the man who seemed so pleasant and helpful was hiding such pain. She was even more surprised that he managed to hide that amount of pain from her own master-level empathy. "Does he know who did it?"

Louve shrugged. "Whether he does or not, he has never told me, and I would not wish to pry into such a private matter. I have never spoken at length to him of what happened to Catherine either, so it seems right. We know the basics of our pasts and that is all. I think he would find the details of what she did even more troubling given his past experiences."

"Interesting. I'm surprised he has never said anything to you, being as close as you are. Perhaps he has simply tried to put it all behind him and build a new life."

The Frenchwoman nodded. "Yes, I think you are correct."

Something was nagging at the back of Keller's brain, but she couldn't pinpoint it so she let it go. There were more important things to worry about right now. "When do you want to set up a meeting between all of us? Sunday afternoon? That should give Raphael and his sons plenty of time to settle in before we talk."

"*Oui c'est bon.*"

Keller looked at her longtime friend for a few seconds, trying to decide if she should broach the subject that had being going through her head. "Have you been able to go see Jill?"

Louve's lips dipped at each corner as she frowned and her eyes were downcast. "Non, but we have spoken on the phone many times since her attack. She is — " She fidgeted with her hand on the stem of her martini glass. "Mon Dieu, but she has been damaged by all of this! I think she is afraid to see me in person."

"She may be. She's fine with Jesse but she doesn't see Jesse as a threat because of her relative innocence and her connection to Annie. Has Jill spoken to you about any of it? Has she opened up at all? She's been closed on the subject with us and Sarah and I worry about her."

"We have spoken at length about a great many personal things." Keller raised her eyebrow. "I have told her about Catherine, and about how much her loss hurt me. I suppose we are both broken things, no? But I will admit to you, my longtime friend, that I am afraid."

Keller looked at Louve in surprise. "Afraid? Are you afraid for Jill? Because I can assure you that she is in no danger now — "

Louve cut her off with a wave of her hand. "Non. I am afraid *of* her!"

"*Quelle?*"

Keller could barely make out Louve's quiet sigh. "Even though we have not known each other very long, I am drawn to her. I am feeling things that I have not felt in nearly a century. Now that she has turned, she is too much of everything I've been looking for. The last time all my desires were met..."

Keller swallowed the lump in her throat. "Catherine."

"Oui, Catherine. So I am afraid, you see. I am afraid that she is too good to be true, that things will go badly again. I do not think my heart could bear it."

Keller covered her friend's hand with her own. "Have faith in her. I think you two could be good for each other if you both give this thing between you a chance. You've opened to each other and

I think that connection is something you have *both* needed for a long time. Let her all the way in; she is not Catherine. Trust your heart."

Louve smiled. It was tentative but Keller could feel the truth of it. "I will. Merci."

Keller waved to the bartender for her check. "So to change the subject back to the bigger situation, you will continue to patrol the woods near the farm? Sarah and I will keep an eye on the news to see if we can find a pattern outside the Alum Creek area."

Louve gave her a grim smile. "Oui." She finished her drink and both women left money on the counter to cover their bill and tip.

After leaving that bar, Keller headed for another one. The Merge wasn't open yet but it was her replacement's first night on the job. Lissa Watkins had previously managed Tully's for two years before deciding she was ready to move on to something bigger and better. Tully's was another establishment that was part of Diamond Enterprises, the same company that owned Merge. Keller's boss Joanne had been working with Lissa for a while and knew she would be fully capable in handling all the demands of a duel format nightclub. Once Keller sat with her through two interviews, she too was convinced that Lissa would be a good fit.

The new manager's first day was all about acclimating to the basic workings of the bar. She would be introduced to the staff and the computer system that handled everything from the ordering to employee time tracking. In an unpopular move, Keller had scheduled a mandatory meeting at three for all employees. It was only a half hour and everyone would get paid regardless of whether or not they were on the work schedule that day. No one liked coming in on their day off but Keller knew it was important to get the introduction out of the way as soon as possible. She wanted the transition to be smooth because in all honestly she was ready to be done with the current phase of her life. Especially with all that was going on, she really wanted to spend more time with Sarah and to be able to focus on their current crisis. In all the years Keller had been alive, she'd come across a plethora of bad and unsavory individuals. A few of them she would even classify as blatantly evil. She knew without a doubt that the wolves responsible for their trouble fell into the last category.

Shortly after she arrived at Merge, Keller's phone rang. Lissa was out meeting the staff so Keller stepped into the office for some privacy. She answered the call from her girlfriend, immediately sensing that something was wrong. "What's the matter?"

Sarah laughed on the other end. "How do you do that?"

Keller's shrug went unseen. "It's our bond, you know that. When you get stronger you'll be able to sense me just as easily. Now tell me what's up."

"The dogs have struck again. Someone broke into my studio sometime after I was here yesterday. The door and lock were both destroyed and they wrote the word 'WHORE' in red paint across my back wall. I have the shades down in the front window so it can't be seen and I've cancelled my lessons for the day. Should I call the police?"

Keller sighed. "Yeah, call the police and get the incident reported. I need to spend a few hours here with Lissa before I can turn her loose on her own for the night. We can go get some paint for the back wall and I'll give John a call and see if he can take care of your door. We can make a night of it. I'll swing by the condo and get some of our old clothes that we don't mind ruining. Once you're finished with the police, you can run to the hardware store for paint and supplies, and I'll stop and pick up dinner."

Sarah laughed wryly, "It's not exactly a romantic evening but I'll take it. Keep me posted on when you're going to get here. I'll call the cops now."

Keller frowned, knowing that Sarah was more upset than she was letting on. "Stay strong, my love. We'll get them." Before her girlfriend could ask, she answered the singer's next question. "Annie is fine. She's busy working with Bruce to finalize the stage shows. They're also coordinating with volunteers to get the posters up all around the city. Bruce's boyfriend Rico did an amazing job designing them. He was just volunteering his time but I think I'm going to cut him a check out of my discretionary budget anyway. He's talented and I know he's not making much over at the coffee shop."

The singer let her lover ramble for a minute, understanding that she had a lot of things going on at once right now. "Okay, fang babe, I'll let you get to that. I'm going to say goodbye and report this, if one of my neighbors haven't already. Text me later!"

Keller ran a hand through her spikey blonde hair. "Will do." She hung up and dialed John, her favorite contractor, and made arrangements for one of his guys to repair Sarah's door and lock. As soon as she finished the last call, the office door opened. Lissa poked her head in.

"Everyone is here, are you finished with your call? Is everything okay?"

Keller nodded. "Ah, nothing too terrible. My girlfriend's music studio was vandalized so I'm afraid I'll need to cut out of here in a few hours. Annie, the assistant manager of Voodoo Pony is on until close so she can help you with anything you need, or answer any questions that come up. I really am sorry."

Lissa raised her hands. "Hey, it's okay, I completely understand. You gotta do what you gotta do, right? Let's get this meeting over with and then we go over some of the most important items before you take off."

"Sounds good, and thank you." The meeting went smoothly. Most everyone knew at that point that Keller was leaving. Some recognized Lissa from her time as the manager of Tully's and most were excited to hear some of her new ideas. A few would always be resistant to change, and everyone was sad to see Keller go. But overall it was a productive and positive meeting. Keller filled Annie in on the latest incident involving the rogue wolves, then spent some time with her and Lissa going over the essentials. After that, she left the new manager in Annie's capable hands.

Over the past few months, Keller had noticed Annie's second, Bruce, taking on more and more responsibility on the Voodoo Pony side, filling in for Sip and Chug work whenever Annie wasn't available. The young man had a great head on his shoulders and a knack for pointing great bands in Annie's direction. She'd have to remember to mention it to Joanne and Lissa if Annie ever decided to move on to something new as well.

By the time Sarah and Keller finished cleaning up the mess in the studio and repainting the back wall it was well past sunset. Luckily Sarah had saved an old paint swatch from when she originally remodeled the place the previous year, so the new paint was a perfect match to what she had before. Keller was busy washing brushes in the small bathroom while Sarah pulled up the drop cloth. The singer called out to her girlfriend from the main room. "Did I tell you that the police think this is related to my sister's vandalized car?"

Keller laughed from the other room. "You don't say? They're very astute, the Columbus PD." Sarah snorted as her girlfriend walked out carrying the clean-ish tools. "I don't think these are salvageable."

Sarah looked from Keller to the gunky paintbrushes. "Just toss them out with the used rollers. Hopefully we won't be doing this again any time soon." Once they finished cleaning up, Sarah looked at the time on her phone. "This took a lot longer than I anticipated."

Keller grinned. "What's the issue, do you have a hot date?"

"Maybe." Sarah walked toward Keller and backed the shorter woman up until she was against one of the unpainted walls. Then she dropped her shields so Keller could feel exactly what her intentions were. "What do you say we cut out of here and spend some time getting this paint off in the Jacuzzi?" Not losing eye contact, she slowly ran a finger along Keller's cheek and swiped a bit of pale orange paint down the smooth skin.

"Why wait until we get home?" Keller grabbed Sarah's hand and spun them both around until the brunette's back was against the wall. Before Sarah could respond, Keller pulled her down into a kiss. The doors were all locked, John's employee had finished the repair a few hours earlier. There was no one there to interrupt. As the kiss deepened Keller ran both hands up underneath Sarah's shirt.

Sarah broke away panting and Keller continued to run lips along her neck. "Wait, we have to let Duke out—" She moaned when talented fingers danced across her nipples.

Keller spoke between kisses. "It's a good thing I let him out on my way over here, isn't it?"

Sarah's breath caught when one hand wandered down her body. Before Keller could wander too far, Sarah caught her wrist. The other hand took a firm hold of Keller's blonde hair. She abruptly pulled the other woman's mouth away from her neck. "I have a couch in my office."

Her proclamation was met with another grin. "Well then, to prevent you from getting rug burn, lead the way."

The singer laughed and reached down to pick up her lover. Keller was quick to wrap legs around the taller woman's waist. "Who says I'm going to be on the bottom?" They started kissing again before Sarah could even take a step. If it hadn't been for her hyper-enhanced strength, they would have both been on the floor. But Sarah managed to hold tight all the way to the couch in the back room. They hit the worn cool leather with a muffled *whump*. She impatiently unbuttoned Keller's jeans and tugged them down her legs. There was a brief scuffle when Keller's shoes wouldn't come off. Both women laughed at the absurdity of the moment. Sarah's clothes went much faster, if only because her shoes were slip-ons. Naked, Keller quickly flipped them around so Sarah's back was against the cool leather. The woman on the bottom flinched and arched away from it. "Jesus, that's cold!"

Keller smirked. "I know." Then with her mouth, she took the singer's mind off the chilly couch.

Lips wrapped around Sarah's very hard nipple and the singer grabbed her lover's shaggy blonde hair. Both women had their shields wide open to each other. Their link was solid and their soul mate bond complete. It had been complete for quite some time now. Every single thing that Keller did to her, the bar manager could feel the echo of it on her own body. Just as the tugging of Keller's hair was echoed back to Sarah. Sarah moaned when her lover switched to the other nipple and pressed a knee against her wet center. "Oh fuck!" She writhed against the well-placed leg and Keller could feel her fast approaching the edge of release.

She pulled her mouth away, ignoring the tugging on her hair that begged otherwise. "It's a good thing your couch is leather." Sarah moaned again as Keller's fingers wandered down between her legs. Keller whispered in the singer's ear as she teased the taller woman's opening. "You're so wet, so hot. You want me inside don't you; you want all of me inside?"

Sarah grabbed her head and pulled it farther down to her neck. She hissed her desperate reply. "Yesssss!"

Keller pierced her with fangs and fingers at the exact same moment and Sarah shuddered with the sensations coursing through her body. When Keller's thumb began rubbing Sarah's clit on each stroke inside, she could feel her lover's muscles clench around her fingers. Just as she sensed Sarah tipping over the edge into orgasm, Keller entered her with the last thing at her disposal. The vampire's aura seemed to swell and pulse deep inside the singer. The pleasurable explosion ripped through both of them and their cries continued for a handful of minutes. Suddenly, Keller's aura pulled back inside her body as she released Sarah's neck. She left her fingers inside, in deference to the aftershocks that continued unabated through her unconscious lover. By now, Keller was used to Sarah losing consciousness after her most powerful orgasms. When Sarah started to come around again, Keller removed her hand. Even though the action was slow, Sarah still shuddered.

Both women were now side by side on the couch, facing each other. Sarah looked at Keller with wide green eyes. "What the hell was that? What did you do to me, Keller?"

Despite the fact that it had been nearly a century since the last time it had happened, Keller remembered well what it felt like to have a vampire push their aura inside her. She laughed quietly. "That is something that only vampires can do with each other. It takes a lot of control, but as you found out, it's highly erotic."

Sarah leaned toward her lover and kissed her deeply. When she pulled back and spoke, her voice was serious and full of wonder. "Teach me, please."

"Oh, you don't have to beg. I've been waiting a long time to feel that again." She sat up and offered her hand to the singer. "This will be easier with clothes on."

Her lover cocked her head in confusion. "Why with clothes on?"

Keller laughed. "Because you're distracting me, wench!" Once they were clothed again, Keller had them sit cross-legged on the couch, facing each other. "Okay, you're familiar with your aura. It's that part of you that merges with your power to become your mental shield." Sarah nodded, and Keller continued with the lesson. "Now, just imagine that instead of merging it with your own power, inside your body, you send it into the body of another. Try it on me now. Sometimes it helps to close your eyes and envision it first..." Keller trailed off at the first metaphysical touch. It was like a warm wind at first, blowing through her. "Focus now, direct it into me instead of through or around me."

Sarah's eyes suddenly opened and she met the vivid blue of Keller's. Sarah smiled and Keller felt the first directed touch of her lover. She could feel it entering her through the seven chakra points. It wasn't that Sarah knew about such points, more that her aura knew the best way in. It was simply the path of least resistance. Before Keller could give any other pointers, she sensed Sarah's aura rubbing along what felt like the inside of her entire body. The smaller woman shuddered and sucked in a breath. Sarah noticed every reaction Keller made and continued the motion of her numinous self, but she wanted to try something new. She didn't know if it was possible but she was going to find out.

Starting small at first, she began trickling power in with her pulsing aura, creating a tingling sensation along with the rubbing feeling inside. Keller abruptly froze and her lips parted as her breathing increased. Sensing that she would be able to bring her lover to the edge and beyond simply by using her aura, Sarah added more power. At the same time, she swirled it all inside the smaller woman, focusing on the lowest point. She didn't know that the lowest point of entry was Keller's root chakra. In a matter of seconds Keller seemed to seize before throwing her head back in a primal scream, her entire body shaking with release. When it was done, she collapsed backward onto the couch, and Sarah pulled her aura back into herself. She followed her lover down, to be sure she was all right. "Love—Keller, are you okay? Did I do it wrong?"

Keller's eyes fluttered open and she blew out a breath. "Crivvens! I forget how quick a study you are with the mental stuff. I'm fair puckled!"

Sarah slapped her arm. "I don't know what that means but it sounds gross. So I didn't do it wrong?"

"No lass. What you did was—I've never seen it before. I would have never thought to push power in with the aura." Keller looked into her lover's deep green eyes. "But you have to be careful with that, you could seriously hurt someone by forcing power into them if they don't have the capacity for it."

The singer nodded. "I understand." Glancing at the clock on the wall, she was surprised to see it was near midnight. "Now we really have to go. Duke's bladder can only wait so long, the poor guy!"

Keller laughed. "All right, let's grab our stuff and get out of here. I parked next to you so we can walk out together."

"Sounds good." Sarah abruptly stopped. "Oh, I forgot to tell you that Joe texted me earlier and asked if I wanted to do a gig this Saturday at Woodland. I told him I'd let him know tomorrow. What do you think?"

"I think I have plans on Saturday to watch my girlfriend play in a band." The two women walked out to the parking lot arm in arm, happy in the moment.

KELLER AND SARAH arrived at seven to pick up Jesse and Annie for dinner, before the younger Colby had to go into work for the night. Annie was bummed that she would miss seeing Sarah play but work was work and she couldn't skip out. When they pulled into Jill's driveway, Annie was standing next to her own car looking irritated. The vampire couple got out and Sarah gave her a curious look. "What's up, A? I thought you were riding with us?"

The younger woman sighed. "Julie just called and she's got some sort of stomach virus and has to leave work, like, right now. So, it looks like I'm going to be eating there. Sorry I have to bail on you."

Keller walked up to her. "Is she okay?"

The assistant manager's face wrinkled in disgust. "Uh, proba-bly. She said that she's, and I'm quoting here, 'Pissing out her ass.' Apparently she's spent more time in the bathroom than out of it since she got there at three. So yeah, I'm gonna hose the place down with disinfectant spray and send her home."

Sarah made a nearly identical face. "Ick! Okay, well that sucks but I understand. We'll have Jesse home by the time you're there, and make sure Teddy walks you out to your car at the end of the night, okay?"

The younger woman rolled her eyes. "Yes, overprotective one!"

"And don't forget that we'll be meeting with Raph and his sons out at the farmhouse on Sunday. I'm assuming that you, Jesse, and Jill will all ride together so we'll meet you there."

Annie made a face. "Hello? I'm not ten, I got it already. I'll see you Sunday, and Sarah?"

"Yeah?"

The younger woman smiled. "Blow them away tonight."

Annie's love and support of her music career always touched a special place in her heart. "Aww, thanks, A."

Annie snorted. "Of course I want you to do well so you drum up a bigger following for your performance at Pride! Okay, gotta go now!" After that she hopped in her car and left for The Merge. Keller started laughing and Sarah just shook her head at her sib-ling's antics.

As they approached the front door, Jesse opened it. "I thought I heard you and Annie talking. We're going to be a little longer here. When Annie had to go into work, Jill suddenly decided that she'd like to come along. I figured the more the mer-rier, right?"

Sarah yelled up the stairs. "Jill! What the hell is taking so long, you're a vampire for Christ's sake. You can move faster than that, Red!"

Just then Jill came running down the stairs looking like she just stepped off the pages of a fashion magazine. "Sorry, I couldn't decide what to wear."

"What's the big deal? We're just going to Medea's for dinner, then Woodland. It's not like either place is five star."

The tall veterinarian blushed. "Uh, well Louve texted me and said she was going to meet us tonight."

Sarah looked at Keller. "Did you know about this?"

"Actually I did. I was the one who let Louve know what we had going on tonight and invited her out to see you perform. I assumed she would invite Jill, but I wasn't sure." Secretly, Keller was very pleased that Jill would be going with them. It meant a healthy step forward in her relationship with Louve. Base on her conversation with Louve, she knew the veterinarian still harbored some resistance to seeing the werewolf in person. The fact that Jill took so much care with her outfit was a good sign. It meant that she cared what Louve thought of her in a physical sense, and that she was ready to get closer to the Frenchwoman.

"I see. Well, okay then. If everyone is ready, let's get out of here. I'm starving!"

Jesse laughed and headed for the door. "Now that sounds like a Colby!" The rest joined in her laughter as they headed out. Luckily, the tavern had saved a four top table for Sarah and her guests, otherwise they would have had to stand for the entire show. The place was packed. Jill said Louve was supposed to arrive around nine. Since Sarah would be on the stage by then, Louve would just take her chair.

After a half hour, Keller looked over at Jill. "There's a lot of energy circulating tonight, how are you holding up?"

Jill shrugged. "I'm fine; I've got my shield up. It seems clean though, can I feed off it? Safely?"

Sarah smirked at her. "I am. I have been since we walked in. You just need to take it slow. You'd be surprised how much just a trickle can be from a crowd this size."

Jill threw a wadded up napkin at her head. "Show off!" The other two at the table snickered.

Sarah laughed and batted the napkin away. "Oh I am, make no mistake about it!" She changed the subject, just to torment her ex a little. "So, Jill, have you actually seen Louve since the change?"

Jill blushed. "No, but we've spoken on the phone many times. Why?"

Sarah chuckled under her breath. "No reason." Before Jill could demand an explanation for what she meant by her comment, Sarah noticed movement over by the stage. "Oh hey, the guys are waving me over. Gotta go!" She bolted from the table and laughed again as she walked away.

Jill cocked her head at Keller. "I don't get it; what's so funn—" She trailed off as she sensed someone approaching. Someone with a lot of power. When she turned her head toward the door, Louve was standing two feet away.

"Hello, Doctor Cole. *Tu es belle.*"

Jill was frozen in place. She blushed with the compliment but was unable to form words of her own. She thought she would be afraid when she saw Louve in person again, but the smaller woman had completely captivated her with the amount of power she was emoting. After strengthening her shield, Jill finally found her voice. "Hello, Louve. What have I told you about calling me Doctor?"

Louve gave her a sad smile. "Ah, but that was over the phone. And the last time we met in person, you said those words thinking there were no animals in the room. But I am a dog, no? Therefore you will always be Doctor to me."

Jill reached out her hand. "I see no dogs, merely a beautiful woman. Now come have a seat over here by me. The show is about to start."

Keller watched her old friend and then turned her gaze to Sarah's ex. The chemistry and potential for a deeply emotional match between them was obvious. Now if only all their problems could be resolved so the two women could realize that potential. Jesse was busy texting throughout the entire exchange. If she were a member of Louve's pack, she would have owed the woman deference to her status as Alpha, but after much discussion between the two, it was determined that Jesse would remain a lone wolf under Keller's protection.

The younger woman said hi to Louve when she sat down but went right back to her keyboard. Keller shook her head at the rapidity the young werewolf was typing. Even with her vampire speed and reflexes, she was still slow at sending messages on the little devices. She mentally shrugged at her failings.

Sarah's old band didn't write their own songs; they were almost exclusively a cover band unless they had a guest singer like Sarah. They introduced their special guest to the audience, which elicited a few whistles and cheers from the crowd in general, and a cacophony of noise from the table full of *other* blood women. For the evening, the band went back and forth between cover songs that Joe would sing lead on and songs that Sarah would sing lead. They even covered a few duets, ones that best highlighted their ability to harmonize. It was clear that the group had a familiarity with each other that only long established bands had.

Keller was impressed at the seamless way that Sarah and her style fit right in with The Standalones. She also found it humorous that a band with the name, "The Standalones," would even have a guest singer. After about five songs, they ventured out and played one of Sarah's new ones. Despite the fact that the crowd was completely unfamiliar with it, it was met with a lot of positive enthusiasm, as were the other four they played throughout the night. Each time they would announce that it was one of Sarah's songs they were performing.

When the band was wrapping up for the evening Joe came back on the mic. "If you liked Sarah's stuff, you can hear all her songs from tonight plus a few more on her newest album, *Blood Ties*. Of course you'll get to hear The Standalones backing her on those same songs." He turned to the tall brunette then. "When can we expect the album, Sarah?"

She dazzled the crowd with her trademark smile. "Actually, you can download them online right now. My website is listed on the cards that are scattered around the tables. Otherwise I should have the first discs for sale at Columbus Pride on June eighteenth. It's being held at the Battelle Darby Creek Metro Park."

Joe took over again after that. "All right, you heard the lady, check her out!" He waggled his eyebrows comically. "And check out her music too!" This elicited a laugh from the easy-going crowd. "Now, we're going to perform one last song. We'll let the crowd decide this one. We can either do 'Cataclysm,' or another new song that was written by Sarah called, 'Blood of My Blood.' I guaranteed both will get your pulse pounding. Max back here — " He turned and pointed to their drummer. "He's going to be the judge. So by virtue of loudest applause, you decide. Resurrection's song 'Cataclysm?'" He paused while the crowd went wild with his suggestion. After a minute or so he calmed them back down. "Okay, okay, now who wants to hear Sarah's new song 'Blood of My Blood?'" This time the sound from the audience was noticeably louder. "Well Max, what's the verdict?"

The handsome drummer was the epitome of what was now considered by all of society as a "lumbersexual." He had a trimmed beard with hair that was pulled back into a man-bun. While most men managed to look ridiculous, instead he made many of the women in the crowd dream of days filled with flannel, wood smoke, and hot sex. He gave an easy smile to the crowd and answered his friend and bandmate. "Not that it matters, because I have a good part either way, but I'd say Sarah won that by the length of a drumstick!"

Joe laughed. "You heard the man, and you're all in for a real treat. Don't forget you can find all these songs on her website." He waited a minute while Max set up a few special drums then they started.

The crowd was blown away and Keller was particularly

impressed. She had liked the song immediately, even unfinished in the living room of their condo. But a real performance with a band that had practiced and recorded it with all the little changes Sarah had worked out in that impromptu jam session really made it come alive. Just as Joe had predicted, the crowd was stomping and clapping by the time Max did his drum solo in the middle. Overall, the song had a very earthy, primal beat. And by the third chorus the audience was even singing along.

The song was a hit, and every musician on the stage knew it. Everyone was pumped at the end of the show, especially Sarah. Keller could see it in her eyes, and feel it through her bond. Keller previously tried to explain how it was different performing in front of a crowd when you had *other* blood, and now the singer knew first-hand what it was like. When Sarah came back to their table, she was practically glowing, and Keller could detect a fine tremor in her lover's hand as is rested on her thigh. "You were amazing, love! I think the audience is your new mistress." Everyone around their little table agreed with Keller.

Sarah laughed. "I'm not even sure what that means but thanks." She shrugged. "It was good to get up there in front of everyone and make music again. I forgot how much I love playing live to a crowd." The music and the feedback from the audience was familiar and soothing in the midst of her own private turmoil. While Sarah still hadn't been able to write anything new, it was nice to be creating something. Playing music was as much an outlet as writing music. They just provided different stimulations and connections for her emotions. Not to mention the added bonus feedback from her new empathic powers. The singer shivered with energy overload and arousal.

Louve cocked her head at the singer, sensing exactly how wound up the woman was feeling. She could smell it on her. "Will the band also be playing with you at Pride? I look forward to seeing all of the shows that weekend. I have never been to an American Pride celebration before."

Sarah shook her head. "No, it's just going to be me that day. So if I want to play that last song, I'm going to have to recruit someone to play the hand drums for me. Perhaps a young werewolf I know who has been practicing."

Everyone looked at Jesse, and her eyes widened with surprise. "Me?" She held up the hand that wasn't gripping her cell phone. "Oh no, I couldn't do that! I'm not a musician at all, just a computer jockey!"

Sarah squeezed her shoulder. "Oh come on, you know the

song. You'll do just fine. And I bet you'd score some major points. You know how Annie loves to watch live music."

Jesse blushed. "Well, maybe. I'll think about it, okay?"

"Fair enough."

Jill had been watching her ex intently after she came off the stage. She was very aware of the state her friend was in. She wasn't sure why Sarah seemed so sexually charged. She noticed Louve also watching Sarah and gave the Frenchwoman a curious look. Louve returned her look with one that was full of simmering heat and Jill blushed. Louve leaned over and spoke quietly into her ear. "You'll have to ask her, *Ma chère*."

Sarah noticed the exchange. "Ask me what?"

Jill flushed at being forced into directness. "You seem kind of, uhh—" She glanced at her temporary housemate, hoping for a little help. Jesse looked at her, then at Sarah, and finally back to Jill. "I noticed, and I'm pretending like I didn't. Sarah's like a sister to me and thinking about that is squicky!" She quickly turned her gaze back to her cell phone in an attempt to block out what was about to be brought up.

Keller cracked up laughing. "Squicky?" She shook her head and told Jill what she wanted to know, since it was taking more and more of Sarah's concentration just to keep her pulsing need in check. Keller was tempted to simply drag her girlfriend into the bathroom to relieve some of her pressure. "When someone of *other* blood is the direct energy focus of an entire crowd of people, it can be a highly charged, erotic experience. Music evokes a very passionate response in people, which carries over a lot like lust. You understand?"

Jill swallowed, knowing exactly what she was talking about. She made the mistake of feeding at the nightclub one night when she was there with Jesse and Annie. Just a small amount of feeding from the crowd sent her straight to the bathroom to take care of her own needs. Much like Sarah, without the age and practice of Keller, she was unable to keep the sensual energy in check. She looked back at Sarah. "Do you have to leave?"

The singer gave her a wry smile. "Eventually, yeah. But I'm good for a little while longer." A look came over her face then, one that promised mischief. Sarah was contemplating directing a bit of lust toward her ex; just enough to make Jill a little hot and bothered. Keller noticed immediately the change in her girlfriend's mood.

"Sarah, no."

Twinkling green eyes looked back at her innocently. "What?"

Keller gave a slight shake of her head and the singer pouted. "Fine." Though she was standing, Sarah squirmed a bit more and her hand clenched against the solid thigh of her lover. She looked around the table at her friends. "So, what do we do next?"

Jesse looked up from her phone and shrugged. "It's your call, I rode with you."

Jill agreed with her. "She's right; I guess I'm kind of along for the ride. What do you want to do?"

Jesse suddenly snickered and looked up from her phone again. "Annie says we should all come to the club, it is weirdly dead and she's bored."

"Well? What's the verdict?" Keller glanced around their little group. "Stay here, go home, hit The Merge, or try a different club?" The word "Merge" went around the table in a unanimous decision. Before she could say anything else, Keller heard Sarah's breathing and heart rate start to increase. Sarah wasn't anywhere near as old or experienced as the members of Resurrection and there was no way she'd be able to hold out much longer. She turned to her longtime friend. "Louve, do you mind giving Jesse and Jill a ride to the club? We have to make a quick stop on the way there."

Louve looked at Sarah with barely restrained hunger. The singer's energy was leaking through her shield, yet at the same time drawing the werewolves' energy toward her. It was beginning to affect the whole table. "It would be my pleasure. I'm sure your stop is very important so take your time."

Keller turned to the other two. "Are you guys okay with that, riding with Louve?"

"Yup"

"Fine"

The truth was that Jesse and Jill would have agreed to walk at that point, rather than get in a vehicle with Sarah. Especially Jesse. Keller stood from her stool. "The tab is paid, so there's no point in hanging around. Sarah, is there anything you need to wrap up with the band?" Sarah had her eyes shut, and Keller realized that her lover hadn't heard a thing she'd said. "Sarah?"

A fine tremor ran through Sarah's entire body. She could barely whisper her words. "Just my guitar."

Sensing urgency in the moment, Jill spoke up. "Joe knows me. I'll run and get her guitar. We can bring it with us to the club; just get her out of here."

Keller nodded and took Sarah gently by the arm and started leading her toward the nearest exit. Many people told Sarah how much they liked her stuff. She was able to smile and say thanks but Keller knew the singer's control was almost gone. They made it to Sarah's blazer in the dimly lit parking lot when suddenly the taller woman spun Keller around and slammed her into the back of the vehicle. Sarah's mouth was on her immediately and the brunette's hands started wandering up the front of Keller's shirt. When Sarah's teeth began cutting into her lips, Keller forcibly grabbed Sarah's hands and pushed the woman back. "Wait!"

Sarah growled back at her. "I don't want to wait. I can't wait!"

Keller shook the half-crazed woman to get her attention. "Sarah! We can't do this here, it's too exposed. Give me just a minute, love." When her lover's eyes still seemed to lack understanding she shook her again. "Sarah, do you hear me?"

The taller woman's nostrils flared. "Y—yes. Please hurry!"

Keller opened the back of the blazer and folded the seats down flat. When she was done, she guided Sarah inside and shut the back gate and window again. The extreme tint provided absolute privacy from prying eyes. Despite the restricted space, Keller had no problem stripping Sarah down to her socks. The carpeted interior was rough on Sarah's skin but she was in no shape to notice something so mundane. By that point she had nearly lost all control, so Keller pinned the brunette's body below her and held Sarah's hands to either side of her head. When she finally had her lover's attention she spoke very clear.

"I will take care of you, my love, but you must leave your hands right here. Do you understand? Don't move your hands."

Sarah's lips parted with anticipation and she nodded. Then with the speed of her *other* blood, she released Sarah's hand and quickly buried three fingers in the desperate woman's wet depths. Sarah arched her back and moaned at the welcome intrusion. Keeping her fingers curled and shallow inside, Keller was able to apply pressure to Sarah's clit with each thrust. Sensing the singer was close, Keller dropped her shields and got Sarah's attention. "Sarah." Even though it was too dark to make out their vibrant green color, Keller could still tell when Sarah's eyes finally opened. "Open to me and share your burden of power. If you need to be inside of me then do it."

Sarah gasped. What little reasoning she had left was drinking Keller's words like life's blood and she knew she was close. Before another word could be said, the singer hunched forward and bit deeply into the side of Keller's neck. At the same time she threw open her shields and pulsed into Keller with a megalith of aura and power. Keller stiffened at the sensation of being filled so full. Keller's arousal built exponentially as Sarah continued to thrust her aura inside her. Sarah started keening at the simultaneous somatic and psychic feeling of both filling and being filled by her lover. As Sarah swallowed the warm liquid down, her body began to jerk with the force of her orgasm. The movements and mental feedback carried over to her lover and she abruptly let go of Keller's neck, screaming her release. It was only once she sensed Sarah fade to unconsciousness that removed her fingers from their warm embrace. Then Keller collapsed next to her girlfriend, unsure if she'd ever been overflowing with power at the same time she was also wrung out. The sweat was beginning to cool on their bodies by the time Sarah managed to rouse herself from somnolence.

Keller smiled at her, and she smiled back. The smile quickly turned into a frown of concern when Sarah lifted a hand to her lover's face. Using her thumb, she delicately wiped something from Keller's upper lip. It was dark, and as Sarah rubbed it between thumb and forefinger she realized that it was blood. "Keller?"

A pale brow raised in the darkness. "Hmm, interesting."

Sarah looked at her in shock. "Shouldn't you be more concerned?"

"No. I'm not bleeding now. My guess is that's what happens when I'm stuffed with power beyond my capacity." She gave Sarah a wry grin, nearly unseen in the dark. "I'm old, and as a result I have a lot of capacity. But even I have never felt such a glut of power rippling through me until it overflowed. It was amazing and painful at the same time. Does that make sense?"

Sarah chuckled. "Big Pink."

Keller merely blinked back at her, momentarily confused, before nodding and breaking out into a grin. "Yes, exactly like that!" Sarah was an unabashed size queen, and their largest toy had been affectionately named Big Pink. It made Sarah scream with pleasure every single time, but it was a lot to take. More often than not before the singer's infection with *other* blood, there would be a little bleeding after sex. But she always insisted that there was nothing like the feeling of being filled so completely and refused to give up Big Pink. Keller imagined that having Sarah's power and aura stretch her to that point between pleasure and pain must feel very much like a vigorous round with Sarah's favorite toy. After lying in each other's arms for a few minutes, Sarah finally squirmed uncomfortably.

"This carpet is shite on the backside!" This prompted a round of laughter from both of them as Sarah began re-dressing herself. The singer had already decided that she'd start keeping a spare blanket in the back, just in case another sex overload occurred in the near future. As they got back into the driver and passenger seats, Sarah turned to her lover. "I can't wait to perform again!"

Keller looked back at her with a naughty smile. "Me either."

LATER, AFTER THEY closed the bar down, Louve took Jill home while Jesse rode with Annie. They sat in the car while the younger couple went inside. Louve desperately craved to spend the night with her beautiful new friend, but she didn't want to push. Their silence was broken when Jill reached over and took her hand. "I was afraid to meet you tonight."

Louve looked at her with sadness. "I assumed you would be. It is to be expected after such an attack." She laid her other hand on top of Jill's, trapping the woman's fingers between her own very warm ones. "But I need you to know that I would never hurt you, *mon ange de feu*." She looked into Jill's eyes, noticing that their distinctive light blue irises were hidden in the darkened car. "In all of our conversations, I have shared things with you that I have not spoken of in a very long time. For whatever the reason, I have found myself drawn to you. And all of our conversations have only served to bring me closer."

Jill smiled back. "I—I feel the same way. Had we not been talking on the phone, I could have just said we simply shared some amazing sexual chemistry. But I think it is much more than that, much deeper. I have told you my oldest fears, and my deepest ones. That is not something I would share with just anyone."

Louve sat in the driver seat of her car, lips parted slightly. The beautiful woman next to her was saying more than she had ever let herself hope for. She licked her lips. "Oui. *Je suis d'accord.*" She wanted to pull Jill down and kiss her but fear of the other woman's emotional vulnerability kept her still. The werewolf was not used to tempering her desires. She was used to taking what she wanted and having it freely given in return. She wasn't the head of her wolf troupe because she was timid. But with Dr. Jillian Cole, she felt like nothing more than a shy pup. So she said and did nothing, forgetting that the veterinarian was a vampire now and could read all the desire and emotion roiling just below Louve's surface.

But Jill did feel it and her heartbeat moved faster inside her chest. Before her fear could scrape her insides bare, before she could talk herself out of it, Jill grabbed Louve roughly and pulled her in for a kiss. That was the point when they dropped their shields to each other and a mild struggle for dominance ensued. Suddenly Jill broke away from the kiss, panting. Louve looked at her in concern. "Are you okay, ma chéri?" Jill shook her head and Louve looked at her in alarm. "*Ce qui est mal?*"

Jill smiled and cupped Louve's cheek in reassurance. "Nothing is the matter, silly woman. Well, other than the fact that I'm desperate to have you come inside with me." She looked into Louve's bright eyes. "Will you stay the night?"

Louve smiled and pulled the taller woman down into another kiss. She was hungry for her in so many ways, perhaps the night could be her feast of ages. When she pulled back, she shut off the car and unclasped her seatbelt. "I believe you have finally succeeded." Jill looked at her in confusion and Louve laughed. "You have thoroughly charmed the pants from me."

Jill looked down at the Frenchwoman's denim covered legs. "Well not yet. But the night is young." With that she gave Louve a wink and exited the car.

Louve exhaled in a rush. "Mon Dieu!" The night silence was broken by the chirping sound of Louve's car locks.

Chapter Nine

EVEN THE SPACIOUS kitchen of Louve's farmhouse seemed crowded when stuffed full of werewolves, vampires, and a lone human. Raphael and his two sons, Ranier and Romaric were introduced to Keller's group before they could get down to business. Only Louve and Alain were in attendance out of all the wolves currently employed at the Temple du Loup. While Annie, the lone human, was simply nervous being around so many powerful beings, Jill was experiencing something completely different. During introductions, Jill balked at greeting Louve's business partner. When Alain held out his hand to shake, Jill shuddered and stepped back. Sarah immediately wrapped an arm around her shoulders to comfort her and let Louve explain the veterinarian's reaction.

After finally spending the night together, Louve felt even more protective of her "fiery angel." Their night of passion prompted another long conversation about their fears and what they were ultimately looking for from a lover. She even went so far as to admit to Jill that she was looking for someone that completed her soul. Neither had been in a real relationship for a long time, but both were willing to try. Louve thought it would be good enough for now. And for now, the passion was beyond expectation. Their night with Keller and Sarah had been amazing, but just the two of them in the bedroom took things to an entirely new level. It was a place that Louve sincerely wanted to visit again and again. But for this very moment, with their situation so precarious, the Frenchwoman would have to be, as Keller would say, "all business." She explained her new lover's reaction to the men in the group. "Jill was the one who was assaulted by the rogue werewolves. I'm afraid Doctor Cole has not many good feelings toward strangers and wolves right now. Please understand and respect her space."

Keller watched as Alain merely smiled pleasantly and pulled his hand back. She sensed something off about his reaction, and possibly his initial actions as well. He and Louve both knew it was Jill who was attacked. Someone who could so easily connect with people should have known that she would be sensitive to strangers still, especially male ones since there were two men in the trio that attacked her. Keller let the fleeting thought pass by as Raph spoke. His voice was a deep rumble, which seemed to intrinsically fit the bearded and broad-chested French Canadian. He may not have started his days in North America but Keller thought the man had acclimated quite nicely. She noticed that he had even lost the European flavor of his French accent when she heard him speak to Louve during their arrival. "My apologies, Doctor Cole, we are deeply sorry for the suffering that you have been through. Ranier, Romaric, and I will do everything we can to make sure that my nephew atones for his crimes."

Jill swallowed the lump in her throat and nodded toward him. Strangely, she didn't feel apprehensive about the giant auburn-haired man or his sons. But when she glanced back at the much shorter Alain, she felt some small bit of memory twist inside of her and fear followed in its wake. She thought maybe it was because what she could remember of her unknown attacker was that he shared a similar build to Louve's business partner. She suspected that she'd feel the same way about any skinny blonde woman or big strapping bleached-blonde man. "Thank you, Raphael, I appreciate any help we can get. I just want this whole thing to be over, and to return to my life."

The big man gave her a sad smile. "I understand. And please, call me Raph."

Jill smiled back. "Only if you call me Jill."

"Done."

Annie had stayed glued to Jesse's side from the moment they stepped out of Jill's Jeep. Even once they were all seated around the giant trestle table in the kitchen, Annie sat between Jesse and Sarah. It was the place she felt safest in a time that most definitely wasn't. She was relieved when Keller started talking because she didn't want to stay any longer than necessary. Even though Jill's house wasn't really her home, she still wanted to get back and chill for a while. She didn't want to be surrounded by so many strangers with *other* blood. The vampire didn't bother beating around the bush. "So what have you done on your end Louve; what have you found?"

Louve pursed her lips. "Sadly we have found no signs. I ran as the wolf around the lands on this side of the lake, and Alain ran the other side where the attacks happened. Neither of us could catch scents of another werewolf. I too have read about the burglaries and animal attacks in the local papers, but I truly do not know what to make of it. Perhaps the next time you are van-dalized you can call one of us to *sniff around*." Romaric, being the younger and less serious of Raph's sons actually chuckled at

Louve's poor attempt at a joke, but one look from his father silenced him again. Sensing the somber mood, Louve apologized. "Forgive me for my crude attempt at humor."

Raph spoke up. "Actually, I think that is a very good idea. I have studied the maps of this area." Louve gave him a surprised look and he shrugged. "Google is an amazing thing, *ma copine*. My guess is that they are staying in the city proper and only hunting for food and money in the surrounding areas. Marcel is a devious sort, even from his time as a boy. I think that he would cause trouble in the region around the farmhouse simply to throw us off the scent, and to make Louve worry that investigations would bring authorities to her doorstep. Perhaps we should stay in the city too so we can run the streets at night and see if we can pick up any traces of him."

Annie, a born planner and organizer, saw an opportunity to give some input. "Um, excuse me?" Sarah looked at her younger sister curiously but otherwise didn't interrupt.

You can take the man out of France, but you cannot take France out of the man. Always the proper gentleman, Raph answered. "Yes, Miss Colby?"

The young brunette made a face. "Eh, it's just Annie, please. So anyway, Jesse and I are staying with Jill for a while. They felt it was safer for me if I had more people around at all times until the rogue wolves were caught. This means our house is currently empty. You three could stay there for the time being and you wouldn't have to pay for a hotel. Not to mention coming and going at all hours would be easier if you were staying at a house."

Keller slapped her hand on the table causing half the people to jump. "That's pure dead brilliant, A!" Annie blushed and waited to see what the rest would say.

Jesse chimed in to sell her girlfriend's idea a little more. "The upstairs has the main living room, kitchen, two bedrooms and a bathroom. And the basement is fully furnished with a bedroom, living room with a futon, and a full bathroom as well. There's plenty of room for everyone."

Raph looked at his sons. "What do you think, should we take them up on their offer?"

The younger men answered as one. "Yes, Papa." Ranier added a bit more. "It does seem to fulfill our requirements while we search for Marcel."

Louve's long-time friend nodded, his beard twitching slightly with the movement. "It is decided then. After this meeting we move to Mis — Annie and Jesse's house for the duration of our stay."

There really wasn't much to talk about after that. Raph and his sons would follow Keller and Jill's cars back to Annie's house. Romaric was speaking with Jesse as the others were bidding goodbye to Louve and Alain. "So, are there any good takeout places near your house?"

Jesse cocked her head. "Well, it's near enough to everything that you can get just about any kind of food you want delivered. Do you all like Thai?"

Romaric grinned. "That's like asking if we like hockey!"

The nerdy werewolf laughed. "Well, you never know other people's tastes. Anyway, if you like Thai food, you're in for a real treat. I'll show you the take-out menus when we get to the house. And we should all have dinner together tonight and get to know each other." She called out to Annie who was standing next to the car ahead of them. "Hey, babe, Romaric says they like Thai food! Let's all have dinner tonight at the house."

Romaric made a face. "Just call me Aric, please."

Jill was standing next to Annie as Jesse and Aric walked up. "Thai Guys? Ooh, I'm in!" The four of them laughed but Jill's laughter cut off abruptly as an icy chill seemed to wash over her. Following her instinct, she tightened her shield and turned her head in the direction of her discomfort. In the distance she could see two blonde women approaching from a large pole barn set in the back of the property. The women looked fairly non-threatening, but she stiffened none the less.

Sarah noticed Jill's reaction as she walked up to the group. "What's wrong?" Jill merely shook her head and continued to stare at the approaching pair. When Sarah followed her gaze, she swore under her breath. As the two blonde women got closer to the group Marie looked at Annie and then turned her gaze to Jill. Sarah almost wrote off the gaze as simply Marie being antagonistic. Almost. When Marie was looking at Jill her expression turned to that of hunger, and she licked her lips seductively. When she noticed Sarah watching, she smirked at the singer. In that exact moment, rage blossomed in Sarah's chest. In an instant she was across the lawn slamming her body into Marie's in a spectacular tackle. The Frenchwoman easily flew twenty feet through the air before landing with a muffled thud onto the grass. Before she could rise, Sarah was on her again. She pinned Marie to the ground and forced a sharp shaft of power–infused aura through Marie's shield. She screamed as she held the struggling blonde down. "It was you! You will never touch my family, you will never hurt another person again!" Sarah watched with satisfaction as blood started to trickle from Marie's nose. She heard a popping sound and knew the werewolf was trying to change form. Before she could drink the Frenchwoman's energy to prevent her from changing, she was plowed into from the side.

Keller sensed Sarah's anger but not before the singer attacked Marie. She knew Sarah's anger could easily take over and lead to serious injury or death of Louve's employee. If Marie was innocent, it would truly be a tragedy. Once she knocked Sarah away, she pinned her lover to the ground. "Sarah, no! This isn't the way, and I won't let you take someone's life in anger."

Sarah struggled below her lover but she was no match for Keller's powerful reservoir of strength. "Let me go! She did it and she has to pay!"

Before Keller could respond, they heard more popping and a choked scream. When they glanced toward the sound, all they saw was Marie dashing toward the woods in wolf form. Everyone came rushing toward the two women on the ground. Sarah bucked Keller off when the smaller woman was distracted by Marie's escape. "Look what you've done!"

"You can't just attack her, Sarah. We have no proof, you could have killed her forcing your power like that. And even if she is guilty, you would be no better than she is. What you were doing was mind rape!" She looked into her lover's green eyes and tried to drive home her point. "Do you want to be the same kind of person that hurt Jill? You're not like that!"

Sarah's fury boiled over and she shoved Keller away from her with all her strength. "Don't you ever accuse me of that again! If anything happens to my family or friends, it's on you!" The singer stalked away from the shocked group. Keller watched her go with a look of fearful worry on her face.

The younger Colby watched her sister walk away, then turned to her friend. "Are you okay?" Keller just shook her head. "I don't get it, I've never seen her angry like that. It was like when she was caught in that rage loop thing with Marcel, but Marie wasn't angry when Sarah attacked her. What could have set her off?"

With her words, something clicked into place for Keller. She immediately looked around their gathered group. Louve stood a few yards away speaking with Alain. Raph, Romaric, and Ranier were back by the vehicles where they had retreated during Sarah and Keller's private falling out. Keller was puzzled. Annie was right, it really wasn't like Sarah to carry that much anger. The singer was a fairly laid-back person. But someone could have triggered her anger; someone powerful could have directed it toward her. She cast out her senses to see if she could pick up Marcel in the area. She was familiar with the feel of him but unfortunately he was nowhere around. She discounted Marie because the blonde wasn't strong enough to direct that much emotion. She continued to search all the people with *other* blood. She felt what she would consider the "flavor" of them all in her head, with the exception of Alain. His shields were so tight that nothing leaked through. Keller raised her eyebrow at such an unusual state for a werewolf. It was in that moment that he looked up from his conversation with Louve and met Keller's eyes. For just an instant his eyes flashed a challenge, then it was gone. It was certainly nothing she could call him on, but she remembered it regardless.

Now she just had to deal with her irate girlfriend. The problem was that Sarah was right. If Marie did anything to Annie, Keller would feel responsible. She realized that her thoughts had wandered off while Annie was speaking with her. "I don't really know, A, but it worries me. I should go talk to her." She looked around, just realizing that Sarah was nowhere in sight.

Jesse noticed her confusion and chimed in. "She went up to the house, and Jill followed her. Jill said she was going to have a talk with her and try to calm her down."

Keller felt a brief flash of jealousy before quickly pushing it away. She knew she didn't have anything to worry about with Sarah and Jill. But there was a small part of her that was always aware of the solid bond of friendship the two women shared. It was a bond that had lasted many years, and through many heartaches. While Sarah and Keller were soul mates, it was still a fairly new bond. And Sarah was known for running from things that were emotionally difficult. "Maybe I'll just let them talk it out for a bit. Perhaps Jill can get through to her while she's so angry at me."

Jesse, ever the optimist, tried to reassure her. "Don't worry, Keller, She'll come around. I just don't think she was thinking clearly. Sarah's not a killer." Jesse wandered off toward the visiting French Canadians and Keller glanced at the unusually silent younger Colby sister.

"And what do you think?"

Annie gave her a worried look. "I think we both know that the death of our parents seriously affected Sarah. And right now I'm not so sure she wouldn't lose her mind to protect me. I think she would do anything to make sure I'm safe." She shrugged. "Keller, she sacrificed her life to save me once. I don't think she'd bat an eye about sacrificing someone else, especially if it was someone she saw as the bad guy."

Keller nodded. "That's what I'm afraid of. Don't get me wrong, I'd sacrifice anything to protect you all. But if it comes down to taking someone's life, I don't want her to do it. I'd rather it were me. I've been there many times. It's a dark road that I don't think she'd do well to travel down."

The younger woman looked at her and realized that there was still a lot she didn't know about her friend. "Will you tell me some time?"

Despite the fact that she was among friends who knew and supported her, Keller always found it difficult talking about her past. There was a gulf of experience that many just couldn't bridge to be able to relate. But more than that, Keller had done many things over the past few hundred years that she regretted. She killed many men in her own personal quest for justice. Yes, they were abusive, some even being murders themselves, but they still deserved consideration by the law of more than just one. The world was a different place back then, and death was a common thing. Whether it was plague, war, childbirth, or the difficulties of life in general, people died often and died early. Her actions of retribution had no real impact on the world as a whole, but she still felt the weight of them. After hundreds of years, the stain remained on her soul.

No, she didn't want that future for her lover. She gave Annie an answer that the younger woman would accept. "Maybe someday." Annie nodded and Keller decided it was a good time to probe the younger Colby for a little information. "Has Sarah talked to you about her nightmares?"

The younger woman looked back at her in surprise. "She's having nightmares again?"

Keller looked at her curiously. "Again?"

Annie nodded sadly. "She had them for years after our parents died. I think she was afraid for a long time after that. I don't know if you've realized, but she likes to push all her emotions down where she doesn't have to deal with them. She started it when Mom and Dad died, I think as a way to be able to cope and focus on me. The only way they seem to come out is when she's writing music. As long as she's writing, she's okay."

"She's not." Annie's eyes widened. "She hasn't created anything new since she finished the album. And she has nightmares almost every other night. It's all I can do just to soothe her back to sleep when it happens. I'm starting to get worried, A."

Annie looked down at her feet. "I feel like this is all my fault. She wouldn't be so out of her mind if she weren't so freaked out about my safety. I'm worried she'll do something stupid."

Keller sighed. "I am too." With those words rolling off her tongue, Keller thought it was time to find her girlfriend. She looked around and saw Louve, Jesse, Raph and his sons all standing in a group. Sarah, Jill, and Alain were all missing. "I'm heading in to find Sarah. Stay close by Jesse and Louve." When Keller walked into the farmhouse, she didn't immediately see Sarah and Jill. Instead she came face to face with Alain. He gave her a benign smile that jangled her nerves. Something was off with him, but she didn't have time to dive deeper into it. "Have you seen Sarah or Jill?"

He nodded at her. "Oiu. They asked me for a place of privacy, so I directed them to the *repaire*."

The jealousy she felt earlier returned and it coincided with a surprise push of power from Alain. She immediately knew that he was responsible for her earlier lapse. Before he could walk around her toward the exit, she tightened her mental shield and grabbed the stocky man by the throat. Her own power far eclipsed the werewolf. "Do not think to play your games with me or my people, wolf! If I find that you had any parts of the emotional turmoil today, you will pay dearly!" She released him abruptly with a slight shove and he sucked in a raspy breath. His skin was already bruising from the force of her grip but she knew his enhanced healing would have it gone in a matter of minutes. Despite the rage she could see in his eyes, she noted that the rest of his face remained an impassive mask, and his shields were locked tight.

He gave a single jerky nod. "*Mes excuses, sangsue*. I was only trying to *liven* things up in here. It will not happened again. Now if you will excuse me?"

Keller stepped aside and watched carefully as he made his way out the door she had entered minutes before. Her thoughts were running like the wind but one stood out above all the others. She no longer trusted Alain. But she did trust Louve, and she would have a talk with her friend later. More determined than ever to find Sarah, she went through the house toward the den. She felt her lover before she saw her. Keller slid open the pocket door to Louve's favorite room and paused. In light of her encounter with Alain, she could only assume he was responsible for the scene she was faced with. Sarah and Jill were locked in an embrace, mouths feasting on each other.

Keller could immediately sense the women were overcome with lust, much the same way Sarah had been overcome by Louve their first time at Temple du Loup. Anger was the first emotion she felt but she quickly pushed it away. She was aware of what Alain had done, but not his true intentions. Instead of being furious at the two women in front of her, she did something much more productive. Using her power and aura, she sent a wash of neutral emotion through both women. The effect was similar to dousing them with a bucket of ice water and they immediately jumped apart. Confusion washed over their faces, which quickly turned to dismay. Jill looked at Keller and then back at Sarah. "What the fuck?"

Keller sighed. "What the fuck, indeed." She knew why they did what they did, but she still didn't like it.

Sarah looked like she was going to cry. "Keller, I swear I don't know what happened. We came in here to talk and—I don't know. It was—I was overwhelmed and the next I remember was feeling something wash through me and you were standing there. I swear, I don't know what happened." She took a step toward her lover and held out her hand. She had been furious with Keller earlier, but she couldn't bear it if Keller thought that Sarah would break her trust, or worse yet, didn't love her. She was relieved when Keller took the offered hand and held it tight in her own.

Keller glanced at Jill, then looked into Sarah's teary green eyes. "It's okay, love, I know exactly what happened. Let's all sit down, we have another problem."

The veterinarian was first to speak. "What do you mean we have another problem? Don't we have enough? And what happened to us? I swear I'd never fuck around like that without consent from both of you. I like to have fun, Keller, but not like that. Besides, I, um, Louve and I have been getting close. I wouldn't mess that up either."

Keller gave her a reassuring smile. "I know you're not like that and I'm glad you and Louve are getting close. I think you are good for each other. First I'm going to ask if either one of you had your shields in place when you came in here to talk?"

Jill shook her head and Sarah answered. "Of course not, it was just Jill. She was the only one here and I trust her with my life!"

Keller held up a hand to calm her girlfriend. "I know you do, but you weren't the only ones in the house."

A shudder ran through Jill as she whispered a name. "Alain."

"Yes, Alain. We had an altercation when I came into the house. He tried to force emotion-laden energy on me, to fuel jealousy. But I am no novice to be caught by his games. I gave him a warning, but I have lost my trust in him. These are serious times right now and I have no interest in pathetic squabbles."

Jill stared at her in confusion. "What do you mean *forced energy?*"

Keller looked at Sarah. "Do you remember what Louve did to you the first time we went to the club?"

The singer's mouth made an 'O' shape as she recalled the night that they first had a threesome with Louve. It was the incident in question that led Sarah to tell the Frenchwoman to go fuck herself. Sarah turned to her ex. "A powerful wolf can overwhelm with emotional energy. Lust, anger, and jealousy, just to name a few. They can even do it to people with *other* blood if we aren't well shielded." She looked back at Keller. "But if Alain did that to us, he must be very powerful. I've never sensed anything like that from him."

The elder vampire scowled. "That's the problem, I've never felt anything from him, period. For a wolf, he is shielded incredibly tight. It takes a lot of strength for a werewolf to hold that much power in check, rather than let it emote naturally."

Jill looked down at the ornate throw rug and swallowed the lump that had formed in her throat. "I—I think that he—"

Sarah stood and walked over to Jill. "What's the matter, Red?"

The veterinarian looked up at her longtime friend. "I think he's the third man. From the moment I first saw him in the kitchen, I felt something. My stomach twisted and I was afraid, but it's more than just the fact that he is a man because I don't feel uncomfortable around Raph, Romaric, or Ranier. At first I thought it was because his build is similar to the wolf I remember, but now I think it's more. I just—I can't remember!"

"Jill." Keller called out softly, to get her attention. "I'm afraid that's my fault."

"What do you mean?"

Keller sighed and ran a hand through her perpetually messy blonde hair. "When you were attacked, I clouded some of your memories to help you distance yourself from them a bit. It's a healing technique I've used many times in the past."

Jill looked at her in shock. "You did *what?*"

"It's like putting salve on a wound so that it doesn't hurt so much while it's healing. While you were physically healed after your attack, your mind was still hurt. I simply numbed some of the pain, psychically. Unfortunately, the side effect was that it also muted some of the more vivid images of your experience. I did intend that, but I did not realize the other difficulty it would pose when trying to positively identify your attackers. I apologize for that."

The veterinarian took a few minutes to absorb Keller's words. She was a doctor; she was a person of extremely rational mind; and she was a survivor. And Doctor Jillian Cole knew that it was time to face her fears. "Is there a way you can undo what you did?"

Sarah looked at her with dismay. "You don't have to do that, Jilly. We can find another way." She glanced at her lover. "Right, Keller? There's another way to find out if Alain is her third attacker?"

Keller shook her head and gave Jill a penetrating stare. "There is no other way. I can reverse what I did, but are you sure about this? If you're not healed enough yet, it could send you into a depressive spiral and it would take even longer to get back to a place of normalcy."

The tall doctor leaned forward and rested her elbows on her knees. "Since reconnecting with Sarah and Annie, and meeting you, Jesse, and Louve, I feel like I've finally got a family again. It was just me and my mom growing up, and we were never very close. Since she moved to Florida a few years back, we rarely even speak with the exception of mandatory phone calls on birthdays and holidays. She likes to pretend that I'm not gay, and I like to pretend she's not a hypocritical bitch." She looked up at Sarah and then turned her gaze to Keller. "You are my family, and I'll face any hardship I have to in order to keep this one intact. So yes, I want to do this because we need to know."

Satisfied, Keller nodded. "Okay. In order to do this, I'll need to take some blood from you to help establish a bond that's a little deeper than normal. It's harder to undo than it was to initially cloud your memories."

Sarah stood up. "Wait, you're going to do this now? With everyone waiting outside and Alain potentially causing trouble someplace else?"

Keller gave her a serious look. "This is the only time to do it. We need to know as soon as possible. Can you keep an eye out and don't let anyone interrupt us until I'm finished. And keep your shields tight, no matter who it is!" Sarah nodded once and walked out of the den, sliding the doors shut behind her. Keller could sense her lover on the other side and knew that she'd watch over them. She looked at Jill. The taller woman was still sitting forward on the couch. "Now it's your turn. I'm going to sit on the couch with my back facing one end. I want you to recline in front of me so I can be comfortable and still have good access to feed. Okay?"

Jill swallowed hard; her nerves were obvious. She moved and waited for Keller to get situated on the couch, then she reclined back between her legs. She tried for a bit of humor, if only to calm her own nerves. "This would be fun on any other day."

Keller chuckled. "How do you think Sarah fed from you the night we all slept together?"

Jill smiled, her nerves abated slightly but the memory of their threesome only served to heat her up in an uncomfortable way. There was no time for that, they had to be serious. She kept her response deceptively light, but was very aware of Keller's breath against her neck. "That was a hot night."

Keller's left arm snaked across the front of Jill's chest, and she gently cupped the taller woman's right cheek and jaw. Jill tilted her head to the left, leaving plenty of room on the right side of her neck for Keller to feed. Keller could feel the nearby pulse start to race and sensed the woman's rising heat, but she did her best to ignore it. She would need all her focus to undo what she had done. Keller tried hard not to think about was how sexual feeding from Jill would be. Like Sarah, Keller didn't want to do anything to cause her lover to question her commitment. Not wanting to delay any longer, Keller entered Jill's mind at the same time she pierced her with sharp fangs. The feeling of biting the other woman immediately made Keller wet. She couldn't help her body's autonomic response, but she could do her best not to let any lust leak through to the compliant woman. She knew that Jill was just as turned on, but that was something they would both have to ignore. As the taller woman's blood slid down Keller's throat, the older vampire used the bond that was forged to delve deeper into her mind.

Jill could feel her inside, but she also felt as if she was floating. The room and world around her faded away the further down Keller went. Suddenly, images appeared to both women. They were hazy at first, but Keller did something to clear it up. It was as if she had peeled away a veil from the screen of Jill's mind. Jill gasped and her body jerked in Keller's grip as she was overtaken by the memories of that night. Fear rolled through her at the memory of her assailants' faces, and she whimpered in terror as she relived their assault. One by one, the three people in her memory took turns breaking her, the remembered pain of it making her stomach roil. And when they were through, the real fear began. She watched the movie of her memory as each person changed into something that she'd only seen before in horror films. The agony that followed was nearly unbearable, and she cried out with her eyes closed tight, tears leaking around her pale lashes.

Sarah could feel her friend's pain and hear the anguish coming from the other room, but she knew she could not leave her duty or interrupt. And Keller was inside Jill through it all. She felt the other woman's torment; she understood her shame and sorrow at what had happened. Instead of clouding those things, she sent wave after wave of positive energy to the woman in her arms. Jill's memory ended when the last of her bones had been broken and she passed out. But she saw enough to know and someone was going to pay. Keller pulled out of her mind at the same time she withdrew her fangs. Her tongue licked away the remaining blood, sealing the wound on Jill's neck. The taller woman shuddered at the sensation. Despite the horrors she had relived, she was unable to fully stop her reactions to the intimate act of feeding either. Keller continued to hold Jill as the taller woman's breathing and heartrate began to slow. "Are you okay?" Jill didn't speak for a minute. Instead, she took slow measured breaths. Keller grew concerned and prompted once more. "Jill? How do you feel?

Jill abruptly sat forward and stood from the couch. The woman that turned around and looked into Keller's eyes wasn't the wounded creature that Keller had feared. Instead, she saw resolution and strength of mind. Jill could feel the slow burn of anger in her belly and was ready to find the wolves responsible for her pain. "It was Alain, and the woman that Sarah attacked earlier. Marie. Which means I can only assume the other person is Raph's nephew, Marcel."

Keller stood as well. "Let's go find Louve. This will need to be handled delicately. I sense that Alain is very powerful and we don't want him to suspect that we know until we can make sure he won't get away." They opened the den door and walked out, startling Sarah. The singer turned quickly and looked back and forth between Jill and Keller.

"Well, did it go all right? Are you okay?" She put her hand on Jill's arm in concern.

Jill looked back at her ex and gave her a sad smile. "I'm going to be. But more importantly right now is that I remember everything. We need to find Louve and warn her about Alain. It was him."

Anger blossomed in Sarah's gut as she thought about the abuse her friend had suffered at the hands of the three rogue wolves. And to find out that one of the wolves was someone she had trusted, it fanned the flames of rage higher. "I swear, I'll kill them all!"

Keller immediately stepped in close to her lover. "Sarah, focus, my love. We just need to catch them first and to do that we need to stay calm and clear. Please, you need to push away that anger and stay with us."

Sarah listened to what her girlfriend had to say and tried her best to comply. She shut her eyes and pushed the anger and emotion down and away from the surface. It was one thing she could easily do with so many years of practice. She opened her eyes and nodded to the shorter woman in front of her. "I'm good. I'm okay now. Let's go catch some dogs."

They were met by Louve as soon as they walked out the door onto the wraparound porch. "Where have you all been? Raph and his sons are ready to get settled in so they can be rested to run the city tonight." Louve noticed the grim look on Keller's face. "What is wrong, mon ami?"

Keller glanced around for Alain but didn't see the stocky man. "Come, we must speak with Raph immediately. I will tell you all at the same time. Where is Alain?"

"I'm afraid he is gone. I was coming to tell you that Alain received a call from one of his good friends in France. Apparently his friend is on his deathbed, and Alain left immediately to be by his side. We will just have to make do without him."

In an uncharacteristic fit of anger, Keller slammed her fist into a nearby planter. "In the name of fack! Can we na' get a break?"

Louve looked in shock at the exploded pieces of wood and earth, and the brightly colored bits of flower scattered on the deck boards and ground below. In all the decades she had known the vampire, Louve had never seen the woman lose her temper. "Mon Dieu! What is so wrong?"

Keller looked at her longtime friend and knew she was going to bring her sorrow. "I lifted the veil from Jill's memories so she could remember her attackers." She paused, sorry for what she had to say. "I am so sorry, my friend, but the third man was Alain."

The Frenchwoman stepped back. "Non! It cannot be!" She glanced over at Jill, perhaps hoping the tall woman could tell her that Keller was speaking false. "Truly?"

Jill gave her a look of sorrow mixed with anger. "It's true. I felt something when I first met him in your kitchen earlier. But it wasn't until Keller lifted the veil over my memory that I knew."

Louve's heart was breaking for the beautiful woman who had finally made it into her heart. But her own heart was also breaking for her seeming betrayal by Alain. "But you said you never saw his face? How do you know this is true?"

Jill closed her eyes to speak. "He wears a signet ring on the middle finger of his right hand. It has a snarling silver wolf set in onyx. My attacker was wearing the same ring."

The petite brunette sagged in place. Everything she had been building, her circus nightclub, her friendships, this new feeling with Jill, and her trust, they were all teetering on the edge of a black abyss. Her voice was a whisper, but the three people closest to her heard it with ease. "He was my friend for many years, how could I not know this thing about him?" She turned to Keller. "I am responsible for everything, I brought him here with me! Why? Why would he do these things?" Then her thoughts turned to her new lover and she looked at Jill in dismay. "Mon dieu! Your attack, all of those horrible things that happened to you—" She covered her mouth. "They are my fault! I am so sorry, *ma amore*. So very sorry." The normally dominant woman was at a loss when faced with such betrayal and guilt. She was afraid she would lose her ange de feu before all the trouble with the rogue wolves could be resolved. The fear of suddenly losing all she had built, and all that she had found, was nearly overwhelming.

Jill took the distraught woman's hand. "Louve, it is not your fault. I don't blame you for this at all."

Keller rested her hand on her friend's shoulder. "I don't know why he has done these things, Louve, but together we can make sure he will not continue to do them. Let's go speak with Raphael and the rest. We need a better plan. Alain is very powerful and it is essential that we stop him."

Keller's words brought back memories of another time, when the vampire's confidence and surety had soothed her once before. And Louve knew without a doubt that as long as Keller was with them, they would prevail in the end.

THEY LEFT LOUVE to arrange things with her people. She

decided to have a meeting with everyone and explain the situation in full. She would let everyone know that Alain, Marcel, and Marie had gone rogue and were all extremely dangerous. She told Keller and Raph that she would come speak with them later. So after handing over Annie and Jesse's address to the Alpha, Keller got into her car and followed the other two vehicles back to Annie's house. Once the three men were settled into the cozy little house, it was decided that food should be the first order of business. Annie and Aric went off to order enough food to feed an army from their favorite take-out place, Thai Guys. And Jesse took Jill on a tour around the house since she had never visited before.

Ranier had retreated to the spare bedroom to call his girlfriend and Raph followed Keller and Sarah to the kitchen. The big man was especially concerned to find out that Alain was one of the rogue wolves. He looked at Sarah with worry. "I don't trust that our rogues have left your sister's place alone. I'm going to change and do a quick check around the house and yard to see if I can smell any of them. I caught Marie and Alain's scents at the farmhouse, and I definitely know what my nephew smells like. It's shouldn't take me too long."

He started to turn away but was stopped by Sarah. "But wait, I thought you couldn't turn furry and then turn back without food, or sex, or something?"

The big bearded man looked at her in surprise. "Non, *pant-oute!*" He gave a hearty laugh and turned to Keller. "What have you been teaching them here in America that they would think a grown wolf would have such limitations?" He roared with laughter and Sarah's face turned red. He got himself under control but continued to chuckle.

Keller explained the best she could. "The only real exposure Sarah and Annie have had to wolves is Jesse, and she is still quite new. And of course being so new, she has such *limitations.*"

The singer huffed. "Well, how was I supposed to know any different?"

"No, you are right. My apologies, Sarah, you would not know how it is with us. Even my boys would be able to change back with minimal difficulty, but it is still easier yet for me. I will go out and search the house and neighborhood and be back before your much touted takeout arrives." Without any care for modesty, he simply stripped near the back door and changed, easy as Keller had ever seen. Once the transformation was complete, she let him out the back door. Sarah could only stare in awe at how fast and effortless the man made it seem. As promised, he was gone no more than twenty minutes when the doorbell sounded.

Jesse called out from the living room. "I'll get it, it's probably dinner." When she opened the door, the biggest wolf she'd ever seen was standing on the step. She looked at the wolf, then at the doorbell, which was nose high on him. Recognizing Raph's scent, she stepped aside and let him in.

He pushed his way through the swinging door into the kitchen and simply changed back. Annie walked through the door behind him and was just in time to see the hugely muscled nude man dressing himself near the back door. She covered her eyes and walked right back out of the room. Keller burst out laughing, and Sarah shook her head and followed her sister out of the kitchen. Dangling man-bits just weren't her thing, no matter how buff the package was. Once dressed, he turned around and noticed that Keller was the only one left in the kitchen. "Did I do something wrong?"

Keller smiled. "No, my friend. They are simply not used to your lack of modesty. But they are fine. Now, what did you discover?"

He grimaced. "Nothing good. The female's scent is all around the house, and it is most concentrated near one of the bedroom windows. My guess is that is the main bedroom."

"The west side of the house?"

He nodded his head. "Oui. But I also scented Marcel. The good news is that they both head off in the same direction. Has it rained in the past week or two?" Keller shook her head no. "Then I'd say they are a few weeks old at least. The smell is faint, but not undetectable. Now we have a direction, we should probably pick up a few more maps of the area, or one big one of the city. We have a direction from here, and I assume they are still in the city somewhere. I'm not sure what to do beyond running the streets hoping to catch a scent of them. I doubt the faint trail that leads from here will take us far but it's all we have." He looked up as Ranier, Sarah, Jill, and Romaric entered the kitchen. "I have discovered a scent around the house, and it leads northeast from here. Perhaps tomorrow night we can follow the trail."

Ranier nodded somberly and Romaric grinned. "That sounds good, Papa, we'll find them in no time!"

The doorbell rang again and less than a minute later, Annie and Jesse entered the kitchen loaded down with boxes full of delicious smelling take-out bags. Annie spoke as Jesse set down the two large boxes she held tightly in her arms. "There is pop, juice, and bottled water in the fridge. Help yourself!"

The young wolf looked in the fridge and wrinkled her nose in disgust. "Um, babe, scratch the juice from the list. Based on the amount of mold growth, I'd say it's been in here since we left to stay with Jill."

"Grody!"

Jesse nodded. "Yeah, grody." She gingerly grabbed the plastic bottle of orange juice and walked it right to the trash. This earned a disdainful look from her girlfriend.

"You're not even going to empty it and put it in the recycling bin?"

Jesse leveled a brown-eyed gaze at the younger Colby sister. "Babe, do I really need to answer that?" She pointed at her own face. "I have an extremely enhanced sense of smell, as do three other people in this room." She held up the bottle of vaguely orange liquid. "This has at least a half inch of slimy mold in it. I wouldn't open this bottle if you paid me!"

Annie giggled. "Fair enough. Carry on then."

After that, they managed to find a few folding chairs downstairs and a leaf to extend the table to fit six people. Annie and Jesse sat on stools at the breakfast bar. The group of eight laughed and joked as they ate their meal together. But underneath there was still a current of tension. Everyone knew it was only a matter of time before the rogue wolves struck again. Keller didn't say it aloud, but she wondered how much more dangerous Alain would be now that he no longer had to hide his secret. They would just have to see.

Chapter Ten

PRIDE WEEK FINALLY arrived in the city of Columbus, Ohio. Raphael, Ranier, and Romaric had been searching the streets for weeks with no luck. It was a big city and they frequently caught scents all over as they checked block by block each night. The rogue wolves continued to make the news, though the news had yet to make the wolves. Multiple burglaries each week moved the mysterious thieves to the top of the Columbus PD's radar. There were advertisements on billboards asking people to call a tip line with any information leading to the arrest of the thieves in exchange for a small reward. There was even another pair of deaths near Westerville that was attributed to the roaming "wild dogs" of Alum Creek State Park. The collection of vampires, werewolves, and the lone human had put all the pieces together but they were trapped in that they couldn't go to the police with their information.

Everyone was stressed out by the situation. Jill and Louve had not been able to spend a lot of quality time together because of Alain's disappearance. The Frenchwoman had relied on him heavily to keep things running smoothly at the Cirque du Loup. Much of her time was taken up of late between managing the club and putting together the promised two stage acts for the Pride festival. Between work and babysitting Annie, Jill was starting to go stir crazy. Louve had come over a few times but both women decided it would be a bad idea to leave Annie and Jesse alone in the house overnight. That meant that they were limited in the nights they could spend with each other because of both their jobs and Louve's duties to her club. They grew close though, despite both their fears. Jill's continued attention and emotional openness had convinced Louve that the veterinarian did not hold her responsible for her attack.

Keller had officially completed her last day as the manager of The Merge the previous weekend. She had been working on a special surprise for Sarah and Annie but whether or not it would work out all came down to timing. Instead of the responsibilities of a normal job, most of her time was now spent helping coordinate Raph's crew with their own. They had a large section of the northern half of the city darkened on the giant map at Annie's house. Only the previous night had the Quebec wolves started

searching the other side of the river, west of downtown. But more
than anyone else, Annie had been bearing the lion's share of
stress on her stubborn human shoulders. Not only was she trying
to keep up her regular work schedule while being potentially targeted by homicidal werewolves, but she had been deep into the
final planning of the Pride stage show for weeks.

Since it was the Friday night before the festival, the younger
Colby sister was finally able to breathe a sigh of relief. All her
hard work over the past few months had paid off. She had a band
shell scheduled for delivery to the park first thing in the morning.
The festival organizers had volunteers that would rotate through
in shifts to help set up and tear down the stage gear, directed by
Voodoo Pony staff volunteers. They would use a lot of sound
equipment from Pony, plus bands would be bringing in their own
stuff. Bruce was going to take turns with her in running the stage
show so they wouldn't miss the entire festival. And lastly, all the
bands and other performers were scheduled and ready to go
starting at noon the next day.

It was only three in the afternoon on Friday, June seven-
teenth, and Annie was slouched down on one of the leather
couches in the bar. Even though she was done working until the
festival the next day, she couldn't leave yet. The assistant manager of Voodoo Pony blew out a long sigh. Jesse was working,
Sarah was working, and Jill was off at some continuous improve-
ment seminar for her veterinary clinic. There was no one to play
guard until one of them was free. Annie growled to herself, irritated at not being able to celebrate her months of hard work, and
at having to have a chaperone like a child. To make matters
worse, she'd been dropped off that morning by Jill, so she
couldn't drive herself anywhere even if she wanted. Bruce giggled from the open garage door near the stage. He was loading
the straight truck with the last little bit of equipment so they
could drive it over to the park in the morning.

Despite the fact that the bar was air conditioned, the breeze
felt refreshing coming in. She watched the man she'd been working with since they both started at The Merge. He never had an
issue with her being promoted as lead bartender, then assistant
manager over him. He was an all-around great employee and had
been a real savior in helping her keep the Pony shows going
while planning for the Pride festival. He and his boyfriend, Rico,
had also been good friends to her over the past few years. She
could see him potentially growing into the assistant manager role
she currently held, should she ever just say screw it and find a

daytime job. The thought popped into her head more and more lately. She was starting to really resent working such dramatically different hours from Jesse. Thinking about their vastly different schedules only made her growl again, prompting another laugh from Bruce. She scowled at him. "What's so funny?"

He stopped and grabbed his water bottle from a nearby table. After gulping a good amount of it, he sat it back down. "I'm laughing at you, all growly like a bear over here. What's the matter, hon, are you and your squeeze already into the LBD stage?"

Annie cocked her head at him. "LBD?"

"Like duh, lesbian bed death. Everyone knows what that is!"

She blushed and made a face at him. "No, we have plenty of sex when we see each other. It's just hard since we aren't staying at home right now." They told everyone that they were remodeling the main floor of their house to explain why they were staying with Jill. They also told people about her car being vandalized and said she was getting threats. This was so no one would question why she needed a chaperone to and from work.

"I bet it's harder when you're home, with that gorgeous hunk of butch between your legs." He made obscene thrusting motions in her direction and she blushed even more. Prior to her relationship with Jesse, Annie had been saving herself for the "right one." Because of the fact that she hadn't been having sex that long, she and Jesse really hadn't explored much with toys. But she was definitely intrigued by the thought. Instead of admitting any of that to a legendary gossip, she simply scrubbed her hands over her face trying to dissipate some of the heat. "Oh my God no, it's not that either!" She threw a pen at him but he ducked. "You're such a letch, Bruce, how does Rico put up with you?"

The blonde man raised a perfectly manicured eyebrow. "Seriously? My hot Latino lover is with me because I'm a letch!" They stared at each other and then burst out laughing. "All kidding aside, why are you still here? There's nothing left to do here and you're working tomorrow."

Annie pointed at him. "You're working tomorrow too!"

He pointed back. "But you came in early, and I only just got here an hour ago. Quit arguing with me and go home already! Or, wherever it is you're staying now."

Annie laughed. "Don't tell me what to do! I'm your boss you know. But anyway, I can't go home because everyone is working and I don't have a ride. Plus there is nobody there right now."

Her friend and employee looked at her with concern. "Is it really that bad that you can't spend a few hours home alone?"

She immediately sobered thinking about all the things that had been happening. "Yeah, it is. But we're taking care of it, and the police are looking into the matter." The last part was a blatant lie since there was no way the cops were looking into the matter of rogue werewolves. But they were looking into the vandalism. "It's a little complicated right now, but things will work out."

Bruce sensed she was done talking about it and felt bad that there was nothing he could do to help. "Well, I'm going to finish this stuff up and go take inventory to make sure we're set for tomorrow night. And Annie?" She looked at him curiously. "If you ever need to talk, I'm here for you."

Annie nodded and smiled. "I know, and thank you. You're a great guy, Bruce." He shrugged and a faint blush washed across his smoothly shaven cheeks, then walked out the garage door. Once he was gone, Annie called her girlfriend. She didn't normally call Jesse at work; usually they just texted throughout the day. But she really wanted to hear her voice. She should have known that Jessie would worry about why she was calling.

When Jesse answered, her voice was hushed and had an edge of panic. "Is everything okay, what's wrong?"

Annie rushed to reassure her. "Nothing's wrong, sorry for scaring you. I just missed your voice."

"Aww, I miss you too, A! But you'll be done soon, right?"

Annie pouted, lip sticking out for no one to see. "I'm done now, and I'm bored, damnit!"

Jesse laughed. "Your adorable bottom lip is poking out, isn't it? Stop pouting cute stuff, I'll be done at five and we can have a little fun before all the craziness hits at tomorrow's festival. Are you nervous about tomorrow?"

Hearing her girlfriend's words, Annie sucked her bottom lip back in and made a face. "Are *you* nervous? This is your fault you know! If I totally suck I'm blaming you!"

Laughter was loud coming through the speaker of her phone. "If you totally suck, so will I and we can suck together! Wait, hold on a sec —" Annie snickered at her girlfriend's choice of phrasing and waited patiently for her to come back on the line. The silence abruptly ended with laughter. "— sorry, apparently my phrasing was too much to let go by without Jason saying something not safe for work. So anyway, you're going to do great up there tomorrow, and I will try not to bomb too badly. You wouldn't have had to worry about it at all if you hadn't volunteered me to play drums in Sarah's song. And if you hadn't volunteered me, I wouldn't have mentioned that you've been practicing it a lot on the guitar Sarah loaned you."

"So now we're both roped into playing 'Blood of My Blood' with her tomorrow. On stage. In front of everyone."

Jesse made a weird growling noise over the phone. "When you put it like that, it makes me kind of queasy. So not to change the subject, but I'm totally changing the subject. Did you only call to tell me you were bored?"

Annie whined. "I'm bored."

The woman on the other end of the phone laughed. "Really? Nothing else?"

"I want a beer."

Jesse laughed even harder. "Babe, you're in a bar. Go get yourself a beer, jeez—" She cut off again, but only for a few seconds this time. "Whoops, gotta go, babe. Boss man wants this code re-written before I leave at five. I'll see you soon, okay? Text Sarah, maybe she's done with appointments and can hang with you for a bit."

They said their goodbyes and hung up. Annie immediately texted her sister.

I want a beer.

She laughed when she read the reply a few seconds later.

Don't you work in a bar?

The younger Colby laughed at how her sister's response was so similar to Jesse's. She sent another text.

yeah but Im done here and want 2 go home

Too bad I've got another client here after this one. Sorry A, but not done til 5. Text 2 see if Keller is free

Annie growled with frustration and looked at the time on her phone. It was only three twenty. Undaunted, she texted Keller next.

whatcha doin?

This time she didn't get a reply for a few minutes. When it chimed, she laughed at Keller's proper spelling and punctuation. There was a reason her old boss was the slowest texter she knew, even with her enhanced speed and dexterity.

```
    I just finished giving Duke a bath and trimming his
nails. Jill showed me how to do it a few weeks ago and
I think I'll leave it to the doctor next time. He was
not a fan. I have no plans now. What's up?
```

Annie sent her frustrated response back.

```
    done w/work and want a beer. All my sitters are
busy. Want 2 hang?
```

Two more minutes went by before her phone vibrated.

```
    Actually, I do want to hang out. I've got some news
for you. I'll be there to pick you up in ten minutes
and we can grab a drink somewhere.
```

Annie's stomach knotted at what her old boss might have to say.

```
    news?
```

Luckily, Keller texted back quickly to reassure her.

```
    Good news. ;)
```

The younger woman immediately sent messages to her sister and girlfriend.

```
    Keller is gonna pick me up. happy hour, ya suckers!
enjoy wrking! :P
```

Happy once again, Annie skipped off to the office to grab her satchel. Lissa was sitting at her desk going over a spreadsheet on her laptop. She looked up when Annie knocked and came in. "What in the world was Keller doing to go through so many office chairs?"

Annie laughed. "I have no idea. You'll have to ask next time you see her. I'm out of here, but I'll be meeting Bruce at the park tomorrow at nine. He's got the truck loaded and he'll swing by here in the morning to pick it up. The volunteers will be there at ten and we can get the stage set up. Everything seems all set for the festival. Anything else you need before I'm gone for the day?"

The new manager of The Merge looked up at her and smiled.

Lissa was continuously amazed at the stellar crew that Keller had managed to put together during her time at the bar. She only hoped she could do half as well. "No, I think you've got everything well in hand. And after six tomorrow evening, consider yourself off until Tuesday. You've done a lot of work lately and I want you to know how much I appreciate it."

The younger woman smiled. "Thanks, boss!" She started to walk out the door but was stopped.

"Oh, and Annie?" When Annie glanced back a Lissa, her boss gave her a reassuring smile. "Good luck tomorrow!"

She mumbled a quick thanks and scooted out the door. She got to the front of the bar just in time to see Keller roll up in her midnight blue Audi. The top was down so Annie quickly pulled the ponytail holder from her wrist and secured her shoulder-length hair. She laughed as she got into the car. "People are going to gossip about attractive women in fancy cars picking me up when my girlfriend's not around."

Keller snorted. "Riiiggghhht. So what do you feel like?"

"Beer and wings."

The driver raised a pale eyebrow as she navigated the streets. "Really?" Annie nodded and grinned. "Bawks & Barley it is then." She aimed her car in the direction of the popular beer and wing place that had opened in downtown Columbus in the past year. "Just so you know, we're never going to get parking."

"Oh ye of little faith!" When they were within a block of their destination, Annie abruptly called out. "Turn in here!"

Keller did a quick right and stopped just shy of the parking lot gate. "This is the lot for the fitness place, and I know my car is small, but it's not going to fit under the gate."

Annie rifled through her bag for a few seconds then came up with a white card in her hand. "Aha! No worries, fangalicious, I've got a membership." Keller scanned the card and the gate lifted like the arm of a great wooden sentinel. Annie murmured. "You shall pass."

Keller snickered. "Have you even seen those movies?"

The younger woman sighed as they got out of the car and Keller locked it with its distinctive chirping sound. "Every single one. Jesse insisted."

"And did you fall asleep for any of them?"

Annie giggled. "Every single one." Once they were seated at a table outside with cold craft brews in front of them, Annie slipped the leash on her curiosity. "So, what news do you have? Did the guys find our asshole wolves?"

Keller took a drink of her beer and gave it a puzzled look before shaking her head slightly and setting it down. "Not yet. I have a question for you about Sarah."

Annie looked at her in concern. "Is she still having nightmares?" She shook her head sadly. "When she suffered from them years ago, I begged her to talk to someone. I think that is part of the reason I got so rebellious after our parents died. I was selfish and angry that Mom and Dad were gone, and I knew that Sarah was suffering too. But she refused to share it with me. To this day it's the one thing that we never shared, our grief. It made me angry at the time, which only made her life even harder. I've apologized but she always shrugs and says we made it through healthy and happy so everything is fine. Since the accident, she's always bottled things up inside."

Keller looked at the woman across from her and realized just how insightful the younger Colby really was. "She is still having the nightmares, but that's not what I want to talk to you about right now. It's about Sarah's set tomorrow. Have you spoken with her about it lately?"

Annie made a face, relieved that their conversation was going to be lighthearted instead of dark. "I'm not talking to your girlfriend about her music right now."

Keller laughed. "You mean your sister?"

"Not since she blackmailed me into performing a song with her at the festival tomorrow. Now she's merely your annoying girlfriend.

Keller choked on her beer at the other woman's adamant words. "Well, how do you think Sarah would feel about a guest band playing with her tomorrow? And would you be able to extend her spot to a full hour?"

Annie cocked her head. "What do you mean? I thought she said her normal band was playing a gig over in Virginia tomorrow? Who would know her music well enough to play with her? And you're treading on some thin ice by asking me to rearrange my well-planned schedule."

"I know I am but I've got a band lined up that has been listening to all her CDs and memorizing her songs."

Annie took a big gulp of her beer and raised her eyebrows in surprise. "What about her new stuff? She's only had the CD's a week, they're not even for sale yet!"

"Well, one may have found its way to the band in question."

"All right, Keller, spill it already. What's the big deal about this band and why are you just coming to me now about it? Who is it?"

They paused their conversation when a server placed a jumbo platter of boneless wings on the table in front of them. Keller's mouth dropped open. "Wow! I have no idea how we're going to eat that." She looked back at Annie to answer her previous question but was interrupted by the younger woman's phone vibrating on the table.

Annie flipped it over and broke into a wide grin. "It's Jesse! She said she's off work a little early and wants to know where we are. Just a sec while I let her know. She can help us eat the wings."

Keller nodded and snickered. "Your wolf will probably eat *all* the wings!"

"Okay, she should be here in about fifteen. Now, you were saying?" Keller started to answer and was once again interrupted when Annie's cell started to vibrated persistently.

"Hold on, Jill's calling." She hit the send button and greeted the woman on the other end. "Hey, Red, are you done already?"

The veterinarian growled back at her. "Hey, *Kid*, what have I told you about calling me Red? And yes, I'm done and I'm starving! Are you still at work, do you need a ride?"

While Annie was talking to Jill, Keller wondered about the young woman's seeming popularity. She shook her head at how Annie's phone was always going off for one reason or another. Sometimes it seemed like things were more different in the past ten years than all the other decades she'd been alive. As she was contemplating the advancements of the world her own phone vibrated. She looked down at the screen and smiled. She typed a reply and by the time she hit send, Annie was finished with her call. Annie loaded her plate with wings and grabbed a dipper of blue cheese dressing. "Jill's on her way. Who was that?"

"Your sister. Her last client of the day had an emergency and cancelled so she's on her way here."

Annie looked at the food on the table and then looked back at Keller. "Are you thinking what I'm thinking?"

Keller gave her a blank look. "Probably not."

"I'm thinking we need to order more appetizers and a few pitchers of beer! Now, what were you going to tell me before we got so popular?"

Keller smirked. "Actually, I may as well wait until the rest get here. Just tell me if you can extend her spot."

Annie gave her an aggrieved look. "Hold on." She grabbed her satchel where it was hanging on the chair. She pulled out a printed sheet and started running down the list with her finger. Then she nodded at Keller. Setting the paper on the table between them, she pointed at the three fifteen minute buffer spots she had added in. "I added some time just in case bands went over. So we should be able to extend her set with no problem. But is it going to be worth it?"

Keller just gave her an enigmatic smile and swallowed a bite of chicken. "Oh, it will definitely be worth it."

"Ooh, can I guess?"

Keller shrugged. "Sure."

"Is it someone from Columbus? Is it someone famous? Is it—?"

The vampire burst out laughing. "I'm not going to tell you until everyone else gets here."

Annie pouted. "But you just said I could guess!"

Mischievous grin met her words. "So I did."

"But you were never going to tell me if I guessed right, were you?" Annie leaned across the table and swatted Keller's arm. "You're such an ass!"

Keller dropped her shields and let a little menace seep through to the woman across from her. "You better watch out, I am a power to be reckoned with. I could snap you in half or simply drain your life in an instant." She held up her hands like menacing claws. "Blah, blah, blah, I vill suck all your blood! I am zee beeg, bad, wampire who only haahhnts at night!"

A voice cut through their laughter. "Don't bother, I already tried that with the big bad werewolf line. She laughed at me too."

Keller looked at Jesse and snickered. "Well, I mean—" She waved her hand vaguely toward the young werewolf's shirt. "Do you blame her?"

The dark-haired androgynous woman looked down. "What's the matter with my shirt? It's casual Friday."

Annie snorted. "Babe, it's a tropical shirt. It doesn't exactly scream 'tough' now does it?"

"What? It was a tropical theme today, I can't help that. You should have seen last week's theme, Keller. I got to wear a bow tie and carry a screwdriver around all day. Totally epic if I do say so myself!"

By the time her girlfriend was done speaking, Annie was laughing so hard she was nearly in tears. "Oh my God, and you think that instills fear in anyone?" She grabbed another wing and waved it in Jesse's direction. "Think again my furry little nerd!"

Jesse ended the teasing by snatching the wing out of Annie's hand so fast the young woman didn't even see it. Annie blinked at her and proceeded to grab another wing off her plate. "Fair enough."

It wasn't long before the other two had arrived, along with another platter of appetizers and two more pitchers of beer. Their server set down the last pitcher and gazed at all the food on the table, and the five women. "Will there be more joining you?"

"Just me." The waitress was startled when a petite woman with a French accent came from behind her to take a seat next to the redhead.

Jesse looked up from dumping a large pile of wings on her plate. "Hi, Louve! Hope you're hungry." Then she gave the poor server a toothy grin and plowed into her plate of barbecued poultry goodness.

Always impatient and insanely curious, Annie prompted her old boss. "Now will you tell us?"

Jill looked up from her uncomplicated admiration of her new lover. She had been missing Louve more than she would have ever thought possible, considering they hadn't really known each other very long. Louve's hand was on her leg under the table, distracting the taller woman slightly. "Tell us what?"

Annie huffed. "She has some sort of good news but she wouldn't say until all of you got here."

Sarah jerked her head around to stare at her lover. "Did the guys find our asshole wolves?"

Keller stared at her for a second then burst out laughing. "Annie said those exact same words to me about thirty minutes ago. *Exact*."

"So?" Nearly twin-sounding voices answered her statement, prompting the rest of the table to laughter as well.

Jill chimed in. "You may as well give up, Keller. They have no idea just how alike they are. It's like they were twins, but born ten years apart."

The younger Colby stuck her tongue out at Jill. "You are so full of shit, Jilly!"

Jill pointed at Annie's plate. "What's on your plate right now?"

"Wings. Fucking duh, Red." Louve raised an eyebrow at the interaction between her lover, and the Colby siblings. It was a side of Jill she had not seen before, though she knew the three women were like family to each other.

"And?"

Annie sighed. "Sauce, like everyone else."

Jill kept pushing. "No, not like everyone else. You both have blue cheese, barbecue, and mustard. And you are *both* swiping your wings through all three sauces before each bite. Literally no one else does that." Keller had to concede that Jill had a point. Jesse made a face but continued plowing through her food.

Sarah took a swig of her beer. "What exactly is your point, Red?"

"My point is that you're both disgusting!"

Jesse snorted with laughter and choked on a piece of chicken. Annie was busy slapping her on the back when the waitress made the mistake of coming by their table again. She looked up at the assembled group just as Sarah was flipping off her ex, and Keller was recording it all on her new smart phone. Even Louve was smiling at their antics, a far cry from the somber mood she had been in as of late. The poor server didn't even speak, she simply circled off to another table. Keller eventually stopped the video and spoke to the rest of the table. "You're all a bunch of mad rockets! Now who wants to hear my good news?"

"It's about freakin' time!"

The table settled almost immediately and Keller looked over at her girlfriend. "Annie has agreed to extend your set to a full hour."

Sarah cocked her head in confusion, prompting another chuckle by Jill. "Why would she do that?"

Keller leaned back in her chair and locked her hands in front of her stomach. "Because I found a band that really wants to play with you for the festival."

Sarah looked skeptical. "Um, Keller, there's only one band that knows my stuff and right now they're on the road to Virginia. I think I'm gonna pass on this one."

"I wouldn't be too sure about that." Keller leaned forward and grabbed her phone from the table. She unlocked it and hit play on the music she had previously cued up. Everyone at the table could easily recognize the fact that it was one of Sarah's songs from her new album but no one knew who was playing it.

Sarah thought it sounded familiar. Suddenly a violin started to play, an instrument she had never before featured in her music. Shock came over her face. "I'll be a bucket of fuck! Is that who I think it is?" Keller nodded and smiled. "Okay, I'm in. I'm incredibly honored that they took the time to learn my songs. I thought they were touring?"

Annie squealed. "Oh my God! You're talking about Resurrection, aren't you?"

Keller nodded and everyone was startled at Jesse's immediately reaction. She slammed one hand onto the table causing the beers and wings to jump, the other fist pumped the air. "Yes! This means I'm off the hook!"

Sarah started laughing. "Yes, you're both off the hook if you want to be. Or you can still perform with us, it's up to you."

Jesse shook her head. "Nope, I'm good with just watching; thanks though!" She turned to Annie. "What about you babe, you still going to play?"

The younger Colby took another bite of overly-sauced wing and chewed thoughtfully. "I'm not really sure. I mean, a part of me is terrified, but another part of me wants to meet the challenge. You know?"

"So what's the harm in doing it?" Keller looked at the younger woman seriously. "If there's one thing I've learned over the years, it's that you're more likely to have fond memories of a 'what was I thinking' moment than a 'I wish I had' moment. Live a little, A."

Annie looked at Sarah. "And what do you think?"

"I think that you will be great, and I would be incredibly honored to share the stage with my little sister."

The younger woman was quiet but pleased when she answered her sister. "Thanks, Sarah. And I'll do it, provided there's room for me with the guest band. I mean, it's only one song."

The small group of friends ended up staying for a few hours before everyone headed off in separate directions. Sarah had walked to the restaurant from her studio, so she rode with Keller, which left Jill and Louve to say their private goodbyes. Louve had invited everyone out to the farmhouse for a Sunday brunch the day after Pride, so even if circumstances occurred that prevented them from meeting up the next day, they would still see each other before the weekend was out.

Instead of going back to the condo like Sarah expected, Keller took them farther downtown. "I thought we were heading home, I have plans for you."

Keller smiled. "Relax, my love. Grace invited us over to their hotel and I thought you might want to stop by to say hi. They got in about an hour ago, but figured it would cause a small riot if they met us out in public for happy hour."

Sarah nodded. "Good point." Then she slapped Keller's arm with the back of her hand. "I can't believe you've been keeping this from me!"

"So you were surprised then?"

A warm smile met Keller's words. "Of course I was surprised! And delighted, and amazed that I have such an awesome
and well-connected girlfriend." Sarah was silent for a few more
blocks then a thought popped into her head. "Oh crap, how are
we going to rehearse? We should at least play through a few
times together so we can get a feel for each other. The impromptu
jam session in our condo months ago doesn't count."

Keller gave her a very self-satisfied smile. "Ah, well being
the consummate planner that I am, I arranged for a few hours of
studio time tomorrow morning. So you have all the space you
need between ten and noon. And since you don't perform until
three; that gives you plenty of time to chill before you all go on."

"Studio Seven?" Keller nodded and Sarah felt an entirely new
appreciation for the woman she shared her life with. "You really
are kind of amazing, you know that?" The singer had her head
cocked to the side as she watched Keller maneuver the streets
during the tail end of rush hour traffic. The look in her eyes was
full of a love that Sarah never thought she'd feel for another person. Yet here she was. Keller glanced her way and returned the
look. Yes, here they were.

After meeting up with the members of Resurrection at their
hotel, they all opted for a late dinner in the restaurant downstairs
rather than have the celebrities brave the Columbus nightlife.
Before they bid the band goodbye, Sarah gave each person a big
hug and thanked them for all the work they had done in prepara-
tion to play with her at the festival. Then they bid farewell until
the next morning.

When the two women walked into the condo they were met
by an anxious husky. After Duke was fed, Keller volunteered to
take him out to wee in the park behind the condo. Once she was
out the door, Sarah put on some music and started filling the
Jacuzzi. Candles were next followed by a bottle of bubbly on ice.
As soon as Keller re-entered with Duke, she was met by Sarah.
Keller removed the dog's leash and harness and hung them both
by the door and watched her lover approach. Sarah was wearing
nothing but a silk robe and handed her a glass of champagne and
Keller raised an eyebrow. "I thought you'd want to relax this evening and just chill since tomorrow is going to be so hectic."

Sarah grabbed her hand and tugged her toward their bedroom. "This is how I relax, now come on."

Keller smiled. "What's with the bath? Is one of us dirty?"

Sarah gave her a heated look. "Only my thoughts, love."
Before Keller could come up with a retort, the robe dropped into a

puddle of silk on the floor. Sarah smiled and reached across the short distance between them to close Keller's mouth. "Guess what I'm going to do?"

Keller wet her lips, wearing hunger on her face like a veil. "What?"

"I'm going to give you a preview of what you can expect tomorrow after my show." Before Keller could answer her, Sarah grabbed her hand and led her to the bathroom. Once Keller matched her nudity, Sarah got into the tub and pointed at the water between her legs. "Come on hot stuff, let me show you how much I appreciate everything you've done." It took mere seconds for Keller to sink into the tub in front of Sarah. Her exhale turned into a light moan as her body dropped into the steaming hot water. Sarah smiled unseen behind her and lathered her hands with body wash from the shelf next to the tub.

"Now relax and let me love you." Slippery hands easily traced along Keller's skin. She kept her touch relaxing, skirting all the places Keller wanted her most. She continued the gently caressing wash for quite a while until she could feel Keller's frustration practically radiating from the body in front of her. Eventually Sarah whispered in her ear. "Can you feel me?"

"Yes." Keller sighed.

In the next breath, Sarah let down her shield and opened herself fully to Keller's mind. "What about now?" She brought her hands up and cupped Keller's small breasts, rolling her nipples between thumbs and forefingers. Keller's back arched into Sarah's touch and the abrupt movement caused the water to slosh precariously. She chuckled. "Careful lover, we don't want to make a mess now." Using her longer legs, she draped them over the top of Keller's, holding her down. At the same time Sarah grabbed her around the waist with her left arm, pulling them tightly together. When the fingers of her right hand began moving down Keller's body, the blonde gripped Sarah's left wrist tightly. As soon as Sarah slid her fingers through Keller's slippery folds, she felt her lover tense then start to writhe. She simply tightened her grip to keep the other woman from moving around too much.

Keller's head was leaning back against Sarah's shoulder, her neck smooth and inviting. With strokes that took her fingers down the length of Keller's sex, then back up to circle around her clit, Sarah knew that Keller wouldn't last long. They were linked now and as Keller's breathing increased, so too did Sarah's. Keller, typically a quiet lover, loudly moaned. Even if she couldn't feel what Keller was feeling through their bond, Sarah would have taken that to mean her lover was rapidly approaching orgasm. In a perfectly timed mental and physical motion, Sarah sank her teeth into Keller's skin at the same time she entered the smaller woman with her aura. Five seconds later it all became too much and Keller pulled her over the edge into ecstasy.

Sarah released her grip on Keller's waist and moved her legs as they both relaxed back into the tub. They stayed there until their breathing slowed and the water began to cool. The women were basking in the intense afterglow that always seemed to follow the feeding/aura probe/orgasm combination. Their silence was eventually broken by a deep breath and long exhale from Keller. "I think that it just may be your turn now."

Sarah laughed at the smaller woman's languid voice. "I came with you."

Keller shifted so her ass pressed firmly into Sarah's crotch and she smirked when the woman behind her gave a little gasp. "I'm aware that you came, but I also know it's different from when I actually touch you. You're throbbing right now, aren't you?"

Sarah bit her bottom lip and ground herself against her girlfriend's ass. "I never said I was opposed." Keller laughed and abruptly sat forward, breaking the contact between them. Sarah growled at her. "Tease!"

Keller stood and grabbed a towel hanging nearby. "No, slowly and torturously washing my body for nearly a half hour while skipping all the good spots is a tease." She dried herself then held the towel in front of her when she was done. "I'm promising to fuck you with your favorite toy until you pass out. No teasing, just fucking. Interested?" She dropped the towel, and before Sarah could answer, disappeared through the doorway back into the bedroom. The singer was out of the tub and drying herself in seconds.

As soon as she crossed the threshold into the bedroom, she was stopped in her tracks by the sight of her soul mate standing near the bed in nothing but an oversized strap-on. The large pink toy jutted out from her hips obscenely. It was big enough that the singer knew had she not been a fast-healing vampire, she would be sore the next day. But now that she was infected, indulging in her size-queen tendencies with no aftereffects was just another perk. She noticed the lube on the nightstand and smiled. Healing or no healing ability, they weren't foolish. Another thing that drew her attention was a palm size bug-looking toy with dangling elastic straps.

She walked toward Keller and tried to figure out what the thing was. "That's new."

Keller smiled and held it out to her. "You like it?"

Sarah took it from her and investigated the item. There was a cord with a power box connected to it but she still couldn't figure it out. "I don't know, what is it?"

"That, my love, is a butterfly." She pointed to identical power box that was tucked into the waist strap of her harness, the cord disappearing underneath to places unseen. "And we're going to play a little game called 'Loser Comes First.' Are you ready?"

Sarah swallowed, suddenly understanding the purpose of the butterfly. She turned the wheel on the power box and the rubbery pink insect came to life. She shook her head and grinned at her lover. "I'm so going to lose this game, and I'm going to love every minute of it! Now help me put it on."

Keller laughed and helped sort out the tangle of thin elastic straps that would secure it to Sarah's waist and upper thighs. Once the toy was nestled in place, she gave the wheel an experimental flick. The sudden vibration against her clit made her jump and Keller laughed again. "Better dial it down, love, we don't want ya' to become Speedy McRacer again."

Sarah turned it off completely and clipped the hook on the back of the power box onto the elastic waistband. "You're so funny, you never let me live that down." She looked at the toy strapped to her lover, then over at the bed. "So how do you want to do this?"

Keller gave her a smoldering look. "I want you on your knees. And—" She pointed at the taller woman. "No cheating. Keep your shields up, keep your aura tucked away inside your own body. This one's going to be all physical."

Sarah cursed under her breath. "I don't even know if I can keep my shields up during sex anymore."

"Think of it as practice then. You need to be able to keep your shields intact no matter what the distraction." Sarah sighed and nodded and both women crawled up on the king size bed. Keller struggled a bit because the big toy kept getting in her way. "Jesus Jenny but I don't know how you take this monster. It's hard enough just to move around in it. I have short legs you know!"

Sarah was upright on her knees, directly in front of Keller. She turned her head and looked over her shoulder at the short woman. In a voice that had lowered with anticipation, she licked her lips and spoke. "Are you at least going to kiss me first?

Keller sorted herself out and with her left hand, she grabbed the bottle from the night stand and lubed the toy. With her clean right hand, she turned on her vibrator and then turned on Sarah's. Sarah's eyes widened in surprise and her breathing immediately picked up. "What's the matter, still wound up from earlier?" With the two lubed fingers from her left hand, she slowly penetrated Sarah's depths, forcing the tall woman onto all fours.

Sarah's eyes fluttered shut and she nodded, then she opened them again and stared back over her shoulder into Keller's blue eyes. "No kiss?"

Keller withdrew her fingers and positioned the toy at Sarah's entrance. Then she gave her lover a mischievous smile and responded with one easy word. "No." Before Sarah could say anything else Keller thrust her hips forward and slid the strap-on all the way in. She immediately set up a moderate rhythm, rolling her hips with each thrust.

"Holyshitjesus, oh God!"

Keller could feel a little trickle from her lover so she called out to her. "Shields, Sarah!"

Sarah cursed and her breathing grew ragged once again, but she managed to tighten her shields. Despite the lube and underlying arousal from earlier, it took her a few minutes to get used to the sheer size of the dildo. She managed to be both loose and tight. Keller eventually increased the strength of her thrusts, which caused the soft rubber tip of the toy to lightly bump Sarah's cervix. A lot of women didn't like it that deep, but Sarah wasn't one of them. She started moaning and clawing at the bedspread below her hands. Sarah could feel every single inch moving in and out of her as she spiraled higher and higher.

Despite the coolness with which she proposed the game, Keller was rapidly approaching her limit. She knew she wouldn't last much longer between the pounding of the strap-on between her legs and the vibration from the butterfly. And without cheating by using her powers, she was left with only her physical skills. She started changing up her rhythm, shallow then deep, fast then slow. Then when Sarah seemed to relax a bit, she began thrusting fast and deep. Very fast. The sound of sweat-covered bodies slapping together at a rapid pace was easily drown out by the woman on her hands and knees. Sarah was yelling unintelligible words and phrases, whatever came to mind as she was fucked senselessly by her lover. Keller felt it and knew she wouldn't last any longer. She cursed and cried out as orgasm took control of her body. "Fucking hell!"

Hearing her lover coming was all it took for Sarah to follow. Her screams were primal and raw and they continued for the length of the unusually long orgasm. Keller eventually shuddered to a stop and quickly turned off the vibrator that was creating havoc with her overly sensitized clit. Sarah gave a final shudder and promptly collapsed on the bed below her. Keller quickly withdrew the toy and shut off Sarah's butterfly as well. Then, with all the grace of a land-bound walrus, she collapsed onto her back next to her unconscious lover. She noted the rips in the sheets next to Sarah's hands and shook her head with a smile. Their sheets didn't seem to last much longer than Sarah's underwear but she wasn't going to complain. She had the harness and vibrator removed before Sarah finally came around. When the singer was fully aware, their eyes met and Keller smiled.

Sarah returned the smile and hoarsely added two words. "Promise fulfilled."

Chapter Eleven

THE NEXT DAY dawned beautiful and clear, and weather reports predicted the temperature would be in the upper eighties. Keller told Sarah that she wouldn't have to worry about being drained by the sun because she would be gaining an enormous amount of energy from the crowd for the hour that she was scheduled to perform. The sun would actually help because it would drain enough that Sarah wouldn't feel overloaded after her performance. They just had to be careful the rest of time they were out in the sun. The two vampire members of Resurrection would be taking the same precautions.

Practice went very well. The two hours that the five musicians spent going over Sarah's music practically flew by. Sarah was impressed with the way Grace, Colton, Corentine, and Mozzie had taken the time to learn her music, on top of their own busy tour schedule. But then, they had all be doing music in some shape or form for a very long time. They made regular seasoned professions look like amateurs. By the time the session came to an end, they had created a set list that included both new and old songs by Sarah, as well as a few songs by Resurrection. They even chose two other cover songs by another popular band. They were able to run through everything at least once, twice for a few of the trickier ones. All in all, Sarah felt pretty good about her upcoming performance. Standing in the lobby of the studio, she looked at the four members of her guest band. "So how do you want to do this today?

Colton look at her quizzically. "Do wut, luv?"

"How do you want me to introduce you? I mean, are you here on the sly? Do you want your presence in Columbus kept on the down low, or can I introduce you as Resurrection? If you want to be anonymous, I can do that."

Mozzie spoke up in his quiet accented English. "Won't you get more notoriety if you play with a famous band?"

His wife chastised him. "Mozzie! Do not assume that everyone is out to ride our coattails."

He inclined his head toward Sarah. "My apologies, Miss Colby. I did not mean to imply you were another of the many leaches we meet in this business."

Sarah laughed. "Please call me Sarah. And no, I don't need

the notoriety. I do well enough with my music instruction. And truthfully, I'm only playing this gig as a favor to Annie. Otherwise I probably wouldn't have volunteered, given our current circumstances right now."

Grace looked at her in concern. "Circumstances?"

This prompted Keller to finally speak up. "We have some loose wolves in the city. They have been robbing and killing in the surrounding region. Of course, the police have not put together wild 'dog' attacks and the string of burglaries that are currently plaguing metro Columbus. The worst of it is they have been targeting our people specifically. They attacked and brutalized Sarah's best friend, Jill, and have been threatening Annie."

The lead singer of Resurrection spun her gaze toward Sarah. "Your friend, is she okay?"

Sarah sighed and ran a hand through her hair. "She's fine now, at least physically. Keller was forced to infect her minutes after discovering her body. But they tortured her. She's a strong woman, but I think it'll take a while for her to get beyond everything."

Keller noticed another band coming in to the studio so she got everyone's attention. "Why don't we take this back to our condo? We can order lunch and further discuss what's been happening and what you want to do on the stage today."

Colton perked up at the mention of lunch. "That is a grand idea, I'm famished!"

"When aren't you hungry, Ra-ta-tat?" Everyone laughed at Grace's comments. "Though I suppose I could eat something too. Do you have a good Thai place around here?"

Colton snorted. "Rubbish! S'all she ever wants when we're in London!"

Keller burst out laughing and Sarah gave Grace a big smile. "*Do* we? I'm sure we can get your fix!"

Over the next hour and a half the members of Resurrection had amazing takeout from Thai Guys, were filled in on all the issues involving the rogue werewolves, and decided on a plan for taking the stage with Sarah. When they left Keller and Sarah's condo, they promised to meet back up with them at the festival around two-thirty. After they left, Sarah grabbed a bottle of water from the fridge and collapsed on the couch next to Duke. He wagged his tail briefly but otherwise didn't acknowledge her presence. She looked up when Keller joined her. "Well, what do you think of our plan?"

Keller bumped her shoulder against the singer's. "I think it will be hilarious. Especially since you're not telling Annie. Hope-fully they can get everything they need in time."

"Oh, the place I sent them is top notch. They should be able to find everything they need in that store, or the one next to it. This is gonna be great!"

Keller shot her a grin. "You're so sure of yourself! So what do you want to do now, rock star?"

Sarah leaned forward to set her bottle on the coffee table. She illuminated the screen of her phone to check the time then promptly turned and straddled Keller's lap. "I can think of a few things." Duke merely made a chuffing noise and moved off the couch to his dog bed.

SARAH AND KELLER arrived at the Metro Park earlier than intended after giving the word "quickie" new meaning. They walked through the festival, having already dropped off her instruments near the stage. Bruce was there organizing things, but they didn't see Annie and Jesse yet. Duke paced next to Keller, his lead firmly in hand in the busy park. The husky loved people and was a very social dog, so he was excitedly sniffing and wagging at every person he met. They made sure to circle back to the vendors near the stage show in anticipation of meet-ing up with Sarah's four temporary bandmates. However, they still hadn't seen them and Sarah was beginning to worry. Keller tried to reassure her. "It'll be fine, love. They'll be here, they probably just got hung up in traffic."

Sarah dropped into a crouch to pet Duke, her nerves forcing her to take solace in her faithful companion. While she was down on his level, she took the opportunity to fill his portable bowl from her water bottle so he could get a drink. "But wouldn't they have called if that were the case?"

"Hey! Where have you two been? And where is your band?" Both women looked up and saw Annie striding toward them with Jesse trailing behind her.

Sarah gave her a look. "I don't go on for another twenty min-utes, so chill."

The younger Colby sister looked around. "And where is Grace, Colton, Corentine and Mozzie?"

Keller tried to reassure the overworked Pride festival stage manager. "Easy A, they'll be here. I promise."

"Major nerves, beware!" The comment was said in the faint-est of whispers by Jesse, unheard by Annie, but easily picked up by Sarah and Keller. The two older women nodded to show that they heard her, but it wasn't anything other than what Sarah was already expecting. She knew her sister well.

Sarah leaned over and gave Keller a kiss before taking Annie's hand in her own. "Come on, let's go make sure the guitar I loaned you is in tune."

When they were gone, Jesse turned to Keller. "So where is Resurrection anyway?"

Keller shrugged. "They're not here yet, at least I don't think they are." When Jesse raised a questioning eyebrow, she laughed and filled the younger woman in. "So here is the plan..." When she finished, both Jesse's eyebrows were up and her mouth was open.

"Oh my God, she's going to kill you both! She's already nervous about being on the stage in front of hundreds of people!"

Keller shrugged and hefted the two camp chair bags higher onto her shoulder. "She'll be fine. Now come on, I want to set these up where I have a good view but won't be too loud for Duke."

At five minutes to three, Annie was really starting to freak out. "You said they'd be here! Didn't you practice with them this morning? Did they give any indication that they might have to bail?"

Sarah took a deep breath and used her power to send calming emotions to her sister. Truthfully though, she was starting to worry as well. "Listen, it's going to be all right. Let's go up on stage and do one of the easy songs that we've been practicing together to kill some time. After that I'll just play by myself for a bit until they show up. Then you'll come back up when I play the song you and Jesse were practicing, okay?" The younger woman swallowed and gave her a nod. Sarah handed Annie her guitar and picked up her own, signaling to Bruce that they were ready.

His voice carried well through the large speakers that were facing the crowd. "Many of you know our next singer. Columbus born and bred, she's traveled the country living the dream. Currently she gives private music lessons to the fine folks of our city. Please welcome the very first performer for our Sip and Chug series, Sarah Colby!" Applause chased the sisters up the steps to the stage. They plugged in and the sound guy hit the switches to bring the microphones and instruments live.

Sarah stood in the center of the stage and looked out over the gathered crowd, Annie a little to the side and behind her. "Hi!" The crowd laughed and said "hi" back. "Some of you may know me, I play a few local gigs here and there. You may recognize me from my occasional stint with The Standalones." She paused when the mention of her sometimes band garnered applause and wolf whistles. "Sadly, they are playing in Virginia today so I brought my sister. You may recognize her as the assistant manager in charge of the Voodoo Pony, and the very same miracle worker who put this little show together today. You see, she's responsible for me being on this stage, and I may have blackmailed her into joining me." She leaned toward the crowd conspiratorially and whispered into the microphone. "She's nervous." The crowd laughed again. "Say hello to the nice people, Annie."

Annie smiled and shook her head at her sister's antics. "You're such a jerk, Sarah!" This prompted more laughter from the crowd. "Anyway, my name is Annie Colby and I don't know about you, but I'm ready for some music! You with me?" More cheers from the crowd caused her to hit a few chords on her guitar.

Sarah thought she saw someone familiar in the crowd and raised her hand, turning toward Annie. "Wait, wait, where's our band?"

Annie looked back in disbelief. "What do you mean 'where's our band?' You were supposed to get the band!"

"But I thought you were going to set it up? You're the one who books all the bands for the club!"

Annie's grumbling was picked up by the sensitive microphone. "I'm so going to kill you."

Sarah turned back to the crowd. "All right, all right, no need for that. We'll just have to find someone, yeah?" She shaded the sun from her eyes with her hand and scanned the growing crowd of people. "Let's see, we need a drummer. Anyone?"

The crowd was silent. Then people turned when short guy with bad surfer dude blond hair and a Hawaiian shirt raised his hand. "Like bro, I totally play. I could probably help you out."

Annie groaned and covered her eyes as Sarah waved the man toward the stage steps. "Well get up here then! What's your name, drummer?"

"Dude, you can just call me Banger."

Annie looked at the man as he walked toward her on the stage. "Banger?"

"Yeah man, cuz I can go like all nig—"

He was interrupted by Sarah. "Okay, thanks, Banger. Go ahead and have a seat behind the drums while we find the rest.

Now we need someone who plays the piano. Anyone?" A tall woman with long flowing hair stepped forward in a blouse and hippie skirt. Sarah looked at her skeptically, trying to see if it was a disguise or if she was setting herself up for failure. She recognized the drummer dude as Colton in drag, but if the hippie chick was Mozzie then he had clearly shaved his chin strap and was amazing looking as a woman. She motioned for the tall hippie to come onto the stage. "What's your name, hon?"

It was a quiet feminine voice that answered. "Moonbeam. And I can play all the songs from Tetris." There was a faint accent and Sarah knew she was saved.

"Okay, that's perfect. Go over by the keyboard then while we find a few more people." She looked around and noticed an odd couple by one of the large speakers. "You there, by the speakers! What are you, Danny and Sandy? Do you two play anything?"

The guy in the black t-shirt and jeans with slicked back dark hair nodded. He sounded like he was from Brooklyn. "Yeah, I can sing a little." He pointed a thumb at his similarly dressed companion. "And she's real good with her hands, ain't ya, babe?" The dirty blond merely nodded and smiled.

Sarah cheered. "Woo, sold! All right, get up here you crazy kids!" By that point the crowd had grown even larger and they had no clue what was going on. All the stage antics had taken up six minutes of time. Normally six minutes would be enough to chase people away if there was no music happening but the audience was intrigued. Once the band members were situated at their instruments Sarah once again addressed the crowd. "How about we start with something that everyone knows, just to warm them up." She looked around at crazy assembly of musicians. "Do you all know 'Bite Like You Mean It' by Resurrection?"

Banger responded immediately. "Bro, that band's nothing but a bunch of hacks!" Colton's words prompted a massive amount of booing from the crowd.

Sarah laughed. "I think the crowd disagrees with you there, *bro*. So let's give them what they want." Banger/Colton shrugged and Annie looked as if she was going to vomit on the stage. "All right, let's do this Columbus! Sing along if you know it!"

The song started with a driving beat and deep notes on the keyboard. Sudden bass notes jumped in and Sarah could see that Sandy, aka Corentine, had found her stashed instruments. At just the right moment, Sarah started to sing. Her backup chorus was none other than Annie and the regular singers of Resurrection. The song "Bite Like You Mean It" rolled off her lips like she had written it herself. Eventually the blood-pumping song came to the end and the crowd went wild. When they settled Sarah spoke again.

"Well that went better than expected, didn't it?" She shuffled a little bit, then looked back out into the sea of people. "Actually, I have a confession to make. These aren't random people behind me. They are a real band that's helping me out today. And with that, let's move on to one of my new songs. You can find it on my brand new album, which will be for sale at the Voodoo Pony booth, or you can download it online. See me after the show if you want my signature!" They played two more songs of Sarah's, one old and one new, before she stopped to engage the crowd again. "So, why don't I introduce my mystery band? How many of you want to know who's sharing the stage with me? They're phenomenal, right?" She waved Annie back onto the stage, who had left after the first song.

The crowd roared their approval. Annie looked over at her and smiled. "Well, sis, I think they want to know so you better tell them before there's a riot."

"All right, why don't I start with the back? Broseph, the surfer dude, can you tell the crowd who you are?"

Colton stood up and removed the blonde wig, tossing it to the ground. She ran hand through her hair to straighten the dark Mohawk then began unbuttoning the offensive shirt. Underneath she wore her trademark black tank top. She stood with drumsticks held high over her head. "Gawdon Bennet! Good afternoon. OKAY? 'A 're ya? M'name's Colton Shep and it's a pleasure!"

A few people in the crowd screamed, starting to catch on, but louder yet was Annie's voice over the mic. "Oh my God!" Sarah chuckled and pointed at the hippie chick on the keyboard. Mozzie doffed the wig and glasses and removed the blouse to reveal a muscular chest that was surprisingly smooth.

"*Guten Tag*. My name is Mozzie and the pleasure is mine as well." He gestured down at the long flowy paisley skirt. "If you don't mind, I will keep the skirt on since I didn't bring with me any short pants. It is surprisingly comfortable."

Sarah gave him a thumbs-up and a grin. "Hey, you be you man. I'm not going to judge." She turned to the last two random women who had graced the stage earlier. "And you two are?"

Corentine smiled and removed her curly dishwater blonde wig as well, tossing it to the side. Her long hair was pulled back into tight French braid. "My name is Corentine, and the man in the long skirt is my husband. He is quite the catch, no?" All the men in the crowd began hooting in agreement about the handsome man on the stage.

And lastly, Grace stepped forward. She pulled off the wig and underneath her own dark hair was slicked back away from her face. She put on the aviator sunglasses that had been hooked to the front of her shirt and gave herself a little shake. "As you may have guess already, I'm Grace Cadence and this is my band Resurrection! And I have a request for Sarah. I would like the next song to be 'Blood of My Blood.' I know for a fact that we have all been looking forward to playing it on stage with you ever since we started practicing your songs a month ago."

Sarah laughed and looked at the crowd. "Who can say no to that, right? Okay, let's do this, take it away, Colton!" The song started like thunder with a driving drum beat that set the tone for the rest of the set. The crowd was pumped and wanted to go higher, so the musicians on the stage gave them what they deserved. Even with the bright sun shining down, Sarah still felt almost light-headed from the energy she was siphoning off the crowd. She looked down at her lover who was seated off to the side and opened her shields to her. She sent Keller some of her energy and what she got back was a surprised wash of pleasure and excitement, and a lot of love.

Eventually their time came to an end and they had to leave the stage, much to the crowd's displeasure. Sarah noticed the anxious faces on the band that was scheduled to perform after her. She knew the band; it was the one that played opposite Fridays from her for that first Sip and Chug engagement. Mary's Angels was an amazing group but she could understand how intimidating it would be to follow after a band like Resurrection, so she shot confidence and calm to each member of the band and waved Bruce off when he was going to come on and introduce them. "I know you want to hear more, but believe me, you're not going to want to miss the band that's up next. I just want to say that today is very important to all of us. It's about coming together to acknowledge the ongoing fight for the freedoms that are still missing from the community. It's about celebrating the freedoms that we have won. And more importantly, it's about coming together and seeing that you have family out there, wherever you go. We are all family and we know the struggle. We're here for you. Now please give a huge welcome to a band that's going to be huge themselves, Mary's Angels!"

The rest of the afternoon flew by for the group of people with *other* blood. Jill eventually arrived after spending the day at work. Louve followed an hour later, just in time to see the second performance of her troupe members. Her booth had games set up to win free passes into Cirque du Loup, as well as coupons for free drinks and different swag. The Merge, Club Diversity, and a few other bars, had similar booths at the festival. The Merge even had a dunk tank set up and the proceeds were to be split between the local LGBT resource clinic and the local no-kill animal shelter.

Annie was one of the employees who got roped into volunteering for that one. The band had finished signing albums and autographs, and people at the festival were being surprisingly cool about letting the band members of Resurrection walk around unmolested. They gathered near the dunk tank and Annie began removing her shorts and tank top. Underneath she was wearing s simple black bikini, which displayed all her best assets as she maneuvered her way into the tank and perched precariously on the seat. Jesse was transfixed. The nerdy werewolf looked at Keller. "Please tell me you have some cash on you because this girl is totally getting dunked!"

Keller smirked at Annie's notoriously un-athletic girlfriend. "Do you even know how to throw a ball?"

Annie snorted and called out. "She knows how to fetch one! Bring it on, babe!" When Keller and Sarah snickered, she gave them an evil eye as well. "I'm not afraid of any of you here. Give it your best shot, losers!" Despite the motivation of seeing her girlfriend wet, Jesse spent twenty dollars proving just how bad she was at throwing a softball. Sarah and Keller watched as many people tried to sink the mouthy Colby sister. She catcalled, she jeered, she teased and taunted all her friends and bar patrons that walked up. After twenty minutes of her thirty minute volunteer stint, she was still sitting dry on the seat and Sarah was tempted to just go push the bullseye to make her shut up.

"What, are you all giving up already? Come on, keep trying! This is for a good cause." Annie's look of bravado quickly turned to one of dismay when Jill and Louve walked up.

Sarah pointed at Annie and cracked up laughing. "Oh, you're in for it now!" She called out to her ex. "Hey Jill, Annie's been talking about how gingers don't have souls again. You should show her how the dunk tank works, she's looking a little dry in there."

The younger Colby immediately called out to Julie, one of the lead bartenders at The Merge. She was the one who was selling the balls. "No matter how much she offers, do not give that soulless redhead a ball!"

Jill looked at Julie. "Where is the money going again?"

Julie smirked. "Rainbow Resources and Bailey's Sanctuary."

Jill held up two twenty-dollar bills. "I'd like twenty balls please."

The bartender tried to protest. "But it's only a dollar a ball!"

"Consider the rest part of my donation then."

Louve looked at Keller, then Sarah. "I do not understand, why does *ta soeur* seem so upset? This is for charity, no?"

Keller shifted her gaze to Sarah as well. "Yes, why is she so upset? Does Jill play sports?"

Sarah smiled. "Jill played softball all through high school and got a full-ride softball scholarship for college."

Louve blinked. "Oh."

Sarah added four more words. "She was a pitcher."

Keller nodded in understanding. "Ohhhh."

Other people in the area had recognized Jill and more of a crowd started to gather. Colton and Grace had even wandered back and were interested in seeing Annie drop into the tank. For the sake of efficiency, Julie brought a five-gallon pail full of balls out to the throwing line. Jill loosened up her arm a bit before picking up the first ball. "You're lucky, kid, I'm pretty rusty so I probably won't make half of these."

Annie was hunched in on herself with spread fingers over her eyes, waiting on the inevitable. When the first pitch rocketed by the bullseye and thudded against the canvas backdrop, she gave a little squeak. The second one prompted a heartfelt single word. "Shit!" The watchers all laughed. When the third ball thundered past she sat up straight and blew a sigh of relief. "Haha, Red, looks like it's more than just your hair that's rust—" She never finished her sentence as the fourth ball hit the bullseye with a muffled clang and dropped her into the water. The tank below the water level was made of some sort of clear material so all the spectators were treated to the view of her surprised face amid a flurry of bubbles. And a middle finger pointed up toward the sky, aimed directly at Jill.

The veterinarian chuckled and waited patiently for Julie to reset the bench and bullseye paddle. Then, despite Annie's begging and pleading between dunks, the redhead without a soul proceeded to sink her the next fifteen throws in a row. She had one ball left when Annie's replacement arrived. The younger Colby wasted no time scrambling out of the tank so The Merge's new manager Lissa could take her place. Jill called out to Annie as the younger woman was swaddled in a large beach towel by her girlfriend. "You're lucky, kid!" Annie stuck out her tongue at the veterinarian and looked very much like a drowned rat.

Keller quickly handed Duke's leash to Sarah and before Jill could wind up on her last ball, she stopped her with an outstretched hand. "Do you mind if I take the last one?"

Jill smiled and handed it to Keller. Anyone watching the dunk tank would have seen Lissa sigh with relief. It was short-lived. Keller didn't throw the blistering underhand fast pitch that Jill had been using. Instead, hers was just an old-fashioned overhand throw with a good amount of heat. Her aim was dead on. When Lissa came back up sputtering, Keller called out to her with good humor. "Welcome to The Merge family, Lissa, and good luck!" The new manager just shook her head and smiled before crawling back onto the reset bench. Their group eventually made their way back to the stage in time to catch the end of Shaker Station's performance. When they were finished, the stage would have an hour break to tear down all the music equipment, then the people running the drag show would take over. Bruce was all set to handle the teardown and truck so Annie was free to leave with the rest of the group.

Initially they were planning on going to The Merge after leaving the festival, but everyone decided that might not be a good idea with their surprise guests in town for the night. Jill offered up her house and backyard with its massive outdoor grill, and the group unanimously decided it was a great day for a barbecue. No one wanted to fight the crowds at the local restaurants on a Saturday night, especially with a famous band in tow. Keller asked Louve to invite Raph, Ranier, and Romaric over to join them and the evening turned into an impromptu party. Eventually dinner was completed and devoured and a bonfire was lit. The musicians brought out their instruments and the entire group had an evening of relaxing fun. At the end of the night, everyone said their goodbyes to the Resurrection band members. It was the end of their tour and they would be flying out the next day. They thanked Louve for her invite to brunch but had to decline so they wouldn't miss their flight back to London. Louve stayed the night at Jill's house with plans to leave early the next morning to set everything up at the farmhouse. And Sarah and Keller made their way back to the condo with a husky that was exhausted after his day of excitement.

THE VERY NEXT day found everyone gathered at Louve's

farmhouse once again. She had a full spread of food for brunch and everyone was gathered around the large table in her kitchen. Since her bar was shut down for some roof repairs, she had given the entire troupe the next five days off. They would return by Friday of the coming week, in time to get some practice in before they were to perform on Cirque Samedi. Otherwise known as Circus Saturday, which was the only day the circus actually performed. All other days of the week the Cirque du Loup was an ordinary nightclub. Only a few stayed behind to keep watch for the wolves who had betrayed the troupe. Beale and Bastien, the fire-breathing twins, were patrolling the park on the other side of the lake. And Joseph, one of the wolves who was present the day Jesse was infected, was patrolling the woods behind the farmhouse.

Jill looked at the Frenchwoman and smiled. "So what you're saying is you have a few days free? What a coincidence, I have the next few days off as well."

Annie groaned. "Oh no, you guys are so loud!"

Louve pointed at her with a smirk. "Non, you are the one who is loud, *ma petit demon*. We are merely average for two people having the 'little deaths.' I cannot count how many times I heard you call out to your 'Furry Nerd' in passion. It was very distracting."

Both Annie and Jesse's faces turned bright red and Annie covered her face. "Oh my God, I can't believe you just said that."

Jill snickered. "I believe you mentioned God a few times as well."

"Shut up, Jilly!" Annie threw an olive from her Bloody Mary at her and the entire table erupted in laughter.

The laughter cut off abruptly as one of the twins burst through the French doors a few feet from the large table. He was panting, having run more than five miles from the opposite side of Alum Creek Lake. Louve stood quickly, knocking her chair to the ground behind her. *"Bastien, que s'est-il passé?"*

He bent over, panting, and his words came out in gasps. *"Nous avons trouvé Alain!"*

"Shit!" Keller and the rest of the French speakers stood immediately. The others followed a little slower, at least understanding the word, "Alain." Keller looked at Louve. "He is very powerful, we have to be careful."

Louve nodded. "You are right, mon ami. This could also be a trap, he is very intelligent." She turned back to Bastien. "Did you see Marcel or Marie as well?"

He shook his head. "Non."

"Okay, we should not have everyone go to him with the other two still missing. Raph, you and your sons need to stay in case Marcel shows up. I, Louve, and Sarah can go—" Keller was cut off by Sarah.

"I'm staying with Annie."

Keller met her eyes for a few seconds before nodding. "Okay, we'll take Jill and Bastien." She looked back at Louve. "Do you need to change, or can you keep up?"

Louve grimaced at the thought of changing in front of her lover. She had not wanted to do it yet for fear of seeing Jill's face respond with disgust. She knew her ange de feu still struggled with dreams of monstrous beasts. She looked at Jill then, trying to gauge the taller woman's reaction. "Êtes-vous *d'accord avec cela , mon chéri?*" Jill nodded that she was all right with it and Louve turned her gaze toward Keller. "If we are keeping up with the vampires, I shall surely have to change." She called out to her employee. "Bastien, you should drink some water and do the same. The run will be much easier on you if we are in half-wolf form. I shall just pray that no one sees us before we can change back."

"Oui, Louve." He grabbed the pitcher of water from the table and drank straight from the large vessel.

Once Louve and Bastien had changed, they all went outside. However, their leave-taking was interrupted by Joseph. He was in half-beast form as well but he was covered in various injuries, including wicked looking claw marks across his ribs. "Louve, Marcel is in the woods behind the house. He says that if we let him have the human, he will leave the rest of us alone."

Sarah snarled. "No fucking way!"

Raph looked at her. "No worries, friend, we will handle him."

Keller looked around. "If we're set, let's go!" Keller, Louve, Bastien, and Jill took off and were out of sight in a matter of seconds.

Sarah looked at Raphael with concern. "If you need help, just yell. I'll hear you."

Raph nodded and Ranier gave her a grateful look. He touched her shoulder on the way by. "Thanks, Sarah."

She nodded back to him then they too were gone, speeding away on foot. The injured Joseph following at a slightly slower pace. Annie stood next to Jesse and hugged herself. Sarah saw her sister shiver, despite the fact that it was nearly noon and over eighty degrees outside. "Come on you two, let's go sit up on the porch where we have a good view. No one has seen Marie yet and I don't trust her." They moved up and around the porch until they had the best view of the tree line. Jesse and Annie took chairs in front of the large picture window and Sarah stayed standing near the railing. Sarah hated waiting. And she hated worrying about Keller and Jill, and all their new friends. But there was no way she was going to let someone else watch Annie. Before she could dwell any further, both people with *other* blood heard a scream come from the woods where Raph and his sons had disappeared. Then Sarah heard her name. She was torn until she heard her name again followed by another scream.

Jesse stood and looked at her. "Sarah? Do you want me to go?"

Annie, not hearing any of it, stood in a panic. "What? Go where? What are you talking about?"

Sarah looked at her younger sister and frowned. "There is screaming in the woods and they are calling for me. I have to go. They wouldn't call if they didn't really need me."

Annie looked like she was going to cry. "I'm scared, Sarah."

Sarah stepped close and gave her a hug. "I know A, but don't worry. It will all be over soon. Hopefully I'll only be gone a few minutes."

"Okay. Annie nodded and stepped back and Jessie was suddenly there wrapping her in an embrace.

"Sarah, go. I'll take care of her, and I'll yell if there's a problem." Jesse nodded toward the woods as they heard another hoarse yell.

Sarah took off. The trees were a blur as she ran in the direction of the fighting. She arrived minutes later to see Joseph impaled on a large tree branch and Romaric on the ground unmoving. Ranier was slowly getting up but still too far away to help his father. Marcel had the older man pinned to a tree by his throat. Raph had a grievous wound in his side and it looked like one of his arms was dislocated. Marcel had changed halfway and was slowly crushing his claws into Raph's throat. His voice was a growl as he addressed his uncle. "You failed, old man. Your mistake was that you tried to take me alive because we're family. But I don't have the same feelings about you three."

Before she could even think about the consequences, Sarah yelled to get the crazed man's attention. Marcel looked at her and laughed. "Oh look, its Louve's little vampire bitch. If you wait your turn I'll give you exactly what your redheaded friend got.

Then I'll start on your sister." He started laughing and abruptly stopped. Without thought of consequence, Sarah linked with him and pulled. She drank his energy so fast that her temples were pounding. She watched surprise flit over his wolf-like features and his grip went slack, dropping Raph to the loam beneath their feet. But Sarah didn't stop. With massive effort she pulled even harder until he gave out a strangled cry and collapsed to the ground next to the French Canadian. It took less than ten seconds for his form to change back to human.

Ranier had managed to rise and he came over to check Marcel's pulse. "He's still alive. We are all still alive except for Joseph." When he didn't get an answer, he looked up at their savior. "Sarah?"

Sarah was lost in her own head. The energy she had pulled from Marcel was nothing but pure hate and rage and she stood frozen, shaking with it. Ranier could feel her anger, could practically see it rolling off her. Even her scent had changed. He wasn't sure what to do but the choice was made for him when they both heard a scream coming from the direction of the house.

"Jesse!" The voice was high and fueled by terror. Before Ranier could say another word Sarah was gone. Vanished from sight. He looked down and said a prayer, then began tending to his father and brother's injuries.

THE SECONDS BEFORE Annie's scream were surprisingly calm. They were still sitting on the porch, the only movement coming from Jesse's nervously jiggling leg. Jesse turned to tell Annie that she couldn't hear any more fighting but never got the chance. The picture window behind her exploded outward and a split second later Jesse was pulled backward into the living room of the farmhouse. Before she could fully register what was happening, Marie swung a bat at her head and everything went dark. "Sorry, lover, but we need more wolves in our little group and Alain told me that I could have you. I promise to kiss it better later." The werewoman laughed and dropped the bat to the floor. Then she turned and climbed through the window onto the porch.

Annie being Annie, she wasn't going to wait idly by while a homicidal wolf came after her. She picked up one of the chairs and brought it down on Marie's head and shoulders as hard as she could and then took off running for Keller's car. She knew her friend had left the keys in the center console and thought that would be her best chance to get away. Marie shook off the blow and caught up with Annie as the younger woman started to pull away. Since she was in half-wolf form, she leaped on top of the small car and used her claws to dig into the canvas roof to improve her grip. Annie found herself careening down the long tree-lined drive trying to shake the wolf loose. Sarah had broken from the trees in time to see the car take off and piled on more rage-driven speed to catch up with them.

Annie was panicked and running scared, but she was also angry at the woman who was terrorizing her. Her stomach roiled with the fear of not knowing if Jesse was dead or alive. "Get off this car, you bitch!" She could hear laughter then the canvas ripping above her head and knew she only had seconds to get rid of Marie before the wolf woman killed her. When she felt Marie's claws graze the top of her scalp she didn't think, she merely reacted. Despite not having time to put on a seatbelt, she took the only option available to her. Annie swerved Keller's pride and joy into the nearest oak tree. The car came to an immediate stop, but not the people that were along for the ride. Marie flew through the air and slammed into the trunk of the tree before falling to the hood of the car. Annie was stopped mostly by the steering wheel but her legs were pinned in place from the impact.

Sarah saw the accident and feared the worst. When she got to the car, she ran to the driver's side and nearly ripped the door off in an effort to get to her sister. All she could see was Annie slumped against the steering wheel with multiple cuts all over her body. There was a large gash on her head and she was covered in blood. "Annie!" She didn't dare touch the lifeless body for fear of doing further harm, but her sister seemed to be breathing and her heart was steady. Sarah heard a groan and looked over at the woman on the hood. All the fury and burning anger that was rolling just below the surface came boiling out. With a scream, she grabbed the recovering woman and threw her from the car. "How dare you touch my family!" She picked her up and threw her again before she could do more than sit upright. "How dare you hurt my friends!" This time she was on the wolf woman even faster, pinning her to the ground near the back of the totaled convertible.

Keller had felt what was happening through their shared bond and took off running back to the farmhouse as fast as possible. She felt all the rage that Sarah had pulled from Marcel and knew the singer would do something stupid unless she could stop her. Her soul mate was brimming with stolen energy and combined with her own, it would be more than enough to kill Marie. Keller was still too far away to stop Sarah when she saw her lover pin Marie to the ground "Sarah, no! Sarah!" Keller had two choices, she could let Sarah kill the werewolf, or she could open her shield wide and take all the violent energy into herself. Then she would have the same problem as Sarah. She knew there was no choice to make, she couldn't let her lover kill another being in front of her. She felt Sarah open her shield as she got ready to force her aura into the woman below her. In that instant Keller drained her and Sarah slumped.

Marie sensed her moment to escape had come and shoved Sarah off her. She was so preoccupied by her healing injuries and Sarah's apparent weakness that she didn't see the vampire that was rapidly approaching. Keller slammed into her with the speed of a train, though not quite the force. And once Marie was down, the vampire was going to make sure she never got back up. Keller knew that taking the emotion-fueled energy would merge with her own. And since she was feeling the same emotion, it would be multiplied exponentially. So when angry Sarah stole angry Marcel's energy, Sarah was filled full of the resulting rage. However when an angry Keller took the power, she saw nothing but red. The rage had blossomed and completely taken control. Her rational mind was fading fast, and she knew there was only one way to get it back. She had to get rid of all the stolen power.

Keller climbed on top of a panicked Marie and pinned her to the ground. Then using the same technique that Sarah had so recently tried, Keller shoved her aura deep inside the blonde werewolf below her. Marie struggled but she was easily overpowered by the centuries old vampire. The screaming began when Keller started pumping all that energy into Marie, more than the wolf could ever hope to hold. Eventually, when all the rage was purged from her system, Keller became aware of where she was. When she came to her senses, she looked down at the now human woman below her and knew she'd never be a threat again.

Marie's eyes were dead, vacantly staring at nothing, and there was blood coming from her nose, ears, and mouth. She reached down and carefully closed her eyes, and mourned one more death added to her history. Keller noticed Louve and Jill approaching from the farmhouse and could hear sirens in the distance and suspected that the screaming in the woods around the farmhouse must have prompted the nearest neighbors to call the police. She was also relieved to hear the distinctive sound of an ambulance siren. Keller stood up and looked down at the dead body at her feet, then looked at the wreck of a car right in front of her. In a move that surprised everyone watching her, she picked up Marie's body and threw it with all her strength into the tree that the car had hit. It was almost exactly the way the werewolf had originally hit in the collision.

Sarah looked at her in shock. "Why did you do that?"

Keller pointed in the direction of the rapidly approaching sirens and addressed Sarah, Jill, and Louve. "They're going to get here and ask what happened. They've got an official record that Annie has a stalker. Marie is her stalker and died when the car hit the tree. That's what they're going to think because that is what all the evidence will point to. We will have to get Marie's body from the morgue before they can perform an autopsy or draw blood, but that shouldn't be a problem. We only have one problem left."

Sarah looked at her and received a solemn gaze in return. "What is that?"

Keller shook her head sadly. "Annie is pinned in the car and she has a large laceration on her head, and from what I know of car accidents her ribs are probably broken. I suspect her injuries are far more serious than I can tell here but there is nothing I can do about it. They will be here any second and if we lose her on the way, there is nothing I can do to save her, Sarah." Jill made her way over to Annie and used the button down shirt she had over her tank as the scrap material for make shift bandages. She didn't want to move Annie, in case there was a spinal injury, but she wanted to get the worst of the bleeding stopped.

Keller called out to Jill. "Can you tell if she was scratched by Marie's claws?"

The veterinarian looked at the dozens of little cuts and lacerations on Annie's body then glanced over her shoulder at Keller. "No, there's too much damage."

"Damn." Sarah went over to help Jill, still in shock over everything that had happened. Keller could feel her lover emotionally shutting down but there was nothing she could do to help her at that moment. Too much had happened at once. As the ambulance turned into the drive, Keller looked at Louve. "Where is Jesse?"

The Frenchwoman spoke quickly, not wanting the response team to overhear. "She was injured by Marie and I left the twins with her to take care of her." She stopped talking as the ambulance and police cruiser pulled up. They moved out of the way so the first responders could get in to stabilize the younger Colby sister. They also put a call in for the Jaws of Life, afraid they wouldn't be able to get her right leg out from under the dash. Jill had to forcibly pull Sarah away when one of the medics said Annie's blood pressure was dropping.

Keller was the one who spoke with the sheriff, explaining the accident when they found it. She also explained that Annie had filed a report about a stalker with the Columbus police department. She said that Marie had bothered her at work and other places recently but that they didn't realize the woman was the one that vandalized Annie's car and Sarah's music instruction studio. After taking Keller's complete statement, Sheriff Canerry left to confirm the reports of vandalism and stalking with Columbus PD. When he investigated the scene upon arrival, he had noted that the deceased was in possession of two switchblades, information that he passed along to the Columbus police as well.

When Annie was finally released from the car, they loaded her into the ambulance and told Sarah which hospital they were going to. The sheriff took down everyone's names and contact information and told them that they may need to come down to the sheriff's office and make another statement later. Sarah spoke up as the four of them where heading back up the driveway to the farmhouse. "They asked if I would donate some blood for Annie because we're both O-neg."

Jill looked at her and then looked at Keller. "Can she do that? What will happen to Annie?"

Keller ran a hand through her hair as they approached Jill's Jeep. "Truthfully, I don't know. They shouldn't pick up the changes in Sarah's blood when they test it because those changes are on a cellular level. Their tests aren't that in-depth. However, I can't say with one hundred percent certainty they won't pick up any anomalies at all. I've only ever given my blood when the person was on the edge of death. And in all those instances, it was a much more personal donation. I don't know what giving someone vampire blood would do to them if they weren't dying, perhaps nothing. I would say err on the side of caution and only donate if they don't have any of her type available, and only if she is going to need it." Keller shifted her gaze when Ranier came out onto the porch and called out to the owner of the house.

"Louve! Romaric is awake. With his help, as well as Bastien and Beale, we have moved my father up to one of the spare rooms. Aric and I also wrapped Joseph in a sheet and placed his body in the garage for now. We weren't sure what you would want done with him."

A look of immense sorrow flooded Louve's features. "That is fine. Thank you, Ranier. Is Jesse well enough to leave yet? They will all be going to the hospital because Annie was gravely injured when the car crashed down the drive."

Jesse appeared in the doorway then stepped through the screen door when she didn't immediately see Annie. "What do you mean she was injured?" Panicked, she scrambled down the steps, still weak from her injury. "We have to go, I have to get to her right now!"

Sarah rushed over to help steady the wobbly werewolf. "Easy, Jesse, she's alive and she's going to be okay. We're heading there right now, let's get in Jill's car." Sarah, Jesse, and Jill piled into the Jeep but Keller hung back for a few seconds. She glanced at the garage then looked into Louve's sad brown eyes.

"I am so very sorry, my friend. I wish we could have prevented all of this."

Louve waived away her words. "Non, it could not be helped. Alain was powerful, but so were the others. They simply made us play their game and it was a dangerous one. Now go. You need to be at the hospital with Annie. And I think Sarah needs you more than anything else right now. She is empty. I can feel it even through her shields." Keller stared into her eyes for another second and then nodded. She got into the back seat of Jill's Jeep and they sped away.

The hospital was a twenty-minute drive but it felt like an eternity to Sarah and Jesse. It was a quiet car ride because Jesse was full of guilt and self-loathing for not being able to protect her girlfriend. Sarah was feeling much the same way because she had left them alone to help with Marcel in the woods. Conversely, she was also feeling guilty because she wasn't fast enough to save Joseph when they called her. And her only vengeance was literally snatched from her grip when Keller stole her anger.

The fact was, Keller stole more than her anger. There was no emotion for Sarah to push down, despite the fact that Annie's life hung in the balance. The singer felt like she was hollow inside, like she would never feel again. When they arrived, Sarah was immediately taken to donate blood while Jesse, Jill, and Keller took seats in the emergency waiting room. The singer had just finished up with the last of her donation when one of the nurses came into the curtained alcove in a rush. She spoke briefly with the nurse who had taken Sarah's blood then grabbed the blood and was back out the curtain in a flash. Sarah looked at the other nurse. "What was that about?"

The woman looked back at Sarah with sympathy coloring her features. "She's taking it for immediate testing. Your sister has internal bleeding and is being rushed into surgery. Don't worry, they will only use the blood if she requires it during surgery, just as you requested." She pushed the curtain the rest of the way open and motioned with her hand toward the front desk. "Now if you can please follow me, I need you to fill out some paperwork. You said that you are her medical power of attorney, right?" The solemn elder Colby sister nodded and followed numbly behind her.

Fifteen minutes later Sarah returned to the waiting room to sit with the other three. She sat on the plastic chair with her cheek resting on the knees of her drawn-up legs. Her feet were resting on the edge of the chair. Jesse spent her time pacing the waiting room, working off a seemingly unlimited amount of worry and energy. Jill and Keller were bookending the shell-shocked singer. More than once Keller tried to send positive energy to her lover but Sarah wasn't letting anything in or out of her walls. Jill looked at Keller over top of Sarah's lowered head. "If she was rushed to surgery for internal bleeding, chances are they will give her Sarah's blood. What do we do now?"

Keller shook her head. "Now we wait. And we hope for a miracle but at the same time we are hoping a miracle will not be needed. If she is infected by Sarah's blood, then the questions and tests will never end and our lives here will be over."

Sarah turned her head and looked at Keller with dawning horror. The realization of their situation had finally sunk in, and it wasn't good.

Chapter Twelve

HOURS WENT BY before a doctor appeared in the doorway. "Sarah Colby?" He looked around, waiting for someone to answer.

Sarah jumped up and rushed over, startling the man back a step. "I'm Sarah Colby. How's Annie?" His name tag read Dr. Reider.

"She's stable right now, though we're not sure how. As you probably know, her injuries were extensive. Her vitals began to drop in the middle of surgery and we were forced to use the blood you donated earlier. She leveled out almost immediately so we were able to continue. She had broken ribs on both sides, her right lung was collapsed, and she had some bleeding around the lungs. The blow to the head also caused a large laceration and some intracranial hemorrhaging. We initially thought her right ankle and leg were broken based on reports from the EMS team and the ER x-ray. But examination in the O.R. and subsequent x-rays show that it's just sprained, though I wouldn't rule out a hairline fracture. All in all, your sister is a very lucky woman for someone who hit a tree head on and wasn't wearing a seatbelt." His judgement was clearly written all over his face.

Sarah stifled a sob and hugged herself. "Wh—when can I see her?"

The doctor looked at his watch. "She's been in recovery for about twenty five minutes now, so she won't be waking up for a few more hours. It just depends on how fast the anesthetic works its way out of her system. You can wait in the recovery room until she wakes, but I ask that you limit it to two people at a time." Sarah nodded and suddenly found herself flanked on all sides by her friends. "Do you have any more questions?"

Keller looked up at him. "How long will she be in the hospital? When can she be released?"

The man gave her a strange look. "Miss Colby has some very serious injuries. Ultimately, healing time is determined by the person's body, but she could be here a while. For now she needs constant monitoring in case she starts bleeding again or suffers other complications from her injuries." When they all nodded in acknowledgment, he tucked his chart under his arm again. "I'll send a nurse to bring two of you back. Have a nice day, Miss Colby."

He walked away and their little group went back over to sit down and wait for the promised nurse. "Shit!" Everyone looked at Jill. "I just remembered that standard procedure is to run a blood alcohol test in the event of an accident. Annie was drinking because I was the driver today. She doesn't need the fallout of a drunk driving conviction on top of everything else."

"She won't have to worry about that."

The group gaze shifted to Keller. Sarah cocked her head to the side at Keller's emphatic statement. "But how do you know that? We don't know when they took the blood sample."

Keller ran a hand through messy blonde hair. "It doesn't matter, no alcohol will show up now."

"Keller?"

"When the doctor came out here he was confused, perplexed. I could read it on him. He was also excited. He also mentioned a few other things, such as the fact that her vitals were dropping until Sarah's blood was introduced. And he also said they thought her ankle was broken, but the second set of x-rays didn't show the break."

Jesse sucked in a breath. "Are you saying that she was infected with Sarah's virus?"

Keller sighed and scrubbed her face with both hands. "Jill, when would they have taken the initial x-ray?"

Jill looked at her strangely. "As soon as she got here she would have had chest, head, and ankle x-rays. At least that's what I would assume based on the injuries she had. Why?"

Keller looked back with an unreadable gaze. "I was pretty sure that ankle was broken, weren't you?"

Jill nodded. "Yes, I thought so too, it was quite obvious. So what does this mean? You think she was infected by Marie, and the werewolf virus kicked in and healed her ankle? But why would she crash in the middle of surgery?"

"Sonofabitch!" Jesse's face wore a look of sheer surprise. "She has both!"

Sarah jerked her head around to look at her sister's girl-friend. "What? But that's not possible." She looked back at Keller. "Is it?"

Keller rested her elbows on her knees and looked thoughtful. She tapped her bottom lip. "Hypothetically, you can't catch the vampire virus unless you are near death. Since werewolves have rapid healing and higher energy, they would never be infected with what we have. However, if they suffer massive enough injuries, their rapid healing would not be able to compensate. It would be the rarest of events for someone infected with the werewolf virus to be near death and then be infected with the vampire virus. I would have said it was impossible before now."

"So why isn't she healed yet? I believe it only took about twenty minutes for Jill to come around, and you said the same for me. She got my blood in the middle of surgery and she's been out for a half hour now." Sarah looked at Keller fearfully, not sure what the two converging viruses would do to her sister's body.

Keller shrugged. "I don't know. This is something I've never even heard of before."

Jill chewed at her bottom lip for a few seconds and then finally just said what she was thinking. "What if — Keller, you told me that both the vampire and werewolf virus work on the body and make changes at a genetic level." Keller nodded and she continued. "How long did it take for Jesse to wake up after she was infected?"

Sarah answered. "Hours."

The veterinarian continued with her thought. "Annie only has so many resources available to make all these changes. What if they are both working, but slower?"

Understanding washed across the nerdy werewolf's face. "Holy shit, it's like a computer!" When she got blank looks from the others she continued. "Computers only have so many resources to process information and programs. When you're running one program, it will run at a certain speed. However, when you are running two programs, your processing speed slows down. If you're running two giant programs, it all slows to a crawl and you probably need a faster processor for whatever you're doing."

Sarah looked up slowly. "I think I actually understood your nerd speak for once!"

Jesse, Sarah, and Jill all turned their gaze to Keller, to see if she agreed with Jesse's thought. "It actually makes sense. At least, it makes as much sense as anything else right now. Like I said, this is all completely new. I've never heard of someone that had more than the werewolf virus in them."

Jill looked at her curiously. "But you've heard of someone with more than the vampire virus?"

Keller's face went blank and Sarah felt her lover's shields tighten. "That is a story best left for another time."

Before another word could be spoken a nurse came in. "I'm here to take Sarah Colby back to see Annie. Which one of you is Sarah?"

Both Sarah and Jesse had stood when they saw the nurse. Sarah looked at Jesse, then back at the nurse. "The doctor said two of us could go in."

She gave them a serious look. "Yes. Two people, no more." They followed the nurse back to the recovery room where they found Annie still asleep and swaddled in warm blankets. She had a large bandage on her head and multiple visible cuts along her face and neck. Jesse and Sarah each took a side of the bed and grasped one of Annie's hands. Sarah couldn't speak yet. When their parents were killed in the car accident nearly a decade ago, their deaths were instantaneous. So waiting in a hospital with what felt like a lead weight on her chest was new. The void that she had been feeling earlier, right after Annie's accident, was slowly filling with dread. All she could do was keep it together and be here for Annie. That's all she's ever been able to do.

Jesse leaned over and lightly kissed the unconscious woman on the lips. "Hey, babe. I'm glad to see that you're alive but you better wake up so we can go on that date you promised me the other day." Her breath caught but after a second she continued on. "I love you, Annie, and I really need you to come back to me, to come back to all of us." At a loss, the werewolf settled into the seat next to the bed but didn't relinquish the hand she was holding.

Sarah reached down and gave her sister's ear a little tug. "Hey there, A. You're so quiet right now. I could get used to this. Just kidding. I would give anything to hear your voice right now. We all love you, Annie, and we need you to fight for us, okay? No matter what has happened, or what will change in our future, we've always got each other." They sat by the bed for over an hour but Annie didn't wake. Finally Sarah flagged down a nurse. "Excuse me?"

The nurse stopped and smiled at her. "Yes?"

Sarah glanced at her sister, then back at the woman dressed in scrubs. Her pants were weighed down by a pager and starting to sag on one side. "The doctor told us it usually only takes a few hours to come out of recovery. Do you know why she isn't awake yet?"

The nurse went over to look at Annie's different monitors, then took her pulse and listened to her lungs. When she was finished, she straightened and stepped back from the bed. "I'm not really sure. People take different amounts of time to wake after surgery, and her injuries were pretty severe. However, her pulse rate is normal, maybe even slightly elevated, and her lungs are surprisingly clear given the injuries she received. Much better than she was right after surgery. Let me speak with the doctor, but I'd say just give her more time. Some people have stayed under for as long as five hours; it really depends on how they react to anesthesia. Has she had surgery before this?"

"Yes, she had her appendix removed when she was in high school. But she woke up less than an hour after she was out of surgery."

The nurse had stopped making a note in Annie's chart and tapped her bottom lip with the pen. "Hmm, I'm sure she's fine but I'll speak with the doctor."

They waited another hour and Annie still didn't wake. Sarah went out twice to update Keller and Jill, but returned each time to sit by her sister's side. Finally, three hours after the end of Annie's surgery, another doctor came to look at Annie. He asked Sarah and Jesse to step outside while he performed the exam. From outside the door they could hear the doctor call one of the nurses over and they had a hushed discussion at the head of Annie's bed. Between the noise of the hospital, the solid closed door, and the fact that the doctor was whispering, they only caught snippets of what the man was saying.

" — they're gone."

"Have you checked...skin looks fine...?"

" — only happened this morning..."

Jesse looked at Sarah in alarm. "What are they talking about?"

The singer frowned as the doctor that performed Annie's surgery came down the hall at a fast pace and pushed into the room. He walked over to Annie's bed and started talking to the first doctor. "I don't know but I'm going to find out!" When she opened the door, one of the nurses immediately rushed over.

"Excuse me, but you can't be in here right now!"

Sarah pointed at the unconscious woman on the bed. "That is my sister, and I have medical power of attorney over her. If there is something wrong with her I want to know right now!"

Hearing the commotion, Dr. Reider came over. "Calm down, Miss Colby, your sister is doing just fine."

"If she's doing fine, why did you come rushing down here and why is everyone gathering around her like that?"

He sighed and looked at the wall above her head, searching for words to explain what he had no explanation for. "Your sister is showing complications, strange complications."

Sarah started to get a clue, even if he hadn't. "Please explain."

He frowned. "Some of her superficial wounds have healed already, something unheard of hours after an initial injury. We need to run some tests to be—"

Sarah interrupted him. "No."

He looked startled. "Pardon?"

"Is her life in danger?"

"Well, no but—"

Sarah continued. "Is she healing? Have there been any negative effects of her injury?"

He looked flustered. "No, I just said that."

"Then I do not consent to the tests."

The doctor's face flushed. "You signed a consent form when you filled out the paperwork for your sister's care."

Sarah's green eye's turned hard. "I signed a consent form for her emergency treatment, so you could provide lifesaving practices and medicines. Tests costs money, do you normally run unnecessary tests here? If so, I'm turning you in to the insurance company!"

"Ms. Colby, please! I'm only trying to do what's best for your sister."

The singer crossed her arms in front of her chest and stood firm. "No sir, you said yourself that Annie is healing and there were no issues with her progress—"

She was interrupted by the good doctor. "But there are anomalies in her blood, and I would like to see if that could be responsible for her strangely accelerated healing."

"Anomalies which I also share, Doctor Reider. It is a family trait and I can assure you that it has done neither my deceased parents, nor myself, any favors. If you cannot respect my wishes then I will remove my sister from this hospital and place her with a private doctor. And I will call our insurance company!"

His face darkened at her threat. "As you wish, Miss Colby." He glanced at his watch impatiently. "Now if you'll excuse me, I have other patients to attend to and I believe visiting hours are over. I'll have your sister transferred to a room and we will continue to keep you apprised of her condition." He went over to Annie's bed to return her chart and say something to the other doctor and the nurse in charge of the recovery area, then walked stiffly from the room. Jesse came in as soon as he was gone.

"Well, what did he say? Or maybe I should ask what you said. His scent screamed anger when he left."

"He told me that she was healing faster than normal, and that they had found anomalies in her blood. Then he told me they were going to run some more blood tests to see if those same anomalies are the cause of this new development. I told him the anomalies were a family trait and that I did not consent to the blood tests. I also threatened to put her in private care and report him to the insurance company if he insisted on running unnecessary and expensive procedures when he already stated she was fine and healing well."

The younger woman's eyes widened. "Oh. I can see how that might piss him off."

Sarah noticed the nurse approaching out of the corner of her eye. "And now they're going to kick us out since visiting hours are over and they want to transfer her to a room."

When they got back to the waiting room, Keller jumped up from her chair. "What's wrong?"

Sarah explained the situation to Keller and Jill. One of Jill's good friends was a doctor, they went to undergrad together. She said she would speak with her friend to see what they could do about getting Annie transferred out of the hospital. After that the four women decided to go to dinner together and head to their separate homes. Louve had called Keller earlier to ask if they could all come over the next day. They still had to deal with the rest of the fallout from their confrontation with the rogue wolves. Alain was dead, Joseph was dead, Marie was dead in a morgue somewhere, and Marcel was still very much alive. There were other issues to deal with as well that were loading both Louve and Keller's shoulders with guilt. Keller knew she would have to fill Sarah in on the details once they got home.

Jill dropped the couple off at the condo before driving herself and Jesse back to her house on Auburn Street. They were still a little shell-shocked when they sat next to each other on the couch. Jill looked over at her temporary roommate when Jesse gave a quiet whimper. Jill could feel the younger woman's fear and heartache with her empathy. She reached out and put her arm around Jesse's shoulders and drew the werewolf to her. The unfamiliar comfort was all it took for Jesse to break down. She sobbed on Jill's shoulder and her pain tore at the older woman's own heart. For Jill, Annie was like the younger sister she always wanted. She'd been practically adopted by the Colby family all those years ago and she couldn't imagine a life without both the sisters in it. Jesse's voice was muffled against Jill's sleeve. "She has to be all right, she has to. I love her so much!" She pulled her head up and turned tear-filled eyes toward Jill's. "What happens if she doesn't wake up?"

"Shh, she'll wake up, J. The kid is tough, she's going to be okay" Inside, Jill was wishing she had someone to hold her. But she knew that Louve was dealing with the death of one of her troupe members, no, pack mates. She understood that the French-woman had her own responsibilities right then, but Jill's heart ached for her nonetheless.

WHEN THEY GOT home, Keller left Sarah seated on the couch with a glass of wine while she took Duke outside to do his business. When she returned she ran a bath in the Jacuzzi tub and coaxed Sarah to join her. Then, while the singer was as relaxed as she was going to get, Keller filled her in on the events with Alain.

Sarah didn't think she could be shocked by anything else that day but she was wrong. "So Alain had been holding a grudge for decades because of something Catherine did?"

The two women were facing each other in the large tub instead of their usual back to front position. It made it easier for them to talk. "Well, Catherine did kill his children and wife in front of him. I think it drove him a little mad and he just wanted someone to pay. When he found out that Louve was her lover, I think he saw a way to get his revenge."

Sarah shook her head. "But you killed Catherine, shouldn't that mean something?"

"Yes, it means I stole his revenge from him."

Sarah sighed and closed her eyes. "That's crazy." When she opened them again, she gave Keller a worried look. "And you're sure he's dead?"

Keller started massaging Sarah's feet with slippery soaped hands. "Don't worry love, he is gone. He confessed everything while I was holding him. After that it turned strange. With the twins as witnesses, Louve judged Alain as *Varoullac*."

Sarah stopped running the sponge she had been using, across Keller's leg. "Varoullac? What is that? And what did she do?"

Keller laughed and brought Sarah's foot up to her mouth. After taking a ticklish nibble of Sarah's big toe she answered her. "You are always so impatient! The word is a portmanteau of *varou ullac*, meaning werewolf outlaw. It is a title as much as a description. As soon as she said the word, he really started to struggle. I think he knew what was coming. All three of the wolves were in their half-form, just like Alain. And they — well they tore him to pieces."

The singer raised an eyebrow. "Harsh."

"Really?"

Sarah frowned and a dark look came over her face as she thought about all they had done to her best friend. "No. And just how did you manage to avoid the bloodbath?"

Keller managed to look offended. "I'm a vampire."

"And you what, magically willed the blood away from you? Or maybe you ran around and caught all the flying blood in your mouth?"

The blonde wrinkled her lip in disgust. "Don't be vile. I'm a centuries old vampire who is both faster and stronger than all of them. I knew what was coming and I moved out of the way before it got messy."

"And Jill?"

Keller chuckled. "Let's just say that when the nice sheriff showed up, not all the blood on Jill's clothes belonged to Annie."

Sarah sunk deeper into the tub. "And what are they going to do with Joseph? Does he have any family?"

"No. Apparently he was a refugee living in southern France; Louve found him on the streets years ago. The Troupe was his only family. They will bury him at the farm. Alain's remains will be burned, per tradition. I don't know yet what will happen to Marie's body at the morgue. I'm guessing that someone from the troupe will pose as a distant relative in order to get the body released for cremation. Maybe give them religious reasons to avoid an autopsy."

The singer put the sponge away and sat forward. "And what will happen to Marcel? He is just as guilty as Marie, maybe not as much as Alain."

Keller looked thoughtful. "Actually, I think Alain was responsible for a lot of Marcel and Marie's aggression. He was a master at mental manipulation. I suspect he used what they already had inside and stoked the flames. As for his fate, his family will take care of him. They will return to Quebec tomorrow, after we all meet."

"How can they keep him in check?"

Keller tickled her foot. "The wolves have their ways, trust me. We won't have to worry about him again." Sensing that Sarah had no more questions about the events of the previous day, she decided it was time to question the singer about her own feelings. "How are you doing with all this?"

Sarah shrugged. "I'm fine." She skimmed her hand through the water, not meeting Keller's eyes.

Keller grabbed the moving hand in her own to still it. When

Sarah looked up, she looked calmly back. "No, you're not." Keller saw Sarah swallow and watched her lover's green eyes fill with tears. "Talk to me, love. Let it out, I'm right here for you." Sarah turned away from her lover's probing gaze and stared at the candle on the ledge around the tub. When Keller gently cupped her cheek and pulled her face back toward her, Sarah's bottom lip began to quiver. "Please Sarah, let me in."

All at once Sarah's hands came out of the water to cover her face and she started sobbing. Keller turned her around until Sarah was seated in front of her, back to Keller's front. Then she wrapped her arms around Sarah and gently rocked her. "It's going to be okay, love, just let it out. I'm here for you and everything is going to be all right."

Sarah's shoulders shook with the force of her crying. "Bu— but how do you know? H—how do you know it's going to be okay?" She shuddered in her girlfriend's arms and wailed her fear to the heavens. "She almost died, Keller!"

Waiting a beat, Keller continued to hold her. "But she didn't die and you have to focus on that. Even better, you won't have to worry about her anymore because you're both going to live very long lives. You know that, right?" Keller rubbed her soul mate's arms, continuing to soothe the overwhelmed woman. "All this fear and anger have been building for a long time and you just need to get it out. Everything is going to be okay, you'll see."

Eventually Sarah's crying slowed and then stopped. She turned red-rimmed eyes back to Keller. "Everything's going to be okay? You promise?"

Keller stared back, knowing that there was no certainty with anything in life. But she also knew that Sarah needed reassurance and she would do anything to make her lover happy again. "Yes. I promise." She gave the taller woman a little nudge. "Now come on, the water is getting cold and I'm starting to prune in here." Sarah gave a quiet hiccupping laugh.

Once they were both standing, Sarah turned around and took the shorter woman into her arms before they could get out of the tub. She looked into the blue eyes that held so much love for her. "Thank you." Keller smiled and nodded. "Now I think you're right. Let's get out of the water and dry off. I need you to hold me tonight." She looked at her girlfriend with uncertainty. "Is it okay if all we do is cuddle?"

Keller leaned up and gave her a sweet kiss on the lips. "Always. I love you, Sarah. Always." The least Keller could do was make her soul mate happy. Tomorrow and their situation with Annie would arrive soon enough. Tonight would be just for them.

THE NEXT DAY, Jill and Jesse picked up Sarah and Keller, then drove out to the farmhouse. Keller noticed that her car had been towed as they drove down the long drive. The Audi definitely didn't survive its meeting with the oak tree, and based on the damage done to the trunk, it looked like the tree wouldn't survive either. The four women were shocked when they saw Marcel. The usually arrogant man looked strangely defeated. He was sporting a spiked collar around his neck, but the spikes were facing in instead of out. Jesse rubbed her own neck, understanding that changing would be impossible without irreparable damage being done. He would kill himself. Sarah understood its use as well and thought the dog certainly deserved it. Jill merely shivered; it looked like an extreme version of a choke collar to her. The mood was somber at the farm. The Columbus women said their goodbyes to Raph, Aric, and Ranier. Louve said that Joseph had been buried that morning and that Beale was carving a headstone for him. Bastien had left to claim his "cousin's" body from the morgue and had instructions to take her to a crematorium that Louve had made arrangements with.

The police had all the evidence they needed to pin the robberies on Marie and had no problem releasing the body. Apparently she had a few personal items, including a necklace, which had been stolen recently. Everything seemed to have wrapped up nicely, with the exception of Annie. It was still early when they left the farm, just after nine in the morning. They went directly to the hospital to see if Annie was awake. When they arrived, all four of them went up to the room number Sarah was given by the front desk. Clustered around the bed, Sarah looked at Keller in confusion. It was obvious the younger woman had healed even more overnight. "I don't get it, why doesn't she wake up?"

Jesse tilted her head and peered closer at her girlfriend. "Does she look thinner to you? Look at her cheeks." She pointed to Annie's cheeks, which were noticeably hollowed out.

Keller shook he head. "I don't know. Something is working on her or she wouldn't be so healed. But it's like something is missing."

Jesse chimed in again. "It's like two programs that aren't compatible with each other crashing the system. How do we fix her?"

"She looks like she's starving." Jill pointed at Annie's bony wrist and collarbone. "Could she be using too much energy, but maybe her body doesn't know how to feed yet because there are two different viruses inside her?"

"Losh! You're right! I have been so stupid!" Keller locked her blue eyes with Jesse's chocolate brown. "She needs blood."

The younger woman swallowed and paled slightly. "Mine?"

Keller nodded. "I have a theory. I think that the vampire in her is hungry and trying to heal her, but it doesn't know how to feed because it's confused by the werewolf side. The two sides aren't balanced. She had a pint of Sarah's blood, but only a scratch from Marie. I don't really know how that equals out in the scheme of things but maybe she needs more wolf in her."

Jesse looked at her fearfully. "How do we do this? I won't bleed for long and she's not even conscious."

"Let's see if her body takes over. Jill, can you watch the door?" Jill nodded and moved across the room to keep anyone from entering. "Now give me your wrist." Jesse reached across Annie and before she could even protest, Keller brought the limb to her mouth and pierced Jesse's wrist with her elongated teeth. The young werewolf closed her eyes tight to avoid seeing her own blood. She didn't think it would be good to pass out while they were trying to fix her girlfriend. It took a lot of Keller's self-control to pull back and not drink any of the warm flowing liquid that seemed to sing to her. Jill could smell the blood but kept her back to the hospital bed.

Sarah was also staring hungrily and when Jesse opened her eyes to see why the vampires in the room suddenly had increased heartrates, she began to feel uncomfortable and quickly shut her eyes again. "Um, guys, I'm going to drip." Keller quickly turned the opened wrist over and placed it against Annie's mouth. Sarah saw Annie's finger twitch as the first few drops hit her tongue. Then the younger woman's entire body convulsed and she brought her hands up to Jesse's wrist and pressed it tighter to her mouth. Eye's still closed tight, they could see Annie's throat moving as she swallowed the blood that Jesse offered. As soon as the younger Colby's hands had moved up to Jesse's arm, Keller had moved hers out of the way. She kept them close though, in case something went wrong.

Abruptly Sarah gasped. "I just heard her!"

Keller looked at her sharply. "What did you just say?"

Sarah pointed at her sister. "I just heard Annie in my head. Words, Keller, not images or emotions. She said words."

The veterinarian called out from the door. "Well, what did she say?"

"I called her a blood sucking freak."

Sarah laughed and Jesse pulled her arm away from Annie's face. "Um, babe?" With her left hand, she gestured at Annie's lips where there was blood still coating them like lipstick.

Annie licked her lips and her eye's widened. "Touché. Sorry, Sarah."

"Guys! Not to break up the little reunion but there's a nurse headed this way." Jill stepped away from the door just before a petite blonde walked into the room.

"Don't mind me ladies, I'm just here to check Miss Colby's vitals." She put her stethoscope into her ears and came around the bed only to be startled back when she met smiling hazel eyes.

Annie smiled at the surprised woman. "Good morning!"

"Oh! You're awake, good! I'm going to go get the doctor. He's going to want to run some tests on you. We've been calling you our little miracle!"

Almost as one voice, Sarah and Annie spoke. "No tests!" Sarah was startled a second later when she heard her sister's voice clearly in her head again. *Don't worry sis, I under-stand.* "I would like to speak to my doctor about getting released."

The nurse looked shocked. "You can't be released, you just had major surgery yesterday! You need to be monitored with twenty-four hour care!"

Annie sat up with no obvious discomfort. "Do I look like I need monitoring? Now please get the doctor."

When she was gone, Jill helped disconnect Annie's IV and various wires while Jesse gave her girlfriend the duffle bag full of clothes and shoes. Annie looked at her girlfriend with obvious love and Jesse startled. "How are you doing that?" She grinned at the idea, then abruptly frowned. "You can't read my thoughts, can you? Oh shit!" The women around the bed laughed at Jesse's discomfort but were interrupted when Dr. Reider walked through the door. He managed to be both surprised and annoyed when he saw that Annie was alert and pain free.

"I see you are feeling much better today and the nurse tells me you would like to go home. I'm afraid that is not possible until we run some tests, Miss Colby."

"My name is Annie, and I will not consent to testing. I'm checking myself out of the hospital, against your advice if it comes to that."

The man's face darkened. "You've had quite a head trauma, Annie, and many people aren't in the right mind for a while after—" He was surprised to be interrupted by her laughter.

"There is nothing wrong with my head and if you try to declare me mentally incapable of making my own medical decisions then my sister, who is my medical power of attorney, will surely agree with me. I'm going home. Are we clear?"

If he was surprised at the way she seemed to know what he was thinking, he didn't show it. "I'll have them draw up your paperwork right away. I wish you the best, Annie."

Everyone blew out a sigh of relief when he left the room and Annie went into the bathroom to change into something that didn't have a draft up the back. Although she did enjoy Jesse's lascivious thoughts as she walked away from the trio.

AN HOUR LATER they found themselves back at the condo with bags of fast-food piled in front of the younger Colby sister. "Oh God, I'm starving!" After eating and filling Annie in on all the developments that had unfolded after she was injured, they all sat in silence and let her process the news. "So what does this mean? Am I a wolf or a vampire?"

Keller nodded. "Yes."

Annie smacked Keller's arm. "Smart ass!"

"Babe, you're like a Vampwolf, or a werepire!" Jesse looked just as giddy as when she found out she was a werewolf. "And you can read minds. That is so cool!"

Jill cracked up laughing. "You say that now, but tell us again how you feel in a month when she's talking your ear off both in and out of your head."

Annie made a face. "Hardy har har, you're a riot, Red!"

The nerdy werewolf was going to say something else but jumped instead. Sheepishly she pulled out her cell phone and read the incoming text. "It's Sam." She received blank looks from the three older women but Annie looked at her curiously.

"What does our neighbor want?" She looked at Keller, Sarah, and Jill to explain. "Sometimes we watch her dog when she's out of town."

Jesse groaned. "She says there's a news truck parked in front of our house. What the hell?"

Keller stood and walked away. Sarah's eyes followed her worriedly. "Keller warned us that the hospital would give us grief for not allowing them to run tests. I'm afraid that your miracle healing is a bit of a sensation. One of the nurses probably spread the word; I don't know when it's going to die down."

"It's not going to die down. She isn't just a medical miracle, she is a miracle that they witnessed heal overnight. To them she did the impossible and that will never die down." Keller had returned carrying a large orange envelope. After clearing the fast-food bags out of the way, she opened the envelope and spread the contents out on the table.

Sarah looked at the photographs and various documents that were spread in front of them, then up at her soul mate. "What's this?"

"This is how I've stayed alive and out of the spotlight for hundreds of years. Number one lesson is to always have a backup plan."

Annie picked up two of the documents. "These are deeds." She looked at a few other papers and shook her head in confusion.

Jesse cocked her head and sorted through the photos. "Where is this place?"

Something clicked inside Sarah's brain and she sucked in a breath. "It's in Michigan, the second largest city if I recall. You really did what I think you did?"

Jill looked back and forth between Sarah and Keller with a sinking feeling in her gut. "Did what?"

The younger Colby nodded, already picking up what Sarah knew. She couldn't read anything from Keller, but she suspected it had more to do with Keller's advanced training and mental shield. "She made a fresh start for us."

The werewolf looked at her in concern. "I don't understand. What do you mean fresh start?"

"I mean a new life, someplace else. A completely fresh start, Jesse."

Terror skittered across Jesse's face. "You'd leave me?"

Annie grabbed her girlfriend and held her tight. "No you idiot, you're coming with us!

"But..." The young IT professional's face was awash with confusion. She thought of her job and how much she loved it and her company. It was her first job since graduating college. "But what about our jobs here, what about our families?"

Keller shifted and got everyone's attention with nothing more than a sigh. "All three of your lives changed irrevocably the minute you became infected with *other* blood. Having our powers, and all the benefits of the werewolf or vampire virus, is also balanced by the fact that we always have to take precautions. One of the major downsides is that our longevity makes it impossible to stay too long in one place. Eventually you have to leave your family and friends behind before too many questions are asked." She cast her gaze to each of the three of them, meeting their eyes one by one. "But in exchange, we get to live many lives. We get to do whatever we want, to discover all of our dreams, try things that we would never have had the time, money, or health to before. So you can either stay here now and be hounded for years, or move on and try something new. But it has to be a personal choice for each one of you." She looked at Sarah. "What do you think?"

"What are we going to do with ourselves there?"

Keller smiled. "Whatever you want to do. But I was thinking about running a recording studio."

Sarah cocked her head curiously. "Thinking about it?"

"Okay, you got me. I've already bought a currently existing one and put together a layout for remodel. I got lucky because the previous owner wanted to retire and I made him an offer that was too good to refuse. Also, it's the only recording studio on that side of the state. I just need people to run it and someone that knows IT to help set it up." She looked at the younger Colby sister. "Annie?"

Annie looked around the table then settled her gaze on Jesse. "I don't want to lose you, but you know I can't stay here now. Will you come with me? Us?"

Jesse looked torn, and she sighed. "Annie, I have a job here that I love and a career. My brother was starting to come around."

Annie gave her a sad smile. "I know baby, but he hasn't called in months. Not since the time you went over there when Sarah was infected after the hit and run accident. I know it hurts, J, but I think they've all made it pretty clear how they feel. And I don't have to tell you that we are your family too, every one of us. And you're not going to lose us for a long, long time. Right Keller?"

Keller nodded. "The oldest werewolf I've ever met is nearly two hundred, and the oldest vampire I've ever met is ten times that. As for Annie's longevity, I really have no idea. I've only met one other vampire hybrid but the blood of their other half was otherworldly."

Sarah raised a dark eyebrow. "What exactly does that mean?

Jesse smiled. "I'm not saying it's aliens...but it's aliens!"

Keller shook her head, recognizing the popular quote from

the History Channel. "No, not aliens. I was referring to a Manbo, or Vodou priestess, that was infected by the vampire virus centuries ago. She is still alive down in New Orleans but it doesn't help me estimate Annie's potential age since she's kind of a—"

"She's kind of a freak!"

Annie made a face at her sister's teasing. "Really, Sarah? We're trying to be serious here." But Jesse started laughing.

"She's right, babe, you are kind of a freak. But I love you and I'm going to follow you to the end of the Earth and back if I have to." She turned toward Keller. "So do you really have a job for me?"

Keller smiled. "Absolutely! And if you don't like it, we'll get you something else. It's a fair-sized city with a lot of job opportunities."

Sarah looked at her ex, realizing for the first time how quiet the veterinarian had been. Jill's face showed nothing but pain and sadness. Waves of loneliness radiated through her shield. "Jilly, you okay?"

Jill swallowed and her eyes teared up. "I can't believe you're all leaving. You and Annie are like family to me and I feel like we've just started to reconnect again. I love you guys." She looked at the four other women around the table. "All of you."

Sarah glanced at Keller, then back at Jill. "You could come with us you know. We consider you part of the family too."

Jill shook her head. "No, I'm not ready to start over again. I've finally built myself up here. I have clients who trust me and depend on me, and I'm not certified to practice in Michigan. I'd have to go through certification all over again..." She trailed off and looked around the table at the faces that were staring back at her. "And then there's Louve. I don't think she can just pick up and move so easily and I can't leave her behind. I've only just found her but there's something there that I've always been missing. I can't give that up."

"Jill." Everyone looked at Keller, surprised that she was smiling when the rest of them were so sad. "Take the time you need, there's no rush. We'll miss you but we can come back and visit any time. So what if you spend the next ten years here with your practice and Louve with her nightclub? You both can spend the next one hundred living near us, or traveling the world. You can go to school and become something completely different. The choice is yours and you have a long future ahead of you. I think you and Louve can be very good together, just remember not to rush things. You have plenty of time to take it slow."

A look of wonder came over the doctor's face. "I have all the time in the world. I don't have to worry about retirement, or getting too old to practice, medical bills, minor accidents and injuries, rabies —"

"Rabies? Like Old Yeller?" Jesse made a face.

Jill looked pained. "Yes. And the vaccines are a real bitch. Veterinarians have to get a lot of different vaccines to stay certified."

Annie blinked at her, never having liked shots. She shuddered then turned to Keller. "So tell me more about this music studio. It doesn't involve vaccines does it?"

Keller laughed at the younger woman. "Not unless you want it to."

"Kinky, babe!" Jesse rubbed her arm after Annie punched it. "Ow! Your hits hurt now!"

Jill smirked. "And she can read your mind. You better watch out, Jesse!"

"Damnit!"

They all broke up in laughter, finally getting the reprieve they'd been looking for. When they seemed to wind down, Sarah looked around the table. "So how do we do this? I mean, I can't just pick up and leave, I have clients. I have to give them the news that I'm moving and I have to close the studio. You still have the condo, Annie has the house and her job at The Merge, and Jesse would have to put her notice in as well. This is a big undertaking. And Annie and Jesse can't even go home because of reporters."

Keller ran a hand through her hair, thinking hard. "Okay, here's what we should do. Sarah, you should start calling clients today and let them know that you're closing. You can refund them money that they would be owed and maybe see if you can recommend them to another instructor in the city. Call the owner of your building and find out what the penalty is if you leave before your contract is up. "Jesse, you'll have to put your notice in right away. Maybe do it tomorrow when you go back to work. Annie, the same thing goes for you. We can keep the house and condo for now. If you want, we can look into a real estate company to handle renting out the house, but I bet one of Louve's people may be interested in another place right here in town. Especially one that has a reinforced room in the basement. I'll keep the condo so that if any of us wants to come back and visit, we have someplace to stay. How does that sound for now?" She immediately got questions.

"How much notice am I giving them?"

"They need to find a replacement for me at the club."

"Can we make a trip to Grand Rapids this weekend, to check it out?"

Keller held up her hand to quiet everyone. "We need to make sure everything is wrapped up with the Columbus Police first, which means Annie still needs to go down and give them a statement. But other than that, we should move as soon as possible. How about a two-week notice? Also, I think Bruce would be a great fit for your position at the club." She turned to Sarah. "And I think a trip to our new city is a fantastic idea. It's about five and a half hours from here, so if you don't have any clients we can leave early on Friday." When Sarah raised an eyebrow, she elaborated. "I know how far away it is because I did a lot of research on this before taking the steps I did. And if you notice, the house is massive. There is more than enough room for all of us to live together, and have friends stay. I didn't throw down nearly half a million dollars on some shabby little apartment." Shocked faces met hers around the table.

"What?"

"Dude, like how much money do you have?"

Keller had a twinkle in her eye when she answered Jesse's question. "Enough to last a lifetime."

The werewolf's mind boggled at the idea. "Mine or yours?"

"Yes."

Jill shook her head. "Jesus. Maybe I will give up my practice and move in with you guys. I can be your full-time vet, taking care of all furry things great and small." The laughter was comforting and started the transition of what once was, to what would become. Annie stood and started cleaning up her food mess, and Jesse, Jill, and Keller were looking through the photos of the one hundred and twenty-five year old mini-mansion that Keller had bought.

Sarah disappeared into the bedroom while they were all busy. She emerged a minute later but instead of going back to the dining room table with the others, she went over to the baby grand and sat down. The music had been complete for months, but there was never a right time to share it. She took something out of her pocket and set it on top of the glossy black instrument, then she began to play. The song started simple, her voice with the quiet backing of the piano.

Would you be my Juliet?
'Cause you can bet

I'd make a terrible Romeo
I'd go too fast
And maybe I'd go too slow

But look at me sitting here beneath
Serenading to your beauty
Staring up at your window
I can't help my attraction
It's all the living I know

What would I do if I had no fear
If I had another million years
If I could do it all again
Would I roll down the same roads
Would I have the same kind of friends

Well I don't know, but
This Romeo sure hopes so

What would I say
If I never once saw your face
Would I know what I had missed
Would I wind up in this place
Still longing for your kiss

You spend most nights in the glow
Of the street lights, me down below
If we said goodbye to our eternity
Trapped in another life
Would you still cry for me

Now we're left with one thing
It's a pretty little metal kinda ring
Is it worth the gamble and the guess
If I asked you the question
Would you hazard to say yes

Well I don't know, but
This Romeo sure hopes so
Yeah, I don't know, but
This Romeo sure hopes so
This Romeo sure hopes so

Keller had walked over to the piano while she was singing and froze when she saw the rings on the lid. "Sarah?"

A mumbled "Oh my God" could be heard in the background, obviously Annie.

The singer looked up at her soul mate. "Yes?"

"You are really serious?"

Sarah nodded. "Yes."

"Yes?"

"Yes!"

"Okay then, yes!"

Annie snorted. "Does anyone else speak their language?"

Jesse looked at her slyly. "Maybe someday." The nerdy were-wolf got nothing but wide eyes from her girlfriend. "Heh."

Later, when Jill, Annie, and Jesse were getting ready to leave, Sarah pulled her sister aside. "You're really okay then?"

Annie smiled at her sister fondly. "I am, I'm great actually. And congratulations, you finally did it!"

Sarah laughed. "I finally did it. And she loved the rings."

"You knew she would."

The older sibling shook her head and her eyes seemed to be looking far away, to a conversation that felt like a lifetime ago. "No, I hoped. There is a difference." She refocused on Annie. "What about you? Are you ready?"

"Ready for what?"

Sarah cracked a smile. "Ready for everything!"

Annie winked back. "Nope. Where's the fun in that?"

Sarah shook her head and slung an arm around her sister's shoulder as they made their way to the door of the condo. "Where indeed?"

EVENING FELL AND the city grew dark. Two women looked out into the night though the floor-length window. They stared down at the dark serpentine shape of the river below. Sarah had her arm draped around Keller's shoulder, much the same way she had earlier with her sister. Keller lifted her hand to stare at the twinkling band on her finger. "You know, we won't be able to see the river from our new house."

"It doesn't matter."

Keller looked up at her soul mate. "But you love to look at the river here."

Sarah pulled her in tighter and smiled down at her lover. "I'll be able to see you. There is no river in the world worth that."

"No, I suppose not." Keller sighed and looked back out the window, into the city they would leave behind. Just another city for Nobel Keller, just another life. Except for in the next one, all the ones to come, she was no longer alone. She turned her head and looked up at Sarah. "Welcome to the future, Miss Colby, I hope you enjoy the stay."

The singer smiled back. "No, welcome to *our* future, Miss Keller. And I hope to never leave." And then they kissed. Because when someone promises you forever, that's what you do.

About the Author

Award winning author and Michigan native, K. Aten brings heroines to life in a variety of blended LGBTQ fiction genres. She's not afraid of pain or adversity, but loves a happy ending. "Some words end the silence, others begin it."

2019 GCLS Goldie winner
Waking the Dreamer - Science Fiction/ Fantasy

Other K. Aten titles to look for:

The Fletcher

Kyri is a fletcher, following in the footsteps of her father, and his father before him. However, fate is a fickle mistress, and six years after the death of her mother, she's faced with the fact that her father is dying as well. Forced to leave her sheltered little homestead in the woods, Kyri discovers that there is more to life than just hunting and making master quality arrows. During her journey to find a new home and happiness, she struggles with the path that seems to take her away from the quiet life of a fletcher. She learns that sometimes the hardest part of growing up is reconciling who we were, with who we will become.

ISBN: 978-1-61929-356-4
eISBN: 978-1-61929-357-1

The Archer

Kyri was raised a fletcher but after finding a new home and family with the Telequire Amazons, she discovers a desire to take on more responsibility within the tribe. She has skills they desperately need and she is called to action to protect those around her. But Kyri's path is ever-changing even as she finds herself altered by love, loyalty, and grief. Far away from home, the new Amazon is forced to decide what to sacrifice and who to become in order to get back to all that she has left behind. And she wonders what is worse, losing everyone she's ever loved or having those people lose her?

ISBN: 978-1-61929-370-0
eISBN: 978-1-61929-371-7

The Sagittarius

Kyri has known her share of loss in the two decades that she has been alive. She never expected to find herself a slave in roman lands, nor did she think she had the heart to become a gladiatrix. But with her soul shattered she must fight to see her way back home again. Will she win her freedom and return to all that she has known, or will she become another kind of slave to the killer that has taken over her mind? The only thing that is certain through it all is her love and devotion to Queen Orianna.

ISBN: 978-1-61929-386-1
eISBN: 978-1-61929-387-8

Rules of the Road

Jamie is an engineer who keeps humor close to her heart and people at arm's length. Kelsey is a dental assistant who deals with everything from the hilarious to the disgusting on a daily basis. What happens when a driving app brings them together as friends? The nerd car and the rainbow car both know a thing or two about hazard avoidance. When a flat tire brings them together in person, Jamie immediately realizes that Kelsey isn't just another woman on her radar. Both of them have struggled to break free from stereotypes while they navigate the road of life. As their friendship deepens they realize that sometimes you have to break the rules to get where you need to go.

ISBN: 978-1-61929-366-3
eISBN: 978-1-61929-367-0

Waking the Dreamer

By the end of the 21st century, the world had become a harsh place. After decades of natural and man-made catastrophes, nations fell, populations shifted, and seventy percent of the continents became uninhabitable without protective suits. Technological advancement strode forward faster than ever and it was the only thing that kept human society steady through it all. No one could have predicted the discovery of the Dream Walkers. They were people born with the ability to leave their bodies at will, unseen by the waking world. Having the potential to become ultimate spies meant the remaining government regimes wanted to study and control them. The North American government, under the leadership of General Rennet, demanded that all Dream Walkers join the military program. For any that refused to comply, they were hunted down and either brainwashed or killed.

The very first Dream Walker discovered was a five year old girl named Julia. And when the soldiers came for her at the age of twenty, she was already hidden away. A decade later found Julia living a new life under the government's radar. As a secure tech courier in the capital city of Chicago, she does her job and the rest of her time avoids other people as much as she is able. The moment she agrees to help another fugitive Walker is when everything changes. Now the government wants them both and they'll stop at nothing to get what they want.

ISBN: 978-1-61929-382-3
eISBN: 978-1-61929-383-0

The Sovereign of Psiere:
Mystery of the Makers Book 1

Psiere is a world of intrigue where old ideology meets new. The Makers built massive pyramids on each continent and filled them with encrypted texts and advanced technology. The two suns, Archeos and Illeos shine down on a mostly undiscovered planet with a psionic race of people living on land, and violent sea people below the water. The Queen seeks to make the world a better place for all Psierians but her daughter, Royal Sovereign Connate Olivienne Dracore, seeks only to solve the Divine Mystery.

The connate makes her living as a historical adventurist and wants the answer to two important questions. Who were the Makers and where did they go? Because she is the heir, Olivienne travels with a security force and resents it every moment. Every one of her captains has either quit or been injured trying to keep up with the risk-taking woman. That's where Commander Castellan Tosh comes in. Capable, confident, and oh-so-dashing, she is forced to switch career corps to take charge of Olivienne's team. Sparks fly from the moment they meet and things only get hotter as they chase down the clues to the greatest mystery of all time

ISBN: 978-1-61929-412-7
eISBN: 978-1-61929-413-4

Running From Forever

Sarah Colby has always run from commitment. But after more than a year on the road following her musical dreams, even she yearns for a little stability. Her sister Annie is only too happy to welcome her back home. When she meets Annie's boss, Nobel Keller, she's immediately drawn to the woman's youthful good looks and dangerous charisma. The first night together leaves Sarah aching for more, but the second shows her the true price of passion.

ISBN: 978-1-61929-398-4
eISBN: 978-1-61929-399-1

Burn It Down

Ash Hayes was failed by the system at the tender age of sixteen and suffered an addiction. As a result she lives her life weighed down by the guilt of her past. To atone for childhood misdeeds, Ash trained as a paramedic after high school and eventually became a firefighter with the Detroit fire department, along with her childhood best friend Derek. Friend, confidant, brother, he has been her light in an otherwise dark life. When tragedy strikes on the job, injury and forced leave from the department are the least of her concerns. Suffering from even more guilt and depression after the loss of her two closest friends Ash is set adrift in a sea of pain.

When Mia Thomas buys the house next door, Ash finds friendship in the most unlikely of places. It's Mia's nature to help and to heal. Many would say she has a knack for finding the broken ones and leading them into the light. But Ash's secret still lives deep inside her. Before the firefighter can even think of a future, she has to amend her past. Like the phoenix of legend, Ash has to burn her fears to the ground before she can be reborn.

ISBN: 978-1-61929-418-9
eISBN: 978-1-61929-419-6

MORE REGAL CREST PUBLICATIONS

Melissa Good	Red Sky At Morning	978-1-932300-80-2
Melissa Good	Storm Surge: Book One	978-1-935053-28-6
Melissa Good	Storm Surge: Book Two	978-1-935053-39-2
Melissa Good	Stormy Waters	978-1-61929-082-2
Melissa Good	Thicker Than Water	1-932300-24-4
Melissa Good	Terrors of the High Seas	1-932300-45-7
Melissa Good	Tropical Storm	978-1-932300-60-4
Melissa Good	Tropical Convergence	978-1-935053-18-7
Melissa Good	Winds of Change Book One	978-1-61929-194-2
Melissa Good	Winds of Change Book Two	978-1-61929-232-1
Melissa Good	Southern Stars	978-1-61929-348-9
Jeanine Hoffman	Lights & Sirens	978-1-61929-115-7
Jeanine Hoffman	Strength in Numbers	978-1-61929-109-6
Jeanine Hoffman	Back Swing	978-1-61929-137-9
K. E. Lane	And, Playing the Role of Herself	978-1-932300-72-7
Kate McLachlan	Christmas Crush	978-1-61929-195-9
Kate McLachlan	Hearts, Dead and Alive	978-1-61929-017-4
Kate McLachlan	Murder and the Hurdy Gurdy Girl	978-1-61929-125-6
Kate McLachlan	Rescue At Inspiration Point	978-1-61929-005-1
Kate McLachlan	Return Of An Impetuous Pilot	978-1-61929-152-2
Kate McLachlan	Rip Van Dyke	978-1-935053-29-3
Kate McLachlan	Ten Little Lesbians	978-1-61929-236-9
Kate McLachlan	Alias Mrs. Jones	978-1-61929-282-6
Lynne Norris	One Promise	978-1-932300-92-5
Lynne Norris	Sanctuary	978-1-61929-248-2
Lynne Norris	The Light of Day	978-1-61929-338-0
Schramm and Dunne	Love Is In the Air	978-1-61929-362-8
Rae Theodore	Leaving Normal: Adventures in Gender	
		978-1-61929-320-5
Rae Theodore	My Mother Says Drums Are for Boys: True	
	Stories for Gender Rebels	978-1-61929-378-6
Barbara Valletto	Pulse Points	978-1-61929-254-3
Barbara Valletto	Everlong	978-1-61929-266-6
Barbara Valletto	Limbo	978-1-61929-358-8
Barbara Valletto	Diver Blues	978-1-61929-384-7
Lisa Young	Out and Proud	978-1-61929-392-2

Be sure to check out our other imprints,
Blue Beacon Books, Carnelian Books, Quest Books,
Silver Dragon Books, Troubadour Books,
Yellow Rose Books and Young Adult Books.

CPSIA information can be obtained
at www.ICGtesting.com
Printed in the USA
FSHW021124031019
62557FS